Little Petrock

Martyn Benford

Fed Pel'
+ MALE.
MB x

Published by New Generation Publishing in 2020

Copyright © Martyn Benford 2020

First Edition

ISBN 978-1-80031-806-9

www.newgeneration-publishing.com

New Generation Publishing

A Precious Sound

No-one can hear a teardrop fall
No little sound comes at all
Silently sliding slowly at first
at some news of a kind the worse.

Tears are soundless like silent rain
slipping down cheeks they fall and stain.
Blinking eyes allow their flow
to cheeks puffed and red with glow

Sadness, a loss, a friend passed on
Wife, husband, a lover, recently gone.
These tricklets begin to gather and form
as if at the beginning of a sudden storm

But wait, listen, sadness never lasts forever
There is something else, far more clever.
As crying stops, comes soon after
A most precious sound, the sound of laughter.

Pablo

Prologue

Simply telling it as it is, how origins are important.

My words at the completion of the initial biography of Maccy Tamryn stated 'this is not the end, it is just the beginning'. I'm not sure I believed those words myself back then. I should have, as once more, I am here.

Much has happened since I wrote that note; Maccy is almost ten years older and through sad personal circumstances he is once again alone apart from Macdonald Junior, a juvenile, a son. Maccy still has the greatest family and friends in the world, he just lacks that one thing he thought he had found in his 'Cornish Queen' Jen'. Doubting, with good reason, he would ever replace her, Maccy has little idea where he should be and what he should be doing. His fascination with a Kansas ghost town still appeals to him. He will return again and again without really knowing why. What is the point of fishing if you don't want to catch a fish? Is it not true fishermen only catch something one percent of the time, on a good day?

I'm a great believer in fate, we do what we have to do not always what we want to do. Maybe if we go against the grain, things that should happen are not allowed to. On the other hand, how do we know we are choosing the wrong side of the coin of fate? We don't flip it, we just call. We don't know what will happen until it lands. And even then the coin is only setting the wheels in motion, if you allow it to. The wheels of fortune can go backwards as easily as they can go forward. They might not even move at all. I believe we each have to want them too.

I once heard the sayings, A Kentish man and a man of Kent. I had no idea there was a difference until I was told by one or the other, I don't remember which. It suddenly became clear later when I myself was described as a 'man of Cornwall'. I had never thought of myself as anything different. It did make me feel good to be told as much. The odd thing was that he who mentioned it was from Cambridgeshire. I shall have to ask him if he sees himself as a man of Cambridgeshire or as a Cambridgeshire man, meaning I know where he lives but have no idea where he originates from. I myself originate from Middlesex and so that would suggest I am both a Middlesex man and a man of Cornwall. My good friend Macdonald is a true Cornishman, he's not confused. At least not all of the time.

In the early 1870's Maccy's great grandfather emigrated to the United States. He stayed until the day he died. He never returned to Ireland, he stayed and lived his life in America. Henry Tamryn born an Irishman, became a man of America and died an Irish hero.

Simply telling the truth, how it was.

These memoirs of Macdonald Tamryn some might say lack honesty. 'Verisimilitude in action' some might tell you. 'it never happened this way'. Take my word for it, it really did happen this way!

Martyn

Chapter One

No hiding Place

"Nobody goes there, Sir."

"Yes they do."

"No, they don't, Sir."

"I'm telling you they do."

"I'm tellin' ya, yes, I mean no, they don't, Sir."

"Look now matey, I'm going there, I've been there, now I'm going back there. I might come back here again to go there next time. I might bring a busload of friends with me to take them there."

"There ain't nuthin' there, Sir."

"There will be."

"When will that be, Sir?"

"When I get there. Just give me the bleddy keys then your car will be there too. Have a nice day, eventually." Jobsworths, don't they just love it. There's one behind every pair of sunglasses in America. In England they don't stand on ceremony, they don't have mirrored shades that make it easier to look down their noses at others. Maybe they have some sort of jobsworth college, how to be a pain in the backside without even trying. A couple of years learning how to tell people they can't do what they like, even if they've paid for the privilege to do just that. They must sit an exam, get a certificate and off they go to spend the rest of their working lives doing what this bloke does so well.

"I don't like your tone, Sir!" This last 'sir' is accompanied by flying saliva.

"I don't much like your hire car buddy. I already paid for it, so it will have to do." I just had to prove him wrong, it was no hardship. I went to college too, to be fair, catering college might not count for much when dealing

4

with an over-zealous, American rental car operative, I mean tosser! One small worry is I might end up like him if I stay around here much longer. I don't think I have ,made his day, I am satisfied, I got my way.

McCarthy City and the vast Plains of Kansas await me once again. This time it's not on a whim. I have returned here as I don't want to be around other people, I don't want others around me, I'm banking on solitude. The old Indian geezer, that's 'Native American' to you and I, plus of course anyone who might be minutely interested, had loaned me the 'fishing pole' and everything I needed to shut myself away into my miserable world. I am determined to lose myself for a few hours, maybe days. The old feller won't bother me much, he has a garage full of spit stains to take up his time. I'm not suggesting he's going to clean them up, just make them bigger. I can't decide if he has any regular customers. I mean where would they come from and where would they go to around here? I doubt the town ever has sightseers, apart from my brother Dusty and I a few years ago. We two came here as teenagers, we returned home a couple of weeks older.

Here I can be in a bad mood and not bother anyone. I no longer feel like the King of Padstow. Jennifer, who had been my queen, is now gone but not alone, as she departed this life in the company of our second child. Her reign was short! I'll never see her again until it is my own time. 'The queen is dead. Long live the queen.'

Padstow itself will be the worse off for her sad and sudden departure. Well known and well liked was Jen'. She would do anything for anyone and pretty much did. The town won't miss me much while I'm away, however long that that might be. I'm easily replaced. My intention is to get away as far as I could for as long as possible. It did seem like a good idea at the time.

Kansas has once again beckoned me. I had nowhere else to go. The Alsatian looked miserable when I left my home in Little Petrock. The mutt reminded me of me, except for his ugly mug. Pardon my modesty! It wasn't his fault he had an argument with a power boat. On second thoughts, maybe it was his fault, most dogs chase cars! The Alsatian, so I'm informed, had been swimming in the quay at Padstow and unfortunately had got too close to a boats' propeller. It must be true; a dog doesn't get ugly by sniffing lampposts. It's not even my dog but I had thought of giving it a name. I had an idea Donald might suit but I doubt the mutt got near three hundred miles an hour, as the celebrated Mister Campbell once did in Bluebird. I doubt he had a dog chasing him at the time. Obviously, the Alsatian couldn't do it twice. Dying while trying has no future in it. To be fair, the dog was lucky. He may not look like a character from a James Bond movie, but he has got to live twice so far, unlike Mister Campbell.

On thinking about it further, Donald will be ideal. It is rhyming slang for luck and the dog was lucky it wasn't turned into dog food the day it tried to do a four-minute mile in three minutes. Maybe Roger would suit better. Nope, it should be Donald. Roger the Alsatian has connotations that should not be aired in decent company. For now, the hapless dog - until something better comes along - shall be known as Donald, if I remember! It's not important in any case as I never call to it as it wouldn't take any notice anyway. As I don't of him when he barks at me.

The dog was not the only thing I left behind. I left a pub full of my friends, my own pub, my friends, maybe not full but on occasion it rocks a tad. Dusty, my brother, regularly takes a boatload of Padstow's finest to Newquay on a Friday night. More often or not, they hardly ever come back again for various reasons. My brother's 'sea bus' venture is quite successful.

I left my family, which had grown somewhat over the last few years. The identity of the most recent member is Padraig, my father. I hadn't seen him since I was a tacker and all of a sudden, he appeared, stayed and eventually slotted in perfectly. Padraig didn't attempt to take over the role of head of the house, he just became one of us. My sibling, Dusty, tried to run him out of town once. Dusty's a trier but for once he failed. Next came Jennifer. We married and eventually extended the clan by two more for a short while. She and a tiny infant departed over a year ago, leaving me with our first child. Jen and the little one are both at rest now in 'Gods' Half Acre'.

I have returned here to Kansas. I brought my misery with me. Right now, as far as I know, I am about to fish my very own stream, catch my own fish with something akin to reluctance. I'm not saying I don't want to be in Kansas, just that I don't need any fish. It would have gone off by the time I get it back home to Cornwall. * Some years ago, Dusty, my little brother - I use that term unwisely as he is just a tad smaller than me at around sixteen stone – had visited Southern Kansas to search for and discover a ghost town. McCarthy City had at one time been the home of our, great grandfather.

Henry McCarthy had left Cork, in the Emerald Isle at around the same age as I am now. Henry had arrived here in the States in eighteen seventy-something. Henry and his new-found associate, Tafflyn Edwards, had met and teamed up as a double act along the way. Taffy and Henry had begun a friendship which would last until a final sad parting when Henry died in a fire..

The two, it has been chronicled, had won a tented saloon in a card game and the men had stayed and settled, eventually replacing the temporary canvas walls for solid wood and adobe. Ma has old letters. She would occasionally find one we hadn't so far read, though we have done now.

The two friends had been instrumental in the town's growth and civilising. Taffy, Ma had told us before we left Padstow, had been the town's first Marshal. Henry had been, amongst other things, mayor for some years. Nobody ever wanted to vote either man out of office it seemed. The two had never been challenged and would stay in their respective offices for a lifetime, though Henry McCarthy died a relatively young man, a hero apparently, while attempting to rescue his friend Frederick, from a burning building.

Henry couldn't have known his friend was already dead as he lifted him on to his shoulders. My great grandfather's heart gave out, his last breath was exhaled while trying to save a man's life almost a hundred and twenty years ago. The letters had said Henry had only been in his thirties when his time came. The old lady, Renee, our great aunt who Dusty and I had met her on that first visit had confirmed everything. Her information came out in dribs and drabs when we two first arrived in Kansas.

So, with the wondering nature of teenagers, Dusty and I had to come here and see for ourselves what our Ma had told us about. Dusty and I had come here and discovered a town with just one remaining inhabitant. We kids met the ancient pocket-sized aunt no one in the family knew still existed. To be honest, Renee gave us the early impression she would like to make sure we didn't. After some erratically close shooting and some heavy whining and begging from me and the kid, Renee had eventually relented somewhat. She had put down her large ** 'Yellow Boy', Winchester rifle to eventually give us a less warm welcome on that day of our arrival. A day neither of us boys will ever forget.

Dusty and I have laughed over it many times. It's true to say, at the time, it wasn't that amusing. Target practice quickly ceases to be popular when you're the target. She was a one-woman firing squad; blindfolds were not provided. It was also true she had told us 'get out my town' after the first half dozen shots. To be fair she did admit to her eyesight not being too clever. Weren't we the lucky ones. We didn't know at the time she needed glasses.

We stayed on with Aunt Renee in the Plainsman Hotel, a hotel Taffy and Henry had built virtually with their own hands. Renee told us everything there was to know about the old place, a city in name only, it's a small village at best. She missed little out. Before we departed, she showed us the tiny cemetery where almost every member of McCarthy City's population now resides, all but Renee, though she is there now. At least none of them had needed to go far on their final journeys.

Local records state almost all the final inhabitants had died of prolonged age, except Henry. It's a good habit. So, few of them went kicking and screaming. Knowing Aunt Renee, she would have been the exception to the rule. She did nothing quietly. It's no wonder the town is bereft of any lingerers.

We looked on our trip as a holiday in the beginning. It wasn't so much that, more like a living history lesson. My brother and I had left Renee at the end of our time in McCarthy with promises of a return visit ringing in various ears. Now, for my own purely selfish reasons, I have kept a part of that almost ten-year-old bargain. Dusty had been far too busy to be with me this time and in fact I was glad that he had. I didn't crave his or anyone's company. My recent companions have had rather a bad habit of dying! I'm hoping to put a stop to the habit.

Jennifer, my own Cornish queen had done just that. We two had been together for eight, almost nine years. We had one son. I have a son, Macdonald Junior. There would have been a brother - mother and child had no time to flourish. Though it feels like it was just yesterday, I lost Jen' almost five years ago. I have been in a bad mood ever since. Now I am back in Kansas to spend some solitary time remembering how my life had once been and will never be again. I'm here for peace and quiet. I'm here to give myself earache only. With a bit of exaggeration, it is so far, so good.

For the second time, I had arrived at McCarthy City in the rental pick-up that may or may not have seen better days, looked around the old empty town and paid a modest rent for a ramshackle room at the nearest gas station a mile or so away from the buildings of the crumbling village. It couldn't have been called a guesthouse unless one was a cockroach. The old Indian geezer had lent me his ancient fishing tackle and directed me to mine and Dusty's very own stretch of creek. It could just be compared to Lost Souls Creek that runs through Little Petrock towards Padstow and passes The Mermaid and Bow Inn at one point. This Kansas stream meanders, unlike Lost Souls, which tends to gush more often than not. The fish aren't what you might call related either. We have salmon in Little Padstow if you know where to find them, here in Kansas they have catfish.

To be fair, we do have dog fish. Obviously, we couldn't have both and neither could Kansas due to the 'age old problem'. They would be fighting all the time, especially when there is a bunch of each; if it's raining heavily, it doesn't help!

Renee, in her last will and testament, had left Dusty and I the deeds to the Plainsman Hotel; in fact, she had left us everything. McCarthy City, though it is more a hamlet - I may be guilty of exaggeration; it's no bigger than Little Petrock, quieter anyway - legally belongs to me and the 'kid'. It is also people-less now apart from the Indian and myself, albeit only temporarily on my part. McCarthy could be called a One Dog Town if there was a dog in residence. It doesn't seem to be the case; it might have been chased off by a cat!

I had taken some time to explain all of this to the old bloke who had nodded and smiled knowingly while I spoke. Without question, he had accepted everything I related to him. My overlying impression was I was wasting my words and time. I believed he already knew who I was and what had come about regarding the will. I can't say for certain he is the last inhabitant of McCarthy as the 'Gas station' is only a mile outside of town. Obviously, it isn't a Cornish mile as they can be any distance. The useful thing about a Cornish mile - at least from the emmets' point of view - is they are in Cornwall longer than they think they are.

And now, as I am prepared, unprepared to be truthful, to catch one of my very own fish, I am to be 'ambushed' as they tend to say in Hollywood cowboy movies.

My hook and line are already thrown out and the stubby little float is settled on the water's surface. I settle back and prepare to catch supper or nothing at all. Who am I kidding? I'm only here to be somewhere. Nothing at all of the fish variety will suit me just fine. My eyes are just half open. The Kansan sun is already hot on my face. I pull the battered Stetson down over one eye. The old git at the gas station had told me not to come out here without some headgear and had lent me what was definitely not his Sunday best. He had also sent me off with a long-barrelled pistol. The old man told me the ***'Peacemaker' six-shooter had the nickname the 'Equaliser'. Seems to me if it is as suggested, then there would be no point in shooting at someone else who had one. Two people could have not a hole in one but a hole in each other.

Apparently, I am to shoot snakes with the gun. I might too, if I knew which end to point at a 'Rattler'. I just hope the snake doesn't have a Peacemaker. I wouldn't know which end to point at anything. If one appears, I will just have to strangle it, or more than likely bore it to death. Not a difficult task, right up my street.

I have settled on a comfortable spot with shade and begin to meditate lightly under a gloriously blue sky. Surely that's what all anglers do when they aren't catching anything, which is ninety-nine percent of the time, sometimes more. Of course, the skies are a different colour back home, grey mostly. The thick fishing line is twisted lightly about my fingertips to warn of a bite. I don't expect it to tighten. In truth, I hope it won't. This recently reacquired pastime is uninteresting as far as I'm concerned, which is just what I need right now.

I'd spent half my childhood fishing in Padstow and never became particularly good at it. I am a Cornish fisherman in name only. Exploitation was sparse, I never made money at it.

Absolute silence surrounds me, I believe myself to be completely alone. This is the very reason for my second visit to the United States. There are a lot of Yanks here

11

apparently. They seem to be well spread out. I have only seen a couple close-up so far. I hope the trend continues; I don't need nor want company.

I nudge the battered Stetson a little further forward and attempt to doze. My mind travels back to Cornwall and the creek at Little Petrock, 'Lost Souls Creek'. A sad place where a tiny humpback bridge passes over its fast flow. To us locals the span is the Bridge of Tears. It's the saddest place I have known. The creek, an ancient waterway has a dark reputation of having been used for the disposal of unwanted newborn babies over the centuries, which is the reason for its shiver inducing titles. Those in the know or who have experienced its paranormal oddities, will never forget. It's true too, the creek was used by smugglers in its long and murky past. On thinking about it, they may well have been the reason for so many human offerings.

We locals are lucky, we know what to do when crossing the bridge at night which has spanned the creek for around two centuries. Our palms are employed to block out the sounds of infant misery. It doesn't quite work. We know they are there. Nobody has to see them, and nobody has as far as I know. They are there! My lifelong buddy, Lenny, blocks his ears while crossing in daylight. My mate likes to be different; he is rather successful at it.

Us boys had fished from Padstows' granite quayside plenty of times and with a tad more to show for it. Fish with legs, claws anyway, Crabs mostly, very small. We had fished from the Bridge of Tears on many occasions, only to be slightly better rewarded. One of the older locals told us boys the bridge would be netted in days gone by. Nets were hung down from the parapets, fish were caught in abundance as and when the tide rose and fell. It's a pity the old bloke hadn't informed us before. We wouldn't have gone home disappointed so often.

It seems my life has been encircled by little ones who never got to grow to full size. I shake off thoughts of Padstow, the creek and the misty visions of Jennifer and my own lost child. I half concentrate on my present task. I know my Ma, Dusty and Padraig are looking after my lad. Macdonald junior will come to no harm in my absence. Being a Tamryn will guarantee his safety. The youngster and I share the name. I am certain that like me, he will also become Maccy. Hopefully an improved version; it would not be difficult. Right now, he is most likely being spoiled rotten by my Ma, Padraig and my brother, the kid, Dusty. MJ and I share two motionless railway carriages. The carriages are our home. My description is sparse, the carriages are not. They are unique in that at one time they were used for transporting livestock, now they provide a roof over our heads. In the past I have berated a certain Doctor Beeching for dismembering our rail transport system. It's a good job he did, otherwise MJ and I would be homeless. We would be sleeping under the stars.

I find myself drifting into the past until suddenly a tiny, gentle plopping sound brings me back to now. I look across at my cork float, it is perfectly still though the water around it is moving away. Minute, delicate rings are travelling outwards from the piece of cork. I stare, waiting for my float to bob again. Nothing is happening. It sits silently in the water, unmoving, the last of the tiny ripples disappearing before my eyes. Stretching back and once again delving into my memory of foggy sadness, my intentional melancholy it seems is not to last.

For a second time, I hear the same faint sound. This time it is just a tad louder. My eyes open immediately, and I again look to the cork float. There is little or no movement. I tug at my line, it is weightless. New ripples are still travelling outwards in perfect symmetry. I don't understand what's happening here. What kind of fish do they have in Kansas? Fish that tease, fish that are here just to annoy idiots like myself? 'Catfish' the old geezer had told me. If I was lucky, I would get me a catfish. To be honest, I didn't want any fish at all. I am just here on the stream bank with a long stick, minding my own business.

The catfish can stay where they are. I don't need fish slime all over my hands. For a third time, I pull the battered hat down and rest on my elbows, determined to reach and search my erratic past and pull some of it back to my more recently disturbed present. It is not to be. I am about to become mildly irate.

Something solid hits against the tatty Stetson, something small but hard has collided with my borrowed headgear. I take the article off and search for the missile. I can find nothing until I have turned the hat completely around in my hands, then I see it. Stuck to the wide brim is a tiny seed of some kind. It feels sticky when I touch it. I have no idea what it is or why it's there. Stuff doesn't happen this way in Padstow. Plenty happens, much of it even weird but nothing of this sort that I know of. I'm certain I have never been attacked by a seed before. I doubt anyone has! It's not something you can tell your friends, is it? 'How's it going Maccy?' 'Yeah really good mate. I'm just waiting to find out how many sticky seeds might attack me today.' 'Guess what happened to me today, I was bombarded with seeds.' It doesn't quite work, does it?

Author's notes:

* Maccy and Dusty first visited McCarthy City in The Mermaid and Bow by this author.

** The 'Yellow Boy' The Winchester rifle, so called as the firing mechanism of the rifle / Carbine was made from brass. The model was first manufactured in 1866 at The Winchester Repeating Rifle Co. Calibre 44-40 cartridge. It weighed 9.5 lbs – 4.3 kgs barrel length thirty inches.

*** Colt Peacemaker: The Colt Single Action Army, also known as the Single Action Army, SAA, Model P, Peacemaker, M1873, and Colt .45 is a single action weapon with a revolving cylinder holding six metallic cartridges. It was designed for the U.S. government service revolver 1872 The pistol had the nick name 'The Equaliser'.

Chapter Two

Spittin' Image

I twist the hat in my hand as I scratch my head in puzzlement. On doing so, the back of my hand is stung, or more likely bitten! My first thought is a Rattlesnake has just announced to me I am about to die in severe pain. I think about the pistol I had been given by the old Indian for my safety and wonder why I had left it under the seat in the pick-up. The truck is fifty yards away, more in metres I'm led to believe. My next thought is 'what's the point of shooting the snake now anyway'? It's already given me a lethal dosage of something very nasty. The 'rattler' is also invisible. I admit I didn't hear a rattle either. I had no warning sign. The snake isn't playing the game!

Lastly, I think about the seed on my hat and now realise there is another stuck to my hand. My 'penultimate thought' could only occur if I am still surviving. For now I am, which is a positive. It's a well-known fact, fads in the States usually become fads in the UK. I just don't see this one following the tradition. We don't have any rattlesnakes in Britain for one thing.

So, there is a bad-tempered, invisible Rattlesnake somewhere close by, which instead of biting and poisoning people to death, projects sticky little seeds at humans generally and it seems, Cornish fishermen – I use the term 'fisherman' loosely - in particular. I wonder if snakes are capable of humour? I think about the absent pistol again. I am only allowed to think for a moment. Okay, so I am in America and I've heard strange things happen in these parts; this sort of thing may be an everyday occurrence, who knows, just the Yanks I suppose, which could be a good thing.

"You, fish man!"

Here we go! It's my day for being stunned. Stunned and by a vocal Rattlesnake it seems. It's like being in a version of Jungle Book. I turn towards the source of the voice and I realise there is no snake as another seed hits the brim of my hat. She is almost fifteen yards away from my position and sitting cross-legged on a high grassy ridge above me. She is not alone, she has a very large companion. Either that or she is unusually small. A hand grasps the reins of a huge grey horse. I have time to wonder if they have just arrived or had I unknowingly walked past them when I approached the stream? It's possible. I have never considered myself to be perfect in the eyesight area. We don't have an opticians in Padstow. If we have, I've never seen it! Every picture can only tell a story if you can see it.

I want to say something, I can't form any useful words. I don't have a clue what to say to this seed-spitting Yank girl. It might be best I keep shtum!

"Are y'all fishing for your supper, stranger?"

"Nope." One pathetic word, it's all I can manage in my reply. At least I think I sound as if I belong around here. She has the nerve to suggest I'm strange. I haven't attacked anyone with seeds today, I'm certain it's a pastime I have never partaken of. She has the nerve to call me 'stranger'. Women couldn't possibly be any stranger than this one!

"You're an English guy, ain't ya?"

So much for my thinking, I convince myself to do less of it. "Nope, I'm Cornish sweetheart and that is something entirely different. Have you finished spitting?" I'm certain there is something in her small but lively mouth. She hasn't stopped smiling all through our short exchange. Maybe she is working out how to get me between the eyes? Newspaper headline: 'Cornish Fisherman found dead in deserted Kansas town'. 'Almost certainly the cause of death, a sticky seed, variety unknown. Verdict –

Misadventure', which might signify I should not have been here fishing at all. There is no snake!

I have forever thought I would be the most eccentric person I would ever know. I am in danger of becoming a loser!

"Cornish, eh? Do ya mind explaining what 'Cornish' means?"

"Explain?"

"Yup, just for my benefit, if y'all don't mind."

I don't know if I mind or not and my short silence is evidence of this. I don't have a clue how to reply to this young woman. I would guess she is twenty-five, maybe more, maybe less. She might be fifteen or fifty. I have no idea. I am reminded of someone, I have no idea who, and so I suppose I'm not. But I am. Her speech is long drawn out, like a slowed down record.

"Catfish got your tongue, Brit?"

I become defensive. "Come closer and try fishing, Yank. Same thing might happen to yours; it would be a shame." Now I am suddenly annoyed with myself. I have been unnecessarily rude to her and with just a small amount of provocation on her part. She did start it.

"I apologise if I have made you feel uncomfortable, Brit."

I untie my tongue and answer her question.

"Not at all. I live in Cornwall, England. I'm Cornish." I reply honestly.

"So, you're English and Cornish! You can be both I guess. Thank you Brit, for enlightening me. I best get along now and let you get back to your fishing pole. Good luck with your supper hombre, see ya around.... mebbe!"

It served me right for being so touchy. I watched as she stepped up from the ground into the stirrups, in one smooth movement. She is indeed tiny, almost childlike in stature but unmistakably a woman. I know about these things. She had climbed into the high Western saddle with ease. For some reason, I feel a tad of guilt. I try to retrieve the situation. "Hombre"?

"Okay, dude!"

"Wait up, I'm sorry for being such a pain in the arse. Snakes make me nervous. I'm not used to such things, especially on finding out they can kill me." I told her of my fears of earlier, she laughed.

"No, please don't apologise, you do it rather well, Brit. Most snakes around here are fast asleep right now."

"Tired of chasing folks?"

"Hibernating, Brit. It's winter!"

She clucks gently and digs in a heel to get her horse into forward movement. I am a little disappointed in myself. Just before she disappears, I notice she turns in the saddle momentarily and smiles a smile that lights up her face. A smile I realise now I'm certain I have witnessed once before, a very long time ago. I believe it may have done the same to my own. Around her small neck dangles a chain with one single silver star. I know I have seen it before. I am suddenly burning. I don't think it is the Kansan sun. She has lit up my own face. This can only be the same girl I had seen from a distance on my first visit to McCarthy almost ten years ago. She didn't spit at me at our first meeting. It could be a term of endearment. I will never know now anyway. I might have been too far away the first time. I was hiding most of myself in the stream. We didn't in fact speak. I'm positive now she is one and the same.

For me the fishing is over. I just can't be bothered now. I had hoped a few hours in silence and solitude would have helped me rearrange the insides of my head into something resembling neatness. To be honest, it hadn't been working before the appearance of the spitting girl. The chances of it happening after her departure are small to say the least, which pretty much is the same thing.

It is unlikely I will see her again. I'll never even find out her name now. Why should I be bothered? I do regret my rudeness to her. I'd been brought up well enough, just forgot myself for a moment. Maybe I had resented the intrusion, now she's gone I believe I resent her departure.

The short meeting had become a welcome distraction, no bad thing I realise too late. It looks like I won't catch anything at all today. No one to blame but myself. If she had been in Cornwall, she would have received much better treatment. As I said and it's not an excuse, I was ungentlemanly. I'm not myself right now. It's a lousy excuse. I must be more bothered than I realise.

I soon lose any minute interest I might have had in the lack of fish, pack up my gear and leave. I am ready for the old-timer's questions as I hand back the fishing equipment, the disintegrating headwear and the useless pistol. It wasn't really the pistol which was useless. The bloke refused the offered gun. I'm not sure why he gave it to me in the first place, the snakes are 'sleeping'.

"Where'd you put your catch son?"

"Left it in the bleddy stream, seems to me fish can't swim out of water." I feel like a fish myself right now. A fish out of water. Or one that spends all day swimming around inside a glass bowl and getting nowhere! "Why the gun?"

"Thought it would give you something to do while you don't catch any fish, youngster."

So, the old sod knew I wouldn't catch anything. Why the hell did he let me go fishing?

The old man eyes me carefully. I'm sure I can read his mind. He's thinking I should be in the stream! Maybe he's right but for now, all I need is a shower, that's as far as it goes. The old man is waylaying me. Obviously, a shower amounts to taking a dip in a creek devoid of fish. Maybe like the snakes, they are hibernating?

"So, why'd you say you're here, son?"

I hadn't said anything at all as to why I was here, the old fart knows it. The old geezer is fishing now. "I'm taking a holiday, a vacation, I was."

"Here, in * McCarthy City?"

What kind of questioning is this? "Here, it's where I am. I don't believe I'm somewhere else!" It might be better if I was.

"A feller would have to have him a good reason to vacation here, son?"

"I don't!" He didn't catch me out!

I begin to wonder if this old Indian might be related to 'Spittin' woman. He is chewing something. I just know whatever it is, is about to exit his mouth. Thankfully it is just tobacco juice and isn't aimed at me. I look down at the concrete floor of the untidy workshop. I see the evidence this is not something he has just taken up. There are black stains everywhere, walls and floor. This bloke is an expert at staining, anything. He might once have been a French polisher. I wouldn't want to use his bathroom. I have two choices: I can stay yakking and become a target or find somewhere to sleep. I can't quite make my mind up. The old bloke does it for me.

"So?"

"The truth is old feller, I came here to learn how to spit. We don't have a lot of spitters in England, there isn't much call for it, only at football matches and they don't really count. I forget; Punk Rockers used to spit a lot too. I think they are all gone now we have 'goths'."

"You came to the right place, son."

"I think I did." I refuse the packet; I already had my hands full of junk. I inform the old feller I'd give it a try after I'd eaten. I know how to spit, I'm just not in the mood. I have plenty of bad habits, I don't really need another one right now.

"Where're you thinking of eating, youngster? There ain't a lot of choices."

"Somewhere they have food would be best."

"There's a diner along the road aways."

"Is it far?"

"Depends on how hungry you are I guess."

"My stomach thinks my throat's cut."

"Twenty miles or so, about forty minutes away." The old man's face seems to crackle as he laughs. The sound reminds me of Renee, or an empty crisp bag being screwed up in a hand.

"Oh joy!" It seems as if the old guy is intent on winding me up, it is time to go. If I find the diner fine, if I don't, I'll leave a note for my finder.

"Word of advice, kid."

"What's that?"

"Out by the river, did you see a girl, a young woman?"

"Can't say I did, why?" I'm not sure why I lied.

"No reason, it don't matter. Don't cause trouble in the roadhouse, and don't talk to strangers okay and don't get in a fight."

Bloody hell, it doesn't leave me much to do, except eat. I only know two Kansans. The horsewoman reappears in my third eye. "I'll remember." The old bloke didn't say I can't spit, it does seem to be the most popular thing to do around here. Maybe I'll spit my food out if I get bored. For just a moment, I think about inviting the old sod to accompany me. That was all, a split second. A vision of him spitting thick black juice all around a diner full of heavily armed cowboys who might also be spitting changed my mind. If I want sauce, I'll ask for it. As for strangers, what else is there in Southern Kansas? I'm just another one. I wondered why he enquired about the girl. I didn't like to ask.

Steering the rented pick-up away from the old man, I take to the open, horizonless straight road that seems to part a sea of gently waving, emerald green. I switch on the vehicles lights as the sky quickly darkens to a deep purple. It doesn't occur to me I am about to find out what other jewels there are in this great expanse, one of which is appearing spasmodically above me even as I pull away from the gas station. A storm must be approaching. I stop the truck again and step outside to watch spindly fingers of lightning crawl, almost impossibly slowly, across the darkening ocean of purple clouds. It is to me a mesmerising scene. The long grass suddenly becomes still as I stare. It feels like the air is being sucked out of the atmosphere.

Lightning has forever attracted me. The narrow, craggy piece of England we call Cornwall does seem to get more than its fair share, Camelford mostly, and well deserved in my opinion. There are almost as many odd people living in Camelford as there is in the whole of Kansas. I exclude myself obviously. I did go there once.

It doesn't take long before I realise this lightning, Kansas lightning, is much different. Here it comes with other less attractive side effects. I can see a peculiar cloud formation in the gathering darkness away in the distance. My eyes follow another heavenly hand of light across the exploding heavens, Again, I see the outline of something in the far distance which would be a complete rarity back home in the Duchy. I've never seen one before. Not very far away, is something that looks remarkably like a kid's toy, a giant spinning top, a tornado! I believe it to be what I suspect. It's a slight worry!

Now, as I am not in a particularly safe place, I decide it is not before time to get back in the pick-up and leave. I'm not well up on such phenomenon. I have no idea how fast the average tornado can travel, another more important point is that I have no idea if this is an 'average' tornado, who does? They might be all be the same for all I know. I'm sure I read somewhere they kill people and to be honest, I don't fancy the idea of dying on an empty stomach. Food poisoning is acceptable, though obviously impossible if a stomach is as empty as mine! As I drive on, I wonder who decides the measurements of such things, someone up there or someone down here. Whoever they might be, they need to get a proper job. I need to get out of here. I don't know how far away it is. It might be a big one far away or a small one close up.

Outrunning the twister hadn't been so difficult. Twisters don't seem to move very fast. This one hadn't. I had been going in a different direction, some of the time, some of the time I hadn't. The rain was a tad lumpy, thunder was noisy, that's about it, show over, apart from a few broken trees; there isn't that many here. I never once saw a cow in full flight. I can live without it. I prefer my meat on a plate anyway. Yes, I admit it, I saw the film, it was okay. At least I still have a windscreen, plus the rest of the vehicle obviously.

I find the diner, which to say the least is scruffy. Bit of a 'greasy spoon' to be honest, the sort that abound back home. It seems the locals only use forks and fingers hereabouts. Perhaps they only use knives for throwing at each other? Not surprisingly there is a certain amount of spitting, a fight or two, nothing serious. I don't even bother to get out of my chair, which just shows I'm not really myself right now. A fight might have done me some good, I just couldn't be asked, far too much going on in my head. Anyway, I would lose, I seem to have gained a knack of losing things recently. I doubt I could even give Lenny a run for his money at this moment.

I make up my mind I wouldn't be returning, I value my stomach lining. I would have to be starving pretty much. There is more fat than burger; most of it in my hand. I have other plans in any case. I'm not certain they are sensible; I never do sensible well anyway. Tomorrow I intend to get supplies at the Circle K store Dusty and I had visited years ago. I would move myself into the solitude of the Plainsman for a week or two, maybe less, maybe longer. When I am ready, I will return to the two old railway carriages in Little Petrock that I call home. I have more than one. I can sleep at the magic mushroom farm anytime I like. I prefer not to. It's not the mushrooms, they're on the outside and made of concrete. I do like my independence.

In my formative years - hark at me, I'm getting ideas above my station – and not that long ago, my grandfather had, let's say attained - it should cover everything more or less - two aged cattle trucks and hidden them at our farm. In my late teens, I had commandeered the two ancient carriages. Bit by bit and with the help of my younger sibling Dusty, not forgetting Lenny, we had managed to fashion my own workable bachelor pad. Lenny helped along the way; Lenny is my oldest friend, I'm pretty sure he always will be. We go together like Starsky and Hutch but without solving crimes, more likely committing them. We could go together like Mills and Boon but I'd rather not, people will talk. Clint and Clyde, Donny and Marie? Nah, I'm not dressing up like a woman. Lenny might.

It can't be said my accommodation have seen better days. They are having better days than when we brought them home for the princely sum of twenty quid. That's how much was handed over by grandfather to the lorry driver whose lorry they didn't fall off the back of. I could live comfortably in the main farmhouse, Maccy Junior and I much prefer the carriages, for now anyway.

When Jennifer departed suddenly, I took Macdonald, my young son and the two of us had moved in. I had lived in them previously of course and over the years they have become a welcome bolthole. My third home is down on the quayside in Padstow, the Mermaid my very own pub. ** Its full title is The Mermaid and Bow. The 'Bow' - which has nothing whatsoever to do with the pointed end of a boat and cannot be worn under the collar of a shirt, or even in the hair - section of the title seems to have been forgotten by most everyone. One last thing, it also cannot be used for gentlemen bending their backs in a formal way as in bowing and scraping. I have no idea what 'scraping' has to do with it either. I make up my mind to reintroduce the item in a literary sense only.

Footnotes:

* McCarthy City was founded in 1873. It came into being due to the building of the railroad and it passes through the same area of Southern Kansas in what would become Ford County, which it is today.

** Legend states a Mermaid was shot by an archer. As she lay cursing and dying, she grasped a handful of sand and threw it into the Camel estuary. Thus, was formed Padstows' infamous Doom Bar! It is said the Doom Bar has taken hundreds, possibly thousands of lives.

Chapter Three

River Rage.

The Mermaid and Bow Inn belongs to me! It had for a while belonged to the two of us, Jennifer and myself. Now it's just there. Not so much a milestone, now it feels more like a millstone. I have little or no interest in the place right now. I should be shot for dereliction of duty. Lenny, my life-long mucker is keeping the pub running with help from his wonderful sister, Alice. I know it is in safe hands.

Next to the Mermaid is Lost Souls Creek. Dusty runs his sea bus business from the creek and it is fast becoming rather successful. My brother keeps an eye on Lenny for me and Lenny keeps an eye on Dusty in the same way, though the kid is unaware obviously. They both are to be fair.

I hardly have the will to stand behind the bar of the Mermaid again. Jennifer and I had been building the trade up slowly but surely. For so many years, it had owned an unenviable reputation. The old pub had been scraping the bottom of the barrel when we took it over from the Blighs; now the Blighs have retired to Plymouth. Jennifer has departed and we won't meet again until I pop my clogs. I don't believe things can ever be the same, I am just not interested. The Mermaid makes money, pays its' way. I know I should return sometime. Maybe I will, I'm just not ready yet.

Cap'n Bligh and Blencathra were our predecessors. They ruled through notoriety. Blen' did anyway. I'm not sure they ever received education in the art of being mein hosts. With those two, it was pretty much, sit down, drink your beer, shut your gob and go home when I tell you to. A knowing where you stood sort of effort.

The Mermaid is holding its own now, thanks to Lenny and Alice. The two manage the place in my prolonged absence. The arrangement allows me to traipse around Kansas as and when I like. It's not a case of like, more a case of being somewhere else. I still live in Little Petrock but pop over to the USA now and then, as you do. To be fair, this is only my second visit. Maybe my last.

The old bloke at the gas station, my temporary landlord, is good enough company. Close company is something I don't need right now. To be fair, he's a right pain in the arse. His nagging is worse than Ma. I'm not even sure what he's saying half the time. There is a fair amount of mumbo jumbo going on, occasionally interspersed with very broken English, so broken it's mostly irreparable. The old feller gives me the feeling I have an inferiority complex. I'm almost sure it is his own. He's just trying to pass it on to me. Maybe it's the other way around? Anyway, one of us has one, the other one might have.

"You sure you ain't had a bump on the head feller?" He had enquired, when I told him of my plans.

I replied the best I could. "Might have. I might even have lost my memory, how the hell would I know." How does anyone know if they've recently lost that faculty? It's all down to thinking, a person has either done or said something or not done or said something they have done or not done, isn't it? The person might or might not have unless witnesses are available. Witnesses aren't always believable, especially if they are suffering the same symptoms as someone who has lost their memory. A bit like Mavis from Corrie: 'I'm not really sure'. Imagine her being in court as a witness, she would quickly be locked up for contempt!

"Beats me. Look youngster, that place is about to fall down, it's turning to dust. It's a ghost town. There's only me left around these parts. You can't stay here even if you do own it."

"We'll see, I'll give it a try. I'll let you know if you're right." I get the feeling he'll know before me. I'm sure he smokes something he shouldn't. It has the effect of him disappearing in plain sight. Possibly it makes me invisible to him also. Now that would make good sense.

The old bloke spits a lot. It looks like tobacco juice, I'm sure it is. The Indian had directed me to the store Dusty and I had visited once before with Renee as a back-seat passenger. Well meant but pointless. I remembered it's twenty miles down the road. 'Down the road'? I use the term as loosely as he did. It's a dirt track pretty much. They don't have roadkill around here. There's hardly anything that can be described as a road, a bit like Cornwall I suppose. There's nothing to kill either. All reptiles are apparently sleeping for a couple of months.

I have everything I need and once again I am in McCarthy City's dusty main street. A street I am certain has only ever seen two automobiles. Each had been driven by me, almost ten years apart. I don't remember seeing the old geezer on the first visit. He must have been away at a spitting convention. He almost certainly came first. I've seen him in action. As far as I know, he's good. I don't think he's thought of me as a target as yet.

The Plainsmans' interior has changed little since my previous visit. The ancient saloon has more dust, more cobwebs, more broken, more live-in rodents. Just the one difference, no Renee. Other than that, it is the same. It almost makes the Mermaid look like a palace. I am sometimes prone to exaggeration.

The building still smells of Renee. I don't mean it in any disrespectful way towards the old lady, my great aunt. It just feels as though she is still here although I know her to be in the tiny cemetery at the end of the main street. I doubt she will ever be followed. There won't be anyone to follow her unless I suddenly keel over for no apparent reason while I'm in residence. My one regret is my younger brother and I did not make it to the old girl's funeral. We didn't know until we knew! We had only met the once, I would not swap that unforgettable time for anything. Time-warps can do that!

The family knew nothing about her passing or our inheritance until the letters started coming from a Kansas City lawyer. Eventually one of those letters explained the kid, my brother and I, had been left everything she had owned. Most of it is just dust, some of what's left is rotten wood and crumbling mud plaster, which will pretty soon become more dust. It seems we own a lot of ancient footprints and some firewood which wouldn't keep a fire burning long.

I stow my meagre supplies in anything resembling cupboards, I leave the fishing tackle at the door. The old git had insisted I use it for emergencies, in case I run out of food. The way I see it, if I run out of food, fishing will not help me if last time was anything to go by. You never know. 'Catfish are your quarry' The old bloke had reminded once again. I'm not too certain I want to eat catfish. If they're anything like their feline counterparts, they eat, dump, sleep and smell a lot as I remember. Catfish sound like a cross between my brother and Lenny.

For now, I store my beer supplies in the darkest coldest part of the old building, but I know I'll be drinking them warm unless I do my drinking in the early hours of the morning, when the temperature might dip below eighty degrees for a couple of hours before it rises to ninety for the remainder of the day. I'm not against heat, I just don't like too much of it against me. Sunbathing is for those with nothing better to do. Hereabouts, no-one does it. They are just naturally a leathery and crispy brown.

I sleep well in my sleeping bag. I fry a decent breakfast over an open fire in the hearth. I eat burned bacon and fried eggs that might have been cooked on a greasy engine block. I'd eaten Renee's food before, just. It could have been best described as 'iffy' but honest. My own efforts were iffy and dishevelled. I am partly ready for action. My first plan of the day is to make something of a cooler for my food and more importantly for my beers. The stream is a hundred yards away from the old saloon at a rough guess and it is here I would have any chance of preserving my food. I get to work.

Every now and then I look over my shoulder and up at the grassy knoll. There is no one. She is not present. She might be, she managed to sneak up on me before, twice. I didn't even hear her horse.

It will be easy enough to make a cooler. I gather as many small rocks as I can find and put them to one side. Next, I scour around for some larger ones. Four large slabs will be enough I decide. I stand the larger slabs up in a square against each other, push them into the mud of the stream bed. I use the smaller stones to help fill any spaces and muddy up the sides until there is hardly a gap. Next, I place a large plastic bag inside and push the sides out to meet the slabs. The bag being an insulated one would surely help my food to keep longer, my beers colder. I throw a loose plastic sack over the top of the bag to keep the sun off. I bring my beer down and just simply put it all in the stream next to my food cooler. It's complete. I will most likely have need to go get more of the liquid tomorrow.

I collect the rod and some bait. I am once more ready to catch any fish stupid enough to allow me to land it. If it's as stupid as me, it will be simple. While I lay here propped up on my elbows, I suddenly realise if I am lucky enough to catch something, I would be sustaining my other supplies even longer. Gradually I decide I wouldn't mind at all getting a bite. I take a lot more notice of the piece of cork than I had yesterday.

While I wait, I use a tad more of the stream bed for something useful. I search for more stones, medium sized this time. When I have enough, I use them to section off a small and shallow section of the bank. Now I have somewhere to keep any fish fresh and they can't escape once caught. I don't have any fish food, they will go without whilst in captivity. All I need to do now is catch some which are fully fed. Almost certainly it will be a long day. On thinking about it, if they are fully fed, I won't be catching any at all!

The inevitable happens. Somehow, I knew it would, which I suppose means the same thing. I watch the tiny ripples as they meander away from the cork and I believe she has returned; somewhere close behind me is Spittin' Woman. I'm sure she and the old feller must be related. For some unknown reason I rather like the idea she is back. I half wish I didn't.

I turn my head slowly and can see absolutely nothing. The glaringly hot sun temporarily blinds me. It doesn't challenge my hearing in any way.

"Fish man."

"Spitting Woman!"

"I don't have any watermelon seeds today, that was my last one, Brit."

"You're in luck, I don't have any fish yet."

"You won't either, Brit."

"What makes you say that?" I am asking a question of someone I still can't see - where have I heard that before - though I have some memory of how she looked yesterday, which means nothing. Knowing my luck, she might be an alien and can change her appearance at any given time. I believe camels spit in a puking sort of manner, spraying their surrounds in the process. I don't mention it. I'm not as stupid as I seem. There I go again, I'm bigging myself up once more. I feel sure she called me a *'Limey idiot' under her breath. I'm not about to make an accusation. I might be stupid; I'm not about to add to it.

Temporary aid appears. A single cloud that must have lost its way shields the powerful rays; she is silhouetted for a moment. She steps down and forward. She approaches like a stealthy mountain lion, I think. I haven't seen one yet and am unlikely to hereabouts. Kansas is far too flat. If the Alsatian was here, I could watch it run away for a couple of days.

She is in pink shirt and blue jeans. The shirt with frills at the edges. Her long sleek, blonde hair is pulled through a multi coloured baseball cap and forms a loose ponytail. She speaks like Miss Ellie. The glinting star dangles loosely about her neck. Each time I have seen her, she has been wearing it. Our meetings equate to three in ten years now.

I didn't like Dallas that much. JR Ewing reminded me too much of me, though he was far better off in the suit department, I just have the one. He had one for each section of the day, more for the following day. I do recall the smart arse Texan from California being portrayed as a Yank, Jack-the-Lad, slimy like a landed fish. At least Mister Hagman's mother was English. There must have been some good in him. Just bad luck she wasn't Cornish!

The wayward cloud still blots out the sun. She still hasn't answered my question. It sounds like she won't.

"So Yank, tell me why you think I won't be catching any fish."

"Easy Brit, you didn't bait your hook."

Embarrassed, I pull the line from the water and discover she is perfectly correct, there is nothing. "How did you know? How long have you been here?" The float and line drift out into the centre of the water as we talk.

"Long enough, Brit. Did you bait up yesterday?"

"I don't remember, far too much else going on at the time. So, are you taking a day off from spitting?"

"Sure, I just rode out here to see if my pistols are working. Are you gonna be rude to me again Limey?"

"To tell the truth darlin', you were spitting before I was rude, don't you remember? Do you have a preferred target?" I am sure she has no intention of shooting me, it still doesn't stop me being nervous.

"Maybe, Brit."

I think the smile grows even wider and it has a hint of deviltry. Now, I see her completely for the first time. I might have shuddered a little as I look at her fully. She has two of everything - obviously not everything, the nose and mouth are singular - and is not afraid to show them off. No wait, I am not considering her built-in female accoutrements. I might be.

This young woman is resting her small hands on two of the longest ** handguns I have ever seen. I'm surprised they aren't banging on her knees. To be fair I haven't seen that many, not this close up anyway. Usually on a TV screen right before I turn it off. The only other is where I placed it, under the seat in the pick-up. I do wish she would stop patting a gun butt!

She is heavily armed and maybe dangerous, definitely veering towards it. As there are only two of us present, I think I should be careful not to antagonise her too much. She might not have been joking regarding checking out her pistols. For some strange reason, the hardware resting on the outside of her thighs makes her seem larger, taller than I at first thought. I also begin to get the impression she knows how to utilise the sidearms if and when they might be needed. I'm hoping the occasion won't arise while she is here, while I'm here. Better for me not to wind her up!

In my defence she did begin the exchanges. I suppose spitting 'watermelon' seeds at a stranger is not a hanging offence. It could be, I have my doubts. What worries me now is, because we have become acquainted in some small way, does it allow her to continue as before, only more so? Will I be caught up in a second bombardment, sometime in my future? That's assuming I have one.

"So Brit, you look like y'all are staying a while."

"Just long enough to catch my supper." I won't catch anything. I can't tell her that, she'll think I'm as crazy as she is.

"I didn't mean that. I meant here, in McCarthy City."

"I don't know. Haven't made up my mind." While I'm watching my step, I'm keeping an eye on her hands. A difficult task for obvious reasons!

"Like the fish. They haven't made up their mind to let you catch them without any bait."

This woman is starting to niggle me. She is pointing out the obvious and I don't seem to be doing anything about it.

I make up my mind and pull the line in. I attach a disgruntled worm, I expect it to be disgruntled, I don't know for sure. I know I would be if someone stuck a metal hook up my arse. I would be downright niggled. I cast the line out again into the deeper section of the slow-running stream where I first saw her while washing. It was the first time we met eye to eye. She couldn't have been more than fourteen. My float settles itself momentarily, before almost instantly disappearing below the water's surface. Now I'm surprised I wasn't half eaten whilst bathing.

I hear her walking away behind me and feel sure my face has dropped, my bottom lip anyway. I look again for the piece of cork and it is nowhere to be seen. I feel panic, I'm not sure why. Which just shows how pathetic I have recently become.

Somewhere below the water's surface a fish is calling me to pluck it out. Somewhere behind me, my small protagonist - not so small to be truthful, it all depends on the beholder I suppose - is leaving me to deal with something I hadn't much thought about previously. The panic is building, I begin to hope the fish will suddenly lose interest and detach itself from my hook. Right now, I am a tad flummoxed. A flummoxed Cornishman and fish should go together easily.

"Give me that, Brit."

She has returned. She glares at me for a second. In her impatience, there is still a hint of the smile. She snatches at my rod and pulls a large flapping fish clear of the water. Before it has a chance to meow, I hear a sound that reminds me of the Cathedral at Notre Dame. Not that I've actually been to Paris. My ears are ringing. The large fish lies on the sandy ground below me. There is a space where its head had been, its body is still flapping, gradually less so. I turn to face her as she replaces the still smoking right-hand pistol. I didn't actually see her take it out of its holster. I was looking at her at the time. The six-gun just seemed to appear in her hand. She would make an excellent pickpocket.

"You shot my bleddy fish!"

"My fish, Brit. I caught it. Anyway, it's better than bashing it with a rock, don't you think?"

I don't know what to think. I do wonder if she has recently escaped from some local madhouse. Fishing is supposed to be a quiet, leisurely pastime. "My fish. It's my bleddy stream so it's my bleddy fish." Bashing it with a rock? We don't do that in Padstow. We just let them flap about until they get tired and cease breathing.

"Your stream? I don't have a clue what you're talking about, Brit. I caught the fish, I shot the fish, that makes it my fish. Even the fishing pole ain't yours." She pats a pistol menacingly. At least I feel it is menacingly, I can't be certain. I don't want to be certain. Patting is pretty okay to be fair!

"Okay, you can have the fish. You can have its head too, if you can find it."

"I don't want the darn fish. I caught it for you, Brit. You were making a mess of it, I helped you out is all."

"Right and you made a smaller mess of it after you helped it out of the water."

"Maybe, its head had to come off anyway, unless you were gonna throw it back and not eat tonight. If you throw it back now, it won't know where to go. Either way, I don't give a damn."

Damn and bugger. Once again, she has made me feel as though my bottom lip should be quivering. I hope it isn't. Why did she have to say 'I don't give a damn'? On second thoughts, why should it bother me? I didn't know the answer to either question. I did know it bothered me; I didn't know why. One thing I did learn about her today, this girl, woman, call her what you will, I'm not about to annoy her. I do doubt she ever landed a complete fish in her life. So much for me thinking catching a fish would be simple. It would be easier to start a world war. Probably less messy! 'It won't know where to go'? This woman reminds me of Lenny, in a much more attractive way obviously.

I look at my beer supply, languishing in the water and consider downing it all in one early evening attempt at drunkenness. I put the plan on hold.

"We could share it?" Now I know I'm sounding like a whining schoolkid, not for the first time.

"Ain't that up to me, Brit? You just now gave me the fish back, didn't ya?"

For a second, I consider snatching one of her pistols and blowing a hole in my own head. Then I remember what happened to the fish. It's a well known fact fish don't feel pain, I know I do. They are cold-blooded, I'm not. We don't get cold-blooded fish murderers in Padstow. On thinking about it, maybe we do. I wonder if this female, this girl or woman, is here to make me crazy. I know, someone is after my town and they have sent her out here to get me sectioned! Once I'm out of the way, job done. I wonder how much she's getting paid by some shady land grabber.

"Okay, half each." I look down at the remains and the fish is still a good size even without its head. It was much bigger earlier. Bigger and ugly.

"You cook, Brit?"

"I went to catering college."

"You went to catering college just so you could cook a fish?"

"No, I went to catering college just so I could cook."

"Thank the lord for small mercies."

"Why do you say that?"

She begins to walk away again. "Simple limey, I don't cook. I don't cook well at all!"

"I completely understand. It must be difficult trying to cook when you're riding a horse most of the time or shooting something to death. Not forgetting spitting. Now that does constitute multi-tasking."

She is already searching for something and I have no idea what. She soon returns with two handfuls of dried sticks and one or two larger broken tree limbs.

"Dig us a hole Brit, need to get a fire burning unless you like Sushi?"

"So, you're staying for tea then?"

"Tea, you mean dinner!"

"I do, if you say so!"

Author's notes:

* The term is thought to have originated in the 1850s as lime juicer later shortened to 'limey' and originally used as a derogatory word for sailors in the Royal Navy. Since the beginning of the 19th century it had been the practice of the Royal Navy to add lemon juice to the sailors' daily ration of grog (watered-down rum). At that time lemon and lime were used interchangeably to refer to citrus fruits. Initially, lemon juice (from lemons imported from Europe) was used as the additive to grog on the Royal Navy ships but was later switched to limes (grown in British colonies), not realising that limes did not contain sufficient Vitamin C to prevent the disease.

** The womans' pistols are seven- and one-half inch long barrel, Colt Army revolvers weighing: 2.31 lbs - 1.048 kgs. Calibre 44. The weapon was first manufactured in 1873.

Chapter Four

Alone again, naturally.

They didn't teach us how to cook Sushi when I went to catering college! I don't see raw fish going down too well with chips, mushy peas and a pickled onion. I do as she orders. I scoop out a shallow pit with my hands. I didn't have a spade with me surprisingly, very remiss! She arranges the twigs and the thicker pieces. I watch her as she spears the fish after pulling out its insides. She had produced a knife of the * 'Bowie' design, it was in the side of her boot. I don't ask. Would you?

She sets the meal down gently on the two uprights. I consider this is some strange woman. Then I remember, she's a Yank. While she works, I have the chance to study her in greater detail. My bet is she's aware of being scrutinised, a temperate word meaning, I am ogling. I try to convince myself I'm not. Somehow my admission would most likely not stand up in court. I do wonder about her confession regarding not being able to cook, I couldn't cook myself not so long ago.

The smile I already know is semi-permanent. The clothes are smart, they look as if they have seen hard work at times. The shape of her body might be called classical by somebody who knows about these things. I know no more than a smidgen. She isn't tall, quite short, her litheness allows for some misinterpretation. She is easy on the eye. Her hair cascades from the red, white and blue baseball cap and she is wearing tight fitting riding boots with Cuban heels. Lastly, she has the wide leather gun belt giving the impression of pulling in her waist. To be honest, everything she has makes her what she is. It scares me more than a little. I'll get over it and then again perhaps I don't want to. The glinting blade of the huge knife is a worry. There was no sign of blood on it until she gutted the fish.

I try not to think about the tight fitting jeans on account they are not only tight but better known as 'pants' this side of the big wet bit we all call the Atlantic. On our side of the pond 'pants' are worn inside, unless you're Superman, an 'all American' weirdo! Let's face it, being afraid of a small lump of rock covered in moss is a tad wussy. We have a Rock opposite Padstow which is much larger than it needs to be. Us locals don't have a lot of time for it though and hardly use its' name at all. I try not to. I know there is a place called Stone in Staffordshire. Maybe they are related in some way. I maybe shouldn't mention it here, but I knew a woman once that didn't wear pants on the inside or the outside. She will remain nameless and most likely remains pantless in the most decent way of course.

Imagine a load of people in the 'lighter ages' - which are slightly brighter than the dark ages for reasons that aren't obvious - building a village? When it's completed, the village elder says 'right, what shall we call it?' Everyone says 'Rock' – obviously they couldn't have a postal vote. Another idiot says 'cool' and that's it, vote over. It's a good thing he didn't say 'Pool', we might have had a village called Rockpool, Cesspool, Liverpool. Just a thought! A nice place apparently. Scousers like it anyway. Are they a good collective judge? The jury is out.

"Hey Brit, do you have anything to eat with about the place?"

Her calm voice snaps my imagination out of its weird wondering nature at exactly the right time; I am certain it is about to become almost indecent. If I said this is the farthest thought from my mind I would be wrong. It is fast becoming the closest and I don't think I want that. She might not be too pleased either to be fair. She does have a huge knife. Averting my gaze is proving difficult.

I thought I had returned here to Kansas to ponder my future. I think I might have to kick things over and start all over again. I thought I was coming here to not have to talk to anyone. I hadn't been expecting conversation. So far I have done nothing but look stupid. Nothing new there. If I did try to kick anything, I would most likely fall over! Jen' would be laughing her head off. She knew how clumsy I could be when attempting something serious. Such as acting like a bloody clown in front of a strange lady. For me it is pretty much par for the course.

I hadn't given a thought to a particularly nice attractive American Lady - I have no idea if she is 'nice' just a reasonable assumption on my part - getting in the way right now and somehow, it makes me just a little bit sad. I still have no idea of her name. I don't know if she is in fact a lady. What the hell am I saying? I have no idea one way or another.

I forget she had asked me a question and is expecting an answer before the meal crystallises. "Nope, just these!" I insert two fingers inside my mouth.

"Fingers it is then!"

Cutlery, she means cutlery. I thought she meant she didn't have any teeth and she may not have. Now she probably thinks I don't. How was I to know. We would have to eat without. I hadn't been expecting company. "I'm Maccy, Macdonald Tamryn." I feel an introduction is long overdue. She doesn't reply immediately. I wait a while. She doesn't reply at all. She is obviously unimpressed!

I did attempt to find cutlery, I returned from the old saloon empty handed. I had completely forgotten why I went there. She ordered me not to try again. I wisely took her advice.

It is peculiar, I can't even decide her age. Her voice is mature, like a mother, a grandmother even. Her body is that of a woman in her very early prime. Her effervescent smile is almost that of a child, it never seems to fade. I feel I am getting myself into trouble; I'm still entrenched in the last lot. I'm not sure how to get out of it right now. I might just be exaggerating. The way my head is working at this moment, she might be a figment of my imagination. It's

39

not the first time my brain has run amok. Chances are, it won't be the last. Another important point would be, if my brain didn't 'run away with me' I most likely wouldn't be able to run at all. I would be static. It's doing it again, I rest my case!

"So Brit, catfish got your tongue?"

"Nope, I'm thinking about something."

"You want to tell me?"

"No way, I haven't finished yet. I might be some while."

"Then I'm gonna swim Brit, join me? Lessen you're chicken."

Now I don't know what to think. Without hesitation she stripped off her outer clothes, leaving just scant underwear in place. "Are you gonna swim like that, Yank?"

"I think only the fish swim naked around thisaway Brit, unless you know something I don't. It is your stream as you keep tellin' me. Do you have rules regarding swimwear, Brit?"

I do, though I'm not about to put my thoughts into words. She is already in the water where I had been half standing the very first time I saw her. She was little more than a child then. She is far from it now. I did the only thing I could do under the circumstances. I kept my shorts on!

"Just the one, you already broke it." She laughed, I laughed, we laughed. We swam about twenty yards before emerging with shivers.

She had swum faster than I ever saw anyone swim without watching the Olympics. She had glided through the water like she was born to it, she hardly left a wake, the water seemed to part without persuasion. I didn't chase her as it would be pointless. At least I wasn't 'chicken'. We had a time of it for nothing more than a few minutes, as she soon strode out of the water shivering, as I did myself. I watched her mesmerising movements.

"Can I use your sleeping bag, Brit? I'm getting cold."

"You should have brought towels maid!"

"I didn't plan to swim. Don't call me maid!"

"I'm sorry, so why did you?"

"Simple Brit, the water was there. Your damned water as you like to keep reminding me."

"I shared it, we shared it."

"Yes, we did, Brit. You do realise I've swum in your creek before, many times since I was a youngster. Not always dressed this way."

Now I'm not sure if she was calling me simple or just telling the truth. They amount to the same thing I guess. It is just my stream, not my water. The water she stepped into has by now moved on to belong to some other idiot. There could be hundreds of shareholders all owning the riverbank, there's no point in owning a stretch of stream. In very hot weather the water can just evaporate and come down somewhere else where someone else won't own it. I put myself in my place. "You have? I'm honoured yank." She is scary!

"Don't you mind, Brit?"

"Not at all, yank."

Catfish to another catfish: 'I don't like it here. I'm moving on.'

'Why, where will you go?'

'There's a stupid bloke comes here looking for us, he never puts any bait on his hook. I can't be bothered with that. What's the point? He's wasting our time and his own.'

'A foreigner most likely.'

'Could be. No idea. What's a bloke anyway?'

'I don't have a clue, but he's got a nice girlfriend!'

'I've seen her, I was swimming with her earlier.'

'Did she have any food?'

'Eventually, she shot one of us.'

'Which one?'

'No idea, she blew the head off before I could recognise it. It wasn't either of us anyway.'

'Such is life.'

'Yeah, for us!'

'So, what time are you going?'

'How the hell should I know?'

'Can't you even tell the time?'

'Erm, no, I don't think I can!'

'That's a coincidence! I have a short attention span too. It's a fish thing I suppose.'

'What is?'

'I can't remember.'

'I'm glad I'm not a goldfish.'

'Why?'

'I don't know.'

'So am I.'

'What?'

She dragged the bedding closer to the fire as she asked the question. I nodded; it would help until I knew what to say. "Be my guest. I mean of course, go ahead." I don't want her to misconstrue my first thoughtless reply, or do I? I'm not certain we would both fit inside the bag and in any case, it's going to be dripping wet. It has to be worth a try. She did exactly as I suggested.

"Thanks, Brit. It wasn't your creek when I watered my horse mister!"

"How would you know that, yank?"

"You might be surprised. I'm all knowing maybe."

In only a short while we were talking like old friends. "We met once before. I'll put it another way, we were both here before. You allowed your horse to drink from the creek, my creek. I remember it like it was only yesterday. You smiled as you rode away."

"Ten years is a long time, Brit."

"You remember. I wasn't sure you would."

"Sure I remember. It's why I'm out here ya damn fool. Damn fool Brits, can't even take a hint!"

"How, I mean, how can that be? How did you know I was here this time?" The latter part of her comment went right over my head almost. 'Damn fool, damn Brit?' That's nice. To be fair to her, she does seem to be a good judge of character. I have been called various worse things. Many times, I've called myself worse things, all unrepeatable in present company.

"You wouldn't understand, Brit. You will someday. Be patient. Just be patient and keep busy."

"I'll try, I'm Maccy. Macdonald Tamryn. I don't do patience that well."

"I know who you are Brit, you already told me ten minutes ago. I ain't senile and forget everything someone tells me dammit. You could try harder."

She reminds me of a schoolteacher now. Back of the class here I come. Now I expect to find out. Still there is no actual name swapping. I look at her, she is already sleeping, she might be shamming. No, I must have bored her into unconsciousness. No surprise there.

I feel it's time for a cigar. It is my last one and I smoke it before sleeping. I'm not sure yanks smoke cigars. Groucho Marx used to. Actually I never saw a film where he did smoke one. He just seemed to waggle them under his nose most of the time. I wonder who invented cigars? Some Cuban dictator more than likely. On second thoughts, possibly Neanderthal man. He might have seen a leaf growing somewhere and thought, I'll dry that out, roll it up and stick it in my mouth. So, he might have done that, got bored with it and decided to burn it. He didn't know how to burn it and so he invented fire. His next thought might have been not knowing what to do with it, so he left it in his mouth and waited for it to disappear. Realising lumps of ash were falling off all the while, he decided to invent the 'ashtray'!

Later this ancient smoker got a friend to try the same exercise. Having invented fire, they built a hearth, chucked a load of leaves and an out of date newspaper – probably The Daily Quake – in it and sat there with rolled up leaves stuck between their lips. The pair may have tried conversation, there might not have been a lot to talk about until a chicken might have walked past. The perfect time for a eureka moment.

"Hey Grunt, bet you a sabretooth tigers tooth you won't eat the first thing that comes out of that chickens butt."

"I already have a sabretooth tigers' tooth."

"Okay what about a mammoths' toenail?"

"Got loads of them."

"Bet you a cigar lighter."

"What's a cigar lighter?"

"Now you're just being ridiculous. I've no idea!"

They might not have had to have wait long and the friend could have done just that. He ate the first thing to come out of the hen's rear. The first caveman might have said: "You're disgusting, it was covered in chicken shit."

Second caveman: "You egged me on, it's your fault. Where's my cigar lighter?"

"Why ask me? I egged you on. Brilliant, that's what we'll call it, an egg. I'm off now, can't stop."

"Where are you going, Groan?"

"Isn't it obvious, I'm gonna see if I can find a frying pan."

"What for?"

"I don't know yet!"

Later:

"Did you find a frying pan?"

"I'm not sure, I think so."

So, what did the egg taste like?"

"No idea, Grunt. I got my mouth full of chicken feathers and eggshell. It was vile!"

"Where's my cigar lighter?"

"Stop scratching on the bloody walls for Christ's sake. One of these days everyone will be doing it. It'll be everywhere you go. Some idiot will probably call himself Banksy one day and it'll be all your fault. That looks like a bloody Giraffe."

"It's my bleddy cave, I'll do what I like. What's a Giraffe?. Who's Christ?"

"How do you expect me to know? I've only been around as long as you have."

"You brought it up!"

"I couldn't help that, Grunt. It tasted disgusting. I wish I hadn't stuck my neck out now."

"We could eat the chicken, where did it go?"

"Over there Grunt, across the road."

"Why did it cross the road?"

"Just a guess, it's mother was calling it in for tea."

"What's tea and where's my cigar lighter?"

"Is it me or is it cold in here, Groan?"

"Bit nippy."

"It's like being in a fridge."

"No, it's not. If it was like a fridge the bleddy light would be on."

"Why?"

"Easy, the door is open."

"We don't have a door."

"Same thing!"

"What's a fridge?"

"Don't do that, someone might want to look at it one of these days."

"What time is it now?"

"Why don't you buy youself a watch?"

"What with?"

Whoever would have thought a chicken, a cigar and a Giraffe would become the three most important things in the whole wide, very flat world? Not forgetting a cigar lighter of course!

She is gone it seems and it's time for me to return home. There isn't much point in me staying here now she is no longer here. It was far too short, it was sweet. It was good while it lasted. I spread the sleeping bag to dry out. A small piece of paper slid out due to my action. The inscription: 'nu nahaniatsa' Macdonald. Great, now what do I do?

Telling me to be patient was not at all helpful. If I was, it would be completely alien to me. It would be like waiting for one's Christmas presents to open themselves, imagine that. Maybe I dreamt the whole thing. There is no evidence of her ever having been here apart from the

45

dampness of the interior of my bag. I couldn't even find the fish head, maybe she took it with her. If I believe that, I'll believe anything. Now I will never know her name. She did tell me to be patient. Best I do as she said. She had made the fire, it is just ash now, there is hardly anything left and nothing at all of her. The chances of seeing her again I believe are remote. I think I dreamt of something. Maybe I should give up on the cigars, I might stop dreaming so often. Dreaming can't be so bad, Bobby Ewing did it for years!

Author's note:

* The Bowie knife is a pattern of fixed-blade fighting knife created by James Black in the early 19th century for Jim Bowie, who had become famous for his use of a large knife at a duel known as the Sandbar Fight. Since the first incarnation, the Bowie knife has come to incorporate several recognizable and characteristic design features, although in common usage the term refers to any large sheath knife with a cross guard and a clip point.

Chapter Five

Down but not out.

The evening on the riverbank with her had been charming; more than that, it helped me make up my mind not to return. She certainly knew how to ask a question in the plural, she hardly stopped. It was endearing in a way. It's not what I'm used to; my usual friends rarely ask why I do anything, they know better! I like to keep myself to myself, unless I've had a few, then I can talk to my heart's content. No one listens.

She had a way with her which made me spill all. It made me think. If she was here now and she's not, she must have reasoned she didn't want to be in my vicinity any longer. It doesn't make any sense. She told me to be patient. How can I be something I've never been before and patient for what? She can't need a miserable git like me in her life right now, nor ever. No one deserves that. I'm not here solely to make others miserable. I could have stayed home, saved the air fare. I really don't do patience very well.

The girl must have far better things to do than nursemaid an eccentric and inept Cornishman. Before she began to sleep, I had told her what was in my tiny mind. The smile had stayed in position and I took it as a sign she accepted it. To be fair, we had only shared a bullet-ridden fish. I'm not certain I trusted the smile. She is gone now, there's no arguing that.

Slight exaggeration regarding the fish, though it is now formally deceased. Only Freddie Starr eats his food live. I wonder if he is a full-time Hamster breeder? I can imagine him sitting next to a glass tank full of pregnant rodents, waiting impatiently, suddenly yelling 'here comes breakfast'!

It had been an interesting evening and I won't forget it. She most likely already has. I had talked about myself mostly, she asked a lot of questions. She asked why I'm here; I told her little. I've done little of what I had promised myself I would do. So far I seem to have spent a fair bit of time dodging spit and picking on fish. We had talked for hours, mostly about Little Petrock, Padstow and McCarthy City.

I had a feeling there was something she wasn't telling me her name for one thing. I didn't venture the question, just assumed she would tell me. She has left it a bit late now. I suppose I'm just not important enough to be, important.

In a way it made it even more difficult. I believe she had done the right thing. She had obviously left to carry on as before. Our parting had been wholly painless for both of us. We had parted where there had been no joining of anything. Had she saved me from myself? It's a possibility. I sure hope I saved her from me. Her invisibility seems to confirm it.

I had one last thing to do before I left McCarthy City, I broke the door in of the ancient newspaper office on the off chance I would find something interesting. In all honesty, I didn't break the door in, it fell in when I touched it, I didn't have to break anything, the place is falling apart. The inside of the building was in a much worse condition than the Plainsman. I found little of interest until I was about to leave, an ancient desk still held a small bundle of documents in a card sheaf. I didn't look too closely as I carefully picked the item up and wrapped it in my empty cooler bag to take it home. There's no harm in acquiring a souvenir.

I endured a crash free return to Little Petrock. All very quiet and thoughtful. Macdonald Junior is sleeping in the warm wooden carriage, I am awake in the tiny add-on sitting room. It must have been added on, cattle don't normally have sitting rooms as far as I know. I have bought a laptop computer since returning home, my first

PC, whatever that means. I doubt it has anything to do with the local constabulary. If it did I wouldn't allow it in the house.

Dusty has been using one for a while, he showed me how to use this. I am not one for modern toys. While we talked and before she fell asleep, the girl, whatever her name is, had given me a small slip of paper. She had written what she called her email address on the scrap. It must be hers it's unlikely she would have given me someone else's. There's little point in giving me the email address of someone I don't even know. It gave me no inkling as to her name; a single X is all that is added. I wrote a handful of notes each of which were almost instantly returned. I had missed one of the smallest things to exist on the planet, the dot. How the hell can something so damned insignificant become so important? It made me wonder why I was even bothering, I didn't really expect a reply.

My brother, Dusty, had coached me in how to send and receive emails and right now, they are all I have. I have Ma and Maccy J of course and I have the ugliest dog in the world beside my feet. I'm not sure which of our feet smell the worst. I'm going with his; he has four, I only have two. His nose is nearer to his than mine is to my own.

As for the internet? It is all totally new to me, new to most people I suppose. I have no idea what it's about. One day there wasn't one, the next day there was. After achieving semi literacy in table-top electronics, I had eventually managed written to write to her, she had replied almost instantly. I couldn't believe she had been waiting for a message from me. At the time it must have been coincidence. We talked for a while, nothing in particular, nothing too deep, just mundane stuff. Still she is nameless. Unless X is a name. There may have been something between the lines, I wouldn't have noticed. I had difficulty reading the lines I could see. Soon there was nothing. It seems she will remain nameless. There was one thing; 'be patient Brit, keep busy' that was her signature.

A second day nothing arrives electronically. A third day without word from Kansas and I am making rather a poor job of feeling indifferent. I suppose I'm not trying hard enough to not try hard enough. She hadn't signed off with anything even resembling a name, just the cross. What am I to do with a kiss, maybe it wasn't a kiss. It was a cross for No! It's far reaching but what does it say?

I realise what an idiot I am. Why on earth can I expect her to spend all her time writing to me? She has a life. I have no idea what her life entails, it has got to be better than sharing mine. I had more or less told her so by the creek. Of course, she may have already been asleep by then. I hadn't told her the worst bits obviously; she would have left a lot earlier.

It is time. My patience is almost spent. I jab a finger at the button and the machine springs into life once more. I wait for the opening programmes to run through their routine. I almost curse aloud in my frustration. At last! My fingers tremble with anticipation and I clumsily hit the wrong key. 'Sod it!' Another wait.

I watch the opening page appear and my eyes flit to the tiny envelope that might open to show me I have an email. The electronic envelope stays closed. My disappointment grows deeper with every day as the realisation hits me; it is becoming obvious now she will not write again.

I push the button to bring my laptop to a sudden halt. Under my breath I count to ten before I restart it. Again, I wait for the opening page and the reappearance of the envelope. Still there is no tell tale movement. A fully formed tear exits freely. The droplet spreads across the sheet of paper I had printed off and read many times, over and over. I look down and wonder how such a small thing can grow so quickly. I can't do patience; I can do pathetic well enough.

This has been the fourth day now without news. It's a tad disappointing. I feel like launching my coffee cup at the already stained wall. Somehow I control my temper and lean back into the deep leather chair. There could be a good reason for her not writing. She isn't so stupid after all. She might be sick, might have a husband. She might have discovered she didn't even like me. Maybe she accidentally shot herself? It's the age-old problem for bigheads like myself. They, we, I, need to be liked. Don't we all!

I look at the ugly Alsatian lying stretched out at my feet, one ear drooping down flat. The mangled other standing taut and alert, I'm not certain how alert. He tilts his head, maybe waiting for me to break another coffee mug in mock temper? I rub my foot along his back, he settles down with a deep sigh that sounds more like a groan. One eye is left open as he pretends to sleep. He can hardly shut it anyway. The mutt is two-faced; a smile one side and a filthy look on the other. A useful attribute.

The dog had his life changing accident with a powerboat engine when he was a youngster. He's as ugly as sin for it. He doesn't have a name either, but somehow he's mine, though I deny it at every turn. Maybe I'm his. Anyway, he appeared from nowhere some years ago and stayed. We're both pathetic now, rather fitting really. The dog is a has been and I'm a never been!

My hand rests on the mouse and I search successfully for the icon which will enable me to adjust the sound volume. I raise it to maximum and settle back in my chair, one foot gently on my desk, the other firmly on the dog's back. The ugly mutt groans a long complaint and shuts some of his good eye. I wait!

I begin to doze. It is a long period of time. The time difference between us is taking a toll. I will sit here all night, waiting, praying for Joanna Lumley to announce, 'you have mail'. Still the voice of the well lusted after actress - not by me of course - stays silent. What the hell is she even doing in my 'PC'?

A sudden clatter brings me around. My eyes seek out my 'virtual' mailbox, nothing. I realise the noise is from the letterbox in the front door. The morning post has arrived. I have bills! They can wait, they will wait for some time.

Once upon a time another clatter at the door would signify Chalky entering. Poor Chalky is long gone now and I miss him. Cats are great company. They do seem to know when you need them and make it clear through weird noises and crawling all over you when you're trying to watch something on the telly. Much like a woman I suppose.

No email arrives. I sleep all day and into the evening. When I awake and dress, I again sit in front of the screen. Still there is nothing but silence. This is the end, it's all over. Whatever it had been is no more. It hadn't been much in any case!

Who am I trying to kid? I used to be able to do nonchalance, not now it would seem. I don't even know how it had all started. It was nobody's fault. It had crept up on me, us. It began with questions, just normal, simple and sometimes silly requests for information. I remember I didn't have all the answers and so a longer discussion ensued. I fell asleep and she didn't; Americans are a bit behind us timewise, it's not their fault Greenwich belongs to us.

Our exchanges had no importance when this began. Now it seems it has run its course. I have no idea why. Maybe I did know. It's possible I had become rude and impatient, perhaps too demanding. I might have been a pain in the arse, it's happened before. I don't remember ever writing so much before.

I do remember once being told: 'never write anything down that will incriminate yourself', it will lead to nothing but trouble. If I had taken the well-meaning advice, you wouldn't be reading this!

It had all begun on a riverbank in Southern Kansas. I had been quietly fishing. Truth be told, I had been non-fishing. I was just there with a long bendy stick which wasn't working. As a total stranger, she had spat fresh watermelon seeds at me from an almost impossible distance and I was hooked. I might have wriggled and fought a tad or two, I now know it had been pointless. From my point of view, I had been landed for no apparent reason. Now I'm gutted and brainless, a bit like the catfish.

So why would a total stranger spit seeds at another stranger just for the hell of it? 'Excuse me, do you mind if I spit at you? It won't take long if you agree, it will take a lot longer if you don't'.

Just what is construed as a 'perfect stranger', how does anyone know if they're perfect? The 'stranger' word says it all. You can't tell if a stranger is perfect because they are strangers until they're not.

I fished again and she returned. One of us caught a large fish. She shot it. I suppose shooting fish is a Kansan thing. It's better than playing around with it for half an hour while it's still swimming, saves a lot of time. 'Just going out to shoot some fish'! Anyway, we shared it and that was that really. I knew it wasn't a dream, Bobby Ewing wasn't in it. Why does Dallas keep coming into it? I've never even been to Texas!

I call Ma. It is two a.m. and she isn't in the best of moods. I know how she feels. I've been in a bad mood on and off for a couple of years now. I must get out of the carriage and I need someone here with the youngster. Ma agrees to come right away as I knew she would.

As I walk away from the door, I know ma is already cuddled up with the boy and I won't have to worry about him.

Saddling one of Ma's nags, I ride across the fields and down over the rising headwater of Lost Souls Creek, I crossed the creek and never heard a sound that wasn't bats. So much for babies wailing. In my current state, they may have been and I simply never heard them. On to Padstow.

For a moment I wish I was one of those lost in the creek, then I remember Macdonald the Younger and keep riding hard. It is a full moon. It is easy to find my way towards the few lights still twinkling around the harbour in the small hours of the morning.

It takes me around an hour or so to reach my destination. I have always been one for boltholes, this is one which is always in favour. I can see the tops of the larger sailing boats bobbing above the choppy water, their mast-top bells jingling in the darkness. I make myself a large mug of steaming tea and the Alsatian, which had run alongside us in the dark, is sharing the Mermaids' yard with the nag. The dog had followed me the two miles – it might be two and a half or three and a half - to Padstow.

One must remember: a Cornish mile does not equate to any other kind in the UK. They are different, they can be longer, they can be shorter but no two are the same, they fluctuate throughout the Duchy. I suppose it's a sort of ten percent anomaly. It's what we're used to. Travelling on Cornish roads can be a lottery at times. Piskies can be a real pain. If they're out and about, a journey can be extended by any distance. Being Piskielated has nothing to do with television or computer screens, it just means find another route, or you will regret it. Yes, I've experienced the little folks. We all have. One thing that puzzles me is why aren't emmets subjected to these mysterious beings? Maybe they are and that's why they drive in the middle of the road and are on the verge of suicide. Another thing, why the hell do emmets shut their eyes when we're coming towards them? What's that about? It's a recipe for disaster. I should know, I'm a chef!

Personally, I think there is good reason for the well-practiced 'white line' driving. By driving over the white lines – there aren't that many – it gives them a better chance of changing their minds and direction at a junction. They can leave it to the last moment before deciding and they do!

My pony and the mutt will be safe for the day at the rear of the Mermaid. It's not the first time livestock has been left here in the yard. Dusty and I rode here a few years ago. Heavy snow was abundant, and we needed to be in town for a funeral. It was the easiest way to travel from Little Petrock, the day of One-Armed Frank's send off.

Funny thing about Frank; he went off with one arm and we all got legless.

Bert will arrive any minute. He won't be surprised to see me sitting behind the hot water still. Bert is the semi-retired bloke employed to clean this quayside cafeteria every morning in readiness for opening. Bert knows me as well, if not better, than anyone. Poor old Bert, his days are numbered. Neither of us know the total but he must be close to it. Bert can be a close friend to anyone though not everyone. He doesn't suffer fools gladly, apart from yours truly obviously.

Bert is so old it's rumoured he's reached retirement age twice! There have been many mornings when I have greeted him at his place of work. I know every inch of Padstow. I know how to open almost every lock on every door. Nowhere is unavailable to me. Oh, I wouldn't steal a thing. Well maybe the odd teabag and a bacon sandwich, sometimes even a fried egg but I have always tried to repay whatever I had taken, in kind. These days, I don't need to break in. Some years ago the owner provided me with my own key. It's a shame really, I rather enjoyed breaking in without actually breaking anything other than eggshells.

One Christmas Eve when Jennifer and I were just an item, we had left the parish church after midnight Mass and entered the café to have a quiet brew. Within a few minutes, half the town had appeared and demanded supper and anything we could supply in a glass or a mug. All the proceeds had been left in the till. It must have given the owners a nice unexpected Christmas present. I couldn't have been certain as I rarely see the proprietor. I don't get to Saint Lucia too often!

As I peer through the huge panoramic window past the splodges of seagull shit and over the quayside, I can see the town is slowly crawling to life once again. Nothing ever happens in a hurry in Cornwall. It will never change. At least I hope not. Despite the heavy influx of foreigners from London, the home counties and Birmingham –

maybe not Birmingham - every year, Cornwall somehow still manages to hold on to its lethargic independence, as I do myself. I forgot about the Mancs deliberately, oh and the Scousers, obviously. I met seven-hundred of them once, all at the same time. They were in Devon, supposedly to attend a soccer match at Home Park. They must have been lost. Before you ask, who would want to meet seven hundred Scousers twice? To be fair, they were all quite affable. I left them that day with all my wheels and hub-caps still in situ. I did check, I was very grateful. So was ma, it was her car.

"So Maccy, whaddya know?"

Bert had taken the full mug with hardly a word, just the usual crooked toothed smile. I have no idea if they are real, I'm certain they're not. "Nothing Bert, I don't know much right now."

"It's a woman then, who is she lad?"

I don't have a clue how the old geezer does it, he just does it. It's always the same, I tell him absolutely nothing and he knows all there is to know. "A foreigner Bert, a Yank, from America."

"I knaw where they bleddy come from. Hmm, strange bunch I hear. Where did you meet her, lad?"

"In America, Bert." Well okay he doesn't know everything.

"That was 'andy, if you hadn't been there, you wouldn't have."

"True enough, true enough." Bert is a master of stating the bleedin' obvious.

"How's that young laddie of yours coming on Maccy lad, still growing is he?"

"He is Bert, just like the other one." I hope he is, otherwise, I'll always be the father of a four-foot kid. Nothing wrong with that, it would save me money on buying his clothes and footwear. Only Bert and Dusty know of my late night tinkering with Alice Copestick a few years ago. Well Alice knows too of course, she had to be there. Thank the lord her fiancé wasn't. Anyway, the two of them are bringing up the boy just right. I stop and talk to him when I get the chance. Not too often as people might put two and two together. We two look so much alike they might get the wrong idea. They might get the right idea and that would certainly be worse I believe.

"So Maccy, what about this Yank lady, the foreigner?"

"I dunno Bert, nothing I suppose. She lives there, I live here, it doesn't make for a good relationship, does it?" I realise by my statement I have unintentionally let the cat out of the bag. Bert has an honours in cajolement!

"Naw, I don't suppose it does. Maybe you should do something about it, maybe you should forget about it. Maybe you should do nothing and let her do something about it. Maybe you can't do anything about it, maybe she can't, she might not want to, maybe no one can or can't. Why don't you go bleddy fishing?"

"There isn't one of them a good choice Bert, I'm for just getting on with things. I have the little one to consider." Bert, orator extraordinaire! Me fisherman, unextraordinaire. I recently tried it and failed. The last fish I saw was like a headless chicken without the clucking bit obviously.

"That might be true Maccy, or maybe it isn't. He has your Ma and Padraig to keep an eye on him. Why don't you go back, see how the land lies?"

"I don't think so Bert, I have stuff here needs my attention. My pub won't run itself, will it? Bleddy hell Bert, I only just got back and you're trying to get rid of me."

"Lenny is looking after your interests, he's doing a good job, isn't he? He is a bit late opening up most days but stays open later in the evenings to make up for it. Not very late, 'ardly late at all really."

"Yeah, course he is, I know. But well, I should get off my arse, do some myself. I believe it's time for me to look after my business before he gets me shut down. How bleddy late?"

"I don't bleddy remember. Up to you then Maccy, you likely knaw best."

I leave my ancient wreck of a friend to get on with his work. I have taken up enough of his time, nothing has changed. He'll be scouring the floor now for loose change dropped by yesterday's customers. This time of the year coach parties made up of senior citizens swarm into Padstow like old aged riff raff! If they drop coins on the floor, they never hear them as they hardly ever turn their hearing aids on, that's if they aren't lost down the side of a sofa in a beach hut! Bert doesn't earn much from the job, he does well between closing time and opening time.

For me, now I must get my tiny, dislocated mind back into one piece, get my life back into some sort of regular order. It may take a while. I make the decision there and then to leave the laptop turned off. It has been time enough. It has gone as far as it can. All the staring in the world won't change anything and I'm fast running out of coffee mugs. I throw them for the dog to bring back, it is difficult for him when they are in so many small pieces. It keeps him amused!

Chapter Six

Old Friends, strange Faces

After leaving my old friend, I check on my mount before letting myself into the back of the Mermaid. The Alsatian had eyed me with his good eye, it became vocal as I toed it out of the way of the door. The dog gains entry to the Mermaid through a broken window as and when. I have thought about getting it repaired at some point - not because I wanted to bar the dog from the bar - it can be draughty. The mutt and I don't have a lot in common. I've never entered or exited though the window frame and I rarely sit on the floor and scratch, as for personal hygiene, well like I say, we don't have a lot in common. I have heard they do say opposites attract. I'm not sure how the dog became aware!

I read an out of date newspaper to while away the time awaiting the arrival of Lenny. Apparently some bloke called Bill Clinton is President of The United States and his wife wants to be. Give the man a cigar, or maybe she would rather he didn't have one. Liverpool didn't win the league again. They're pretty crap these days. If the Reds' had any sense they would put two and two together which would result in them having four strikers. It could help. Just my tuppence worth, which isn't worth an awful lot.

Lenny and I have been friends since nursery school. The two of us have been inseparable ever since birth near enough, unless of course either of us had a woman in tow, which is most often in Lenny's case. It's not good having bystanders when you have a woman in tow, though I believe they are better known as Gooseberries! Consider this: if spares were known as grapes instead of gooseberries, there could be a bunch of onlookers.

Lenny could have been equal owner of The Mermaid and Bow but at the last moment he pulled out, I always knew he would. Lenny hates the thought of commitment, don't we all! My mucker has worked for me ever since. Lenny and Alice, his sister, have been looking after the place. When Jen' was taken, the siblings took over as my unofficial temporary managers. And so my mate can be generally irresponsible but surprisingly capable of taking responsibility when employed to. Lenny won't change too much, he'd better not.

"Maccy, how are you, mucker?"

Lenny arrives with a maximum of fuss, he is not at his best, he isn't himself but close enough which is useful. I don't know anyone else called Lenny, one's enough. "Lenny, I am back mucker. Move over."

"Maccy, there 'ave been a problem or two. T'wadn't my fault. Not all of it anyway."

"Okay Lenny. Have it gone away?"

"Not quite, see but I think it best I do."

"I get the picture matey."

"Naw Maccy, it wasn't that sort of problem. There idn't no pictures. Nothing of that sort. Not that I know of anyway."

"Good, that's a relief. So what did happen?"

"Well matey, I have me a tad of trouble right now. Some bloke thinks I have been tinkering with his womanfolk and he have made some nasty threats to certain parts of me I'd rather he hadn't. Being dismantled bit by bit idn't bleddy desirable mate. What I would like to know is the name of the bugger that did snitch on me. I'll take some holiday now you'm back. If he comes here looking for me, tell him I am away for a year or two. Tell him I'm in a bit of a bad mood and it idn't likely to go away yet. Tell him, I'm about to be in a long-distance bad mood, it might put him off."

"Who should I tell that you haven't been tinkering with whoever she is and don't want to be found by?"

"I can't tell 'e, in case the bugger is listening. Who told you?"

"You did mate."

"I did, did I? I must learn to keep my bleddy gob shut."

"T'would be best Lenny."

Dear Lenny, nothing has changed at all in the romance stakes where he is concerned. If he wasn't already in trouble it would come looking for him. "Lenny that is just perfect matey, you get off to Spain and leave this to me. You had better take a change of clothes or two. It might be a while before you get back drekly." I don't expect to see Lenny Copestick for at least a month.

"I'm not going to Spain. I am but if anyone asks you don't know, nobody knows."

"I understand Lenny, I do. Apart from where you might not be going?"

"Mum's the word!" Lenny taps the side of his nose and then he taps the other side. It's good to cover all bases.

"You have returned in the nick of time mucker. You might have saved me from partial decapitation, maybe even worse."

"What could be worse, Lenny?"

"Who knows, Maccy, who bleddy knows?"

"What will you do in Spain bud'?"

"This and that Maccy. Nothing different to what I do here I suppose. I never said I'm going to bleddy Spain."

"That's what I thought. Andorra then Lenny, Portugal is nice I hear. You will slowly run out of places to run to quickly."

"What you say is true, Maccy. What if I was to go to Portugal instead buddy?"

"That won't work Lenny, you have to go through Spain to get there."

"Bleddy 'ell, I'm on a plane. Can't they go around?"

"Ask the pilot. Anyway, give her my love!"

"Who Maccy, give who your love?"

"No idea Lenny, I won't be there. Just pick someone, a maid is your best bet!"

"I'll do my best. It won't be easy."

"I guess not mucker!"

"It will take my mind off the other one."

"What other one?"

"I can't bleddy say!"

That's the trouble, Lenny will do as he says, and he'll be right back where he started from. While he's at it he might as well go to Timbuctoo, he's bound to end up back here wherever he goes.

Home sweet home and it seems little has changed. My mate is gone to collect his belongings. Methinks he is in a lot of trouble. It takes him a lot to decide this fast unless there is a female in front of him, a husband behind him. Both at the same time is a dead giveaway, though it can be done without mishap. Lenny isn't fast on his feet. He is good on his toes; Lenny can fall in love between meals. Fish, woman and chips. I'm happy with fish and mushy peas with curry sauce and cheesecake for afters. Obviously I wouldn't want it all on the same plate.

For me, now it is time to give the chef a holiday. I'm not one for keeping a dog and barking myself. To be truthful, I do have a dog and I haven't started barking yet, it all seems to be working well. In all honesty, it's not even my dog, it just thinks it is. It won't be long.

The food business this time of the year is almost non-existent anyway. A bit like Lennys' forward planning. First things first. Lenny just had time to inform me Dusty is behind with his rent for the landing stage that crosses over Lost Souls creek and allows access. Dear Dusty has spent half a lifetime squeezing money out of me one way or another, now it is my turn. My brother is only twenty something, same as me. I am a year in advance as our ma never did have twins.

I bide my time in getting the Mermaid's bar spruced up for opening time. I know the kid will be in sooner or later. Someone once told me 'never chase money, let it come to you'. It sounds good. We will see!

The memory of the little fish shooter will begin to diminish in time I'm sure. She will always have a place in my head. My heart is already too badly damaged! She is beautiful there is no doubt in my mind. I believe now I'm not ready for her. She's not ready for the likes of me in all likelihood. I would make her life an instant misery. And anyway, she talks strange, I can't be doing with that. Nothing like the average Cornish Maid. It is a shame, that's the way it has to be.

I have other things on my mind. I decide I would sell the laptop, I won't be requiring it anymore. I might even give it to Lenny. He can start his own dating agency when he gets back from somewhere else. It would have potential. He could end up in the Guinness book of Records, if he isn't there already.

"Dusty, my little brother. How I've missed you." The 'someone' was right! Dusty has arrived and looks a tad shocked at my appearance behind the Mermaids' bar. I believe he has a sudden look of doom and gloom. He's not fooling me.

"Maccy and about time."

"Are you sure, are you feeling okay little brother?"

"Never better big Mac."

"Good, I'm glad to hear it. We need to talk about financial things. Three hundred financial things, pounds. Three months' rent on the landing stage. Big Mac? That'll never catch on, brother."

"Is that all, I thought it was something serious. Take a cheque Maccy?"

"I might but never from you kid. IOU's are out too. Proper money would be best." It wouldn't be the first time Dusty has tried to pay me with Monopoly money though it was some while ago. I use the term loosely but I'm glad my brother has grown up. I hope he continues. It may or may not be too much to ask.

My brother pulls a large wad of notes from his back pocket and counts out the required amount there and then. It pleases me no end. The last thing I want right now is a heated discussion with the kid about cash. The kid's look of doom and gloom was all a sham. The day is beginning to take just perfect shape after a doubtful start. Whoever it was, was right. I might hang around and see if any more cash appears.

From the looks of things, I now need to get Alice into cleaning mode. She needs regular coaxing in this particular direction. The maid has looks, she has personality in spades, she is no 'maid' in the true sense of the word. She has made my day more than once, the less said about that here the better. I try not to talk in my sleep, though right now, it doesn't matter much. I'm the only one there apart from Maccy J. Like me, he won't have a clue what I'm talking about.

The middle of winter in Padstow sees a desolate place. As usual, the population is in hiding until Spring's arrival. I have my work cut out to find anyone. Just at that very moment, the diminutive Americans' face appears before mine, but she just as quickly fades again. Maybe it will be the last time I ever see her. She might be trying to tell me something. I might need my head seeing too!

On his return, I hand Lenny all the cash given to me by Dusty; easy come, easy go. He has brought me the keys to the Mermaid before hurriedly leaving for Newquay airport. Look out Lloret de Mar. Lenny's coming and hell's a following! Look out Lloret, my mucker will cause havoc wherever he arrives. Lenny had stuck his head in the door.

"I'm off then mucker."

"Have you got five minutes bud'?" My mate sticks his head back outside for a moment. The head returns.

"Yes mate, no longer."

The Mermaid has changed so much while I've been tooing and frowing. I've hardly had time to turn up since I got back. I know Lenny has been doing his bit. I also know Alice has stamped her mark on the place. It's all a far cry from Blen' and the Cap'n. The Mermaid and Bow is moving forward and it's down to brother Lenny and sister

Alice. To be fair if it didn't, there wouldn't be any point. Alice, of course, is still with Mervyn and the lad. The boy is growing fast. Thank god his hair is darkening! She and the nipper had disappeared to the nearest sweetshop as Lenny and I get to yakking.

"Lenny, you two are doing great here. Thanks, Bud'. Takings are hitting the leaking roof, but we could do with some more food sales. Any suggestions."

"Yes mate! We need a seafood stall outside for the season. It'll need refrigeration. That should be easy. Cockles and Winkles, Jellied Eels!"

"Good one, Lenny. I'll let you get on with that when you return from wherever you're not going to. You'll need more staff, I can help there. When you get back, you'll have extra help."

"That will be grand mucker."

"We'll get a chilled counter, with wheels. Either that or a good strong chain and padlocks. We'll need to get some rings put in the wall. That should make it secure overnight."

"I'll be back before you know it."

"No you won't."

"I will, as I 'aven't told you yet when I'm coming back. That way you can't know."

"That's true, so when do you reckon?"

"If I tell you I'll be back in a fortnight, you'll know buddy. So I can't."

"Okay mate, you get going and I'll see you in a couple of weeks."

"Ais, that would be good Maccy, see you then. I'm glad you never asked me mucker. I didn't want to lie to you."

"You'll go or you might not drekly."

"Why might I not?"

"Lenny, if you don't go now, it won't be worth going for a fortnight. You'll have to go for three weeks to make up for it."

"That's true mucker."

"Have you got transport?"

65

"Yes and no."

"Get a taxi."

"I can't get a taxi to Spain Maccy, it'll cost a bleddy fortune."

"Where are you flying from Lenny?"

"Newquay, I thought it best."

"Just get a taxi to Newquay then and get on a plane there mate. Wait, I'll drive you to Newquay."

"But how will you get back?"

"I'll think of something, don't worry."

"Maccy, if I do get back early, I'll have to wear a disguise."

"How will I know it's you mate?"

"I never thought about that."

I would love Lenny like a brother, if I didn't already have one. I can't manage two!

I am both apprehensive and as nervous as the day I first took over the Mermaid. It had been a while since I had stood behind my own bar. Since the day I lost Jen' I had hardly even set foot inside the building. I had discarded my friends and my family. I had discarded the Crew; the Crew being the Mermaids' clientele, its regulars, the hardcore without any rude bits

They are the pubs' bread and butter, minus the 'It's Not Butter'. Personally, I prefer my butter to be butter, not, 'it's not butter', nor do I want 'It might or might not be a bit like butter'. Just plain old butter will do. Butter is far better than Magnolia spread unless you're doing some interior decorating.

I am here now with just the mangled mutt as company. The dog is in his place beneath the pool table and cleaning those which hardly need any further cleaning. I think the mutt has a licking fetish. It is good he keeps it too himself! Wandering around licking everyone else should not be encouraged in a public house, anywhere really. On second thoughts some licking is acceptable. I wonder what he would do if he didn't own those that are attached. Anyway, I'm not taking him to the vets, he's not even my dog! I have never encouraged the Alsatian to accompany me everywhere I go.

Maybe the dog is blind and sees me as a guide person, I haven't thought of that. In any case most dogs see with their noses. They think everything is a lamp post or a pool table.

Every room upstairs reeks of stale air. I open all the windows. I feel a tad ashamed of what has been my dereliction of duty. The place is tidy enough, it just stinks. Might be the dog. It's not likely he's the cause, he has always stunk a tad, I would have noticed a difference. I think he should have a clean. As if by magic, he takes the hint. One of these days they won't be there and there would be no reason for the mutt to exist, it will have made itself redundant. The Alsatian would have 'cleaned up' so to speak!

It's still early, time for coffee and a cigar. I lean back on a stool out on the bandstand and listen to the gulls as they provide their own rendition of Reveille. They are all out of tune as always. It's odd when you think that late at night it's only drunks that sing, first thing in the morning it's birds, though gulls could never be described as songbirds. When I was a tacker we had a remedy for out of tune gulls, we gave them guts ache, we blew them up! I watch as a one-legged fisherman comes around the corner. He's walking as if he's still on the water. Obviously he isn't still on the water, more likely he's been on the rum!

It will soon be time to open the huge door and face the crew, if they are still around. I feel like I had turned my back on them in my time of need. I realise now how selfish I had been. I would have to be on good form. These people are like family to me. Humble pie may need to be eaten in large portions; not something I learned to cook at catering college. I can throw a decent pasty together, I can do Steak and Kidney. Yorkshire puddings are my forte. Once cooked they should be hard enough to do battle within the annual Yorkshire Pudding throwing competition. I'm not sure where it's held but feel sure it is somewhere up north.

It makes me wonder what they do in Lancashire. Maybe they throw uneaten Lancashire Hotpot at the Yorkies and the Yorkies throw their unwanted puddings at the Lankies, or whatever they call themselves. I hope Devon doesn't decide to take sides with either, or the Midlands might be covered in dumplings.

As for Cornish pasty throwing, it's a complete non-starter. No decent Cornishman, or woman for that matter would throw them to anyone in another county. It would be far too ridiculous. I suppose some versions could be used in this way. No names, no pack drill.

There is work to be done and as I'm the only one present, it must be down to me.

Chapter Seven

Battle Lines Drawn

I kick myself up the backside; not literally obviously, as I would just fall arse over tit. Within the hour I am ready and waiting to see who will be first to cross the now, well swept threshold. Okay, maybe not well swept, I did lean on the yard broom for a while as I surveyed the harbour and wondered why I was surveying anything. I knew what the harbour looked like; it hardly changes much in a couple of weeks. I wonder who I await as the huge door creaks slowly open. I could have won money on it only I have no one to bet with until a person comes in which would be pointless as so far unknown person would already know the result! It's becoming the story of my life recently as companions continue to become non-existent, they seem to have all buggered off willy nilly.

"Maccy, my 'ansome, bleddy 'ell, we thought you were gone forever."

I was just about to have a bet with myself it would be Lil, 'Lil the tart' I was just too late! There is the rumour Lil has been on the game since the end of World War One. The tittle tattle is well spread out. We can rule out the Boer war as she was far too young. Many think she hasn't retired yet. Lil's specialty is her make-up, she needs it as she used to be a head bell ringer. To this day the scars on her forehead have never completely disappeared! "Come here Lil, give us a kiss darlin'. Gone where?" My mind must be in a hell of a dilapidated state. Still, these things must be done. Tongues are not employed, small mercies! 'Must be done'! What the hell am I saying? I like Lil, that's it. She's not a potential companion. If she was, she'd probably bugger off moaning I haven't paid her enough.

She did as I requested with sound effects, accompanied with her trademark giggle; she didn't need a second invitation, she's not about to get one. I did have to push her away firmly after a minute or so. I think she was in training mode. Dear old Lil would kiss anything in trousers. Maybe I should re-phrase that. She would snog any male providing they were still breathing and had money in their pockets. Any clothing would not be important. Pockets would soon be emptied anyway. "Gin and Tonic, Lil?"

"You know me well enough, young Maccy. Some of us never change lad!"

Lil is right, I do know her well enough. Thankfully not as well as some. I wouldn't want to know her any better. I have some standards, not many it's true but some. As far as I know, I'm not and never have been on her client list. I have no intention of joining it. I'm not too picky, though a line should be drawn. A strange saying when one considers where it originated from. The officers in command of the *Alamo told their troops if they wanted to stay and defend the old mission to the death, to cross the line and stand with them. Those that didn't would be excused and allowed to leave. I know where I would have stood. One hundred and seventy odd, mostly Europeans, lining up against two thousand poncey looking Mexicans is not good odds. I would have been out of there like liquid thingy off a shovel. To be fair the brave defenders did maim or kill more than six hundred of the well-dressed attackers. I'm not saying the Mexican troops were born clumsy but many of them could have met their deaths by tripping over their fancy swords!

On thinking about it, I felt sorry for the bloke who had drawn the line, he probably got shot up the bum whilst he was doing his artwork. I doubt 'Banksy' ever had to worry about such things. All he has to worry about is the sound of a local copper's voice saying: 'Evening all, what 'ave we got 'ere then? You're nicked sonny!'

Poor old Lil, she is a dear, I wish she would use a mirror when applying her lipstick. For as long as I remember, it has always looked as if a couple of three-year old kids have been crayoning on her face. I wonder how they applied it with a paper bag over her head. Obviously the kiddies would be wearing the same in case hers fell off. This isn't a long term thought for me!

"Good to see you back where you belong boy!"

"Thank you Lil, glad to be back." I did attempt to sound convincing. "By the way Lil, 'ave you heard they're gonna open up a sex shop up the road."

"Which road?"

"Dunno, one out there I suppose. They're looking for staff though."

"Bleddy hell, I didn't hear about that."

"If I were you, I'd ask someone to write you a reference, can't do any harm, you know as much as the next man, I mean woman. You probably know more! You're highly experienced." My face stays straight.

"Who would I ask, Maccy?"

"Someone who knows you might be best."

"What about you, Maccy?"

"Not me Lil, I don't know you that well. Just ask anyone out on the quay."

"I'll have my gin first."

"Might be best, it will dull the pain."

"What pain?"

"I don't know, any pain."

Lil takes her drink and turns away to sit at her regular table. Even now she is screwing up her face in contemplation, not that anyone would know, looking at her from a sidelong glance would suggest it's been done on a regular basis. At least she didn't catch on to my innuendo regarding her clients. Anyway she is the first crew member to be on duty. I'm not sure she ever goes off duty, that's why I suggested the job. She'll be seventy-five soon, and then she'll be sixty-five again. She's shrinking so fast her old mini-skirts will start to fit again, right down to her knees. Trouble is her thigh boots will pop out of the top.

"What do you mean about my 'miniskirts'?"

Damn, there was me thinking I was talking to myself. **sotto voce. I should be more careful. I leave Lil to her own vices; I mean devices, obviously.

I am impatient to see who will be next. I have plenty of time. I use it to allow my memory to travel back to my early days here in the Mermaid. They were reasonably good until the one fateful day. I have hardly set foot in here since. Can I get my mojo back? I have no idea. Time will tell.

I had sneaked inside the Mermaid - if you'll pardon the expression - once or twice, more than that in all honesty, while still under the legal drinking age. I had exited in various ways, unfortunately, never sneakily. I had been thrown out, kicked out and even on occasion had tumbled out while involved in some pointless brawl. I suppose they were all pointless. They do say regular exercise is good. Often I had just fallen out the door, the inability to stand any longer being my only excuse. As I've got older I am less likely to be thrown or kicked out. I'm a big bloke, there are few Padstownians who would attempt to dislodge me from this building. Blencathra has managed it a time or two in the past, the only one. She was my first. The first to throw me out I mean, I wouldn't want there to be any confusion.

Now of course, the ancient inn is my own, thanks to Lil in fact. She sowed the seed if you'll pardon the expression. It was Lil who broached the subject of the Mermaid needing someone younger to bring it into the twenty first century. Not quite there yet, still another one to go. I am here mostly because of Lil, it was her suggestion. Now it is my duty to eject any troublemakers. What's that oldest of sayings? 'What comes around goes around' or it might be the other way around, it doesn't really matter. It really is a funny old world, a completely pointless old saying as it isn't funny all the time, hardly ever.

Next to appear, a couple in their mid-twenties. I know they are in their mid-twenties as I am myself. They quietly order two drinks and retreat to the darkest corner of the Mermaid Bar. For as long as I can remember these two have been coming here for their oral Olympics, their habits never changing. They will stay in the corner until just after closing time. They will snog, giggle and grope each other until it's time to leave. As far as I know they still have never married but they have, like me. been coming here since teenagers. They hardly ever speak to anyone or even each other; it isn't surprising, they can't. The two are almost unrecognisable on account it's rare to see their faces. Saying number three: 'never speak with your mouth full'. Something else best not to think about. They are as regular as clockwork. I can't help wondering if they have a home to go to. When we close they might just stand outside and wait until we open again, sort of 'in perpetuity'. Actually I think most members of the Mermaids' crew do the same thing.

The appearance of these last two has somehow allowed my guard to slip. She has reappeared. The little American with the large guns, the silver star, the smile. Somehow, almost supernaturally, I can see her, I can hear what she is saying. It isn't good, not good at all. The thing is, I don't really know for sure. Everything could be explained by an over-active imagination on my part. It might be I am being a tad immodest. She might not be giving me a second thought. Who can blame her? I do feel she is trying to contact me during some great sadness. Most likely it's my own?

Her nagging insistence is so strong I need to stop myself from speaking out loud again. I would only embarrass myself in front of my friends. It wouldn't be the first time. Changes must be made as one grows up. I've had some unpleasant changes thrust upon me just lately. I'm not best pleased.

When she came to the riverbank in Kansas the second time, she had asked me if I was 'staying a while'. I told her

73

I would be, I didn't know how long. I had left within days and hide it as I may, it makes no difference. I had left early because of her. I had skedaddled as she had herself. I wouldn't normally run from a lady; I have run after a few. We hadn't indulged in anything other than eat a decapitated fish and shared a beer or two. It hadn't occurred to me she could have been underage at the time. She might not have been. I believe the alcohol consumption limits vary in legality, depending on the state of occupation.

We two had just yakked about anything and almost everything, nothing that could be conceived as courting, nothing of any importance. Okay, it had got dark and we had sat close together as a million crickets had tuned up their instruments, but that was it. I never saw her after that. I feel certain I will never see her again. Pessimism is my 'chosen subject'.

Optimism never has really taken off here in the Mermaid Bar, not surprisingly. The trouble with woman trouble is the woman doesn't always have to be present. I think it's all down to metaphysics. Are we or are we not? Should we, or shouldn't we? In this case there is some uncertainty, which is pretty much the same thing. I don't own a dictionary and so it might not be what I suspect it to be.

I have no idea where the girl lives, what she does or even if she has a husband, fiancé or boyfriend. I never asked, she never offered. She never asked me about my personal circumstances. Little personal information was exchanged that might lead to complications. I did in fact tell her a good deal about my place of birth; she was inquisitive. Mostly I had talked about America and Kansas especially. She had wanted to know more about England and Cornwall. Little information was passed due to my overactive stuttering.

Believe it or not, being tongue-tied is a speciality where I'm concerned when in company of strange women. It had been all just idle chit chat. There was some gentle teasing about accents and quaint old-fashioned customs, nothing more. Spitting was only brought up due to errant fish bones.

The image and memory are quickly dislodged. "Maccy Tamryn! I see you're back in town."

"Can't you think of something bleddy original?" Louis Armstrong has got a lot to answer for.

Alice. Now here is Alice Copestick. Alice is another old friend, a very old - older than me anyway - close friend. In fact, at one time, okay on occasion, we had been as close as two can ever become. I'm not certain what the opposite of innocence is but whatever it was, we were guilty of it. Fortunately, or unfortunately, certainly in the case of her fiancé, there are permanent results of our late-night entanglement in a penthouse, a top floor flat anyway. Just once or twice we had amalgamated, it won't happen again. I discard the notion completely as I thought about the result of our last one-night amalgamation. 'One-night stand' sounds a bit derogatory! I did eventually find a tatty dictionary. It might have been more than the one night, maybe it was a long weekend!

Thankfully Alice and Mervyn were already engaged, their wedding was just brought forward a tad which allowed both of us off the hook. I mean no disrespect to Mervyn in this last confession. Poor Mervyn had a terrible time of it when he was a kid. The story goes he was out night fishing - another name for poaching salmon. He had an accident with his fishing lines in the dark. A wayward fishhook got blown into his eye and that was that - Popeye mark two came into being! Mervyn the expert fisherman had caught himself unfortunately.

Let's just say Mervyn is now not all-seeing. As I have already mentioned, their youngster is thriving and occasionally when it is safe, I will spend an hour helping him with his street education. Sort of parental guidance in an unofficial role. The tacker doesn't know of course, it is my hope he never will. Explanations aren't really my thing. I rarely get them right, does anyone?

"So Maccy, where have you been all this time?"

"Here and there, Alice. Nowhere in particular."

"I heard you were in America?"

"I came home." I winked at Alice and she returned one of her own before stepping away to challenge the dishonesty of the fruit machine.

"The boy's looking good, Alice." I shout over the din of far too many pound coins dropping. I should get the damned machine fixed, it is doing something it shouldn't be. Alice is unknowingly eating into my pocket money. Eating is a family trait in the Copestick's household.

"Yes Maccy, he is." It is Alice's turn to wink. Another satisfied crew member on board.

And so, the yank had returned for a moment. Looking at Alice and knowing what I know of the little American, there is little to compare the two. Alice is, well maybe I'd better not go there, let's just say she is Alice. Alice is simple - not in any backward way - she is just a decent, simple, fun-loving girl. Alice is also Lenny's sister, which is another good reason for the youngster's blood-line to stay a secret. Lenny would be unhappy if he discovered he and I are in some part, a large part, related. If he becomes aware, it will be a swift separation. A violent and swift parting!

Lenny is more than a little fightable if he finds someone has been tinkering with any of the womenfolk in his life. One very good reason for his never discovering about his mother and me. Anyway, that's another story and I still cling to the weak excuse; she started it! As for the American, she is as far distant from Alice and Mrs Copestick as the harbour is wide. There are no comparisons. I could be wrong of course, how the hell would I know? She might be a raving, yank sex machine. I doubted it. I will never know!

And so, to the last members of the crew who might or might not arrive on this damp Saturday lunchtime. The Birdsalls, aka The Birdseyes, two peas in separate pods! This odd couple live in the quay, not literally obviously. I suppose their bed may be under the water line. They are proud owners of a very small, two-berth, non-seagoing craft with silk sheets. A cruiser to do battle in. It is their four walls. The Birdseyes inhabit the sloop permanently. They are the real thing, quintessentially English. The roguish pair live the high life, unless there is a hole in Padstows' harbour gate, in which case they would be living on a crab infested mudbank. Why shouldn't these two enjoy their semi-retirement years?

The Admiral and his wife are retired accountants, except in my case they are still employed. When I took on the Mermaid and Bow a handful of years ago the couple had no hesitation in answering my call to utilise their mathematical skills for my benefit. They readily agreed to take care of my business finances; they still do but strictly on a cash or free meal basis. Book cooking I suppose! It's the Padstow way. Bookkeeping doesn't come into it as most are discreetly discarded in case the VAT man calls.

Alma and the Admiral also have what is quaintly called an open marriage. She does her thing, she almost did it with me a couple of times, sort of touch and go, she touched and when I got free, I went! I guess she might be seventy now. The Admiral does his thing, and he didn't, thank the lord. Don't get me wrong, I'm not anti-gay, just anti-gay with me. I don't think he's full time anyway. So, the loveable Birdseyes continue their horizontal antics, mostly but not always, together. The old feller sometimes likes his vice versa. They certainly know how to entertain. They can keep us guessing as to their preferences. The little cruiser is a floating gin palace and I have spent many a pleasant hour in their company sharing the said cordial with tonic, ice and a slice.

Talk of the devil and they shall appear. At last, the Mermaids' crew is just about altogether, as the Birdseyes arrived with a modicum of fanfare. Only the deceased One-Armed Frank is missing. On second thoughts he might be here, who knows? He could be sitting on the optics shelf with the rest of the spirits. For all intents and purposes, Frank is long gone. He passed away in here whilst far gone in sheets and wind phraseology. Still, Frank has an honorary place as he well deserves. His ashes would have been on the mantlepiece but for Frank being buried in a coffin. We couldn't keep them in here, health and safety. We should have buried him at sea, it would have been a lot easier, it's only a couple of yards away. I do know about metres, I am just not sure how they work.

There are other crew members. Lenny is a regular under normal circumstances, he's tied up right now, probably anyway. Lenny and I have forever fought for various reasons. We are the closest of enemies, the best of friends.

It is a strange day. I have the feeling everyone has questions for me but are too afraid to ask them, Alice asked one or two but my answer to each was the same. 'No thanks Alice, I'm not in the mood.' Some things never change. I hope they never do, I do like the maid.

As I clean up the days' mess there is one question gnawing away at me. Of course, it's to do with the American and the question in question has been growing for a while now. I had a reason for being in the States, I had a reason for being in McCarthy City, I had a reason for being at the stream. I just cannot fathom why she had been there, twice. Actually, she had been there three times to my knowledge. I still think there had been something she wasn't telling me. Now it seems, however long I wait, she never will.

The first time I saw her she had been watering a horse. As a young teenager she had approached the stream for a moment, whilst on my first visit to Kansas. I was also a teenager, not much older. It had been so long ago I hardly remember. I do remember the single star glinting about her neck and the nervous smile. Now just what was the reason for the feisty but obviously well-educated girls' second and third appearances in and around the old towns' ruins? I will never know. It is a puzzle I doubt will ever be unravelled. It is a disappointment to me. One of many!

The last time I saw her we had swum in the creek and slept side by side. She was in my sleeping bag and I was on the outside. 'You can't have everything at once' as ma use to say, when Dusty and I were kids. I'm sure we were on a different subject back then.

Author's notes

* Battle of the Alamo (February 23 – March 6, 1836) Mexican troops under President General Antonio López de Santa Anna reclaimed the Alamo Mission near San Antonio de Béxar (modern-day San Antonio, Texas, United States). Co-commanders at the Alamo: Davy Crockett and James Bowie, Col. William Barrett Travis. Not all but most of the defenders at the Alamo, were Europeans, (settlers) not Americans. Some were even British, Welsh and even possibly Cornish. A handful of lives were spared, women and children mostly. The final approximate fatality score: Defenders 200 – 600 Attackers. The only trophy of the encounter being James Bowies' Bowie Knife.

**Sotto voce 'Soto 'voce, Italian: 'sotto 'voce; literally "under the voice" means intentionally lowering the volume of one's voice for emphasis.

Chapter Eight

Time waits for no Woman

On his return, Lenny is raring to go again. He arrived back all in one piece, unusual but useful. He turned up not unlike a bull in a china shop. He wanted to tell everything, I told him to write it down, I'd read it later. Most likely in another life.

I know I made myself a promise, but if you can't break a promise to yourself, when can you? The American will not give up, she is unerring, insistent. It's like she is in my space but invisible to me. I think about Ma and I know what she would say if I told her. She would say 'follow your heart, son'. It's what she would have done. I'm taking Ma's unspoken advice, I'm going back. It will be for the last time. I don't believe in third time lucky, but I might do by the time I return.

I have spent time with Maccy J who has now moved up a school. I have one week to put my mind at rest in Kansas. One more chance and that's it, end of. There will be no going back.

"Look after the dog, Lenny."

"What's the matter with it?"

"Nothing's the matter with it as far as I know, it's always been the same, pretty vile!"

"Why do I need to look after it then? I'm not a bleddy vet!"

"It'll be lonely, and it likes you. It likes the pub too."

"Will it? It only likes the bleddy pub so it can sit under the pool table, Maccy."

"I knaw that. You'll be company for it."

"I'm not sitting under the pool table. I'm not gonna do anything the bleddy dog does!"

"That'll be a relief for everyone. I'm going back to Kansas, last time I promise."

"How do you know it'll be the last time?"

"Because I won't go back again."

"I see but what if …."

"Please look after the dog, Lenny."

"Okay, I'll look after your dog!"

"He isn't my dog."

"He lives with you sometimes, most of the time apart from when he idn't!"

"I didn't buy him, he didn't buy me and I don't have a bleddy dog license."

"You don't need one these days."

"I don't need a dog!"

"But you still have one. What does he eat?"

"Any bleddy thing!"

Dogs' welfare settled, eventually decided in a manner of speaking. The siblings will look after the Mermaid and my mate will feed the mutt. I'm on my way. I have already set the wheels in motion to buy the Maltsters Arms, I have the Mermaid in Padstow, now I want the village local. Why not? The agents and my solicitor will right now be earning an undeserved half fortune from me. I only have time for a flying visit, which of course, it was. I swim well. I wouldn't attempt the Atlantic. I took a plane. I wouldn't steal one, I used one that was there already. Thought it best to clear up any misunderstanding.

I have rented a pick-up, not from the same bloke as before thankfully. I can't be dealing with him again. A very nice lady told me 'have a nice day' when I told her where I am going. McCarthy City is only an hour or two away. I don't have a clue what to do when I get there. My only notion is to do what I did on my last visit; sit on my arse, play with worms and reflect a little, oh and keep my eyes open.

The old geezer is fully alert. He just gives the impression he's half asleep. "Back again son?"

81

See, I told you. The old Indian makes it sound like I just popped out for a newspaper or a pint. "I believe I am. Where's your fishing pole?" We're almost best friends and I still don't know his name. I probably wouldn't be able to pronounce it if I did.

"Same place it always is. Help yourself, youngster." A stream of black juice passes by me at a decent distance. I feel it is something of a warm welcome from the old feller. Maybe he is trying to hit me, and his eyesight isn't great. I have stocked up with everything I need. I have been in the Circle K which is nothing like Spar as those establishments have different staff members every time you return. I'm almost on first name terms with the staff and the local Sheriff. 'Hey Brit, you got nuthin better to do than come back here?' is the regular shout now when I enter the store. 'Yo Yank' I reply each time. That's my idea of being on first name terms. I don't have to remember what any of them are called.

I am improving. I even manage to remember to bait my hook this time. I've no idea why I bothered. My sleeping bag is in place. I'm not really sure why I'm sleeping over the road that isn't, it's just a dirt track and it seems like a good idea. My food is in the insulated bag that has never moved, fresh beer is in the water. The borrowed Stetson is tilted over my eyes once more. I wait. Again, I'm not really fishing, I'm just sitting here with a long stick with twine hanging off it. My intention right now is to forget what I'm doing while I'm still doing it. I'm not here to catch a fish. I've heard that before. I never did catch one, I did eat half of one but I'm not sure who it belonged to. It wasn't all there, just like the yank who shot it! It's of no matter now!

Darkness begins to creep across the prairie, it seems to stretch a thick shadow across my mind. I have lain on the sandy bank all afternoon and without a bite of any kind thankfully. Suddenly I feel a real loneliness for the first time since Jennifer went. I begin to think I should never have come back for this last visit. I should have said something before, but what? I would have sounded like a Limey idiot. 'Excuse me darlin' will you marry me and oh by the way, do you need to get divorced first?' See, it would have been a messy bleddy business! I feel like my brain is turning to scrambled egg. So I'm not sure why I have returned this time. One last throw of the dice I suppose. She is costing me a fortune in air fares. I really should stop doing things on the spur of the moment.

I drink my entire stock of beer after first lighting a campfire to keep out the chill of the star filled Kansas night. It seems there are so many, it's a surprise they don't bump into each other. The glistening shower would keep Mister Como busy, it seems plenty of them are falling. Maybe it is a chill of another kind? The chill of loneliness and almost certain failure. I don't have to give up, I have all the time in the world to be honest, but I have put a time limit on this, my final visit.

The early morning sun is warming me now as I circle the old building and I think about Henry, Taffy and Renee, all the people who had made McCarthy City possible and didn't give up easily. They didn't have time to give up! For me personally there is no future in McCarthy. No one will ever live here again. I know I couldn't. It's a rather fitting monument to those people. I will bend my back and shed some sweat for the old town and its past for an hour or two, it isn't too much to ask. I can't do much but patch up here and there but somehow my assumed task puts me in touch a tad with my forefathers. I begin to listen to the answers to my unasked questions. I can't be certain if the words are mine, or Henry McCarthy's or Renee's or even those of the old Chinese cook, whatshisname. I listen anyway. I listen and I learn. I'm sure someone is telling me to tidy it up. I don't have enough time to do it all obviously.

I know I'll never be a regular church going man, but I am praying she will materialise. What else is there? I'm Maccy, a regular pub going man, a hell-raiser, a woman chaser, a scrapper and part-time streaker long retired. I am learning about myself here and it's a good feeling. All the time there is still no sign.

She is out there somewhere and I can't reach her. She doesn't want to know. I can't see what's in front of my face. I decide there and then I will just do what I must. If she appears she appears, if not, I will accept it and move on to pastures new. Nothing new then. At least I feel I have given us both this final opportunity. Now it's in the lap of the gods, right now they don't seem to be smiling down. I did manage to send off one last email and tell her of my plans. There was no reply!

The second morning the old geezer arrived on the oldest looking motorbike I have ever seen. He steps over the bike and pulls the machine onto its stand.

"Morning youngster, any luck?"

"Nope, not a sign. I don't think she'll ever return."

"She, who's she, son? I was just wondering how your fishing was coming along is all."

And there you have it. I am so wrapped up in myself I can't tell the difference between a beautiful girl, a woman and a Catfish. She would not be amused if she knew. I think now she would run a mile. She may already have done so. That's it, she's legged it, got out while the going's good.

The old man stayed for an hour or two and we talked of the town's great days. He had known Renee and heard tales of her ancestors. The older male members of her previous generation had apparently all gone to war before she was born; none had returned. In the eighteen-seventies even her forebears had gone to war, where fathers, brothers and uncles had fought against each other and died on the same battlefield. So many of those who had come back from a pointless Civil War had hardly anything to come back to. *Carpet Baggers had stolen their cattle and moved into houses that didn't belong to them. Squatters of the day?

For the second day she does not appear. Spittin' Woman is avoiding me. I plan my third day as I empty another stash of cans. Again, I sleep beside my stream.

Unlike my stagnant love life, my stream is continuously moving, sparkling in the firelight and forever washing the dirt off the stones below it. I dream brokenly of Henry, of Tafflynn Evans, of Indian warriors and squaws who had grafted harder than their men. In my dreams, I come to believe I am one of these people. I wonder where my stream starts and where it stops. I try not to think about it after waking up.

I can't explain it, but the old man seems to able to look inside my head. I'm not saying he was reading my mind, maybe I am but it was more than that. He made me feel naked and I wasn't. He is reading me like an open book but giving nothing of himself away.

The old bloke had told me of Wild Bill Hickok and his association with what was originally christened ** McCarthy City and of his friendship with Henry and Taffy. So, the village has two names, McCarthy City and Hickok City. A town with two names. It may be quite empty now, but its many final occupants somehow seemed very real. Hickok isn't buried here, he lies at peace now in Deadwood, South Dakota, next to Martha Jane Cannary, the notorious Calamity Jane. The two had been close in life and Calamity wanted to stay close in death. It was her request to be buried next to the extrovert lawman she had adored throughout adulthood and into her later years. The alcoholic ex-prostitute got her wish.

Late into the night the Native American had said something else, rambling in words I didn't understand, a nasal sounding language. 'Ohoyo oka Taloa'. He spread his arms as far as they would go. His hands fluttered like a hawk watching its prey from above. The under flesh of his muscular arms seemed almost to ripple. Like a bird of prey spreading wings and about to swoop. Somehow, I felt this meant something. Something beyond my comprehension. He had a strange look on his face as if he was on something. For moments he became something other than a petrol pump attendant. He stopped and placed his hand over his heart. It was as if he was in the distance. He wasn't, he was present. I don't remember anything else.

Now I have all the time in the world. I won't give up yet. I'm not convinced she won't suddenly appear and begin to berate me for just any or no reason at all. I'd give my right arm for it to be that way. I have time to wonder if this was something One-armed Frank once said and he got his wish. The loss of a limb wouldn't bother me too much; I don't have to roll cigarettes!

The old Indian visits every day now. I hear the ancient machine a half mile away. Not sure which is the elder. I don't think he has a silencer. He doesn't need one, there is nobody else around to hear the racket from the ancient bike. Each day he tells me more and I am thankful of his company. In a way this old bloke is re-educating me. I'm glad to see him each time. I'm not forgetting why I'm here, but he is getting me through the days. Then one day he brings his pistols and stays the night beside the creek. The two of us drink too much and sleep by the stream, it is easy to dispose of the contents of my beer cellar.

The old man had produced a whisky bottle that wasn't quite full. By the time we were sleeping it was quite empty, unable to drip. We had used all his pistol rounds and I had hit nothing but air. He was a good shot. I still have no idea what his name is, and he will stay as 'old geezer' as far as I'm concerned. We laughed until we had both tipped over. It all took my mind off the girl a little, never completely. I'm not sure as to why I think of her as a 'girl' I have no idea of her age. Twenty-five, thirty-five, who knows, she does and she's not telling. The bloke had sidled down the slope in the semi light, whisky bottle in hand. We had got down to it. How did he know I needed company? This old geezer is different, he is spiritual, he seems to know everything.

By the time I awake he is gone. I rub the sleep out of my eyes to help my recovery, feel more alert. I am disoriented. She is back in my mind. She is always there now it seems. I shake her off. I need life-giving coffee. I am talking to myself in a voice I don't recognise. Maybe I am where the old feller went the previous evening. I can't remember the last time I drank whisky. Telepathy, he's telepathic, she's telepathic. I feel she is trying to reach out to me. Load of bollocks, no such thing. It's nuts! I'm a nut. My head still hurts but more so.

I make my coffee and light a cigar, as I always do at a time of stress. I stretch out my legs and accidentally kick the old coffee pot over. I could have scolded something; I would rather not. I miss by luck! Leaning on my elbows, I wonder if she has been dreaming about me. Can two dreams combine? I need to get out more! I need a swim in my stream, a paddle anyway. It's not much more than four feet deep in the middle. My head clears as I hit the water. I stand in the cold centre, mug in hand. The old git must have spiked the scotch with something, tobacco juice maybe. I don't mind a glass or two of scotch; it was a tad more than one or two. The chipped mug is empty. Where did this stream come from? Wtf, as they say now on the ever-expanding internet! I really should find out what it means. Dusty will know!

The Kansan sun is rising faster now. I am still slightly hungover. I know just how to cure it completely, hard work! I intend to do some more work around the place. The early morning sun is warming me now as I circle the old building and I think about Henry, Taffy and Renee, all the people who had made McCarthy possible.

I continue with my patching up of the old creaking hotel as well as the tiny church and to be honest, each building doesn't look much different. I don't care. I'm not bothered. I am just passing the time; if I get bored I'll spend time weeding the graves in the tiny cemetery and it will somehow be satisfying to know my ancestors are around me, watching, maybe smiling at my complete uselessness as a jobbing builder and landscape gardener. Not to mention failed fisherman.

One morning the oddest thing happens. A hoard of bikers appear, horned helmets and 'leathers' the lot.

McCarthys' main street is suddenly full of Hells Angels. For a moment or two I am scared stiff.

They have arrived seemingly prepared. Surprisingly they don't seem to want to mug me. They have food, they have beer, they have canvas. There are twenty or more of these guys, girls too, as far as I can tell. I assumed the ones with facial hair were men. Maybe I shouldn't assume anything. They didn't all have whiskers. They are quickly erecting tents at the side of my stream and I feel they hardly even notice me, so much for my feelings. Then I remember, this is America, 'The land of the free, the home of the brave!' Leathers and Levi's and long hair. It's hard to tell which is which or who is what. Not knowing a one of them doesn't help. The chest area gives away some clues but it's not a fool proof way of confirming gender. It is a good starting place.

I am approached by their elected leader. He is polite, he is friendly. He might not be elected. He is the first to speak. I would have voted for him. "Y'all mind if we set here a while, friend?"

Like I'm gonna say no, piss off from whence you came you ugly bastard, take the rest of your fat, hairy bummed friends with you and the blokes.' I hadn't thought about the clean-shaven variety. When I say clean-shaven, I mean un-whiskered. I'm fairly certain I know of no one who shaves their bum! My invitation sounds a tad lightweight even to me. "Please, feel free." I'm hardly about to tell them to un-pitch their tents and bugger off. I'm not as stupid as I look!

They take me at my word. 'Free' and easy is their way it seems. I enjoy the company for a time. When the old git arrives from the gas station he can hardly believe his eyes. He suddenly seems to take on a whole new persona. His old bike is surrounded by interested greasers. I just let them all get on with it. I take up the fishing pole and wait. I wait and don't know why or what I'm waiting for.

When the head Angel had asked if I mind if they set a while, I thought they would brew some Magic

Mushrooms, have a knife throwing competition using each other and possibly me as targets, bury their dead and disappear. Not so! The buggers stay longer than I do. I gave the group a wave as I left. I have left the village in their capable hands. I told them they could have the place. I have no use for it. As for the petrol pump attendant, I thanked him and told him goodbye. I would not be back. He just mumbled incoherently again, I think. He was good company and seemed, without me telling him, to know my predicament. He smiled a simple smile and waved as I left.

In a lot of ways he reminded me of old Bert, the café cleaner in Padstow who knows everything about me without asking or being told. I suppose it could be a useful trait. How the hell would I know? I don't have any good or bad habits that I know of. As for the angels, they can stay and pray they don't go to heaven! If they went to heaven they wouldn't know what to do! I'd like to think the odd one or two were female. I'm not a great judge. They all looked the same to me. I'm not about to hang around wherever it is they might decide to pee. It could be dangerous whatever their sex!

I'm going home. It hadn't all been a waste of time. I'd got to know more about my ancestors and their lives. I'd got to know a little more about Maccy Tamryn. I learnt nothing of the intricacies of gardening. I believe the only way I might get green fingers is to continuously pick my nose. There's something to look forward to.

The Spittin' Woman had not appeared in the completed week. It is long enough. She is to be in my past now. Placed in the 'out' tray. It had been just an enjoyable chance meeting. I don't believe there will be another. I leave McCarthy or Hickok in a sombre mood. I can do sombre when required! Sober is much more difficult but both words mean more or less the same thing, not forgetting morose. I realise it's a good job I never owned a dictionary. They mostly were only any use to prop doors open anyway. Right now, mine and hers is shut tight and it seems locked!

Everything at the Mermaid had been as it should be on my return. Lenny and Alice have it all under control. The pub is still where I left it. An Alsatian is under the pool table. The Mermaid is thriving. I am once again on the move. I need to keep going. I not only have to complete getting over the loss of Jennifer, now I must get over the American and her now fast dimming star. It is many days now since I heard from her. It's time to move on. Bloody hell, I can't wait until it's time to stand still. To be honest, I don't do standing still too often. When I do, too much goes past me. When it's gone, it's gone. No amount of wondering can make up for it.

Like the woman once said, without invitation, 'regrets are for losers'. She didn't say it in so many words but I'm beginning to think she was correct, which is a shame. I really hate smart arses. Always, they think they are right. They invariably are.

A sudden and unexpected offer comes in by telephone which will surely help concentrate my mind for a day or two. Plymouth Associated Breweries are in a quandary, they think I can help them out. I think they are barking but not up the wrong tree, or just barking! I accept. Somewhere between Truro and Grampound is a pub which has lost its incumbent. It has recently been sold but not changed hands yet. The late landlord had keeled over permanently. The Merry Maiden at the quaintly named 'Golden Mill' near Tredinnit needs a caretaker. I am to be the chosen one apparently. I get the feeling it'll be like winning the lottery without the financial bit. Well to be fair, there is a few quid in it, or I wouldn't be doing it. So, I am off to Tredinnit!

* Carpetbagger was a derogatory term applied by former Confederates to any person from the <u>Northern United States</u> who came to the <u>Southern states</u> after the <u>American Civil War</u>; they were perceived as exploiting the local populace.

** The village continues to have two names: McCarthy City and Hickok City.

Chapter Nine

Some Thing has Landed

"You sir!"

"Yes?"

"Why isn't this establishment open yet?"

"I can't get in."

"Why not man."

"Erm, because you're in the way."

"That's no excuse man."

"I thought it was. Who are you?"

"I've completely forgotten. Oh that's it, I'm Silent."

"No you're not."

"It's my name you bloody fool, Silent Knight to you."

"Knight to you too. It is only nine O' clock, in the morning. Anyway, sleep well. Don't wake up too early. Sotto Voce 'or not at all.'

"I live across the road. You can't miss my place, it's got a Mosquito in the garden, Gotta Spit' too."

"Get an insect spray. Please don't spit at me. I've had enough spit to last a lifetime. Don't spit in the pub either. Everybody will want to do it."

"A Plane, the Mosquito is a plane, don't you listen man. The damn Spit too you bloody fool!"

"Shouldn't you give them back to the RAF? They might need them one day. Anyway, nice letting you chat to me. Gotta go and wash all the spit off my face." Maccy to Earth, I'm coming back!

Sanity at last. On the other hand. "Who are you?" She had taken the place of the old farmer.

"I'm Lavinia, I'm the head barmaid."

"So there must be others?"

"I was told someone was coming here to help, a man. You'll have to do. It's just me and you for now, and a cook. He says he's a cook."

"What man? So the cook is a man?"

"Yeah, he's all man. I'm not sure about the cooking bit."

I resist the temptation to respond to her statement in a way that may be obvious to some. I'm not telling her I can cook either.

"I am only one. Where's my room?" It is still early, I had my wits about me a few moments ago, half at least. Now I have something resembling a halfwit in front of me, after an earlier one had left, and I believe I am coping reasonably well. I don't profess to be an expert in such matters. She might be more than a halfwit, or even less.

"In the garden. It was my room."

"Was it? I'm sure you'll find somewhere."

"We liked it down there. No one could hear us. You know when we were having how's your father. We had to move out yesterday, so you could move in. Staying at my mum's up down the road in the village over there." The bedraggled looking female pointed unnecessarily at something I didn't think I could see.

"Shouldn't think anyone would want to hear, would they? For your information, I have no idea how my father is right now." I try not to think about her horizontal relationship at all. It may not even have been horizontal. What she got up to at the bottom of the garden and maybe in the car park does not interest me at all, surprisingly. I've done car parks, they aren't all they are cracked up to be. Let me put it this way, I would much rather kerb crawl. Each to their own I say.

"You never know around here. Bloody weird lot."

"I'll keep my eyes open for some of them." I do believe her. I've done the weird thing, I went to Liskeard for a week one day.

"There always seems to be some randy perv' creeping around out there in the dark and grunting. We could hear him in the middle of the night, snortin' and what 'ave you. Dunno what he was doing."

"Are you a cockney?" Do I even care?

Lavinia giggles like a fifteen-year-old version of herself. I think she is around sixteen and a half at least. She may be twenty and a very good actress.

"I love that word, don't you?"

"Not particularly. Don't you have something to be getting on with?" This girl, did I say girl, has the nerve to call others weird. I attempt to stop giving her encouragement. I am failing miserably.

"What would you like me to do, Mister?"

"Maccy Tamryn. I don't know, do what you normally do, I imagine." I have no intention of imagining anything. I have rendered my imagination redundant for my stay.

"Better not I s'pose, you might get embarrassed."

"So, what happened with the last landlord, Lavinia?" I decide to completely ignore most of the daft girl's side comments.

"He snuffed it when 'is wife caught us. You know, having nookie, right 'ere in the bar. There! We only got caught cos he died." The girl has an overactive pointing finger.

"Who died?" I almost asked if it was the same man she was with in the garden. I didn't want to know where 'there' is or was.

"The bloke who had this place, the last landlord."

So it was the same man. This is all too much information. I don't allow my eyes to follow her still pointing finger. Some things are better not known. This is one of them.

"Right, well that won't be happening again." My reply is partly unconvincing. I'm convinced, I'm not certain she is.

She looks as if she has just left her bed and forgotten to dress or just grabbed the nearest items that looked like clothes. If I had been single and ten years younger my answer might have been very different. Obviously if I was ten years younger, she would be. I would get locked up. I also prefer my bedclothes to stay on the bed. To be honest, Lavinia isn't unattractive, she's well formed. She is dressed like a badly wrapped Hippy Eskimo. I am hoping she might say 'I'm going outside, I might be a while.'

"That's what he said the morning we were caught. I didn't like him that much anyway. He had breath like a butcher's underpants and a face like a Hedgehog's backside."

"You didn't like him? Why did you keep, erm, you know, with him then?" I have no idea why I am asking her. I'm not even slightly interested. As for her knowledge of a master butcher's underwear and a nocturnal rodent's rear end, I'm not inclined to venture any more questions. It's worrying me that I even asked.

"Better than working, innit?"

It was enough for me. The two conversations had almost worn me out and I hadn't done anything resembling work as yet. I decide to look for a kettle and make life giving coffee before attempting any further exchanges with the horribly dressed, self-confessed sex goddess who possibly has relatives living in the Arctic Circle or the Bermuda Triangle? Do they need clowns at Piccadilly Circus, This one is going spare.

I take half an hour on my own to get my bearings and gather my recently displaced wits. I can hardly sack her, I'm only here to help out for a few days. I have successfully fought the randy females' suggestiveness. I am pleased with myself. I suppose if I'm honest, I have looked her up and down, nothing more. She is well formed but not my type and no milk has been spilt. We probably don't have any anyway. Five or ten years ago at home in Padstow, things might have been different. Almost without my knowledge I had inadvertently built myself a reputation locally. There was hardly a time when I hadn't a female companion but now those days are well and truly over. Even more were attracted by my little brother, Dusty. It's all been a huge responsibility.

My mind goes into rewind and visions of my short liaison with Alice Copestick. Alice was engaged to Popeye Mervyn at the time, it didn't deter her from dragging me into her rooftop love nest late one evening; it took me until early morning to find my way out!

Alice and Mervyn are long married now. Their chunky blonde youngster will tower over both and is currently eating them out of house and home. A good-looking lad unsurprisingly. I'm glad his hair is starting to darken, I wonder what's caused that!

Danny's a nice well-mannered kid with the gift of the gab. He hardly ever stops asking questions to which I have few if any answers. I stop and chat to him whenever I catch up with him. It's good for a growing kid to have an independent mentor. Kids will often listen to an outsider rather than a parent. Dusty, my own kid brother, is the exception to the rule. He believes he knows the answer to everything.

Alice knows I spend time with the boy. She winks slyly in my direction whenever we meet on the quayside. She keeps me up to date with his educational improvements when it's safe. Danny keeps me up to date with his latest escapades.

Mervyn and I get along. We're not close friends; a pint together occasionally when Mervyn will take the opportunity to brag about the lad being just like his father. 'A chip off the old block' he will repeat at every opportunity. It's always left to me to change the subject, which I do as quickly as possible. I wouldn't want Mervyn to get the wrong idea. I wouldn't want him to get the right idea.

Dear Lenny, treats Danny like a brother. My own brother Dusty treats the youngster like a brother. The youngster is a nephew to both of them more or less. Nobody but Alice, Dusty and I know. But then Dusty knows just about all there is to know about Danny boy. I've had to pay him enough to keep his gob shut. I don't believe he would grass us up, you never can be certain.

I miss my little brother when he's not about. We have a unique relationship for siblings. We get on, always have. We don't squabble. We look out for each other. We look out for our Ma. Dusty does help me look after my wallet, on far too many occasions.

My brother has a well-established business of his own now. A small, well-built craft he fondly calls a sea bus takes holidaymakers by boat to other coastal towns. I always knew the kid would do well. He certainly helped me with my pub, the 'Mermaid' when we were struggling to build the trade after I took it on from Cap'n Bligh and Blencathra when that pair retired to England, over the 'other side' of the wet bit commonly known as the Tamar by us locals. I have no idea what the people on the other side call it. Something similar no doubt.

The kid would turn up in Lost Souls Creek – no sadder place in Cornwall exists than the creek - at midnight with a boatload of lager louts who believed they needed 'one more for the road' even though they could hardly walk and certainly couldn't drive. Newquay has that effect on teenagers. It did me once upon a time!

Every morning, Dusty would need to hose down all the suddenly discarded food and beer the youngsters have sprayed all over his pine decking. Every evening he is at the quayside, taking cash in exchange for tickets for another excursion into the alcohol hell that is Newquay. He can never get too much of a good thing. Who wouldn't?

Dusty is yet to settle down but ma and I live in hope. Despite his own mis-spent youth, the kid will make a good partner for someone, someday. There was one, she disappeared a while ago, a decent enough girl, probably too decent for the likes of the kid. She promised to return at some later point, won't hold my breath.

I take my coffee and step outside for a quiet cigar. Looking out over the rolling hillsides that blot out the television aerials of Truro, I suddenly become aware of a pungent smell. It isn't aromatic. It is the unmistakable scent of the porcine variety. A pig farm is obviously operating close by. So much for the late-night noises I think as I enjoy my smoke in a silent and well-earned solitude. I survey the beautiful rolling countryside which surrounds me.

On returning bar side I find the slightly less lumpy Lavinia. She has discarded the tablecloth, she retains the uplifted shades and the pillows. They are not pillows obviously!

Lavinia is setting out a row of black buckets. I can hardly help noticing she is bending over a tad more than I believe to be necessary to do the chore. The bending motion almost allowing the built-in pillows to make an appearance, it is mildly scary.

I feel better after my short break. I feel safe enough to question the still bedraggled girl, that may have once been a contortionist.

"What's the story on all this then?" I point at the growing line of containers.

"What, these buckets?" She smiles, I know she knows I had been admiring her elasticity and her extremely lively puppies, I mean pillows.

"Yeah, the buckets?"

"It rained yesterday afternoon."

"So?" I remembered the lousy drive and the constant spraying of my windscreen from an endless convoy of articulated lorries, caravans and tractors. I don't remember seeing any cars. I think there might have been one or two of the 'broken down' variety dotted around.

"The thatch roof up there, it leaks." The pointing finger is unnecessary. I know where the roof is. She continued. "The rain takes hours to come through the thatch and I know where all the leaks are."

"So, do I now, all over the bleddy place." The finger pointing is beginning to get on my wick.

"Nah, just along the bar. Kitchen's okay, it's just here. Sometimes we need to have the buckets out when we're open. Trouble is they get knocked over and my T-Shirt and everything else gets wet. When I tell the customers I need to change my T shirt, they ask me not to."

I play deaf although dead might be more useful.

The large caravan park - it's a bumpy field with a standpipe - across the road had suddenly filled up with long weekenders on Thursday evening. Business was frantic, Saturday, Sunday and the bank holiday Monday lunchtime saw the Merry Maiden packed to the rafters. Lavinia showed exactly why she is a barmaid and I should add, a damned good one. She worked her socks off, thankfully that was all. She kept the T-Shirt on, it stayed dry mostly.

Although fully qualified myself in the culinary arts, I have a chef in the kitchen who had virtually emptied all the cupboards of any food stuffs. He had nothing edible left for Monday night. He needn't have worried, Monday night was totally cancelled without our knowledge. Sometime during Bank Holiday Monday afternoon everyone had packed up their buckets and spades and gone back home to Shepherds Bush or somewhere in Essex. All except one, who didn't seem to be local. He looks as though he'd travelled some distance, Jamaica is my guess.

Bob is well over six feet tall and he can drink the hind legs off an alcoholic donkey. Bob also has a habit of carrying around his own tankard. At the completion of each pint, he will just wave the mug in the air and shout the rhyme 'more, more beer over 'ere, fill 'er up, let me sup'! Bob is rather dark hued from head to toe. I couldn't see his toes obviously.

I am pleased to see the bloke slide in the door, not to be confused with a sliding door. He is the distraction I need from the constant suggestiveness of my high-performance barmaid. My chef doesn't need to be distracted. He realises my reluctance to react and uses it to his own advantage. It works out well.

On Monday evening the slot machine is silent, the carpark is empty, and the bar is vacant. Apart from one of us dropping a coin in the jukebox at regular intervals, the four of us do little but empty and refill our glasses.

By nine o'clock I have given up hope of further custom. I pull the door shut and the four of us have a lock-in, paid for by the mountain of tips that have accrued over the long holiday weekend. It was a short weekend in fact, it just felt like the longer version.

One other punter did come knocking at the door late on but we four pretended not to hear. I guess he or she soon retreated to the off license in the village.

Bob is a godsend. He keeps me entertained. He is in fact from 'Jamaica' – not the inn obviously, although he might be – I learn! There is just the one awful point in the evening when Lavinia seems to be on the verge of suggesting she and I retire to the bedroom in the garden. There was a time many moons ago when I might have seconded the motion.

The bored – an assumption on my part - Alsatian yawns and continues to do what it does best. Lavinia's exploits remind me of some of my own. My memory revisits Chapel Porth first. Jen' and I had taken in a restaurant. A little celebration of something, I don't remember what. I do remember the highlight of the evening. We agreed to take a midnight stroll on Porth beach. The taxi driver who had brought us promised to wait an hour and then he was 'leaving' with or without us.

We had walked, talked and laughed. Eventually we set out a blanket on the moist sand. I had got glasses and Champagne from the back of the taxi where I had put the items earlier in the evening. The driver had winked at me as I collected the pieces.

The taxi was parked in the carpark at the back of the beach. The driver was armed with flask and food. I'd told him as I handed over a fifty-pound note, it would be a long night. 'Take as long as you like, Maccy.' It didn't take much to change his plans, the cash helped.

Jen and I watched the moon pecking at the water's surface. Invisible gulls cried a sad message as we stretched out.

Now, I'm a big lad and the Champagne has little effect on me. I had walked back to the taxi and fetched another bottle.

I had opened the bottle, put my thumb over the top and shook it. She had screamed and swore at the coldness of the spray. She came at me. We fell where we stood. Like two giant crabs we fought and squirmed out of our clothes. The blanket was a damp ball. Just at this point, I notice something I consider to be unsavoury.

"What the hell!" I yelled.

"Not now, Maccy."

"There, up there." I pointed at the towering cliffs where flashing lights moved haphazardly.

"Bleddy hell, shit!"

This was a new look into her vocabulary. A dozen or more globes of light seem to hover on the cliffside. The balls of light come towards us.

Jen' and I grab at the clothes we could find and ran across the beach to the taxi. The driver was half asleep in the back. I evicted him, shoved him back in the drivers' seat and we took his place. The driver stared through the screen. The lights were closing on us. We both struggled to get some clothes back on, I was sweating profusely in panic.

They were on us, rapping on the glass and yelling, screaming, baying, naked. Slowly I'd undone the window. Hands clawed at me from all angles.

"Maccy, Maccy, MACCY!"

"Get off me, get off."

"You were asleep. I was telling Chef and Bob about the time me and my man was on a caravan roof and it broke."

"Not now Lavinia, I'm just too bleddy knackered."

"Frickin' men!"

Bob is first to leave, I disappear a little later. I leave Lavinia and the chef to their own devices. I catch sight of the disheveled chef as he creeps out early the next morning.

The end of my time at The Merry Maiden is nigh. The locals must have realised and turned out in small droves to give me a good send off. The area manager had suggested I let Lavinia take over until the new owners arrive, If I want to get on the road home a day earlier, she will manage for the short term.

My last night and the place is half full. A party of sorts is hastily begun. It's nice they are celebrating my leaving, especially as I've only been here for a few of days.

Two aged latecomers arrive. The man is almost seven feet tall, his female companion around five at the most.

"Evening landlord."

"Evening!"

"I am Frederik, and this is my wife Mary."

He had an indistinct accent. I ask the origin!

"I am from the Fatherland. I was a pilot in the Luftwaffe. I bailed out here and was imprisoned. I stayed after the war. I love this place, I feel right at home here."

"Well Fred, you could hardly go back up without a plane mate!"

"It is true landlord!"

A German, it can't get any better than this. At his height, who needs a plane? He can look at everything with a birds eye view. I could see the Squadron Leader beginning to wake. "Why don't you go and chat to Mr. Knight? That's him over there. You two should get on like a plane on fire."

"Thank you, landlord. I will look forward to it." The couple walk away in the direction of the old bloke. Perfect. I'm doing so well, I might consider opening up a 'swingers' agency for very odd couples.

The short time I had been in Lavinia's' company had been more than enough. The new, permanent owners are due soon. I am emptying the buckets myself this miserable grey morning.

Derek called and is obviously excited at the prospect of he and his partner obtaining the Maiden, so to speak. I take the time and trouble to explain to the feller the workings and the peculiar trade patterns of this country pub. I make the same explanations as the girl had a couple of days ago, before I leave. In quieter tones, I tell him all about lusty Lavinia and her fondness and cravings for sexual experimentation, especially on the larger items of furniture, that doesn't include the one-armed bandit. Of course, it doesn't exclude it either, or that he had better be on his guard if alone in her presence.

I flush and wince as Derek eventually explains his partner is called Tim that they are gay and have just spent a month on their honeymoon in the Scilly Isles which is the reason for my having to be here temporarily. Not being anti-gay in any way but the sainted Scilly Isles seemed to be the perfect honeymoon spot for the pair in my opinion.

There is some justice in the world after all. Lavinia will be barking up the wrong tree with the newcomers. I am disappointed I can't be a fly on the wall when they finally appear.

The Merry Maiden nightmare, for me, is almost over. It hasn't been so terrible as nightmares go. It was another experience to be stored away in a file named: Not to be opened until the event of my death. Shouldn't be too long the way things are going!

One thing I did do in my short time at the Maiden was to order a pool table. A side room which was supposed to be a bijou restaurant was never used during my stay. I decided to empty it out and turn it into a Pool room. It didn't quite happen as easily as I thought it might.

"Now then, where's this pool table going mister? You don't have much room." Something about the tall bloke bothers me. I don't know why. He was here promptly at least.

"In there." I point at the door opposite and see this arrival as me finally putting the restaurant out of its lingering misery. I am rather pleased with myself for a moment or two.

"In there?" Now he's pointing just like I did. It must be a local custom.

"Exactly, dead centre. I've made room for it!"

"I can't do that."

"Why the hell not?"

"It's the restaurant, that's why not. You can't have a pool table in a bleddy restaurant. It'll get in the way, people will drop food on the cloth."

Here we go. Every son of a bitch and his dog wants to tell me what I can do and what I can't do. "Right mister, what's your name? I'm gonna call your bloody lot and tell them to get someone else here to do it."

"Call whoever you like. Won't make any bleddy difference. I don't believe I'll be putting my table in there."

"Take your pool table and sling your bleddy hook. I've had enough of you lot telling me what to do and what not to do."

"Have it your way."

"I bleddy well intend to, now 'op it, bugger off."

The table fitter had nothing more to say and promptly left me alone with the phone and a card with the company details on it.

I'm determined to tell the company what I thought and dialed the number printed at the bottom of the card.

It's a mobile and the owner is soon talking to me at the other end.

"I've just had your man here telling me he can't put my pool table up where I want it. What are you gonna do about it? The useless tosser was a pain in the arse and I want you to come here and sort it out, and don't bring the idiot that has just left with you!"

"Can you remind me, whereabouts are you again?"

"The Merry Maiden near Golden."

"Now then, is that the one that have just got a temporary landlord? Yes, I know it."

"That's right."

"Do you have a restaurant there?"

"No! I don't have a bleddy restaurant. I have a bleddy games room, that's why I want a bleddy pool table. It used to have a restaurant, now it doesn't, the restaurant is now extinct, it's no longer here."

"Okay, I'll be with you as soon as I can. Are you sure you don't have a restaurant?"

"No, I don't have a frigging restaurant." Now I am feeling much better, I have made it loud and clear to almost everyone and his dog, the Maiden no longer has a restaurant, not even a café or a free food counter, excepting Sundays when all the regulars expect a free roast potato and a bit of pork crackling. The pub has a games room and a games room it shall stay until I leave. After that they can do what they like.

The front door swings open again even before I have put the phone down properly. It is the same table fitter. He is wearing a wry smile and I am not happy; not happy would be an understatement.

"Now then."

"Bleddy hell, don't people take no, bugger off and shove your pool table up your arse, for an answer around here? Obviously not. I told you to sling your bleddy hook. I just spoke to your boss and he's on his way here to sort this out."

"Who is?"

"The bloke on the phone that runs the pool table business."

"That's me, I'm the tosser you just spoke to. Now, where shall I start?"

He proves to be a pussy cat. I watch the pussy cat put the table together. It is pretty much an art form, at least in his case. The heavy frame is first, then two sections of perfectly flat slate were slid into position by both of us. A new cloth was templated and cut to perfection and glued down tightly underneath the edges where the cushions will be fitted, before ultimately the black dots! The cushions put in place that added to the tautness of the baize and to stop the balls falling off the edge. The pockets were fitted, and the spots were stuck on where an iron was employed. It was useful he had his own, I don't have one as far as I know. I don't want one!

New shiny balls came from a box and I am presented with cues in their plastic wrappers and a box of blue chalk cubes. We unsheathed two cues and commenced our potentially long free session. I couldn't wait to get started. We stopped a while. I made food and poured pints.

The fitter is good. I did manage to make a match of it. Once again, I had no idea what this latest visitor is called, and he never offered to tell me. I could find out by looking at the invoice and the rental agreement.

One thought that did occur to me after he left was how on earth were incoming landlords, Tim and Derek, two confirmed gays, going to manage the Merry Maiden and a Merry Maiden. On second thoughts, Merry Maiden Lavinia is not. I wasn't what might be called reluctant to leave. It had been interesting; it had been a challenge. I have always considered myself to be adventurous. I may have to change my views.

Whatever she is, Lavinia is a great barmaid. She never bothered me again until my last morning. She threw her arms around my neck and without hesitation, slipped her tongue inside my mouth and pushed her groaning pillows into my chest as I was about to leave through the doorway, backwards. No bones were broken in the making of my departure.

For a moment only, I do wonder what Lavinia is going to do to amuse herself now. The poor girl will be bored out of her handful of brain cells, the remainder of which seemed to have been sucked into a black hole.

The Duchy is full of holes pretty much. Most of them are empty now, apart from those being used for disposing of junk. It's no wonder scrap metal businesses are going bust. Most tin and copper mineshafts are now full of scrap metal of one kind or another. If mine shafts are now full of rusty unwanted metal, is it Karma, two hundred years from now someone will be mining Ford Cortinas and Vauxhall Astras. Time Team may be called in to explain to the general public what a car was.

I pulled my car to a sudden halt at Winnards Perch. "Where are you going bud?"

"Padstow mate."

"You're in luck, I reckon I know where it is. Do you want to run behind?"

Chapter Ten

Cider Drinkers do it Slower

"You live there mate?"

"Not yet. Maybe when I get there."

"Good luck with that. Careful what you wish for. You might just want to think again. I'll drop you at the harbour, not in it obviously; maybe later!"

"Appreciate it, where is it?"

"Next to the sea. Maccy Tamryn. Most people know me here, might be better if you don't mention my name mind."

"You don't live here?"

"Couple of miles back, Little Petrock."

"Thanks for the lift, Maccy. It's Peter."

"Good luck, Peter. What do you do by the way, Peter?"

"You name it."

"See you around mate."

The time had gone by fast; the experiences could prove invaluable. I thought Padstow in particular was weird. I should think again. There are odder places to light upon, none weirder than Tredinnit. Oh, don't worry they know it. I believe I did them a favour in the end, more than one. I gave them their pub back - I didn't need it - I gave them a pool table, I promised them a friendly once they have raised a team to play us.

I have left them in the capable hands of Lavinia and most likely they have little hope or none at all. Disaster may well await. They should pray she doesn't stay too long, I'm not certain they're ready for her. She might not cope with the local clientele easily; I suspect she will drive them madder than they already are. One thing for sure, I will miss the people. Eccentric yes, but who am I to point the finger?

For a few days I have been sampling the 'middle' of Cornwall. It's what they told me. They lied of course, the Middle of Cornwall is fifteen or so miles further north and in a churchyard in Lanivet, so Michael informed me once or twice. One has to believe a man of the cloth of course. In Michael's case, maybe not, he does cheat at snooker. I wonder how big the centre of a county needs to be. Perhaps it's like a centre spot on a football pitch? It might be a cross as in X marks the spot. It should be on a roundabout, they could call it 'Treasure Island'.

Now I have returned home and intend to take over The Maltsters Arms. I could not want for better. I'm back home to stay. The carriages are just yards away from where I sit. The Mermaid and Bow is just a ten-minute drive away. Padstow is less than a handful - it depends how big the hands are - of Cornish miles distant, the uninitiated will have to guess how far that is. The answer has nothing to do with crows flying. For one thing, how does a crow know how far it has flown? If the bird doesn't know, how can any other Tom, Dick or whatshisname have any idea?

It had been less than half an hours' drive back to Little Petrock. The Maltsters is in darkness as I make my way past it to get to the carriages where I will bed down. As far as I know no one knew I was back home and I wanted it to stay that way for twenty-four hours. I needed a decent amount of rest. I am determined to get it before showing my face. I did want to see Maccy Junior, but best to let him sleep. No point in waking him now, he'd be yakking all night.

I sleep well and walk the short distance to the Maltsters early. It is pay day! Starkey, the breweries' area manager is to meet me. He will surely attempt to lure me away again. He has no chance. I'll give him his due, he's a trier.

The Maltsters is the centre of a tiny community that is not much bigger than Golden Mill and Tredinnit. To call Little Petrock a village would surely be an overstatement. The Maltsters is a passing trade pub if you can get anyone to stop. A dozen or so cottages and bungalows, a French style miniature church directly across the road and of course the various farms, one of which is Ma's, which is just in a back lane that leads on to St Issey, a slightly larger village. The cottages are squashed into a huddle. A rambling mixture of houses that look like they should have been in an old black and white film, with Alistair Sim in place as the sinister pub landlord, James Robertson Justice as the alcoholic, womanising vicar. The pub is accompanied by various outbuildings, one of which has a reputation second to none. It is the walls of this lean-to which once echoed to the sounds of newborn infants making their first and only journeys pretty much unaided. Almost certainly the babes never having seen the light of day.

There is one other little abode close by. Hidden away in a back lane, just a hundred yards away are the carriages. My home, mine and Maccy Junior's. I had moved into the century old carriages some years ago. My grandfather had acquired them for a small backhander he regularly told us. He did well. In fact, it's my guess the seller didn't actually own them at the time. Possibly he paid a bystander to look the other way when Grandad and two or three of us boys went to collect them from the overgrown remains of the sidings at the ruined Camel's Halt.

Starkey and I are seated on a large circular wooden bench in the garden at the side of the pub. The bench has seen better days. We sit with care. The rambling Lost Souls Creek provides lively water music while we talk. While Starkey talks, a Kingfisher glides past at speed. Within a few seconds the bird is completely invisible.

Little Petrock isn't so much a hamlet, just a couple of dozen or so stone built homes that seem to be there to stop one another falling over. The main coast road is just a few yards away. It is mid-February; the holiday season is still a way off. Until then the Maltsters congregation will be made up of a dozen locals, their dogs and the odd couple who probably shouldn't be hiding there together in the first place, if you get my meaning.

I listen as Starkey wastes his time exercising vocal chords.

"So, I can't talk you into staying on with us, Maccy?"

"No, my mind is made up. I have done my bit, I have done my time and learned plenty. For me, it was all about that. There can't be anything worse than where I've been. Maybe Birmingham and London even Glasgow might qualify. I don't intend to be a landlord in any of those places. So, no. I'm staying home."

"Sure?"

"Yep, if you offered double, it wouldn't make a blind bit of difference. I'm done, it's done. I'll be back at my own place down the road and getting this place shipshape drekly. The sale has gone through here, it's no good trying to change my mind."

"Wouldn't of thought you'd want this place Maccy, it's a bit behind the times."

"It's already mine in everything but name. There's nothing I don't know about this place, don't you worry. I was brought up around here, I have to have it. The wheels were already set in motion before I left to go to wherever it is I have just returned from. Cider drinkers don't drink as much as beer drinkers, they don't need to, it's much stronger. They all fall down for the same reason, but it doesn't take so long to do it."

Starkey gave up, knowing his persistence was useless. The brewery man left after handing me a large cheque for my services at the Merry Maiden. I bet he doesn't drive so fast where he comes from, nobody does. Just why is it emmets shut their eyes when we are driving towards them? It is a recipe for their disaster, theirs mostly!

I take a drive into Padstow to check on the Mermaid and Bow. It all seems to be operating smoothly. It seems Lenny is maturing a tad with age. The place is all spick and span, I will give Alice the credit for that. She would have knocked her brother into shape by now and the evidence is here to prove it. I don't let them know I've been in. Right now no one knows I'm back in the vicinity. It's time I showed my face at home.

The Maltsters customers are a mixture of born and bred Cornish, relocated and cocky West Londoners and the usual passing council workmen. I will feel very much at home again, which of course is where I am. I just need the keys. Any time soon I will have them in my grubby mitt and we can get a shift on.

I already know the pub hasn't deteriorated in quite the same way as the Mermaid and the Merry Maiden had been allowed to. The previous owners here hadn't gone bust, the aged landlord had just suddenly passed away – there's a lot of it about it seems – and his wife had decided she couldn't or didn't want to carry on, on her own. Passing away seems to be a habit in the licensing trade it would seem. I will try not to replicate the habit yet awhile.

The Maltsters has just the one close opposition, The Bells! No, not some imitation of Notre Dame, The Ring O Bells. The Bells doesn't make the Maltsters suffer. They complement each other. They both have a good regular trade when the emmets are hereabouts. Young Chris the landlord sees to it they are welcomed. I will need to follow his lead!

The Maltsters has a steady trade, it just needs to be kept steady. It has plenty of room for growth. There is much to do and I'm already drawing plans in my head. The creek runs close by, a small lake spreads out for a while at the back. An ancient engine house and chimney stack cast there shadows over it at times when the sun is low. Yes, there is plenty can be done with the old place.

The local old timers drink slowly here. Not the youngsters, who would arrive and after throwing down two or three pints of Snakebite - that's cider and lager in the same pint glass - too quickly, end up horizontal after half an hour and have large sections of irreplaceable memory missing the next morning. Snakebite is potent. I should know, I have a shed full of the homemade variety. It's not so much a shed, just an old milking unit at the

111

Magic Mushroom Farm where ma will be at home when she's not in the pub.

Not many of the youngsters can handle more than two pints of the stuff. They are so predictable, each one believing they could handle half a gallon better than the other, each one suddenly achieving glass eye status, partial paralysis and temporary, perhaps even permanent, brain damage. The blindness is not usually permanent.

Those that know better, the older hands, just sip away slowly, certain in the knowledge they had learned the art of cider supping in the very same way, perhaps thirty or forty years ago. It's funny but these drinkers do everything slower. It's as if they are in a completely different gear to everyone around them. They're on a different plain and a different plane seemingly. I make a vow not to touch the stuff when I have total ownership of the Maltsters. It won't last! At least here I will have a decent pool table. There is a team in the local league. I'm never happier than when I have a pool cue in my hand. I would need to speak to the team captain and see if I can get myself a game or two at some point. I can't wait until we have a fixture against the Mermaid and Bow. It'll be like home-from-home for me. The Mermaid and Bow is my other pub and right now under the management of my oldest friend Lenny Copestick and his wonderful sister Alice.

Alice and I were close once, as close as two can be for want of a more apt phrase, Alice and I may have been over friendly on occasion when we were a tad younger. We were fancy free and single - I was single anyway. Her bloke, Mervyn, tended to spend a lot of time visiting his mother. Alice is now the joint manager at the Mermaid. No, not in the kitchen, chef organises the meat products. I get to see the lad quite often. He's at school now, following in the footsteps of his father, I hope. Less said the better!

Needless to say, the two of us hardly speak if we meet. Certainly when others might be around. As for the Mermaid, I've frequented the place almost forever it seems, as a legal customer, not more than nine or ten years on and off. I was away in the smoke, at college for a while, learning to cook various items. As landlord, I've been the incumbent for a year or two now. I bought the place and with some help from Ma and Jen', we managed the impossible and pulled it out of the doldrums somewhat. Since Jen went, it hasn't quite been the same.

My ma uses the Maltsters as she always has done. When she appears she'll look like something from the seventies and there'll be men around her like flies around freshly expedited cow dung.

Ma doesn't live far away, less than a mile. She has her own business - The Magic Mushroom Farm. She makes garden ornaments, concrete mushrooms mostly. In fact forget mostly, it's all she makes. She does everything herself - mixes the concrete, fills the moulds, markets them and sells them all over the country. That way she doesn't have to pay out any wages. Her stuff is in big demand. She tells punters one of hers is in the garden at 10 Downing Street. I am doubtful. It boosts trade though. I came across one or two in my travels. I thought she had been exaggerating, she wasn't. I managed to get up close and personal with one in the Fulham Palace Road, I have the scar to prove it. I tripped over one and headbutted it whilst trying to stand up, not intentionally obviously. I'm not even certain as to why I was in a stranger's garden in the first place.

You can't miss the Mushroom Farm, there's a whole wall along the front made up from rejects. The Mushroom Wall and another lot at my place. Ma gets a few strange looks from tourists passing her place, as do I. They might gawp or stop and buy one. Not many folks pass my place. It's a bit out of the way, which is how I like it. If I can't be found, it's where I am.

As for the shed, it's here some of us locals make our own cider. We have our own press and all that we need to produce it. Sunday mornings, the lads go to the shed before they go to the Maltsters or the Bells. They would have had a couple of pints by the time they get to the Maltsters - here they would just drink halves. It's an old tradition, an operation her majesty's customs office don't know about thankfully.

There will be little to getting the Maltsters improved, it hasn't been closed more than a couple of weeks. The old lady has made her departure. The doors for now are locked but hopefully not for long.

The Mermaid and Bow, my other place hardly fifteen minutes away in Padstow by road, is unusual to say the least. First thing a new visitor will notice is the lack of any barstools. In their place and running from one end to the other of the bar, is a long, highly polished, well-built bench, I guessed it could seat ten to twelve punters, maybe more, at any one go. All a punter has to do is step over and plonk his or her backside.

On one wall is a glass display cabinet which holds the some of the remains of a broken chair and table. There is a carved inscription at the base of the cabinet:

"In memory of a beloved Crew member, One Armed Frank."

"Herein lie the remains of the Mermaid and Bow's last barstool."

We couldn't put Franks' remains there obviously, they would have scared the kids. There is a picture of a Tall Ship at the Mermaid that hanging upside down, - another memory from the past. It got turned that way in a fight some years ago. If it were turned the right way now there would be dust on the top and dust on the bottom!

There had been fights aplenty when I was attempting to grow up in Padstow. Not anymore, now that I'm respectable they have declined considerably in number. Most of them had been caused by me or my mate, Lenny. Lenny has settled down a tad now and Blencathra and Cap'n Bligh have gone over the bridge to live in England.

Blen' was the Mermaids' landlady, she won most of the scraps thereabouts. Blen' was a great scrapper.

Dear Blen' is enormous - a flesh covered Easter Island statue. It wasn't that she would start a fight herself, though there were one or two occasions. Mostly she would bring one to an end - not many of us could best her in a scrap. I bought the place from the old couple. They moved over to Plymouth. I get a postcard occasionally. They are long retired now. She and Bligh had a windfall on the very day they were leaving the Mermaid. Blencathra is almost certainly a throw-back from some bygone age.

The Mermaids' crew has changed a tad since the old days. Some have gone and others have arrived and fitted right in. There's Bessie, a newcomer, once the pervy pirate, now retired by public demand. You can't miss Bessie; he'll be wearing a carpenter's tool belt to hold his trousers up. I don't think Bessie ever takes that belt off. It might have been something I said to him once a long time ago.

There's the Birdseyes. Like old Lil the tart, they are original crew members. Even my Jen' had become a member. Now she has gone and cannot return.

They all belonged, even the ugliest looking Alsatian that ever chewed a bone. Not one that belongs to him obviously. Falling apart now from age, the dog still has the cleanest undercarriage in the Duchy. It just adopted me, years ago. It's been with me through thick and thin. It still has no name. I've called it many things it didn't seem to take too willingly.

It seems I must have a good eye for business. There is no restaurant in my pub as such, wherever the diners want to eat, they eat. If we're full, they can eat in the bog or on the stairs. It hasn't been full that often in the past but we're getting there. Each time a table is vacated, the ugly Alsatian with half its face missing - lying dormant under the pool table licking its bits and bobs to the best of his ability - would get up and vacuum the dropped scraps before returning to its darkened hiding place. It keeps the dog employed and makes the cleaners' job easier.

The kid, Dusty, my only brother as far as I know, has his own business, the sea bus. He ferries folk back and forth to Newquay. Mostly they're kids from the bigger working farms with more money than sense. It's the kids and the emmets that have the money.

Unlike all the other places, where time had passed so quickly, the Maltsters has a much slower pace. It will change in time. Maybe our local brew has an influence on the building. As previously mentioned, these drinkers do everything slower, which I'm sure is an asset in the bedroom if they make it that far. The whole village seems to have the same slow demeanour.

My ma and obviously my younger brothers' ma is Morning Joy as she used to be known way back in the early seventies. It had been her hippy name. This is the woman Dusty and I both idolise equally.

Mine and Dusty's' father had done a runner before the kid had been born. Joy had brought us boys up single-handedly and at the same time she had built her concrete mushroom empire. A successful business that had eventually paid off leaving her very comfortably placed. I'm not sure what got ma started. The clue might be in St Merryn where a local man has a purpose-built stone circle in his front garden.

My absent father has long since returned and there is now a complete rekindling of my parents' early relationship, Padraig is a large part of our lives. He is even now in the process of modernising the Tamryn farmhouse and some of the more dilapidated buildings around the place - not including the cider shed.

Joy, my mother, has a name that reflects her being. She hardly ever needs to buy a drink, she never gets the chance. Any time she gets near a bar someone close by will shout, 'I'll get that or take it out of this', 'that one's on me'. She is just that kind of woman, men seem to be at her beck and call without her beckoning or calling. Not only that, but the other women don't seem to mind. Joy is a free spirit though she isn't a flirt; she is just popular. She is what her name suggests. Every pub should have one but get your own!

Chapter Eleven

Forward Thinking

The incessant gull cries are doing my head in. It's a good job I'm not seventeen again. It takes me back to the bad old days when we locals had inherited a way to quieten them in a more permanent way. A piece of silver foil with a half teaspoonful of baking powder inserted served to quieten them down perfectly. Sent skyward with a Royal Mail supplied elastic band, they were irresistible to the fliers, for a short while anyway. Gulls don't like belly ache it seems, especially when it's terminal. They don't go quietly! I say let them eat your chips and batter scraps from the chippy, that way they will be too fat to fly and will eventually starve to death. It would be a tad more humane, well maybe not. It might solve the problem of the flying scavengers eventually.

I have slipped back into my old routine somewhat reluctantly. The Maltsters is open for business after waking from the dead. We haven't quite performed surgery on the old place, more like we just massaged it's chest, Lenny did anyway. I went to Kansas!

My fond memories of the so far still unnamed American and her one silver star may become foggy, but I fear will never go away completely. Some time has passed, Christmas had come and gone in a subdued manner where I was concerned. We had minor celebrations. Lenny and Alice are still both in one piece. I suspect they are hoping to stay that way. I doubt they will, knowing the siblings.

As for any fond memories of the Merry Maiden – both of them in fact – I don't have many. That's not quite true, variety is the spice of life and all that. The cockney was an excellent barmaid.

Padstow is preparing to celebrate May Day. I won't be around - attendance is optional - my absence is intentional. Jen' loved Padstows' biggest day of the year and never missed it. I'll stay in the carriages at Little Petrock with the boy and be back in time for the summer season of rain, hailstones, gales and the odd thunderstorm. There have been a few odd thunderstorms in recent years.

I do intend to wander down to the Ring O Bells at St Issey for an hour. There is always a breakaway group of revellers in there turning the place upside down. If there isn't, there should be!

The Mermaid is performing well. Obviously she couldn't do a lot. Having no legs must prove to be a major snag. Maybe slithering well would describe her better. The Mermaid is slithering on towards the tourist season. Yeah, that kind of works, for me anyway!

Padstow will burst into life very soon. Easter has already come and gone and the tourist season will stall for a few weeks. Work will have begun back in January for the coming Mayday. The Osses will be smartened up after having lain dormant in their respective stables, one at the institute in Market Square, the other at The Golden Lion. Accordions will be cleaned and shined, drum skins tightened. The big day will take over the lives of real local people for a few days. Mayday to real Padstownians is sacrosanct. No one born outside of the town can even contemplate interference in the machinations of this day of red white and blue. White shirts and slacks will be worn, flowered buttonholes will be inserted, ribbons will adorn and flutter behind the wearer. Drums will echo through the narrow streets; accordions will whine in unison, occasionally a fight might be fought, beer will be spilled, blood too. Hangovers will come and go and return. This could be partly due to Mayday actually starting on, well let's call it Mayday Eve! They officially call it 'Night Song' - it is to be experienced! In the morning the 'kids' Osses will come out after seven and give way later to the real deal, the adults version. Emmets will for the best part be ignored at all times and whenever possible. As Mayday rides into the sunset another stall will occur until Spring Bank. Now here is my problem; how can the first day of summer appear before the Spring Bank Holiday? The May song states 'Summer is a come unto day' but it isn't about here tomorrow? Something doesn't quite pan out, does it? It's like having Boxing Day before Christmas Day, August Bank Holiday in July. Never mind, if you're born a Padstownian it doesn't matter a damn. 'Like it, lump it', or bugger off to Rock!

The pattern will change in early July and the season will be full on until the end of August, rain or shine. Whining snot-nosed parents and their bored kids will be everywhere. It won't be obvious who is in charge of these families. It might be the kids but most likely it will be the one with a bulging wallet. It will be in a much different condition by the time they arrive home. Money doesn't talk in the holiday season, it screams!

Around here is somewhere I don't want to be this May Day. As I have already mentioned, Jen' was a big part of everything about Mayday. I was too but not this time. Maybe never again, who knows, time might tell. I somehow doubt it. It would just not be the same as it never has been over the last handful of years.

I spy Lenny and it is a perfect opportunity to remind him and Alice of their duties during the next few days. Dear Lenny, gives anyone and everyone the impression he's thick. It's all a sham, I know he puts it all on. He thinks I don't know. Lenny isn't thick, he's smart. I couldn't do what he does, I wouldn't be able to keep it up. I believe he's only thick by choice, I'm thick by nature. I'm sure I'm right about both of us.

"You Lenny, are now officially my manager. You Alice, are now officially my manageress, right and proper. I'll clear things with the solicitors. You're in charge guys." I had caught up with the Copesticks at the Mermaid and Bow.

The two had listened as I put my plan to them. They had just the one request. "Maccy, can me and Mervyn and

120

Danny carry on living in?" She asked gingerly. Whatever that means, she's blonde.

"Good idea, go ahead. I might stay at the carriages for a while. One last thing Lenny, if anything goes wrong here, anything important, any emergency, call me. I won't be far away."

"What happens if you have an emergency, Maccy?"

"I'll call you, Lenny!"

"I'm already called Lenny."

See what I mean? "You're right mate. How could I forget?" Why on earth do I put myself through this? Should I consider emigrating? No, it's far too expensive. It used to be just a tenner a head!

"The thing is Maccy, if we do 'ave enough time to call each other if one 'appens, it's hardly an emergency is it because one of us will already knaw. Us won't have time to call anyway, if it is."

"If we have one. We haven't yet. If we do, we'll find out then."

"I see, but you think we will? I hope you idn't far away!"

"I'd bet on it." Now I'm nervous. "Thanks Len."

"So, where are you going, Maccy?"

"No idea buddy, round the back of Bill's mum's, I expect."

"She might not even be home. You could be just driving around in bleddy circles for a couple of weeks waiting for 'er to come home drekly!"

"I hadn't thought about that mate."

"Best you find out before you go then. Make sure you fill your tank up too."

"I will, Lenny."

I love Lenny like family, I'm just relieved he isn't. I'm not comfortable with taking his advice, about anything. I never know if he's telling the truth. Only one person knows, or does he really?

"Right Lenny, I know of a chiller!"

"What's that?"

"Something that keeps things cold."

"Like last winter mucker."

"Yeah, yeah. Anyway, I found a chiller."

"That's bleddy lucky. They can be bleddy expensive if you have to buy one."

"Shut up, Lenny. We have to go to some godforsaken place near Devon to get it."

"Now?"

"I'll pick you up later."

You'll do your bleddy back in."

"More than likely. I'll do myself in afterwards."

Sometimes life can be a tad difficult when Lenny's about. To be honest I did get through to him a bit quicker than usual. My mate will never change, I hope he doesn't. He almost had me going for a minute. I saved myself in the nick of time. It was a close thing, it always is. It does seem to get harder; Lenny does keep me on my toes. There are times when I tend to talk to myself, but I can't do it when he's about or I'll end up talking to myself!

I call Michael, he's far more sane. He's saner anyway! "Michael, are you busy?"

"A tad mucker."

"What's happening?"

"Funeral, got to help the old man with a funeral this afternoon."

"What about now?"

"No, sorry it has to be this afternoon. Lots of people are coming."

"Don't Michael, please don't."

"Sorry Maccy, so what can I do for you?"

"Loft?"

"Yeah, go on then, one hour. You know I can't stick spending any longer than an hour with you."

"Save it for the table, loser!"

Snooker does it for me in times of stress, I hate losing. Michael has the wood over me lately. I feel like getting my own back some. I'm determined to beat the beast of the pulpit, or whatever they have in a Methodist chapel. I'm not overly religious on the outside. I do hold Michael in high regard for following his calling, why shouldn't I? Michael has stuck by me many a time. He would be there for me and I for him if trouble came calling as it has many times whilst we were growing up. He's also got a good right cross when needed. He's called it into use many times over the years. I wouldn't want to feel the front end of it, I've seen what it can do!

A short walk to the huge building where the door is already unlocked. I pick up the solitary bottle of milk from the step and enter. I put the container next to twenty others. They are all full and in different states of congealment. I cross myself and mutter at the same time as I pass the altar: "Dear god, please don't let Michael beat me, it's my turn."

"Maccy, 'ow's it going bud?"

"Not great Michael, I wouldn't be here if I had something better to do."

"True enough. Scotch?"

"Is the pope a bleddy catholic?"

"What are you asking me for, he might be, I'm not bleddy certain."

"Nice cassock mate. New one by the looks of it?"

"My Sunday best. Had an accident with the old one, Lil is repairing it for me."

"I wouldn't let Lil get near any of my garments, especially my cassock mate. She'll be wanting to dress you completely before you know it, then she'll want you to take it all off again. Then you will bleddy know it, you'll be for the high-jump, fairly low on thinking about it." A poor choice of phrase of course. Needs must!

"Don't you worry about me Maccy, I have my faith."

"You'll need more than that. What happened anyway?"

"I had me a skinfull a night or two ago, fell into a flower bed in someone's garden and ripped it."

"Legless, Mike?"

"Felt like it, that's how come I fell, I reckon."

"The old 'God forgive me, I know not what I do malarkey?"

"Yeah, pretty much, Maccy."

"That's what cider does to you mate, you should knaw by now."

"Never again, it's the last time."

"You gonna give up the apple juice, Mike? I don't believe it."

"No, nothing like that. I'll go home a different way next time, if I remember to."

"Would be best I reckon. How's the old man?"

"Playing golf with the mad vicar."

"But they don't actually get on, Michael." For years it's been common knowledge the Methodist Minister and the vicar have been at odds. Not only the current incumbents either. The two jobs around here have been a poison chalice for many that have gone before. It's certain to continue, especially if and when Michael takes over. Personally, I think it's all put on. I would bet the two probably spend their evenings around the same table with a bottle in attendance, dreaming up what they can fall out over next.

"That's why they play golf. They can beat the hell out of each other without raising a fist, apart from taking a tee shot."

"Best all round I suppose."

"Your break buddy."

"I broke last time."

"That was bleddy months ago. You're living in the bleddy past!"

"How would you know. I bet you don't know what day it was when you tore your cassock."

"You win! Now try doing it with your cue in your hand."

"Oh Michael, how lewd, you're in the house of god man. Your dad would kick off big time if he could hear you."

"He's not at home right now. He's gone to Barcelona."

"What's he doing in Barcelona."

"Getting the holy wine."

"What's the matter with English wine? I can't stand the bleddy Spanish plonk, cheap and nasty."

"He's getting British wine. He has a dealer there, gets a good price."

"A 'dealer' in Spain, is he getting some wacky baccy too?"

"Not that kind of dealer. He lives in Barcelona, it's just outside Looe somewhere."

"It's a long way to go to get a spliff and a bottle of plonk, especially if you're not sure where it is."

"Yeah, yeah, but I idn't going mucker! Break the bleddy pack, Mac!"

"Yes Reverend. You make me sound like a pensioners bleddy raincoat!"

"You look like you're wearing one."

"What were you doing in someone's garden, Michael?"

"Practicing kneeling."

"Why?"

"I was throwing up!"

"You shouldn't do that in someone's garden mate. You should practice getting out of a good snooker too."

"Another?"

"You conceding, Michael?"

"Another scotch you plonker!"

The whiskey did the trick. Michael was suitably thrashed in the same way I was last time we played. On thinking about it, maybe it wasn't the whiskey? "How many lessons do I have to bleddy give you buddy?"

"Up yours!"

"Better luck next time, Michael."

"You used it all up, Tamryn."

We don't get together that often, when we do, it is like we meet every day. Michael, Lenny and I went through school together. Inseparable then and no different now. Long may it continue.

"You were lucky, Tamryn,"

"Not at all mate. I had the big feller on my side."

"How do you work that out?"

"I asked him for help when I got here."

"You bleddy hypocrite!"

"Yes I know. So why not go all the way to Spain for some holy wine? It could be an ideal working holiday."

"I don't like Spain, it's full of foreigners, Geordies, wide boy cockneys and bleddy Mancs!"

"You learn something new every day. I learned two new things today."

"What was the other thing?"

"He listens!"

"Course he does, but don't push your luck boy."

"I won't. Best you get someone to collect your cassock for you buddy, or you'll be the one pushing your luck with Lil on the prowl with sharpened pincers!"

Mayday is just over the horizon. On a clear day the drums and sounds of revelry can be heard from the top of Rose Hill, as you leave Little Petrock to travel the three miles to Padstow. The sounds might be wanton imagination to a local. Imagination or not, it doesn't matter. I won't hear it, I'm taking my boy out for the day in the opposite direction.

Maccy J, Lenny and I get an early start to Millbrook on the Rame peninsular to get a chiller at a knock down price. Meaning, if the seller doesn't reduce the price, I might have to knock him down a couple of times! Millbrook is almost facing Plymouth which, if anyone is in any doubt, belongs to Devon. Thank god, I wouldn't want it on my doorstep!

We'd lashed a trailer to ma's back end - the rear of her car - and made Millbrook in an hour. A cafe door is wide open, people are peering in and shrugging shoulders. 'If you wanna brew, you'll have to make it yourself. The guvnor is sleeping like a babby,' said one local.

"Do you eat in here mate?"

"Do they sell food? I never knew that."

We cleared the doorway and entered. The local man had been telling the truth. The bloke is sparko, crashed whilst reading it seems. I look at the book, it's a children's book, I'm not surprised he's asleep, you're supposed to read it to kids; he's read it to himself. I'm not sure why it isn't called the Kernow Bedroom. A smart sign above the door informs any approachee this is the 'Kernow Lounge'.

"We should come back when he's alive, Maccy."

"He's alive, Lenny. Most likely he's just forgotten. I would too if I looked like him."

"What shall we do mate?"

"Put the frying pan on, Lenny."

"On what mucker?"

"On the damn coat rack. On the bleddy cooker. If he wakes up to a breakfast he didn't have to cook, he's likely to be more affable. That way we can knock the price down."

"Good thinking mucker, nothing better than a cheap breakfast."

"Not the breakfast, we'll eat ours before we wake him. We'll get the chaps' chiller cheaper. If he doesn't play ball, we'll fight him on the beaches."

"Or in the park!"

"Yeah, yeah, 'or in the park'. Get cooking, egg and bacon twice."

"If you're 'aving two breakfasts, so am I. I'll cook four. What about the youngster?"

"Three Lenny, just three. Just get on with it before he calls the pigs. Boiled egg with soldiers for Maccy J."

"There's no need to kill a pig Maccy, there's a pile of bacon here already. Soldiers?"

"I want scrambled egg, not fried."

"Who was that mate?"

"Who was who?"

"Don't matter, thought someone said something before I did!"

"It wasn't me, Lenny. Just get on with it. I don't think he's in a coma. He might be."

"Mushrooms in the fridge, tomatoes too. One sugar in mine, milk."

"Thought you'd need a bottle, you've been asleep for hours. Put some milk on, Lenny."

"I idn't bleddy winding 'im. I idn't putting him over my bleddy shoulder."

"Why didn't you wake me before?"

"Before what mate?"

"Before you two empty my fridge!"

"Thought you was a dummy!"

"Don't tease him Lenny, we need him affable remember."

"What's 'affable' dad?"

"Friendly and generous whilst selling a cold cabinet."

You'll be lucky, I'm a Brummy. We don't do 'affable'. Hundred and fifty plus fifteen for the breakfasts."

"Hundred. It's an eighty-mile round trip mate."

"Hundred and twenty-five. Don't go back, it'll save you twenty."

"Shut it Brummy!"

"Beach or park?"

"Can't fight on an empty stomach."

"Me neither, let's eat my food."

We struck a deal at one twenty-five and got a free breakfast. It's only fair, we did cook the Brummys' grub!

"That all went well, Maccy. We taught him a lesson!"

"Yeah, it did mucker, I'm well happy. I was gonna be affable and go to a hundred and thirty."

"Maccy, what is a Brummy?"

"Just go back in Lenny, take another look. It's all you need to know."

"Nah, it's hardly worth it, he wasn't that bad, Maccy."

"You should 'ave heard what he called you!"

"Wait for me!"

"Leave it Lenny, we don't have time for knuckle swapping."

.

Chapter Twelve

Sea Food, eat Food

I call Lenny at the Mermaid. "Lenny!"

"You got home safe then mucker!"

"You know I did."

"It's right what you say, Maccy. You didn't give me any petrol money, tight-arsed bugger."

"It was ma's car."

"I knaw that but I put the bleddy petrol in it."

"And I gave you my card."

"Ais, I remember now. You did, but I did 'ave to sign for it."

"There you go."

"But you bleddy drove it, Maccy!"

"Ffs, give it up, Lenny. Have you got the seafood bar set up yet?"

"I 'ave mate. Bessie 'ave made a damn good counter. We just need something to sell drekly. All we need is the seafood now. What does that mean?"

"What does what mean?"

"All they letters and such."

"Not sure Lenny, nothing important. They'll never catch on. You need to order seafood from the suppliers buddy."

"They all be out at sea, catching seafood, mucker."

"Who is?"

"Them that do catch the bleddy seafood."

"Nah Lenny, stop right there, you can't buy the bleddy stuff local."

"Why not Maccy, they catch it local."

"Too dear mate, they charge too much."

"Owzat?"

"Cos it's fresh, we need frozen seafood, it's cheaper."

"'Ow can it be cheaper than they buggers catching it off the Point?"

"It just is, I'll order it. Don't go buying any from bleddy Padstow. You'll only make some rich tosser bleddy richer!"

"Look Maccy, it stands to reason it's gotta be cheaper from here. It don't have to come so far."

"Tidn't as simple as that bud, it all does have to go to London and come back here again to be cheaper. What they put out hereabouts is twice the bleddy price. It has to be sold for four times the price it's bought for by the restaurant owners."

"Why's that then?"

"So the local restaurateurs can make a fortune selling it to the bleddy emmets that do want them."

"But Maccy, most all them buggers are bleddy emmets. They idn't born and bred bleddy local."

"That my friend is very true. You hit the nail right on the head. I know it doesn't seem right but that's what does happen buddy. It's almost like all the seafood caught here does go to London and comes back dearer, apart from some that does come back frozen, that is cheaper. If you buy local and not frozen it's expensive. If you buy local and it's frozen and done a bit of travelling, it means it has been to London and come back which makes it cheaper. You can't buy local frozen unless it's come off the back of a refrigerated lorry. Sometimes you don't know how long it's been on the bleddy lorry. See what I mean mate."

"I wish I could say I do Maccy, it don't any of it make a lot of sense mind. Why would it come back cheaper? Maccy, I don't have a hammer buddy. I can't hit bugger all."

"Tidn't meant to. Otherwise nobody would sell any and no bugger would buy any. Apart from the ones with the lorries. Because it's older I suppose. Forget about the nail thing for now, Lenny. We need to concentrate on the bleddy shrimps and whelks and the like."

"We should get us a lorry and do it ourselves, we would make a fortune, Maccy and we could drive faster, then it wouldn't be so old. Or if we drive slower, it'll be even older and then it will be even cheaper. We 'aven't any shrimps to concentrate on. We have no crabs, no lobster, no bleddy cockles, no nothing."

"We wouldn't Lenny, cos we would have to buy the lorry and charge ourselves exorbitant bleddy prices to get all that stuff from them that do own the other lorries. Then we would have to charge higher prices to our own customers to help pay for our lorry. They wouldn't buy the bleddy stuff and we'd have to sell the lorry to be able to afford to buy seafood from somewhere else to sell it cheaper. If we did that we wouldn't have a lorry for it to fall off the back of. It won't really matter how old it is or how fast it's going. See what I mean?"

"Now I'm with you mucker. Good job we know what we're bleddy doing."

Didn't take long did it? All's well that ends well!

"Lenny, we do need to talk mate."

"We just did, didn't we?"

"Yes mate, we did. This is something else."

"That was bleddy quick!"

"I haven't bleddy started yet."

"Tell me when you do, Maccy. Shall I go now?"

"No, not now, we're gonna talk."

"What about now?"

"Lenny, shut your rabbit."

"You can't say that, it's unlucky."

"Only when it's on a boat and being stroked by a woman."

"We don't have a boat, Dusty does. What about Lobster woman, 'er that do live out at Mother Ivy's Bay?"

"We don't need her, we don't need her or her mother, we'll stay here and do it. I'll give Molly Malone a call, tell 'er to bring 'er wheelbarrow."

"Fair enough. Do I know her? That's not a bad idea mate, save us buying a bleddy lorry."

"Most likely mate. I have the keys for the Maltsters, Lenny. I'll tell Molly to get a bigger barrow."

"I'll be out of a job then."

"No, I'm gonna manage the Maltsters, you're staying here, and you can help Molly push her barrow down the narrow streets, that'll keep you on the straight and narrow and might bring you in a few quid. You can look after the Mermaid at the same time."

"Why should I?"

"Because it's where your job is. Forget about Molly, she do 'ave a job in the marketplace selling marmalade on the side."

"Okay. And you're gonna work where?"

"At the Maltsters. I have the keys now." The agents had called, and the deal has gone through. I'm already licensed. The Bells will have to wait. Chris won't mind. He's grumpy anyway, no one can tell the difference. I had only planned to visit for an hour or two.

"So I'll be here, and you'll be there!"

"That's it, you got it mate. Same as before. Anyway, keep it under your hat, Lenny."

"I'll need to borrow one of yours mucker."

"I'll order the crustaceans."

"Crushed Asians? Bleddy hell, what happened, bet it was one of them bleddy lorry drivers!"

"Okay Lenny, listen carefully, I'll get the seafood, the crabs and whatever."

"You will need to go to the clinic buddy. They'll sort you out proper drekly."

"Do they sell prawns?"

"Knaw, I don't think they do."

"Catch you later, Lenny." It's enough, I have to get away. I believe I handled reasonably well; all things considered. Who am I trying to kid?

"Maccy!"

"Michael, wasson boy?"

"It's Bert, he's in the bleddy hospital."

"What's wrong with him?"

"No idea, I'm a thingy, minister, not a bleddy doctor, for Christ's sake! The old sod hurt himself while you were away."

"So it's my fault he's in the hospital!"

"I hadn't thought of that. Most likely."

"Is he in the place where you have to do your own operations? I know who you work for by the way!"

"I thought he was working for you?"

"He is, but only on a temporary basis. Between you and me I'm looking for someone more reliable. He won't work Sundays for one thing! I'll get down to the hospital, see what's happening, Mike. Thanks Buddy. I thought you had a funeral to organise?"

"Not much to do really mate, she's fairly dead so no need to rush. Her old man said he was gonna dance on her grave. He'll 'ave to wear a bleddy life-jacket, she's being scattered in the estuary! All I have to do is learn my lines and thingy is your uncle. Not yours obviously. If he was he wouldn't admit to it."

"Thanks for letting me know, Michael. By the way, if you ever want me to put a good word in for you with the boss man, just give me a shout, happy to help. I hope the Almighty will forgive your poor sense of humour."

"Get stuffed you tosser!"

"Guess what he calls you."

"Bye, Maccy."

Mobile phones, don't you just love them. Whatever did we do before they appeared? It's ridiculous, no one ever bothered calling me before. If I needed to see someone I would just stand on the quayside and shout their name. I saw a bloke on the harbour wall not long ago. He had three mobiles, one in each hand another sticking out of his pocket. It was unfortunate for him, he leant over the harbour railings too far to get a better signal and talk to two people at the same time and now he's down to only two. He only has two ears anyway.

"Maccy, is that you?"

"It was just now buddy."

"Which hospital do you do your own operations in?"

"Truro."

"Good, don't go there then mate. He's in Bodmin. He do only have a bad back."

"If he's in bleddy Bodmin there won't be any point in me going bud'."

"Why the hell not, it isn't so far as Truro."

"They buggers in Bodmin would have mislaid him by now." I didn't see that coming. I'll have to take Maccy J with me as ma is busy. Well, I did say I needed to spend some time with him. It's as good a time as any. He can learn about doctors and nurses!

I strap the boy in and put my foot down. Bert is no relation, it just feels as if he is. Then again, knowing Cornwall, he might well be.

"What are you doing in this place, you old skiver?"

"I'm here for my bleddy health boy. You booking in too, Maccy?"

"I'll ignore that. Are you allowed to play cards for money in here, Bert? I thought you was dying, or worse?"

"Naw, I 'ave done me bleddy back in. Can hardly straighten it, Maccy. 'Tis bleddy agony. What's worse?"

"When you don't know if you are or you idn't. So, how did you do that old buddy?"

"I was trying to pick up a two pound coin from under a bleddy table."

"Was it yours? Did you manage it?"

"Naw, the bugger is still there. It wadn't mine, I never bleddy 'ad one before."

"So where did you get money to play cards with?"

"That was easy Maccy, I bet the doctor he couldn't tell what was wrong with me."

"And he couldn't?"

"Naw, bleddy kid didn't have a clue. Ee thought t'was the bleddy menopause, I dare say."

"You're letting him look after you and he's useless?"

"Naw, he's okay, I just lied to him about what's wrong with me."

"Why did you lie to him?"

"So I could win the bleddy bet. Maccy, try and keep up boy. Why is your youngster wearing a stethoscope?"

"He's doing his training, Bert. There was me thinking you could be dead or bleddy worse."

"Your boy looks older than my bleddy doctor! Do I look as though I'm dead?"

"A bit mate to be honest."

"Block that laddie's ears up a minute mister."

"You block them up."

"I can't, I got me a bleddy bad back!"

"You know what they say."

"Who?"

"I don't know. Them that says it I suppose."

"Says what?"

"What goes around, comes around. So, when do you think you'll be going home, Bert?"

"When I be better is favourite."

"How will you know?"

"The doctor will tell me."

"The doctor doesn't know what's wrong with you. You told him a load of cobblers."

"I told him the truth after."

"Then if you know already, he won't need to tell you. You might just as well tell yourself and go home anyway."

"Don't bleddy matter, I'm not going home, I like it where I am."

"Does your missus know you're in here?"

"Naw she bleddy doesn't. Don't you bleddy go telling 'er neither!"

"Where does she think you are?"

"I did tell 'er I was going to the chippy for fish and chips."

"When?"

"Couple of days ago."

"She must be starving. Think I might move in with you Bert, you seem to eat well."

"Just so long as you 'ave your own bed. I knaw what you am like. I idn't in to topping and tailing!"

My friend is knocking on for 'ninety something'. I hope I do as well as he does at ninety. "Your gambling partner doesn't look too good, Bert. Think he might have gone on mate. He idn't breathing an awful lot. Someone should take his temperature or something"

"Don't just sit there thinking about the price of bleddy grapes, Maccy. Pass that cash over 'ere quick. Most of it was mine anyway. What's the point in taking his bleddy temperature if he don't 'ave a bleddy pulse."

"'How should I know. Anyway, you can't take his money Bert, that idn't right."

"The bugger didn't mind taking mine! Something you're not telling me boy. What has happened with the yank woman?"

"Nothing to tell, Bert. I don't believe I will hear from her again, not even drekly."

"Remember, there's plenty more in the sea, Maccy."

"Please don't mention anything that does come out of the sea Bert, it won't help old friend. Have you seen the bleddy state of it lately?"

"I won't. Now you get on and get that youngster home safe. I've got kippers for me bleddy tea. I don't want them to get cold."

He did it on purpose, it was not unexpected. He's still sharp as a tack, ninety or not. I leave the old geezer to count his ill-gotten gains. As for betting, I'd bet he'll be around to get his century. As I walk away his doctor appears in the doorway that doesn't have any doors. "How is he, Doc'?"

"He's an annoying old bastard. Can't you take him with you?"

"Never mind Doc', your mum will be here soon to take you home. It's getting dark outside, it's nearly past your bedtime. Give the doctor back the stethoscope MJ. What's that stuck to it? Where have you been?"

"Chewing gum I think. I was saying goodbye to the old bastard."

"Out of the mouths of babes. Pull it off boy."

"Why should I? It was there when I found it."

"Give it back to the Doc' before he starts blubbing."

"Why should I?"

"He might need it for something important."

The young Doctor must be an emmet. They're always losing things. Clothes, sunglasses, their kids, themselves. I don't really mind them, but they do get lost a lot. It's possible when the emmets come over the bridge at Saltash, there is a big sign saying '**Emmets get lost**' and that's exactly what they do every single day they are here. They shouldn't have a sign at all.. I say if they really want to be useful, they should cycle to Cornwall and leave their 'Chelsea tractors' at home. A cycling proficiency badge could be shown at the bridge at Saltash. Even better, they could leave their caravans at home and hire one that is already here that doesn't need to be parked in a layby all night.

"Dad, they 'ave got your name on that sign look."

"So they have. I'll have to talk to our solicitor when we get back."

"Can I have a burger? What's a solicitor?"

"No you can't. I'll make us some when we get home. Someone who takes all our money!"

Americans have a lot to answer for. Instantly I am confronted with an inter cranial vision of the only one I know, but not by name. I have no idea what her name is, I don't ever expect to find out in this lifetime. I may have put her to the back of my mind lately, but it doesn't work very well. She has the power to move about seemingly.

We finally arrive back at our well-hidden gaff. A bus load of Belgian detectives with weird moustaches would never find it. The post-person did but it took him or her a while. I've had problems with finding it myself on occasion. What the Royal Mail operative doesn't know is that all the rubbish advertising stuff he or she leaves here goes back into the post box in the village. It's not really a village, it's just a huddle. One or two of the letters I don't want to accompany it. I like to think it lends a whole new meaning to the well-used saying 'what goes around, comes around'.

I hear a noise as Maccy J takes off his shirt and shorts and hangs them on the floor. "What's all this Junior?"

"I'm not supposed to tell you Dad. The old git gave it to me."

I look at my palm, it is covered in cash. Who said he was an old git? "Goodnight youngster."

"It's better than calling him an old bastard isn't it! I like Bert. Goodnight dad."

"I like him too, Junior."

The boy has eaten and will soon be sleeping. It's been good to have him around and I make up my mind we will do more of it. I have neglected him somewhat these past months, it's time to put it right.

There is nothing better than one's own bed. The beds Lenny and I had built into the ancient wooden railway carriages are much more comfortable than anything I ever slept in before. I have slept in some odd places. I've even slept on the iron bridge just outside of town. When I woke up, I couldn't remember which way I was going before I fell asleep. I spent the night in a blanket box on one occasion; I wouldn't recommend it to anyone, especially if you're in someone else's public house and you need to leave sharpish. The box was so small, I thought about sleeping on the outside!

I hardly moved for the remainder of the evening and didn't let on to my family I was back. The Alsatian had whined at the door for ages. I'd forgotten him. I let him in, and he slept under the steps for as long as I did in my pit.

The carriages, mine and Maccy J's home, are nestled in a corner of a field forming part of Magic Mushroom farm. The only other inhabitants are a gang of noisy frogs that don't tend to sleep at night. The carriages are partially surrounded by slightly chipped or broken concrete mushrooms all set out like some miniature Stonehenge. I wonder if Ed Prynn has been around to look at my stones.

Ed only lives across the road, Ed's a professional stone collector.

The frogs must have had a public address system during my second night back. I felt I'd been entertained, for want of a better word, by the nocturnal amphibians; they don't bloody stop. Why my cat – it wasn't really mine, I was his – only fancied the back legs I'll never know. Chalky is long gone now but he was good company when he wasn't eating a French delicacy. Obviously, he wasn't good company to the frogs. He was bad news. The frogs hardly had a leg to stand on!

I guess any neighborhood pond will soon be inundated with tadpoles and this time next year it will be even louder here after dark. They say, whoever they are, frogs return to whence they had been started, to begin their procreation process. I'm not even sure if I have a big pond or a small lake. I didn't know I had a pond at all until my brother informed me.

Chapter Thirteen

The Vision

Alice and Lenny did a great job at the Mermaid over the Mayday, Obby Oss weekend. The brother and sister act worked the Mermaid off her feet. They make a great team. I'm aware one of these days one or even both of them might want to go their own way and do something else. I make a mental note of the possibility.

These siblings are like Dusty and I, they get on. Obviously neither my brother nor I have the large bumpy bits in the upper torso area. I wouldn't want to be a landlady and be ogled all the time. I'm reminded of my friend and mentor Blencathra. She had it all worked out perfectly. Blen' in all fairness was hideous behind the bar, she is hideous anywhere. She never had a problem putting the men off. She scared me once or twice with the Stone Frog effect. I could do with Blencathra in the garden. If the frogs didn't shut their row up, she would just have to look at them and that would be it. Frog ornaments! Ma could do a special offer, buy a concrete mushroom and get a free stone frog. I'll talk to her about it one of these days. Maybe Blen could do the same with the gulls!

Although there is plenty of room at the Maltsters for me to lay my head, I just have a fancy for my miniature wooden palace for a while longer. In any case, I will move into the pub eventually, it's only a stone frogs' throw away. The carriages are just a minute or two walking time from the Maltsters. I'm spoiled for choice now I have my keys for the Maltsters.

I am looking forward to a good nights' sleep. I am knackered and tomorrow will be a big day. The dog is under the stairs and I sleep like a bump on a log. My thoughts conjure up the only two loves of my life, apart from my son; Jennifer has gone, never can she return, as for wannabe Annie Oakley, the Yank, it's been months now. It's over, done and dusted. It has been a puzzle. I'm sad our friendship has not approached a higher level of fruition. At one time I would think, easy come, easy go. Not this time. Neither did I when I met Jennifer a second time. We had first met many years ago at our enclave on the beach. When we met the second time, I had no idea who she was. I had to have it pointed out to me, by her. Jen' was a tad pushy thankfully.

Rising early, I take a ten-minute walk across the empty fields and down to the lake, which is really a large pond; it is far enough to complete a whole cigar and another after. The Alsatian follows without complaint. He never questions anything I do. He takes it all in his stride, literally. You can't beat a good Alsatian. I suppose you can, but I wouldn't. He might not have a complete face but most of his teeth are still in the right place. I wouldn't want any of them stuck in my arse.

Today might be a good time to give the Maltsters Arms a Spring clean, - a bit late as the May Song states Summer 'has a come unto day' - a breath of fresh air, some spit and polish. It's nothing like as bad as the Mermaid was in the beginning. Little will change for now, just needs a good smarten up. Dusty has already made a start I notice. Pub regulars by their nature don't like change. Subtleness will be needed. The semi-professional drinker likes to leave home and lean on the same piece of beer stained bar as he always does. Another wants to sit in the same rickety chair or on the same lop-sided stool as he has always done. Dear old One-Armed Frank – now deceased – a regular at the Mermaid, just to destroy any furniture he came into contact with. Others will play the same one-armed bandit losing varying amounts of money and look appealingly at the same barmaid carefully filling his twenty-first birthday inscribed Pewter mug and knowing he had no chance at all of 'pulling' her but continuing all the same because it is the right thing to do at least until the wife or girlfriend turns up with a cold roast dinner and a jug of cold gravy you could lay bricks with.

Our changes need to be almost invisible to the naked eye. Just a spruce up, a few repairs outside and a clean cellar. Good middle of the road pop music should permeate the interior. Occasionally we'll get an accordionist playing, mostly for free drinks and a couple of quid, well earned on a busy night. Television screens, MTV would have no place at Little Petrock; this is okay by me. Padstow and the Mermaid is a little different these days. The kids have all the money. We will mostly only see them for an hour before they take on the dubious delights of Newquay, where they can head bang and bop all night, Dusty will take them down the coast on his sea bus. Little Petrock is no Perranporth and has no aspirations as such to be. They will have a couple of 'liveners' here before moving on to the clubs that stay open until breakfast time. As long as they spend a few quid in the Mermaid first, I'm happy.

In any case, if they didn't want to make the boat trip, there is always the Country Club tucked away amongst the trees a mile or two up Rose Lane. It isn't quite Stringfellows, they play loud music of sorts and stay open until something A.M. mostly with impromptu long-distance puking competitions; the grand finals being held outside in the car park at closing time between the skimpily dressed girls who can't remember their own names or each other's.

At my appearance, the reception is somewhat muted. I was mildly surprised and a tad disappointed nothing was made of it. The important thing is, I am here and ready to get this place on the up.

Along with my Ma, who seems to be somewhat quiet and thoughtful, I do most of the scrubbing and sprucing. I hosed and scrubbed the cellar, Dusty and I did all the tearing around, fetching and carrying, getting stock mostly. Countless fast drives to Wadebridge and Truro in the people carrier - it hardly ever gets a chance to carry more than one person - for garden furniture, cheap but comfortable. A St Agnes bakery run for the first class Cornish Pasties that could only be found in that coastal village. Oh, and by the way, I don't think the valeter wants to come back in the future, who can blame him? Don't eat pasties whilst driving?

An odd job man, a friend of mine, Bessie, is still rushing around repairing and renovating pieces of wooden furniture which belong in the bar but have somehow found their way into a lean-to storeroom at the back of the building. The previous landlord had eventually given up his ageing attempts at mending and replacing these things. I make up my mind never to become a seventy-year-old non-furniture repairing landlord. I want to be the sitting on my arse not completing a crossword in a month of Sundays kind of retiree as my body clock ticks past sixty. Or do I? I'll know when the time comes. Some tosser will remind me!

Talking of 'tossers', Dusty, my brother, has taken time out from his own business to trim and strim the lawns and shrubs in the Maltsters gardens. He is still at it even now. Unusually, he too is quietly subdued.

Everything is different here, there are no syringes to pick up, no smashed pool cues to repair or replace. There is no leaking roof, not much anyway, just a drip here and there. No single trainer – just where do they come from - is apparent. There is no sex mad bar staff, as far as I know. I could be wrong. Apart from myself, oh and Lavinia and my brother too!

The Maltsters has all its beer taps in good working order, the cellar is functioning well, most importantly, there are no ducks of any colour or breed, though I wouldn't mind some on the pond instead of seagulls. No animals apart from Maccy's best friend who, although nameless other than dog - I have called it various things over the years - is not in any way soundless unfortunately. I once decided to call it Stan, it thought I was saying 'stand' and got up every five minutes to do nothing. The dog reminds me of me, apart from the anatomy washing obviously.

The village itself seems even more cocooned than usual, in some mysterious pervading silence of its own. Everything seems to feel a tad mystical today. It makes me shiver without any obvious reason. Unusually I have goose pimples too.

The 'Kid' as I affectionately like to call my younger brother, has the pub garden looking more than presentable by the time the petrol mower is switched off and the trimmer unplugged. It is just as well the task has been completed as he is down to just his shorts and the parading of local teenage girls is becoming monotonous and because of their very young ages, embarrassing. Not to Dusty of course. He's acting like a dog with two thingys, tails!

I'm sure it is to the parading girls' disappointment the kid has replaced his shirt and right now sits contentedly on a bar stool smugly sipping at a chilled pint of very orangey looking cider, Scrumpy! He says little which is even more unusual. I hadn't imported the no stools rule at the Maltsters. I guess it is unlikely we will have a One-Armed Frank here; a one-legged fisherman may turn up one of these days. Dusty is lounging around and looking overly smug now, it's annoying me. I can't put my finger on it. He is unusually quiet as he continues to smirk.

I'm not expecting to be overrun with heavyweight boozers when we finally open the Maltsters doors, we aren't expecting to be flooded with diners either. We are expecting a handful of regulars with their half pints of rough cider, some with their non rough wives in attendance and the odd one or two middle-aged tourist who might ask, 'what kind of cow is that?' It's a bleddy cow, they only have to look underneath! They will wander in quietly to sup a pint and a half of cold lager, maybe a Schooner of medium Sherry before ordering steaming hot jacket potatoes stuffed with potato. Well, it has to go somewhere. I'm not sure which is most popular, the inside of a spud or what goes on the outside. Potato skins are like spud gold now, catering folks sell the skins and chuck the insides away!

****

And so it all suddenly clicks into place. The large copper coin suddenly drops, the alarm bells ring. They alarm me anyway.

Either my eyes are lying or the supernatural does indeed exist. I believe I am seeing it in action at this very moment. A vision suddenly appears in front of me, it is as if she is floating forwards from the lake. My eyes cloud over without the aid of a half-gallon of Cider. A girl, not a girl, a woman. She is sporting a baseball cap, her golden hair sweeping over her shoulders. Tight blue Levi's show her pleasant shape. The smile is dazzling, as is the silver star pendant still in place about her neck. I blink and blink again. This can only be a vision and no wacky baccy or LSD has been employed. It's possible someone is working a smoke machine close by as she drifts towards me.

I see the mouth begin to move. The vision speaks "Hello Maccy! Not fishing today, Brit?"

My own mouth will not work. It's not even trying.

"Catfish got your tongue, Brit?"

I grunt noisily. I'm certain it was me. "What, how?"

"Ohoyo oka Taloa. Easy, Brit. Big silver bird above the water will make your heart sing!"

She stretches her arm out and I almost wish she hadn't for some reason, for two reasons actually. This is what the old man had done before I left Kansas. He didn't look quite so appealing obviously. I wanted to sing but couldn't, I can't sing.

"In here, Brit." She placed her hand over her heart as he had. There the similarity ended. I have no reply. She must have known what I was thinking. Fair enough, most women do, which can be a bind.

The old feller had told me she would come. He told me how she would come. I didn't have a clue what he was going

145

on about at the time. It was all gobbldy gook. Whatever he said and he did say it, it seems he was correct.

I look around as my small - but soon to be growing by one - family appear, one at a time, smiling stupidly; obviously I can't tell with the dog. The hot sun makes me feel like I am wilting. Where do you find a battered Stetson when you need one?

So, she had taken no notice. Some women just don't learn. I'd told her the worst of me, and it had obviously just made her more determined. You think you know someone, you don't, they simply prove you wrong. I went to school when I was a kid. They taught me about nothing that was any use. They could have taught me about these situations. All I learned was how to do sums with letters. Just what was the point of Algebra?

"When?" It was a start. I can't deal with everything all at once.

"A while, Maccy. I knew where to come, you talked about it enough times, You're all talk, period! Your family didn't ask questions, just gave me a bed and told me you'd be back sometime, probably. You took your own damned time. Why did you leave Kansas, Macdonald?"

"I don't know. I didn't think you would notice. You left my sleeping bag with a note in it. It was soggy." I'm not a good liar. I'm like my mutt now, only I have one more tail than he does, I don't eat live food and I don't drool much, so not alike! I feel like an extra in Gone with the Wind. - 'You took your own damned time.' To be fair, she's better looking than Vivienne Lee. Masterful in the vocal department as was the great and beautiful actress!

"You damn fool! We have work to do, Brit. Can't leave it all to your family." My boy Macdonald appears and tightly clutches her hand. He smiles my smile. I am once again lacking in words. I believe it's time now for him to become Maccy Junior! Seems like she's kidnapped my kid. Might as well do as I'm told before she brainwashes me. It may be too late. It was too late in Kansas, I thought. Now I am a 'damn fool'. Fair enough, I'll live with it. At least she remembered my name. I still have no idea of hers. Can't be that important.

I think about my late queen, Jennifer and firmly believe wherever she is, she will be smiling and telling me what a lucky bugger I am and in truth, have always been. She would be right.

"Ma, how many bedrooms do we have?"

"Enough, Maccy."

"Hope you're right, mother. We got two kids arriving later from Grampound. There may be others."

I need to go to Bodmin Parkway and pick them up. Lavinia will be here soon. What the hell was I thinking? Before departing the Maiden, I had at the last minute made Jill and Jack an offer they did not refuse. I had heard them playing and singing in the Dolphin at Grampound one evening when I wasn't working. They are coming here to live, work and entertain. They can have the carriages. They will be better off than in the caravan on the Merry Maidens' car park. Lavinia? Well call me a big softy and a glutton for punishment! I had left her a note to come here when her stint at the Maiden is completed, if she cared too.

"Anyone else?"

Ma sounds a tad exasperated, it won't last. "I don't think so. Maybe, I can't remember. I don't think so."

Last to appear on this momentous day is Padraig, my father. He offers his hand. We shake and smile, like shake and vac without the hoover!

I had a hundred questions to ask her. They would have to wait. Like Vivienne said, 'we have work to do', if she didn't, she should have. 'Frankly my dear, I don't give a damn' wouldn't go down well at this moment in time. I resist!

Jill calls and I'm back on the road again, towards Bodmin Parkway. The Texan sits beside me smiling knowingly. I'm smiling for many reasons. She is just smiling, I don't really know why.

"Well?"

"Well what?"

"I went back. You weren't bleddy there."

"I was there, Brit. I saw you, I watched you and you got drunk with the bikers and a senior citizen."

"Really? Why didn't you come and show yourself?"

"I did. I was wearing my leathers and had my bike. I wanted to know more about you, without you knowing more about me. It worked perfectly, fish man! I'm all seeing, you just remember that, you and I will get along fine."

"Did you have a headscarf or a horny helmet?"

"I'm sorry Brit, what the hell are you talking about?"

"Why I didn't see you."

"I didn't want to be seen! I was around, Maccy!"

"You're pulling my plonker."

"I might be if I knew what it was."

"Leg, you're pulling my leg!" I forget myself. I quickly remember, it is pointless.

"Oh, okay, you didn't mean your wanger then!"

I might have, who knows? 'Wanger?' No idea! This is all too much for me. I feel like I'm talking to Del boys' sister, American cousin anyway. Luckily, we had arrived at the station. I still don't know a lot about this Yank but I'm getting there, mostly thanks to her. Why didn't I just stay home and wait? I'm too damned impatient and I know it! I never thought I would say it but God Bless America! Not all of it obviously. There are some dodgy people there!

The kids are waiting as we arrive at Bodmin Parkway Station, they have little more than shoulder bags and carrier bags each. They tell me it is everything they have. Jill informs me she even has livestock in one bag! I look inside as three sets of eyes look up. Just one more thing to smile about. I know where they'll be living. If she keeps her ducklings in a bag I won't have to tread in crap every five minutes! They will find the lake soon enough. It's too big to call a pond and I suppose too small to call a lake. I can live with lake!

The pair had stared in disbelief when seeing their accommodation as I gave them the key to the carriages. I think they are already in love with their new home, the ducklings already investigating their own new surrounds. I left the kids to sort out their bits, shouldn't take long, and walked back to the Maltsters. I might have been whistling. I don't whistle, it must have been someone else.

Jill had insisted they had informed their parents about coming here. If they had been mine, I wouldn't have bothered from what I learned of them. A local told me they had both been booted out of their respective homes by irate parents.

We opened at six. We stared at each other for all of ten minutes before a first customer appeared.

With the bulk of the spring clean complete, Joy had whisked off her work clothes and took up her place at the other side of the bar, intent on using her effervescent charm and rather well formed but strangely garbed physique to keep wandering locals from wandering off to their next planned port of call. Joy is well practiced in the art of bees to a honeypot. Not many of the wellied and Gurnseyed fraternity had just the one and went on to pastures new. If some middle-aged male customer looked like leaving, Joy would skillfully waylay them and almost all would stay for 'just one more'.

That evening we all of us at some time tend the bar, even the yank. One or another of us kept the pumps moving up and down and any one of the half a dozen of us could stuff a jacket potato and chuck it in the microwave, served up with a little side salad. Toasting a Pizza doesn't take much effort, neither does spreading mayonnaise on egg or ham sandwiches; the Alsatian could have done it but we, wisely in my opinion, leave the dog unemployed. He already has enough bad habits!

The excellent Cornish pasties sold themselves out as I believe from information received, they always had. Loved by all who ate them and eaten by most everyone this side of the Tamar. Might as well move any imposters to the other side and see how the Devon Dumplings like them. Our opening session went well. No fireworks or strippers in cakes and, most importantly, no punch-ups; all very sedate. The vicar from the church around the corner even

149

came in to see if he might potentially have a new flock member. It's quite unlikely but we've always hit it off well enough. We have passed the time of day on occasion.

My mate Michael, a tall, well-spoken snooker exponent and of course, opponent, as well as affable ex-school friend stood at the opposite end of the bar from the vicar. The two acknowledge each other but nothing more than the usual unpleasantries. Michael is the son of the local Methodist Minister, my friend is also a trainee Methodist minister; he's taking his time. Mike is a friendly chap mostly, unless he's losing at snooker or his horse falls at the first fence! I won't even go into his sister's habits here, I've already said too much! Mike is obviously still seething at a recent defeat at my hands, as he calls to me loudly across the bar,

"Tosser!"

"Loser!"

We had a visit from some long retired professional footballer who lives just across the road from the carriages. He was nobody I had heard of. Think he might only have heard of himself. He has cash to splash, that's the important thing. *He has a car under his lawn. How do I know that? I put it there for safekeeping. It's still there as far as I know.

The sight of Padraig, my father and Joy together is a small piece of icing on the cake for me. Finally, every member of my close family are now closer. Padraig has a big building concern in Cork. Semi-retired now, he came here over a year ago with a bee in his bonnet about finding his family. I do believe he got his wish. Padraig had for a short time stayed at the Ship Inn at Wadebridge. I have a sneaking feeling he has moved here permanently now. About time too! I haven't had time to talk to Dusty about such things, I will. My brother almost ran Padraig out of town when he first appeared. Dusty had a change of heart.

The Yank had also been helping Jill in the kitchen until it closed for the evening. She came and sat beside me. She is here to stay now, I'm certain. Her belongings are moving around the world without her. Some of them are already here, some are still traversing the Atlantic with more to come. Now, if I might seem to be taking all this calmly, I in no way am.

I tried to give her more of an insight into my life, my friends and my family. I hardly knew where to start. I hadn't had much preparation time. I attempt to untie my tongue.

"It's a shame you never met Cap'n Bligh, Cecil to give him his proper name, and Blencathra. They pair were a bit like Frankenstein and his monster, only the monster is female. Do you know, I reckon Blencathra shaves more regular than Bligh does. She kissed me once, right on the lips too. It was like rubbing your face with roadkill hedgehog. They two owned my other pub, the Mermaid, until their retirement."

"You have two bars, I mean pubs?"

"Yep, the Mermaid is a couple of minutes away. We'll go there tomorrow if you want?" She only had time to nod her head as I raced along with unnecessary recalls and recollections.

"Anyway, Dusty and I had ridden to Padstow on horseback, owing to the terrible bleddy weather. We were going to One-Armed Frank's funeral. I hadn't seen Blen' for a while and she took it upon herself to make what you'd call unnecessary amends. Jesus, I thought she was gonna crush the tripe out of my guts. It was like as if I was escaped toothpaste and she was trying to get me back into the bleddy tube. I thought my time had come, I really did."

I continued and just when I thought she might think I'm making it all up, I had to think again. You can't make this stuff up.

"I remember the time the Cap'n stole a cardboard cut-out figure of a well-endowed lady - Blencathra was on one of her visits somewhere. The Cap'n pinched the bleddy thing from outside the chemists. There was a half-naked bird on it, and he stood it up behind the bar with him. She just stood there, in her polka dot bikini, all tits and smiles, you know. Old Bligh loved it. He would feel her up like every half hour and tell her all the things he was gonna do to her after closing time. Until Blen' came home a bit early and heard one of their conversations. She kicked the crap out of it and burnt it in the yard out the back. Poor old One-Armed Frank was a tad disappointed when she went."

"Why is that?"

"He'd taken a liking to her as well. I suppose he'd never had both his arms around a girl, and one isn't quite the same thing, is it."

"You should have seen the faces on a bunch of Emmets that came in one day when the Cap'n told them he had a real Cornish giant asleep in the beer cellar. Frightened the life outta their kids when Blen' appeared suddenly behind the bar. Poor little sods were hiding behind their parents, Blen' didn't have a clue why they were screaming their little heads off. The more she tried to speak to them, the more they did scream."

"See, Blen', dear of 'er, weren't no oil painting you might say. She made ugly almost acceptable, around Padstow. It was like as if every other bugger were wrong and she were right. We are used to her see. The holidaymakers must have thought they'd landed on another planet when she appeared in the bar, which wasn't often."

"Another time, the Cap'n nearly burnt the bleddy place down. He was wanting a BBQ. Trouble being neither he nor Blen was what you'd call cooks. He got this thing that looked like a wok on legs and couldn't get the coals to light. Silly bugger put petrol on it and it went up like a bonfire. The wok was a bit buckled from the heat. All of us talked him out of trying again. It should have been outside anyway."

"Did she ever hurt the Cap'n, Maccy?"

"No, no chance, she thinks the world of the old bugger. Bligh most likely never did feel pain anyway. To be honest the two think the world of each other, just a puzzle we don't know which world he found her on. A pity you never

152

got the chance to meet them both. You will one of these days. The Cap'n and Blencathra are like Little and Large, maybe Little and bleddy Huge but they're great folks and I miss them not being about the place, even now. You will meet them."

We had our first proper conversation on our first night together, apart from Kansas where we discussed who a headless fish belonged to. We had talked into the early hours at the stream. Mostly I had, I might be doing it again. I put her to sleep then, I'm in danger of doing it again.

I knew some of her past but little enough. There is plenty of time. She is a personable type, not at all shy and full of good ideas and encouragement for the Maltsters and for us.

"What's Cornwall like, Maccy?"

"Weird, weird place, weird people. It's like they all have a plan all along. No one wants to tell you their names. You have to sort of work away at it." I'm hinting here, she takes no notice.

"What would you change if you could, Maccy?"

"Not a thing!"

"Yeah, yeah!"

"What?"

"Nothing, sleep Brit."

"What did you say, was that some more native American speak?"

"Sleep, Maccy."

I'll be lucky!

Author's note:

* How and why this occurred is explained in 'The Mermaid and Bow' by this author.

Chapter Fourteen

A Second Coming

She sleeps silently as I lay awake trying to take in all that has happened in the last twenty-four hours; making sense of it all does not come easy.

Yesterday, what can I say about yesterday? Just as I felt I had got my head together it is all over the place again. To say I had been taken by surprise by her appearance would be an understatement. I hadn't quite decided to give up completely, I had definitely been hovering. And then it was all taken out of my hands as the vision appeared before me, like the Lady of the Lake from Arthurian times, or even The Lady of the large pond. I'm sticking with 'lake'.

Oddly, Sir Thomas Mallory, whilst writing about the death of King Arthur in Le Morte d' Arthur, could not name his 'enchantress'. In my case there the comparison ended, as for me, the scene that came before me yesterday was one of enchantment, not of an enchantress. On thinking about it, who knows? The yank could be either I suppose and if she is an enchantress, just like Sir Thomas, I am unable to name her.

What got me was everyone else seemed to know what was to happen yesterday morning. Everyone but me. The story of my life; always the last to know! I have a feeling there will be plenty of time to put it right. Three times I had been to the States and met people at varying levels of weirdness, none more so than this yank. There's me thinking Padstow is full of eccentrics. It's probably not 'full', there are a few. I do wish I had been here when she arrived. Remembering Lavinia for a moment – it's all I can spare. Maybe I would still do it all again despite her. I learned quickly to keep well away. She did attack me gently just as I was leaving the Merry Maiden, I can't blame her! A woman's got to do, etcetera. The yank did only attack me with watermelon seeds.

Somehow, I had attracted varying degrees of trouble, like flypaper attracts flies and far too occasionally one's hair! I didn't go out of my way to bring it on, just sort of searched until it arrived. I do like to think I had taught all the folks I had met something from my own short life. Now here I am looking back at my tour of duty. After the last twelve months, I feel like a Rolling Stone without the big lips and the hallucinations.

Perfect days don't come along too often in my experience. The yank tells me she had suffered some trepidation when she discovered I was away on her arrival in the Duchy. My family had accepted her and taken her in without a second thought. We're all like it, us Tamryns. The yank had spent nights in my bed without me knowing or even being there. I would have know if I had been there.

Dusty and I were up and about early. I think it is a good time to have a man-to-man chat. The Kid agreed after asking if I can suggest someone; a typical comment; I expected something of the sort. Dusty is aware I now think of him as a man. Not so long ago something happened between us brothers and our Ma when Padraig turned up here. Before that, we neither of us did anything without talking to the other, we just lived as three. I believe we have all changed a little. Don't get me wrong, we're all here for each other if or when the need arises. Now three has turned to four, four to five and with more to come.

"It was a big deal, the Irishman turning up the way he did Maccy and to think, I nearly sent him packing."

"Good job you didn't, brother. I don't 'ave a clue what the future is for the buggers but whatever Ma decides is okay by me. Like I say, who knows?"

"We two have accepted him and must stick by that." It isn't often, if ever, we two sit and agree with each other. It's a pleasant change.

"Did he ever give you a bill for his dry cleaning?"

155

"Not yet. So, what about your yank then. What is she called?"

"No idea bro', I don't have a clue. It's not important."

"Right, and the way you tell it, I'm the useless one. Still, a bit of mystery is good for the soul, brother."

"Put it this way Dusty, I hope there will be two weddings when the time is right, not one. Thing is, has Padraig asked Ma. Maybe we are jumping the gun here. I thought families got smaller as they got older. We'll find out drekly." At this rate there will be a couple of dozen of us in a year or two.

"We'll just have to wait, see what happens, Mac. Have you asked her then?"

"Nope, how can I ask someone who is nameless? Mike, the minister will say 'Do you take whatshername, or Josephine Bloggs to be your something or other?"

"Fair enough, brother. No need to waste words from what I can see. You're a lucky man."

"That's what I think. I need to thank you kid."

"What for?"

"I know you must have done the same as ma and made her feel welcome while I was away."

"Don't underestimate her, Maccy."

"Oh, I won't. You should see her with a six-gun, scared the hell out of me brother."

"I don't doubt it. Like the old lady, Renee?"

"Worse! Not quite the same Dusty, the yank has better eyesight. You could be forgiven for thinking the pistols are for show, she knows how they work."

"I've seen them. She had to get a permit."

"She most likely twisted a few arms. So, how's the bus doing?"

"Better than I reckoned, about time I got a second, Mac."

"Glad to hear it. You would need to get to doing it. Better safe than sorry."

"I need two boats of similar size. If I got something bigger it'd cost me more to license. Iffen I have two boats out there and one has a problem, I can't use it, I still have one on the water. I'll look into it after we get this bleddy place organised."

"That makes good sense."

"Who's this Lavinia that's coming here then, Maccy?"

"Best you don't know too much about her. She'll chew you up and spit you out in bits, Dusty!"

"Where is she from?"

"Venus, Mars, maybe even further!"

"That's alright, so she's out of this world then?"

"Seriously Dusty, don't go there."

"Scare you, did she?"

"And some."

"Cool."

"Don't say I didn't warn you."

Well, that's about the longest conversation we've had in a while. Most likely the only serious one we ever had. Okay, fairly serious, I didn't have to part with any cash either. Dusty is indeed growing up. I'd bet he won't take heed of my warning.

It had been a long night. We Tamryn boys know how to hold our beer, between visits to the gents of course. It shouldn't be held too long as I found out when carrying two pints during the Padstow Chase. All competitors were naked at the time. When I say 'all' there were just the three of us plus a large audience.

Our mother can put it away, though rarely to excess nowadays. Joy doesn't drink much, she took the bottle of wine slowly but surely. Padraig sat on the sidelines the whole evening, just commenting quietly here and there on some of the varied topics of conversation. He was taking notice for the future I believe. At a quieter moment I told him my plan and was a tad apprehensive. I needn't have been. It was a conversation just between the two of us.

The mystery accordionist had materialised from nowhere, played and smiled all evening and at some point that was unknown to all of us, he must have, if it's possible, de-materialised to whence he came.

Now here I am at the completion of my extended long weekend away which almost turned into a week. My odd jigsaw like Celtic family are in the process of being reconnected, repaired, rehashed, maybe soon to be reunited legally. It's a bit like putting a fuse in a plug that never had one previously; all the wires are in the right places. It really couldn't happen to a nicer bunch of people. There is still a bit to do obviously but the mechanics seem to be back in place. A bystander might think it's all too soon. He or she should go stand by someone else, same as Dusty if he has any sense. My brother won't have.

We had talked into the early hours once we had closed the doors. It had been a long day. Some Scrumpy was disposed of. As for right now, my head feels as if someone has used a lemon squeezer on it and my eyes are giving me the impression they were in the wrong sockets, even my teeth seem to be itching. It feels like I am in a dentist's chair with trainees all around, three of them have drills. This is no time for feeling sorry for myself even though I don't ever remember feeling this worse for wear before.

I'm not and never have been a regular drinker of the golden liquid. I much prefer selling it to someone else and making a profit, as I have done since a teenager. Grandad Tamryn had shown me how and when he wasn't making it in the shed, I was producing it myself. I certainly don't intend to imbibe again anytime soon, well-meant or not. It was enough, no, far too much after what had gone before, the session had cost me my early morning awareness of anything of a human nature.

On waking too early I did eventually begin to go through the motions and slowly my mind caught up with the movable bits on my face and my limbs and they all began to work in unison near enough, which allowed me to get from my shared bedroom to the garden without any serious mishap or sudden personal extinction. It did feel as if someone had left a very powerful light on until I realised it was just the solar globe annoying me. It's an easy mistake to make under the circumstances.

I recall that at the end of the evening, which was as I had previously stated, sometime into the beginning of the morning, Padraig had made a small speech regarding the family. I proceeded to make myself invisible, not literally as I didn't believe it would work. If it could work, I would be a shoplifter, not a publican. I just kept my gob shut and so did my brother. We had already decided it was right. Dusty held out his right hand to Padraig and he couldn't help but show how pleased he was us boys and most importantly ma, had now fully accepted him back into the family.

It all gave me the feeling that the Tamryns are what commonsense is all about. I doubt we'll make a habit of it. The family is in complete agreement and disarray, caused by nothing more than what was or was not in our glasses for a short time throughout the evening and wee hours. Ma said little as she sat on her stool smiling gently and listening. We all spent plenty of time doing that.

Luckily, I remember the most important part. The yank had been my bed partner last night, it would be wise of me to tread gently on the stairs and check she is okay. After all, I'm not certain she has ever partaken of pints of our home produced apple juice before, I doubt it. I had warned her of the consequences. I had no idea how she might react to the cloudy amber nectar. I creep up the stairs for two reasons - I don't want to disturb her possible pain and neither do I want to reignite my own. A half-opened eye from behind the bed clothes tells me to go away smartish. I won't forget that look in a hurry! I quietly return from whence I came.

Right now, I feel I am the only survivor of the stricken Marie Celeste. There is no sign of half eaten meals or anything of that nature, half empty pint glasses, yes. Coincidentally, no bodies are apparent so far in the bar area. I check the kitchen. It is also bodyless, except for Jill. She has a face wide grin and a knowing look. I begin to get the feeling the remnants of last night have just nipped out for a paper, another packet of fags or a pint of milk or maybe they are having a lie in, in some secret bedroom. I wonder if there is still a customer or two in the toilets. The Marie Celeste story sails silently through my mind the longer I wander about the place.

"Breakfast, Maccy?"

"Oh yes, the greasier the better maid. Don't hold the bacon, don't hold anything." Jill gave me a start just as I needed one.

"What about your brother?"

"My brother? Jesus Jill, whatever you do, promise me you will never hold my brother! Not under any circumstances. not ever, promise me maid?" I almost shiver in fear, scared she might ignore my advice.

"I'll bare that in mind, Maccy. Fried bread?"

"Yeah, yeah! Thank you." Believe me, I have no idea why that came out. What's the point, unless you are Paul McCartney or John Lennon, of saying the same word twice when just the one should be explanatory enough, it's just a waste! To repeat it three times in one sentence should be a hanging offence. I leave out Ringo and George intentionally. Those two spent most of their time smiling when they should have been serenading mini-skirted, female members of the early sixties. These days the scouse pair would be reprimanded by the Weights and Measures people, not forgetting Customs and Excise officers or the police, who might charge them with impersonating musicians. To be fair to George, he did eventually learn to play rhythm guitar to a decent standard as well as become vocally responsible. Ringo? What can anyone say, 'he was quite good with two sticks and a foot!' Let's be brutally honest, so was Pete Best; look where that got him!

Let me warn anyone who drinks half a dozen pints of the rough stuff made by an amateur and drunk by amateurs over a period of a couple of hours, he or she will become a first-class raconteur of musical abilities, in their own mind. I'm not saying The Beatles should have been stepped on at birth. I'm not saying they shouldn't have been. I'm just pointing out human deficiencies generally in the music industry and the early sixties in particular, I have no idea why! When I fell out of bed half an hour ago, it was the furthest thought from my mind, it is a fair distance even now.

"How do you like your bacon, Maccy?"

"I like it next to more bacon, Jill. Where's Jack at?"

"Working in the garden, fixing the circular bench. He knows how to graft, Maccy."

"You're right, Jill. Seems he can turn his hand to everything. How are the birds settling in?"

"They'll eat the remainder of your fried bread, if you don't."

I like this girl. She may only be sixteen, she is forthright, she is all about, as we say around these parts. She will be an asset as will Jack.

Just when I think it is safe to breathe normally and having eaten a possible hangover cure the phone rings. My heart rate rises as I hear the voice at the other end.

"Lavinia, what can't I do for you?"

"I don't remember. I had a really late-night last night. They don't need me here anymore here. They didn't need me for anything much, Maccy. I need that job now."

"I can find one for you. You will have to come here obviously."

"Where's 'here'?"

"Padstow, more or less."

"Is it near Newquay, more or less?"

"You've been to Newquay?"

"No. Where is it?"

"It's down West."

"Dunno, might have but no, don't think so. Why?"

"You wanted a job."

"Where, when?"

I knew it. It is the second most harmful conversation I've had all day. It's not over yet, I'm in a sequel of Groundhog Day.

"Here, soon as you like."

"Where is 'here?'"

"Where I am. Don't worry about that now."

"Will you pay my train fare?"

"Yes, I'll pay for your journey." A ticket to Timbuctoo springs to mind at this point. Perhaps N.A.S.A. want a guinea pig to send into space. I'd like to see an alien try to deal with her. Maybe I wouldn't. I suppose she might stop a possible invasion.

"Where will I sleep?"

"A railway carriage."

"I can't sleep on a train. I'll miss my stop."

"It's okay, it doesn't move anywhere. You could have my bed. Unfortunately, you can't."

"Can't? That would have been nice."

"Not the train you're coming on, the one I have here. No, I won't be in it."

"You have your own train and it has a bed? We could be, you know, thingy, friends, FWB."

"What the hell does that mean?"

"Friend with benefits."

"I don't need one right now."

"What do you want me for then?"

"I never said I did. I do need a bleddy good barmaid." Possibly a bodyguard might be more useful. I wonder if Kevin Costner is doing anything right now. I doubt it, counting up his money takes up all his time.

"So, what do you want me for then?"

"Lavinia, listen, find a suitcase, it's a big plastic thing with a handle and a zip, pack your clothes, that's the stuff you wear, inside it, get a ticket for the train and get on it. Don't get off in Bristol, Bath, or Bude or any place beginning with the same letter. Leave the train driver alone, he needs to concentrate and stay on until you get to Bodmin Parkway." I nearly said Bedford, that would be a serious mistake, I stop myself in time. 'Find a phone and call me."

"Bodmin Parkway begins with a B, doesn't it."

"Some of it, just pretend it doesn't."

"This train carriage, is it a big, springy bed? Where will I find a phone. I've never found one before."

"If it isn't, just use your imagination! Just keep your eyes open. Call me later when you're in the vicinity." I believe it is a shame the Funny Farm at St Lawrence near Bodmin has closed now it's needed more than ever. There's nothing more I can do for her. She'll either get here or she won't.

"Right, Bodmin Parkway, how will I know when I've arrived?"

"That's easy, you'll be on a train that's going there."

"I will. Will I?"

"I'm sending Lenny to come and get you."

"Oh no, what did I do wrong?"

"What are you talking about?"

"This Lenny is gonna get me. I didn't do anything."

"Find the phone and call me."

"I have a phone here now."

"Is it a mobile?"

"I don't think so."

"Then best you leave that one where it is and find another one when you get to Bodmin Parkway."

"Okay. What about this Lenny bloke."

"I never said he is a bloke."

"He sounds like he might be, Maccy."

"Lavinia, don't look at Lenny when he gets there."

"Why not?"

"Just don't!"

"That's silly. How will I know it's him if I don't look?"

"You'll know. Just don't touch him."

"Why?"

"Because he's delicate."

"I'll be gentle, Maccy."

"Actually Lavinia, do what you think is best. Just don't cause to much damage."

"Okay, I won't."

I spend the next few hours with shattered nerves. I know they'll be worse when she arrives. As reluctantly agreed, Lavinia does arrive with everything she owns. She had passed the Merry Maiden on to its new owners and travelled to be somewhere she had never previously been. She, with Jill and Jack, will manage the Maltsters for the day. I needed the best. I would make do with what I could get at such short notice, in Lavinia's case. Seriously, I wouldn't have asked anyone else. Sad isn't it!

Lavinia is looking like a single surviving cast member of the ill-fated Crossroads kitchen staff even though that wonderful advertisement for brain damaged and completely mentally disturbed actors has finally disappeared from our screens. She would have been a scream in that. I mean, never mind. I feel sorry for my mate. Lenny looks a tad queasy.

A shed, an old station waiting room from an old station will be Lavinia's home for now. The local Wadebridge to Padstow line had been given unpaid redundancy in the sixties. It is now parked next to the carriages and fully fitted, almost. Looking at the shed and Lavinia, the two are perfect for each other. It might be wise for me to move it to a more distant field. Then I remember, I don't have to. I'll be living at the Maltsters soon enough. I now seem to have become the proud owner of a fast-growing commune. Scratch proud, it isn't at all relevant!

After my cellar checks I return to the kitchen where I find the American is awake and moving. Her eyes are staring straight ahead as if she is an extra in 'Zombies-R-Us' or she might just have returned from a one-night stand with Paul McKenna and in his excitement, he'd forgotten to bring her out of 'trance' at the end of it. It was all rather pleasing for a moment. This poor girl has been sucked into the maelstrom of the Tamryn clan. I doubt she will be imbibing of our locally produced beverage again, not in a pint glass anyway.

Dusty is going somewhere he can't reach, mostly at speed. He went out through the door backwards a moment ago. I noticed through one half opened bloodshot eye. The speedy maneuver must have been successful, I don't expect to see him again too soon.

I like 'the Kid', he makes me laugh and reminds me of me when I was around his age. It was only a year ago. I suppose from what I've heard about him recently, he puts my past into the shade a tad.

I am not and have never been a serious cider drinker and don't intend to be again. Unfortunately, I had put away some pints of the stuff somewhere around one, two and three o'clock this morning. It was enough, no it was too much after what had gone before. The fried breakfast held it in check for a while. I am hoping it is going to be an antidote.

We locals call it 'rough' for good reason. When you're not used to it, perhaps if you are, you're just gonna feel rough as rats a short time later. No hair of the dog for me with this stuff, not unless I'm looking for an early grave.

Like Dusty, I had drunk three, maybe it was more, dark coffees. Unlike the kid, I stumbled around for a lot longer than he did. The 'rough' had given me a temporary bout of numbness and memory loss. I can't be sure as if I have lost my memory, how would I know? I wouldn't be at all surprised if my breath didn't smell something like a dragon's arse might after it had consumed a complete curry house and all its customers.

It had been a trial to get out of bed without waking her. Every time I got up and tried to walk away from it, I had to go back again as I couldn't remember for the life of me why I had got up in the first place. This went on for about an hour or so by the end of which, planet Earth was still spinning a bit faster than normal, as far as I could tell. The grey mushy stuff that might or might not be irreparably damaged inside my head has now become reasonably still, throbbing a tad but off the boil. I couldn't put all the blame on the four pints of cider but to be truthful, it did do the most serious damage. It might have been the fifth or sixth should take the blame.

I do remember her telling me in the small hours why she had stopped writing. Her parents had both died in a motoring accident, apparently the old Indian had come to her in the middle of the night and told her what had happened. She had left immediately after writing the strange note. She tells me she is a single child and after the shock of losing her parents, she had to bury them. She has no other family to speak of, no past to speak of now. She has a 'future' she told me, 'here'. I may have been in a right state, but I didn't forget a thing she said. I'm not certain she told me everything. It felt like she was leaving something out. It'll keep for another time, it can't be too important.

I must be sober by opening time, I can't afford not to be. If I messed up today it would be a sort of Death by Chocolate, without the chocolate. A different kind of brown stuff and a lot more of it hitting a fan if I fail.

My first task on my return is rather gruesome, the yank had mentioned a problem in the bedroom. No, no, nothing like that. I must remove the most revolting item currently inside the Maltsters Arms. I grab at it with both arms right around the middle, I had thought about picking it up by its four legs - I was concerned they may become separated from the torso. It wouldn't have been a bad thing as it would have to stay in the same place unless it was a Crufts champion at rolling. I carried it upstairs and dropped it, still unmoving, onto Dusty's unmade bed. I pulled the door tight shut. There was a small amount of howling and growling as I stepped away. Some of it by me, most of it.

Later, when he comes home my brother will take over the sound effects. May they both be very happy together.

I seem to have regained my faculties and remember Lavinia. God help Little Petrock, God help us all! Life will no longer be boring – to be truthful, it never has been - and I have no one to blame but myself. I can't wait to see Dusty end up on his backside when she gets hold of him. On thinking about it, I don't think I want to know, I wouldn't want to be a witness.

Chapter Fifteen

The Maltsters Arms

The Maltsters Arms sits astride Lost Souls Creek. It isn't a creek that often to be honest. If it's a long hot, dry summer, it might be a creek for a while. Most of the time it can be a powerful rushing watercourse that empties calmly into the Camel close to Sea Mills, meeting the Camel estuary at a gushing rate of knots after heavy rainfall and of course, a Spring tide can raise the watercourse almost to the grassy banks. The creek itself seems to exude evil with its omnipresent danger lurking below the surface. If the creek is moody it will soon become riled; it will be unforgiving, understandably so due to its long shameful history.

There is evidence the creek was in constant use in the eighteenth and nineteenth centuries and upwards. There is also evidence smugglers used it and most likely the Maltsters Arms too, to hide and when the coast was clear, distribute French Brandy, other rich wines and tobacco. Whatever it's given name, the creek and the pub were at one time both employed in nefarious ways. I wouldn't mind betting the vicar was involved. Many clergymen were known to participate in some way in the illegal trade. *One such at Dymchurch in Kent actually marshalled and directed smuggling operations when he was away from the pulpit. He continued to do so successfully on the forbidding Romney Marshes in the eighteenth century, until he was eventually murdered by a traitor amongst his company of cut-throats. A similar operation could have easily operated here in Little Petrock. Funny how the village church is situated directly opposite the Maltsters Arms at the centre of the village. Coincidence? I don't much believe in coincidence.

A much smaller building adjoining the Maltsters is reputed to have looked upon the face of sadness; newborns were deposited in the creek suffering an ignominious fate. It is a well-known secret the one-time hovel was used for the dispersal of many a soul. Souls whose eyes never once got to see the light of day. All the ladies of the night knew where to go after a mishap in their line of work. Even now, many locals will not walk over the tiny humpback bridge in the late or early hours. As a tacker I was warned to keep away or put my hands over my ears if I was about, in order not to hear the wailing of the tiny souls as their mothers turned their backs and returned to carry on their chosen work down on the harbourside at Padstow. Maybe 'chosen' is for want of a better word, necessary might easily replace it. Ladies of the night - whatever name is used - didn't do what they did through choice, unlike those of today who choose to carry on the 'oldest' profession. A well at the back of the Maltsters exists today. It may even have been the drop off point for the poor infants being just yards from the creek. The well still does overflow and fill the yard at Spring tide.

Now, what might have once been a hovel can only be a little different on the outside. It hides its history badly. It is almost easy to imagine how it was in its early days of use, as it adjoined the drinking establishment. The old place has been home to many, one such a doctor, a healer. Did he or she eventually heal the misery of the ancient building? It can never be determined. I like to think the good doctor might have. I hope so. I still consider blocking my ears if I have to cross the bridge at the witching hour and I know many more who would do the same. Tiny bones have in the past been picked up along the creek bank, which steers the water towards the Camel and eventually back into the Atlantic Ocean. In the case of the little humpback bridge it would be a shame if there was no truth, a much bigger shame if there is. Isn't there always some truth in a legend?

**A village elder once told me the Mermaid and Bow was employed as a dressing station at the end of World War one. Troops who had come home from the front with serious wounds could go there to have them redressed. The dressings would be washed and repaired and wait for the next recipient.

As for the 'Bridge of Tears', countless exhaust pipes – with fumes – pass over it every summer. It can be silent on occasion, apart from the almost inaudible sound of tiny bats flitting here and there. Every now and then around dusk they might show themselves for a fleeting moment. They don't hang around long. The 'Lost Souls' have hung around for centuries. You have to think they will do for many more. Maybe there are no human cries at all and it is just the sound of the bats emitting their night song. If they are to blame, how is it they can make your skin prickle and the hair on the back of your neck stand up?

I digress, back to the Maltsters.

Since her unheralded arrival at the Maltsters late yesterday afternoon, we had seen little of Lavinia. I told her to take as long as she needed to settle herself in. She took me at my word. I made it her first task, as I saw it in order of importance, to get rid of the nearly, but not quite, dead dog. It isn't yet deceased. It had found a place that I had no intention of letting it stay and eventually rot in. How it got out of Dusty's room is a bone of contention. Dusty says he didn't let it out, I say he did, etc. I think I have the perfect answer.

"Lavinia, I did ask you to look after my dog. How difficult can it be, get rid of it"

"Where? You told me it isn't your dog."

"It's not my dog, it's a figure of speech. It is my responsibility, it's in my pub. It doesn't mean it's my dog."

"It's not in my job description."

"You don't have one."

"I don't have a contract of employment either."

"Correct. So, no job description, no contract, no argument. Shift the bleddy mutt!"

"Where?"

"Battersea? Give Paul O'Grady a ring. He's into waifs and strays with four legs, you might as well go too!"

"Where's Battersea? Who's Paul O'Grady?"

"I thought you were a cockney?"

"I am, I'm from The Isle of Dogs!"

Music to my ears. I should believe in coincidence after all. "There you go then it's perfect, just hide the bleddy dog. I'll put it in your job description. The last person Paul O' Grady would want to speak to is you anyway. You wouldn't be his type." Think I know how he feels.

"Hide it? Where? I might not want to speak to him either."

"Believe me, you're not his type."

"How would you know?"

"He prefers to be in male company, dear of 'n."

"I could sort him out without the speaking bit."

"Put the dog behind the bar."

"Is it the best place to hide a dog?"

"Put him behind the bar!" That's me done, we have gone full circle. The Alsatian is still where it was and cleaner in the undercarriage area.

"Where is the bar?".

"Look love, there is no way you don't know where the bar is. You fell over it when you arrived."

"I was joking, Maccy. It's your damn dog, you do it."

"It isn't my dog. I'm his man."

"Well if you ask me, he could have picked a better one."

"I agree, he could have. I wish he had." I couldn't think of another answer. She is right, it's not her job to look after my problems. In fact, the dog isn't a problem. It's probably been in as many pubs as I have, maybe more. Here it is home for the first time in its life. I'll smuggle it back into Dusty's room later! Okay, it can sleep outside our room or in Dusty's room. I can't be fairer than that.

Lavinia does have a knack of getting her own way. I don't, especially where women are concerned. They somehow also have the knack of making me talk to myself. Do all females do this? Is there some secret society amongst the fairer sex? A stupid question! Do all females sign the official secrets act at age thirteen and a half? Indoctrination! The thing is where would we be without them? It's okay, I know the answer - fatherless, motherless too, I suppose. The thing is the women know this and hold it against us. We hardly stand a chance.

"Maccy, I only have two legs!"

"Jill, hoover the dog and whatever there is underneath it please. Then ask Jack to hide it behind the bar." I changed my mind as I know Dusty will kick off with the previous arrangement. Delegation works sometimes, you just have to stick with it.

"Okay Maccy, look after my bucket. Jill is a constant source of humour most days, she doesn't realise it. Almost every time I see her dodging about the place, she has a tight grip on the metal bucket. It has water in it and three ducklings. Not the stuff of nursery rhymes but with a bit of thought and a roll of brown paper lagged in vinegar...... I think I might have the wrong story. Anyway I think she will soon need a bigger bucket.

"Thanks maid."

"Mac, Lenny on the phone for you."

"Now what, yank?" It's about time she got up. I'm not about to tell her obviously.

"There have been a fight mucker, in the Mermaid. I did my best to stop it, Maccy. The police have done their job well. It was something and nothing."

"Tell me about both bits but not at the same time, Lenny."

"Firstly, there was an argument about a game of pool. It got heated and all hell broke loose."

"Have this just happened? It's a bit early to have fighting this time of the day."

171

"No mate, it did start last night. Tis all over now I believe."

"So, what's the problem then."

"I'm in the police station in Wadebridge now."

"Right. You said something and nothing. We've had the nothing part. What about the something bit?"

"I need you to pick me up from here, as I have to get back to Padstow. I don't have a car here right now."

"How did you get there then?" Somehow, I know how this story will play out.

"In the police car. We all got here in the police car, police cars. There was more than one. There was more than two."

"Did you start the fight, Lenny?"

"Naw, I stopped it. The others started it, three of them. One was a woman."

"Who won?"

"We won the first one. The police won the one after. They have warned me to behave myself and to not be so heavy handed with folks when I'm in a position of authority. They have said for me not to be so rough next time. Copper with the nosebleed said he wouldn't press charges as it was more or less an accident. They told Alice the same thing. I have to get the window mended."

"What was an accident? What happened to the window? Is it the one that has always been broken?"

"The nosebleed. He got in the way of my hand. It broke. Alice did it. It was a pity your dog weren't here. How will I know if it's the one that was already broke?"

"It's not my dog, Lenny. It's been broken for almost fifteen bleddy years."

"The woman that left through the window broke it again. Alice said she should leave but the woman didn't want to. She only had a few scratches, there isn't much blood on the pool table. The town has quietened down now, so Twotrees says. He turned up with the second lot. The first lot were already here before them. He was very good about it all. Said 'it was one of those things.' I told him, 'sorry about your nose'!"

"Did you break it?"

"The window? Naw, Alice broke it with the other woman, I told you."

"Not the window, Twotree's nose."

"Naw, I don't think I did, tis just a bit red, like his shirt."

"I'll be half an hour mate. Stay where you are."

"We can't go anywhere yet Maccy, they have lost the keys to Alice's handcuffs!"

"Is that the ones with the red fluff on them?"

"Naw, the police ones don't have fluff on them as far as I know. How do you know she has handcuffs with red fluff on them?"

"More to the point Lenny, how do you bleddy know? She's your bleddy sister mate!"

"I 'ad to borrow them when I was going out with that scrawny waitress that time. She was so skinny, they kept falling off anyway. She made me wear them."

"Okay, I'm on my way. I'll bring a cake with a file in it."

"What for?"

"Somewhere you can keep your notes and the police caution!"

"Okay, cheesecake would be grand. I didn't get a caution, Maccy."

"You're getting one now. Don't fight with women, let other women do it, it's less painful and far more entertaining." If I'm honest, I have to admit I've had a few scuffles with Alice myself. That's another story entirely, I always allowed her to win. I'm beginning to wonder whether I should just leave Lenny where he is. I wish he had had the dog with him now, it would have saved a hell of a lot of fuss trying to hide it here.

"I will do my best Mucker. Give your dog a pat for me."

"Yes, I will matey. On the head?"

"That would be proper."

"I need a shovel,"

"What do you need a shovel for?"

"Never mind. Shall I bring a hacksaw, Lenny?"

"What for?"

"I'll be with you in a half hour, might be tomorrow mind. Don't wait up for me."

"Is she still there?"

"Who?"

"You know, thingy. The one that did or didn't leave through the window."

"Maybe, maybe not, I'll check and let you know."

"Okay, tell her she owes for the broken pane."

"You tell her."

"I can't, I don't know who she is."

Someone must get to Padstow and open up the Mermaid. There is no one else until the cons become ex-cons. I'm not a great believer in luck unless it's the bad variety. I become a tad bemused as a sad – I mean pathetic - looking sports car pulls up outside the kitchen window. I watch as the ex-hitchhiker gets out. This is my day taking a turn for the better. Now Peter can go to Padstow. He did tell me he could do anything. Who says praying is pointless? To be fair, I hadn't prayed, I have been thinking about it. It worked at the chapel a day or two ago. It is something I might take up.

Peter is a big man, I would guess around six four. He stoops to enter the door built for anyone under the height of five feet five. Hopefully he will be able to stoop to conquer at the Mermaid, if only temporarily.

"Peter, my friend. How long has it been?"

"About seventy-two hours, Maccy. Sorry I'm late, I had to drive here. My car isn't what most people would call a car. I have to open the door to let the clutch out. Maybe I should get an automatic with a dodgy door. I would still have to be there, but I could hold the door shut."

"It's a soft top, mate. You can get in and out of the top."

"Not really, the catch is knackered. It used to open and shut on its own. I had to secure it with a nail-gun. It's worked okay so far."

"Where are you staying mate?"

"Not far away. Here would be good, I'm out of petrol, I have a slow puncture. It'd be better if it was slower. I need a bath."

"You don't have time, Peter. Take a shower instead. It's in the back of the pub."

"I don't know about that Maccy, I'd rather be doing something useful. I'll have a shower in the shower if that's alright with you?"

"I want you to open up my other pub, buddy. My regular manager is indisposed for a while. It's only down the road a couple of miles. You can use my car."

"Lead me to the shower, mate. What's your manager doing?"

"He's doing a stint of in-house entertainment at the police station."

"Really?"

"Yes, he has an assistant. They regularly work together at Wadebridge."

"Maybe he could have picked a better place!"

"You might think so. Wait 'til you get to know him better, you'll change your mind. Anyway, it's a charity thing for red nose day."

"Comedy?"

"Something like that. Lenny Henry was hereabouts a few minutes ago. You just missed him."

"Is he a comedian."

"It's a matter of opinion."

There is something about Peter, I still can't decide what it is. It is a slight worry that he reminds me of Lenny. I check the bottom of my shoes to see if I've trodden in something. All clear. It must be my day. I intend to make the most of it. Damn! I have forgotten now I need a car to get to Wadebridge. The yank! She can look after this place, I'll get a taxi. No, I'll send a taxi and ring the police station. We can run this place. It will be the first time we have both stood behind the bar at the same time since we opened.

"Yes sir, Mr. Tamryn, someone will be there in an hour."

'Mister Tamryn,' I'll use him again. Even Twotrees is amiable once more. I had to call him to make sure they could come home. No charges were brought which is a shame.

"So, Miss America, are you about to tell me about the old geezer in McCarthy City?"

"Okay yes, he used to help out my dad on the ranch sometimes. He's also a Dog Soldier, of the Comanche tribe, a tribal elder. You better be good to me or he might disembowel ya and drag ya underneath his horse a mile or two, if I don't have to do it my own self."

"Me too, I can ride. Dusty and I both ride, even cows sometimes! We have horses at Ma's place. You should go see them. They are getting on a bit mind. Dusty and I rode them into Padstow last year. They were so knackered, they slept most of the way home. We all of us did. We had snow and ice and couldn't drive, so we rode. Had to get to a funeral, couldn't miss it, it wouldn't have been right."

"So, are we gonna ride together then? Knackered?"

"Knackered, it means shagged out!"

"Knackered, shagged out?"

"Tell you about that later. Why is it you talk so slow?"

"Easy, I'm from Texas, we all do. It's what's known as the Texas drawl. We do everything slow Maccy, we do everything big."

"I thought you were from Kansas."

"Nope, Texas, I'm a Texan through and through. Actually, not quite through and through, some of me ain't."

"I see. Something else I need to get used to, Miss America!"

"Do you have watermelons here in England?"

"No, I don't think we do."

"Maccy …."

"We might do, I never needed one."

"Maybe you don't but I might."

That's me told! "So, would you like a drink, a beer?"

"Yep, I'll have a glass of one of these. That's what you people drink normally ain't it?"

"Yes, it is. The ladies around here usually drink halves."

"Then that's what I want. I never said I was a lady, I ain't about to. When in Rome…."

"This is England. Rome is somewhere else."

"I know that, it's in Italy. I wasn't born yesterday."

"Good, otherwise you wouldn't be able to serve behind the bar, ma'am. You wouldn't be able to reach if you were born yesterday. You would be breaking the law too. I know where Rome is too!"

"So, I haven't met everyone yet?"

"No, Lenny and his sister are in the police station. They'll be here soon enough. Watch out for Lenny!"

"Why?"

"He's different. Lenny can do sharp at times, don't come to expect it. He's mostly harmless."

She didn't have to wait long.

"Lenny, meet Spittin' woman and well, you already know Lavinia."

"Who says?" Lavinia is homing in on Lenny now. It's a scary thought. They could share a brain cell. They might procreate!

"Yank meet Lenny and Alice. They've been away. Before you ask darlin', no, they aren't together.

"What makes you say that?"

"You don't need to know, yank."

I hadn't thought about this. Lavinia is eyeing my mate up like a Praying Mantis as we speak. This is all I need. Lenny and Lavinia a twosome. I never thought, I don't think, it could be worse. I'm not sure how!

"Maccy darlin', what is 'shagged out?"

"Like being tired after hard work. Ask Lavinia sweetheart, she'll explain it better than I can, her being an expert on her chosen subject, so I almost but not quite learned, luckily."

"Maccy, did you know your brother has a Yurt?"

"A what?"

"No, a yurt."

"A what?"

"I told you, a darned yurt."

"Then he needs to see a doctor and get it removed, yank."

"He bought it, a yurt."

"Is it some kind of Russian car or a disease?"

"He's living in it. The dog is sleeping alone. He didn't tell you then!"

"So Dusty is living in a yurt, why?"

"We're not sure Lenny, you could ask him."

"Ask him what Miss?"

"Maccy!"

"What?"

"Help me out here."

"I bleddy warned you maid, I bleddy told 'e. Don't mess with things you know nothing about, especially Lenny!"

Author's notes:

*The Reverend Doctor Christopher **Syn** is the smuggler hero of a series of novels by Russell Thorndike. The first book, Doctor Syn: A Tale of the Romney Marshes was published in 1915. The story idea came from smuggling in the 18th century on Romney Marshes, where brandy and tobacco were brought in at night by boat from France to avoid high tax.

** Over nine million dying or wounded men passed through the army hospitals, with 1.6 million being successfully patched up and returned to the Front, while six million were carried from there to base and 2.26 million were evacuated back to England. Many of the latter would need further attention when returning home. The Mermaid and Bow at Little Petrock is said to have been one such place.

Chapter Sixteen

All and Sundry

I get a message from some obscure nursing home in Wadebridge. Not surprisingly, it was unknown to me. Apparently Bert has taken advice and is now living a life of luxury in said establishment. I doubt his wife knows where he is, she never does. The olden told them to call me. I have been summoned, I need to make a visit.

I will miss having breakfast with Bert at the cafe. It will be like going to church without a vicar. The place will be like a cemetery now without any graves, like going to a pub that doesn't have a barmaid.

Michael had informed me my friend Bert had finally packed up his cleaning job and put his feet up. My unofficial and therefore unpaid tutor and confidante has finally hung up his mop and bucket. The old chap had cleaned the big harbourside café for years. Even when I was still a teenager, I would sneak into the café and make his tea for him before he'd even unlocked the place and begun his work. *Now I have my own key given to me by the café owner a while ago. Back in the day I didn't need a key, I knew how to get in without one. I think the café owner let me have it for services rendered. Maybe he wanted me to take over Bert's duties once he popped his clogs?

"Where the hell have you been Maccy lad, it's been a while?"

"Here and there Bert, you knaw."

"I might and I might not, I'd be willin' to bet you 'ave been up to no bleddy good while you 'ave been away, you bugger."

"I did my best matey, you know me." I have always done my best to stay out of trouble. Rarely has it been enough.

"Ais I do you bugger. So, where did you say you've been?"

"Tredinnit!"

"I don't believe I 'ave, Maccy, if I did I don't bleddy remember."

"You 'aven't, I 'ave."

"You should clean it off boy, I thought I could smell some bleddy thing."

"Look Bert, it's a place. Not a very big place you understand. but it's called Tredinnit, down nearby Truro."

"Right, I understand."

"Anyway, I'm back now, that's my lot. No more wandering around. You could say, been there, done that and Trodinnit! I'm done with travelling around. I have the Maltsters in Little Petrock to take up all my time now. I'll come and get you when I have settled in and all is shipshape. You can come and have a stay old buddy."

"That would be grand, Maccy!"

"How's that youngster, Bert?"

"Coming along fine, Maccy. Alice has been here to visit, she has done good with him, you needn't worry. The young tacker do remind me of someone mind."

"Does he now? I can't think who that could be, matey."

"I bet you can't, you bugger. Anyways, you had better not leave it too long lad, I might not be 'ere. Do you know Maccy, if you juggle the letters around, the word funeral can spell 'real fun'?"

"You won't be finding out just yet old buddy! Only the good die young, you don't qualify at all, pard. How's your bleddy back?"

"Tis bleddy good now lad."

"How's the missus?"

"No idea. 'Er's probably alright, mebbe."

My old friend began to doze. I left him alone to rest, he deserves it. I would bet Bert is clinging on to ninety, I wouldn't suggest it to him. Bert is reaching his twilight years slowly but surely. He is in no hurry.

As I drove home I thought about where I am and where I was going. Some folks do that occasionally, sometimes at the right moment. So, the kid, my younger brother by nine months, Dusty, has acquired a ** yurt. Well why not. When I find out what it is, he can get it shifted, to another place. He can go with it and keep it company. My brother is show-boating as per usual. This news may account for his sheepishness the day of my return. To be fair, it could have been any one of a dozen things. As I even consider what a yurt is, the short-term owner in question appears.

"Yurt!"

"Pardon?"

"You're excused. I hear you do have a yurt, brother. I hope it's not some kind of animal?"

"I do to be sure, you wanna see it? You can feed it if you like."

"Do I want to see it, probably not. 'Feed it', no I don't think so."

"Suit yourself."

Dusty has always had an Irish twist to his voice. Until just a few years ago no one really knew why except our ma. Our father turned up one day and all became clear. Think he went out for a newspaper, full of fish and chips, it took him twenty years to eat them and then he returned. Padraig made himself useful and gradually found and took his place – a tad belatedly – into our family. Not as head of the family as we have never needed one. He's here and it's good. Dusty did kick off a bit once he knew who the stranger was; he chilled out eventually, watched and waited as I did myself. Neither of us call him dad even now and I don't it believe it bothers Padraig at all. He's 'cool'!

"So, it's not an animal then! Is it like seeing a flying saucer, give me a clue boy?"

"Yup, it is a bit like a flying saucer, without the flying bit. It's a non-flying saucer you could say."

"It can't fly, it does look like a flying saucer. Having never seen one I can hardly comment. So what does it do aside from what it can't do, can it do anything of use, can it do anything at all?"

"Not much, apart from keep me dry and warm brother. No bleddy engines. You can laugh Maccy, it's better than your bleddy gaff."

"Is it? Will it make money, this yurt?"

"Not really. It could do I suppose."

"When could it make money?"

"When I'm not living in it maybe."

"Where is it?"

"Outside, it wouldn't fit in here."

"Show me."

"Show you it won't fit in here? I'll give it a try."

"Dusty, just show me the bleddy yurt, comprende?" I think 'comprende' means 'get it'. I'm not sure. I heard it somewhere. Between you and me, she talks in her sleep. I have trouble talking when I'm awake, I would never get the chance to talk in my sleep, I wouldn't want to interrupt her. I'll put that a different way, she wouldn't want me to interrupt her. That's much better.

A more than mild surprise affects me whilst viewing this non-alien owned, non-flying spacecraft. The yurt is huge and to be fair, on closer inspection, I wouldn't mind one myself. I am instantly impressed, I am not about to let my brother know. How he got it here I have no idea. It is massive, twenty feet or more across and as the boy says, 'dry and warm'. It would make a great holiday let. My brother is not happy at my proposal. I think I've heard of them, but never seen a yurt before. I can't remember the last time I went to Russia or Outer Mongolia, I've never even been to Inner Mongolia. Now I don't have to go to any part. What would be the point? If you've seen one yurt, you've seen them all surely.

Another thing to take into consideration is that the yurt actually resembles a circus big top. Worryingly my brother should feel completely at home. He is definitely the clown of the family.

"We could charge people to look at it like they do at Stonehenge only without all the rocks." Talking about lumps of stone, when I was a tacker, Mister Jagger could be seen wandering around Padstow Quay on May Day. I'm fairly certain he wasn't seen 'dancing in the street'. The Boss, Bruce Springsteen might pop in for a dance after dark. How would anyone know? Doesn't mean he hasn't!

"Get stuffed! No chance. It's mine, I bought it, I'm living in it. I don't want people looking in on me when I'm sleeping."

"Dusty, there aren't any bleddy windows boy. You call what you do 'living'? You can't live in it. There's no bog for one thing. Another thing, it'll probably be full of hippies by the end of the week. You'll be making a fashion statement for about half an hour. They'll turn up and there won't be anywhere for you to lay your head boy."

"Bucket and Chuck it! You didn't have a bog when you moved into the train carriages, not straight away you didn't. I wouldn't mind so long as they're of the female variety. What is a hippy anyway?"

"No idea, ask ma, she will know." The kid is right. The thing is impressive. I like it, I just don't want to know how much it cost him. To be fair, his sea bus business is thriving. He must be able to afford it whatever the figure. We only had to part with twenty quid to get the carriages here, that was just for the use of the tractor and a bit of bribery. Money well spent! I'm guessing the kid parted with a lot more than twenty-five quid. Twenty thousand would be more like it. "Where are you gonna wash, kid. You got no bleddy plumbing."

"In the pond. I didn't know ma was a hippy."

"Lake, it is not a pond, boy. She and the old man both were."

"It's a bleddy pond, Maccy. I might grow a ponytail my own self."

"Lake. Anyway if it's a pond, you should feel right at home. It's the perfect pond for you."

"What makes you say that, brother?"

"Here's a clue Dusty, pond life!"

"Call it what you like, I'm washing in it unless I want a hot bath. I might even buy a speedboat and put on the 'lake'."

"That's a novelty. I didn't know you were taking up cleanliness. I'd buy a pedalo if I was you, you couldn't afford much else. You spent all your money on a bleddy circus big top. That reminds me, did you get another boat yet? By the way, do you know what can be found under every ponytail, Dusty?"

"Nope."

"An arsehole every time. Anyway it'll never sail brother, not upside down anyway. If it did, you could use it to take folks to Newquay and charge a fortune. It might take off if we get a hurricane I suppose, or a strong gale. You won't be able to throw up over the side like in a boat."

"I don't get seasick."

"Then you're lucky you won't in a yurt. It'll be up in the air, you'll get air sick!"

"You're jealous, admit it. It doesn't have any portholes anyway."

"Okay, if it'll make you feel better." I'm not jealous of the kid, I am impressed. I'd bet he didn't have much change from ten grand. It'll be handy for chasing the girls round in. More likely they'll be doing the chasing. "What's that in the centre of the roof?"

"It's so I can look out for flying saucers. So what do you think, Maccy?"

"Well brother, you and Peter should be right comfy in there. You can watch out for them together."

"We won't, he won't, I might."

"Why didn't you just get a bleddy gypsy caravan boy?"

"To tell the truth I did consider that Maccy and even looked at one, but there was a bleddy gypsy in it, told me

184

he was a traveller. The bugger never moved while I was there, just sat grinning while he plucked his roadkill! I suppose hedgehogs are pretty easy to catch?"

"That's the trouble with those things. I bet there was a horse tied to the back of it, Dusty. You gonna call it something?"

"He can sleep in my old room. 'Yurtiz'."

"I don't think so Dusty, I wouldn't. Not very original. If you do, put the sign on the roof. That way aliens can find it easier. When they turn up, throw them a party. Give me a shout, I can't wait. Yurtiz? If the wind catches it'll be Wherizit or maybe, Wherethebleddyelldiditgo!"

"I'll ignore all of that."

"The mutt is sleeping in your room right now."

"Glad I don't have to clean it."

"The room or the dog, brother?"

"Both!"

"You never did clean it. The Alsatian has most likely hoovered up all the food you had under the bed. It was bad enough before the dog moved in. He'll have guts ache by now. By the way, I'm gonna fill the lake with fish. While you're bathing they can do that nibbling thing with your feet."

"What bleddy nibbling thing?"

"I don't know. They suck off all the dry skin or something."

"I don't have any dry skin."

"Then you best keep your shoes on brother, the bleddy fish won't know that. They lose their memory after thirty seconds."

"How the hell would you know that?"

"Sorry kid, I can't remember. I'll let Peter decide where he wants to sleep. He might prefer to sleep with the dog, I know I would. Better make him up a bed just in case though."

"He's your mate. You make him up a bed."

"He bleddy isn't, I hardly know the bloke. Only met him a couple of days ago. He was hitchhiking. Anyway, thanks for putting him up at such short notice."

"You'll pick up anything. You've known him longer than I have, let him sleep with you."

"Not sure the yank will be keen brother."

"I like her Mac, she's okay."

"Me too Dusty, you're right, she is."

"I liked Jen too, we all did."

"As you say, everybody liked Jen. Everybody will like the yank."

"You should find out her name Maccy, 'tis only right."

"Why, she knows it. Maybe I should, it won't make any difference though."

"Fair enough, brother."

"It'll be a nice surprise one of these days, Dusty."

"It will for her, she doesn't know much about you either."

"It's true what you say, Dusty. Best I leave it that way and best you do the same."

"Might be best. Mind you, it could come out accidental."

"Don't even think about it kid! You're earning more than me now, there's no need for bribery anymore."

Early start. I need to see a man about a dog. Not a dog of mine, I don't actually own a dog. I know a dog who has a man but doing business with it may prove difficult. I will defer! The place is silent, just the way I like it. The kitchen is mine for an hour or two, it's all I need. What better breakfast could there be than a bacon sandwich or a bacon roll, followed by sweet tea.

I have thirty-six fresh baps – sorry ladies, nothing personal, I'm sure your baps are just as fresh – to smother with margarine – sorry again ladies, margarine is extra – and ketchup. They fit perfectly in a large bains marie and once they are almost ready, I wake her. She is a tad displeased. Never mind 'it's all in a good cause'. I inform her rather puzzled face. We eat one each, wash them down with said beverage and leave. Fifteen minutes later we are

186

at our destination, where we are expected and mildly welcomed by a moody looking matron type who might be the granddaughter of Hattie Jacques. I pick up the large stainless-steel container and carry it through to the large dining room. Miss America is a tad surprised at the reception. Thirty-four smiling faces can do that! One of the widest smiles belongs to Bert. The old feller is as surprised as much as anyone as the yank does her waitress thing at my instigation. She does her task well as I and the staff share around the remaining thirty odd plates. With arms outstretched Bert snatches his chance.

"Morning Bert!" She greets the beaming Bert with a kiss on both cheeks. The old feller stands grinning and staring around the dining room with a huge smile on his face as he takes the offered plate. I separate them fast. The old feller might do himself an injury.

"You must be the 'yank lady'. You don't seem mazed!"

"I believe I must be, Bert. You must be Maccy's best friend. What's 'mazed?"

"I dunno 'bout that maid. Mebbe I be, maybe I mightn't, you might be right, you might not be. I know the bugger anyway. Nothing but bleddy trouble 'e be. He should think himself lucky I 'ave been around to keep him out of bleddy trouble maid. 'Mazed' is like confused. If you idn't, you will be soon, Miss. Tamryns will do that to you, you wait and see."

"That's what I heard, Bert. How do you put up with the buggers?"

"Tidn't easy maid, I do my best. You'll find out soon enough, I do reckon."

"I thought I already did old timer. I'll rope him yet and break him sure enough, don't you worry."

"Best you get to doing it soon, it won't be easy maid. So, what do they call you?"

"Anything they damn well please, Bert. That's about the size of it."

"Well, if it gets too much for you maid, come here and stay, you can look after me."

I watch and listen as she wraps my friend around her little finger within seconds. I believe Bert has done the same with her. It does me good to see my old friend smile. Not once have I seen him look under a table for the possibility of finding the wayward pound coin.

"You bleddy shyster, Maccy Tamryn, there idn't no bleddy fried egg in this boy. You'm slipping laddie."

"Lick your plate and drink your bleddy tea, stop your complaining!" I wink at the still grinning pensioner. I have no idea where the yank is going as she disappears into the kitchen area. She returns with a guitar and I wonder where she could have found the instrument as she already begins to kneel on an empty chair and play. She opened her mouth and began to sing, and it made me shiver. I think to myself, this morning could not have gone better if I had planned it all, which I hadn't. I don't do well with planning. I had no idea she could sing or even play. I realise now, I know hardly anything about this woman and it makes little or no difference. I believe she is mocking me with one haunting melody: 'A sleeve is no Place for a Heart'. I disagree but keep my gob tightly shut and continue to listen to her short repertoire. No one it seems wanted her to stop, including myself if I'm honest. The home had come to a halt for a short while at eight-thirty in the morning. The staff had ceased clattering around to stop and listen, now it was time to get out of their way and let them get on with their jobs. Just one thing puzzled me, how did she know there was a guitar in the kitchen?

As I said earlier 'I don't do planning'. It's a damn good job I don't. Mostly I just do stuff, occasionally it works out but more often than not I fail. This is not one of those times. I'm still a bit miffed at her song choice but I wouldn't have missed it for all the sweet tea in China. I know one thing, she knows me better than I know myself. I need to smarten up my act quickly!

"Maccy Tamryn, come here ya bugger, I need a word."

"Now what?"

"Thank you young man, t'was a real bleddy treat."

188

"It was Bert, you can say that again."

"You didn't tell me everything."

"There's a damn good reason for that, Bert."

"And what would that be?"

"I didn't know everything myself mate."

"Get on with you now and don't come back here with empty hands!"

"I won't."

"Where did you get all that bacon, boy?"

"Same place I always do Bert, I still have my key."

"You pinched the café's bleddy bacon?"

"Naw, I swapped it. I left a couple of nice plump lobsters in the café fridge. I hope they don't get out mind. They were pretty bleddy fresh."

"How bleddy fresh?"

"They was kicking and screaming a tad when I left."

You bad bugger!"

"Keep your boots clean, Bert."

"Are you gonna marry her, Maccy?"

"Wouldn't you?"

"Yes, I bleddy would boy, now bugger off, I've got a woman to talk to myself."

"Thank you, yank."

"Don't mention it Brit, it was my pleasure. Don't expect it all the time, then you won't be too darned disappointed."

"I could never be that, darlin'."

"Road, Maccy."

"Where is it maid?"

"You're on the wrong bleddy side!"

"Wait up, you bleddy yanks are on the wrong side every time you drive anywhere."

I feel there could be no better start to a day. Once again she has surprised me. She can shoot, kick, sing, make my feet tingle and she can rope cows. That is one hell of a combination. On the downside, she can't cook or drive on the right side of the road. She can swear too. She calls it cussing!

189

"That's a damn lie, I bleddy can so. I don't swear when I'm driving so think on, we're nearly home."

So much for thinking aloud. How the women do that! On second thoughts, I don't want to know. I put my foot down but only on the accelerator. There's me thinking butter wouldn't melt in her mouth!

Author's notes:

*This is explained in 'The Mermaid and Bow' by this author.

**A traditional yurt or ger is a portable, round tent covered with skins or felt and used as a dwelling by several distinct nomadic groups in the steppes of Central Asia. The structure comprises an angled assembly or latticework of pieces of wood or bamboo for walls, a door frame, ribs, and a wheel possibly steam-bent. In Russia it is simply called 'Yurta'.

Chapter Seventeen

Lenny gets his Goat.

"Lenny, what have you got there mucker?"

"Tis my new pal, pal!"

"Right mate and does that mean it's yours, you do own it, it's family?"

"Tis right what you say buddy. I got 'n bleddy cheap mind. T'wadn't a lot!"

"Taking it for a walk then Lenny, a bit of exercise?" To be fair, it is a lovely looking animal. A bit scrawny, a bit leggy, a youngster if I'm not mistaken.

"I am, they said at the animal rescue centre it would need plenty of exercise. I'll let it off the lead when I get 'n away from the road and such. They did say his mother did die when it was born, poor maid. They had to hand rear this little one. Poor little pup. Sad idn't it!"

"It is very sad matey, is it a girl or a boy?"

"Tis a boy Maccy, I believe. I didn't think to ask, I weren't bothered. Soon as I saw the little'n, I did decide to 'ave 'n. I couldn't bleddy leave 'n there."

"What's its name then mate, what have you called it?"

"I 'aven't come up with a name yet, I'm thinking about it mind."

"What breed is it?"

"'Tis a mongrel, I reckon. I haven't never seen another like it, have you?"

"I honestly haven't mate, never." Not quite the truth. I don't like to lie to my best friend, this is one of those times it's better I do. Are you gonna show it?"

"How do you mean, Maccy. You can see it, can't you?"

"Oh yes mate, I can. I mean like, Royal Cornwall, at the showground next summer."

"Would you show it, Maccy?"

"No mate, I wouldn't. I don't think I would want anyone to see it. Anyway I don't believe they have a category for such. They might do but I 'aven't heard about it. What will you feed it, Lenny?"

"Usual puppy food until it gets older I suppose. Just the normal stuff, biscuits and a beef bone sometimes."

"It might be a vegan, Lenny."

"Knaw, it's a bleddy puppy, Maccy. It haven't been imported."

"Well buddy, gotta get on, loads to do mate. You two look after each other."

"Will do. Gonna take him for a run and play with his ball. So what do you think I should call him, what would you call him mucker?"

*Sotto voce "I'd call him a goat, Lenny. How about Billy?"

"What did you say, Maccy? I didn't catch that."

"I said it's a bit cold for a pup, get him a nice warm coat. If I was you, I'd call him Billy, Lenny."

"That's a good name Maccy, thank you buddy. Come on Billy Lenny, good boy. Fetch!"

"Wait a minute Lenny, before you go."

Dear Lenny, he is my oldest friend. I love him to bits, though I wouldn't want to go any further. Lenny is like his new friend, easily led, or perhaps not if you get my meaning. My mate has bought himself a baby goat. I can't wait until it's fully grown, it will eat him out of house and home, maybe worse. In fact it will most likely eat his home. I didn't have the heart to tell him they don't show goats at the Royal Cornwall Show, not as far as I know anyway. Someone will have to inform my mate as to what he has. I won't look forward to it, I just hope some other bugger else will point out his mistake to him when I'm not about.

On the positive side, the Kid could make a nice Spiced Moroccan stew, lovely lean meat, a few shallots and other bits and pieces chucked in. I wouldn't mention this to him either. It's a good job it isn't a female. Lenny is rather touchy with regards to his female friends and relatives. Anyway, my friend has made his bed and he shall have to lie in it. Certainly until the goat eats it, which someday soon it surely will.

"Now then Lenny, I need you to get some bulbs to help brighten up the place. Make it more cheerful. We want them everywhere, front, back and on the roof if possible, in the toilets. Some little ones around the bar too."

"That's a good idea, mucker. It would be more inviting and let people know where we are and we're here, idn't us."

"You got it Lenny, the more colourful the better. So the place stands out, can't be missed."

"I will go to the garden centre, they sell everything in that place."

"Now you're talking, Lenny. You get on with that when you're finished playing with your erm... friend. I'll order the not so expensive well travelled seafood."

"Gotcha mate. I might need some help, Maccy. Do you have anyone spare?"

"Male or female?"

"One or the other, a woman would be better I would think. They do know about such things."

"Let me know when you do have the bulbs and I'll send Lavinia out to help you. Alice can look after the pub while you and Lavinia do the donkey work outside. Shouldn't take you long. You will need a ladder to hang them up high so they can hang down low over the outside walls. You might need to borrow the vicar's ladder."

"That'll be in the churchyard mucker."

"I want it looking nice and bright Lenny and colourful. How did you know there was a ladder in the churchyard, Lenny?"

"Your brother Dusty tried to sell it to me once. He said it had only had one owner."

"Who might that have been then?"

"Dusty said it was you mucker. What did you buy a ladder for, Maccy?"

"I didn't buy it, I borrowed it to get up on the church roof. You were there. It wasn't my ladder; I was needing one at the time, Lenny. You should know better, never buy anything from my brother. How is Alice and the tacker?"

"They are both grand, Maccy. Boy's growing up 'ansome. Not much like his dad though. I never wanted to get up on the church roof. Dusty just asked me if I wanted to buy the ladder."

"What would you have done with it?"

"It's bleddy obvious, I'd climb up it mate, but somewhere else."

"Good thinking but don't buy anything offen my brother. Dusty would sell you anything that idn't nailed down. Good job you didn't give him any cash."

"So where did you get the ladder mucker?"

"From out of the vicar's shed."

"Why didn't you ask to borrow it?"

"Because the vicar would 'ave wanted me to make a donation to help fix the church roof!"

"If you were going up there anyway, you could have killed two birds with one stone and done it for him."

"No I couldn't. You told me there was only the one gull up there."

"How did you knaw I was there?"

"You were down below waiting for me to jump off mate remember? Let's get this work done as soon as we can mate, make the mermaid happy. You can't beat a happy mermaid!"

"You're right, you can't beat a mermaid mucker, tis bad luck. The boy reminds me of someone, Maccy."

"He doesn't me, Lenny." I beg to differ about the boy myself. I believe he looks just like his dad. I can't tell my mate that. He would string me up until they fall off!

"It will be done mucker, leave it to us. I will find someone with a donkey, it might come in useful. I would never beat a mermaid Maccy, tidn't on. They can put a curse on folk, anything could happen! I'll just look for the donkey, it'll be good company for Billy Lenny. Now I best get off and find me the vicar's bleddy ladder and I'll bring back a hammer."

"You do that Lenny, you can give kids rides on it then and make some money that way. Dusty will 'ave the ladder." I shouldn't joke about it, but Lenny will never find a donkey around these parts. He'd have to go to Clovelly. I don't think he knows where Clovelly is. I only have a rough idea myself. It's somewhere north of here. My brother is cleverer than I thought. The vicar is unlikely to be happy.

"Kids can't ride on a ladder Maccy, it would be dangerous."

"What you say is true, Lenny. Speak to you later buddy, okay? Hang on Lenny, what do you need a hammer for?"

"Bleddy 'ell, Maccy, your memory idn't good. You said Dusty will sell anything if it idn't nailed down."

"Just forget about the hammer and get the bulbs, mate."

I need to talk to Jack and Miss America about doing the same kind of makeover at the Maltsters.

"Plenty of colour Lenny, don't forget. You'll need carrots too!"

"I will do as you say mate. I'm not bleddy hungry."

This is a turn up for the books. If Lenny isn't doing anything, he's usually eating something or just about to, or he could be with a maid and doing both. 'Not hungry' doesn't sound right coming out of Lenny's mouth. Mostly something is going in.

"Not for you, for your friend and the donkey if you find one. They might both be vegetarian, you never know."

"Do you think so?"

"Could be. Best to be on the safe side, Lenny. See you later. Have fun!"

I tell the yank the same as I had told Lenny. Luckily she jumps at the idea. Peter makes some ridiculous comment about flowers.

"Why not Maccy, I want roses and such around the door."

"It's a pub, you can have roses in the beer garden. I need lights around the pub, so folks can see what they're bumping into when they leave. They won't want to bump into bleddy flowers. They'll be stealing them to give to their wives at breakfast time because they were bleddy late home. It's what I would do dear."

"Not everybody is like you Brit, thank the lord. I sure will remember you said that."

"I didn't knaw you were religious?"

"You do now, you'll need to be soon if you 'ain't careful."

"Idn't careful. It's 'idn't' maid!"

"How can something be 'idn't?"

"Don't ask so many bleddy questions, maid."

"I 'idn't your damn maid."

"That's better, see, you're getting used to it already You'll be a local in no time. God 'elp us all."

"I heard that!"

I suddenly receive a lightbulb moment; quite relevant I suppose. Rooms! We need rooms to let for the emmets when they come visiting. We'll try not to keep them too long. I'll tell them come and stay, have a good kip and a bit of crib, play with the jellyfish and bugger off back from whence you came. Take your bleddy rubbish home with you.

I need to get all the men working together, we need to be getting rooms ready for letting at the Mermaid and Bow in Padstow. When they finish the first, there they can come to the Maltsters and do the same. Backwards and forwards one at a time. It's going to take a while. I'm thinking all the ladies can man the bars and kitchens, all the men can do the renovations. Maybe the other way round? I am fearful of being sexist owing to the amount of birds - I mean ladies - around here. I need to bring everyone together and explain what's going to happen. Lenny might need the hammer and the ladder now.

I'll ask the yank to draw up rotas. I'm not certain she can read. Maybe she can't write? I never asked. She'll know, she goes to church. I won't go into that for now. I try not to talk about things I don't know anything about. There's only one way to find out, though to be fair, she does own a personal computer. So do I. I have little idea what to do with it. It's been a while since I shut the lid on it. Does anyone know? Come to think of it, I think I sold it. It didn't work properly, no one sent me any emails. It was like I didn't exist!

I call all the staff together to explain my intentions. "We need to get rooms ready. We'll start with the worst ones. First at the Mermaid, you, you, you and you two. We need Lavinia, and you Jill, to manage the bar and food here. We can't afford to close. Me and the yank with Jill can keep things going here at the Maltsters for now.

"Can't I go there"

There's always one, Lavinia is definitely one! "No maid. You're not going anywhere."

"That's a shame!"

"Yank, you might have to go there at some point but no fighting."

"Okay, sounds good. Shame about the fighting, I'll try and behave Brit, I sure don't fight more than once a day regular."

"We'll need some rota systems worked out if you could do that maid?"

"What about the kid?"

"Dusty will be busy on his own stuff most of the time."

"Not that kid Maccy, MJ. What's he going to do?"

"He'll look after the ducks and feed them when he gets home from school, I'll make sure."

"If you're gonna be checking up on me, why don't you feed them yourself?"

"Because I already have enough to do, MJ."

"I got stuff to do too. You're getting old!"

"That's good, isn't it, I'm supposed to?"

"You had forgotten your own son, Maccy Tamryn. How could you do that?"

"No, well maybe, not really. I thought you two had stuff to do. I didn't forget him."

"We do. You're off the hook, just. We're going to go and see Lenny and Mervyn about our fish first off. See you later. Don't do anything I wouldn't."

Think it's a bit late to tell me that now! I'm feeling a tad nervous. She has taken the wind out of my sails with her announcement. There is nothing I can do about it, except keep my bum from squeaking on a regular basis until she gets back. I am dependant on Alice also for the foreseeable future. I hadn't reckoned on this. I'm not yet ready for life to bite me on the arse. Right now, it does seem to be nibbling away.

It's a surprise to me when they return so early. They have been gone less than a couple of hours. I look for any sign of a sign I might need to resign. None is forthcoming and I relax nervously.

"Fish!"

"Where?"

"In the back of the car, in black bags."

"What, you're joking'. It's a bit bleddy cruel. They'll be bleddy dead by now. We need them to be able to swim love, we need happy breathing fish."

"It's not. No they won't. They will be."

She's beginning to remind me of Lenny now. Whatever he has must be contagious. They're all going down with it. "Will what?"

"Swim happy, the black bags are in buckets of water. Had to cover them somehow as they kept trying to jump out."

"Because they knew you were bleddy driving on the wrong side of the road."

"No they didn't. They couldn't see in the darned front."

"They were jumping so they could see what was in front." I know how they were feeling. Only these fish are coldblooded. Maybe they didn't know. "Why are you talking funny?"

"Let's get them in the pond Maccy, before they get bored by your constant complaining."

"Can't 'til the kid has made sure the nets are fish proof. They can go in the bath for now."

"One of those buckets is full off eels. Lenny says the Londoners like them."

"They do, but they come in jelly. They eat jellied eels. We can't keep them in buckets."

"I know how to make jello. Where will you keep them if they're not in buckets?"

"We call it jelly. I told you, in the bath!"

"No, not in the bath. No way! The main thing is we now have some darned fish. Another thing, eels breed fast, much quicker in warm water. Lenny isn't as stupid as you look."

"True, he did well." Lenny always does somehow. He just goes about it in a different way to everyone else. "It's jelly, Jellied Eels. Londoners won't eat 'Jello' Eels. They won't know what the bleddy hell you're talking about. What do you know about eels?"

"Eels don't just live in bleddy Great Britain. We got eels in the States too, Fish man!"

"You're not in the States now, someone else can eat them! Dusty, make sure that mesh is small holed boy, we don't want them getting out, use chicken wire, two layers at least, maybe three. Get Peter to help you." Why does it take the best part of a day to discuss eels when I have no idea what they look like as yet? Slimy and long, I guess. The less slimy and the longer the better would be useful. We will have an eel menu, jellied eels and eel pie. * French Matelot stew. Smoked eels, we can smoke them ourselves. Personally I would rather have a cigar. I can't stand smoked salmon just doesn't do it for me.

"We can get up eely dad, go to bed eely. Have an eely Christmas!"

I ignore my son. A good sense of humour is sure to appear one of these days. "Yank, Lenny is a bleddy genius. We'll make a fortune." Lenny has stumbled on something here. Once again he has come up trumps and probably doesn't even realise it. He may have known he was stumbling but not why.

"Dusty, less tents mate, more eels." I explain to my brother he will make more money from eels than he will from tents. Cooking eels can't be easier. Boil for twenty minutes, throw in some chopped shallots, black pepper and gelatine, allow to go cold and hey, thingy, presto, Jellied Eels! I tell him to make it a rush job as I might want a bath later. I make a mental note regarding the building of an extension. It seems like twenty people live here at the Maltsters all of a sudden. We only have one bath and it's about to be filled with live eels.

"So, how do you cook them, Maccy?"

"Just chop them into steaks and let them jump into a pan of hot olive oil. Twenty minutes in the pan. An hour to get them cold, straight on a plate. Heads still on so they can see where the pan is. Bit of rice and Bob's your thingy, uncle."

"No, not heads."

"Yes heads, you won't have to behead them with your pistols like you did the Catfish. The heads stay on. Eels should go on a plate proudly, with their heads held high, it's tradition."

"That's gross, I won't be eating them."

"They might not want you to, me neither. We will sell them, not straight away. We need the ones we have already to breed. We're gonna need another channel to allow the stream to keep running. The water will need heating, or they won't breed. I'll get on to Padraig for a JCB. I had better speak to farmer Bird."

Another channel beside the one we already have will allow the pond to be shut off. In the winter if there is nondescript water running into it, it won't be warm enough for the eels to prosper. I just hope Farmer Birds' cows don't eat them all. To be fair, steak and eel pie does sound interesting. They probably won't unless he bought the beasts in the East End. There are one or two in EastEnders apparently!

Lenny has done us proud today. I doubt he knew it at the time, you never know with Lenny, he might have. Lenny doesn't do straight questions and answers. Lenny doesn't do straight talking at all. I doubt he ever will.

There is a mixture of other breeds in the buckets, such as Roach. Bream, Perch, other odds and ends. Soon the stream and the pond will come to life. I didn't ask Lenny where he got them all from, I didn't want to know. The yank says she doesn't know either. They might have come down in the last shower. That's acceptable, it's happened before!

"Lenny, it's me bud."

"Me who?"

"Me bleddy ow, Maccy, you daft sod. We want some more eels. We need more."

"What's wrong with the ones I got you?"

"Nothing wrong with them, that's why I want more."

"I don't understand mucker."

"Neither do I Len. I still need more eels. Where did you get them from?"

"Out of the water mate."

"I knaw that. I don't know where the water is, do I?"

"I'm with you mate. I don't know where it is either now. I'll ask around."

"Why don't you bleddy know?"

"That's easy buddy, it has moved on. It isn't there anymore."

"Lenny, I will come and see you. Don't move."

"I idn't moving mucker, I like it here. Why would I move anywhere else? I'm born and bleddy bred!"

"That's a matter of opinion. I'll see you later Lenny, you can move now."

"I don't want to move Maccy, I told 'ee. What do you want me to do with all these bulbs mucker?"

"Not now, just put them up a bit at a time when you can."

"Whatever you say, Maccy.

Author's notes:

* Matelote is a French fish soup (also described as a stew or chowder.) It is made from freshwater fish, unlike the better-known Bouillabaisse, which is made from saltwater seafood. The fish used are eel, salmon, and carp. The broth is based on fish stock, and either red or white wine. The fish should be skinned and filleted. The disposable parts are first used to make stock, the rest of the fish is used in the soup after the broth is strained. Eel heads should be served to attention but not consumed.

Chapter Eighteen

Messing about on a Lake

"Maccy, have you seen Lenny, mate?"

"I have, Michael. Why do you ask?"

"When did you last see him?"

"Just before he took the bleddy goat to play football. It might be best he doesn't buy him a shirt. I suppose a scarf wouldn't hurt, unless the animal is double jointed!"

"What are we gonna do, Maccy. Why?"

"The bleddy animal will most likely eat it. He doesn't knaw does he?"

"Someone should tell him. He's up Style Field throwing a ball to it. He was, but as soon as the goat got hold of the ball, it bleddy ate it. I came away sharpish."

"What's the beast doing now then?"

"Not much really, just eating grass when I left."

"What about the goat?"

"It's no joke Maccy, Lenny needs a bleddy license for that thing."

"What about the goat, I think it needs one more. You must tell him, Michael."

"Can you be serious. Me, why should I bleddy tell him?"

"Cos you're supposed to look after your flock, you know about animals."

"It's a bleddy goat, not a lamb. If it was a bleddy lamb, we could eat it on Sunday. Goats are the sign of the other guy; aren't they!"

"Whoa, why didn't I think about that? We could do Lamb Shanks as a one-off special. We could do breast of lamb another time when the animal is feeling better. Anyway, good luck Michael, I'll see you later, Mikey."

It's time for a pint at the Mermaid. As soon as I enter, the Admiral collars me. His news is not of the good variety.

"Maccy, I need to sell the old tub, lad. She must be moved from the quay quick sharp. The old thing isn't seaworthy anymore. The harbour master has decided she must go. It'll be a sad day old chap, a sad day. Dammit Maccy, it's so unfair at our time of life. What will I do without her? She may not be seaworthy, but we don't want to go to sea. We just want a quiet life. Padstow harbour is getting too full of the damned emmets and she must be moved aside, Maccy."

"Are you talking about the lovely Alma, Admiral?"

"Of course not. She has plenty of nautical miles in her tank yet, let me tell you."

"It's okay Admiral, no need, I was just joking."

The old feller is dispensing a tear from an eye. I'm not sure how to handle this, I have never seen him in such a state. Now, I'm not sure if the Admiral is talking about his boat or his wife. I'm not even certain they are married. I've known them since I was a kid, but I don't have a clue. Most of us just know the odd couple as the Birdseyes! It must be the boat, though Alma has tried to give me a tug once or twice in the past, tried but failed I hasten to add. I don't know where she's been, I guess a lot of others do. Anyway, it's none of my business.

The admiral followed me while chuntering away about the injustice of it all. I get the remainder of the ins and outs, mostly the outs. Just the one fortunately.

"Leave me 'ave a think, Admiral. Must be something we can do. We'll come up with something old feller."

"Thank you Maccy, now it's past the noon mark, I have to take a beverage old boy. See you later."

The yank is with Alice at the kids' park at the top of Padstow Hill. I caught up with them as I cut across the ancient greens of the old stately home that had once stood there, before being ripped apart and sold a hundred and fifty years ago. The house was stripped, everything was sold off in lots. The whole lot, fixtures and fittings being sold to all and sundry to repay debts. I told the yank the Admiral and Almas' story. She had met them only briefly.

"What can you do, Maccy? They will be homeless without the boat. You have to think of something."

"I will if you give me a chance. We'll go see Lenny." We continued walking up the narrow street.

It's quiet and the bucket carriers are managing without my mate. He's eating. Lenny eats when there's nothing else to do. He eats in bed, eats in the bath. There might be a sandwich going around in the mixer. As far as I know there is only two occasions when he doesn't eat at all. Both would be whilst in bed. Lenny most likely dreams about food while I have nightmares.

"Lenny, have you heard about the Birdseyes, mate?"

"Yes I 'ave, buddy. Bleddy sad job, tidn't on."

"We do need to get the Birdseyes boat back to Little Petrock. Times running out. I'll get the tractor sorted with old man Bird. Forget everything else for now, Lenny. We need you, me, Peter and Dusty. That should be enough. Couple of hours it'll all be shipshape."

"I thought it was already shipshaped."

"Early Lenny, we'll meet you at the slipway. Let's say eight o'clock."

"Eight o'clock, bang on Maccy. I'll be there at eight o'clock. Shall I bring my waders for when we meet at eight o'clock?"

"Why do you keep saying it mate?"

"You said we should say eight o'clock."

"T'wadn't what I meant, Lenny. Yeah, bring your waders, you might even need them." Lenny must be sickening for something. It might be serious. Ah well, I'll just have to make the most of it. It won't last.

"Too true mate, I've never used them before."

"We gotta do something. I'll sort the tractor out with farmer Bird when I get back to the Maltsters."

"You taking up farming, Maccy?"

"No Lenny, to move the bleddy Birdseyes' boat."

"Where to, you can't put a tractor in the quay mate, there'll be a right kick off."

"We can't, as you say. Since they built the bloody gates, it's always full of bleddy water. We'll tug it to the slipway with rope and pull it up. Then we'll tow it to the Maltsters and put it on the lake, what do you think, Yank?"

"I can drive a tractor."

"Through the streets, Miss Yank?"

"Sure can! 'Miss Yank'? Leave it out Lenny."

"I don't know what she means Maccy, leave what out?"

"Take no notice Lenny, she's been listening to the bleddy emmets. They say it all the time, but I don't think they do what they say. Lenny, you can help, yeah?"

"Course I can, mate."

"Well you can start by not calling the yank, Miss Yank, don't do it again. You're not in Gone with the bleddy Wind. If you carry on, I'll have to do it and I ain't, I idn't. No way! Jesus, we'll all be at it."

"Take no notice Lenny, he sure ain't your boss right now."

"Why's that Miss, er, yank?"

"You're on a lunch break. Tell him to do one, Lenny! I might tell him the same in a moment, goddam Limey!"

"Do one, Maccy! Can I call you Miss something else then?"

"Don't push it, Lenny!"

This is what's known as a sea-change. I doubt I'll ever go to Kansas again, it's bad luck. Every time I go, I come back with something nasty. First time it was my brother, Dusty. Second time it was with a long-distance hangover. No, I wasn't going to say lorry driver. Third time it was another of the same. Then Yank turns up by special delivery. She's here now and encouraging my best mate to mutiny! Maybe I should call Bligh back from Plymouth, he should be used to mutinies. He was the landlord of the Mermaid before I attained it. He tells anyone who might be interested he's related to Bligh of the Bounty. He could be! I might move onto the boat with the Admiral and

Alma. On second thoughts, I won't. My imagination has begun to work overtime. I need to stop it now before it runs completely amok!

"So, I'll get the tractor sorted from the old git next door. I'll call you when we're ready mate."

"Call me what? I never knew they had a tractor next door. A bugger to park around here!"

I turn my back, I can't take a lot more. Sometimes I think Lenny is doing it on purpose. I don't think I will ever know and to be honest, I like it that way. He should not be informed.

"Yank, we're going."

"Why do you do it, Lenny?"

"Why do you think, I enjoy it. So does Maccy, least I think he does. I believe he thinks he does. We could both be wrong I suppose!"

"Don't stop Lenny, don't you dare stop, it keeps him on his toes, exactly where he should be!"

"I'll do as you say, maid!"

"Stop calling me maid!"

"Okay, Miss Yank, but I 'aven't never called you, I don't even know your bleddy number."

"Maccy!"

"It's your own fault, yank. You ask for it. I'm going. Lenny, I'll call you later."

"Just call me drekly!"

"No Lenny, I'm not doing this now, I don't 'ave bleddy time. We need to sort the Birdseyes' bleddy boat out."

"Sort their boat out. That's a new one on me. So what 'ave it done wrong? Can't you just 'ave a quiet word with it. There idn't no need to get bleddy violent."

"Bye, Lenny!"

I need a cigar, I can't even smoke in my own pub anymore. Can't swear, can't tell my staff what to do, though Lenny rarely takes any notice anyway, can't begin to think what I can't do next. She can spit everywhere, curse and fight in the street, I can't do a damn thing. I can smoke a cigar!

"What the heck is that damned smell, Maccy?"

Now I can't even speak too soon!

She had caught me up. Too soon, I spoke too soon. Come to think of it, I hadn't spoken at all. I didn't say anything aloud. I spoke sotto voce. She is psychic. Now what do I do? How is it Dusty can fall in shit and come up smelling of some damn flower? I fall in shit and come up smelling of shit plus cigar smoke! Life is just not fair. She sent me mad when I couldn't find her. Now she's here, she is worse. I do need to let the family know what's happening regarding the Birdseyes.

It's settled, we'll tow the Birdsall's boat up the Camel. We'll use the tractor to tow it across next door's field and into ours and on to the lake. Damn, I was hoping to piss off the emmets who wander around town wondering which gull to feed next. I'll have to think of some other way to do that now. I still need to tell ma and the Kid. I need to make sure to do it when the tide's out.

I found Dusty helping out at the Maltsters' bar, it is ideal. "Brother, how's things with the maid?"

"Which one, Maccy?"

"The one that got you out of trouble. The one with the helicopter."

"Yeah, she's good. Busy at the moment, she is away flying it. Why?"

"Wondered if you are still seeing her."

"I haven't gone blind brother. When I can."

"Does she do any work on the side?"

"On the side of what?"

"Don't you start, I've had enough of that other tosser today. I need a boat moving. The Birdseyes' tug."

Where to?"

"Here, on the lake."

"Course you do."

"You can tow it round to the creek, she can lift it over the land bridge and onto the water. It's not on the cheap Kid, just makes life easier. We can bring it by road, but it'll take ages and will most likely bring the village to a bleddy standstill. Helicopter can do it in minutes. If she can't borrow one, I'll hire one and she can fly it!"

"I'll talk to her. You're nuts Maccy, do you have a clue what it costs to hire a bleddy helicopter and fly it?"

"A fair bit."

"About five grand an hour, plus my cut!"

"Tell her we need to be quick about it, fifteen minutes should be enough. Leave it with you. You don't get a cut. Give her my best brother."

"No chance!"

"On second thoughts Dusty, leave it, it's too much fuss anyway. We'll go back to plan A and use the tractor."

I call the carpenter. "Bessie, we need a mooring and a timber gangway to it on the big pond buddy. We need it quick mate."

"Thought you said it was a lake."

"We need a lot of rain."

"How will that help, Maccy?"

"Because then it will be a lake."

"Fair enough. Need to get some timber. I need the same for the pontoon malarkey."

"You do your measuring up Bessie, let me know what you need, I'll get it ordered. Now the walkway for the pontoon needs to reach out almost to the centre of the thingy, lake but not quite. The other one doesn't. About ten feet from the shore should be plenty. It's only for the Birdseyes' boat. It will need to be sturdy. The boat will most likely never move again once it's here."

"The Birdseyes' boat? How are you gonna get that here?"

"Tractor mate. We have to. They don't have anywhere else to live, here is as good a place as any."

"Okay Maccy, you're the boss!"

"No Bessie, Ma's the boss and when she 'idn't around it could be anyone! I have left it late enough. As soon as Peter is finished at the Mermaid, he can help you here, Lenny too."

"Please Maccy, not Lenny too. What happened to Lenny One?"

"No one knows the answer to that, Bessie. Maybe Lenny One is as he came?"

"That's a tad deep even for you, Maccy."

"You're right, I don't even know where it came from. I'll order the timber. We need to move fast, Bessie." Everything is in place almost. Bessie can get it serviceable for now. The Birdseyes will have a new home. I hope they like ducks! I need to inform the powers that be.

"Ma, I'm gonna bring the Birdsalls' boat here and put it on the lake.

"How big a boat is it?"

"You've seen it, ma. Big enough to make the water come up higher, big enough to turn the pond into a proper lake, almost. It'll make it deeper. Kill two birds with one stone that way!"

"I dare say you know what you're doing, boy."

sotto voce Like hell I do! "I don't have a clue but so long as it's still floating when we get it in here, it should be good enough."

It's an early start. Everything and everyone is in place. What can go wrong?

"Okay, let's do this." The yank, not to be left out, is in the driving seat. She reverses the tractor down the slipway while the rest of us pull the vessel towards it. We get it to swing around just in time as Dusty enters the harbour whilst breaking the speed limit.

"Okay Maccy, leave plenty of rope there, we don't want them banging into each other. It's at least a mile to Sea Mills. Tide is still coming in which is good."

"You boys can get back to Little Petrock and we'll meet you at the creek. Peter, get everyone on the tractor, take them back to Little Petrock, I'm going round with Dusty. Don't let Lenny drive the tractor, you hear me!"

"I ain't no damn boy, Maccy Tamryn."

"Hallelujah to that, yank! You drive it, Lenny can sit on the mudguard."

"Damn you! Who put you in charge, Brit?"

"I did!"

"Rod Stewart didn't know he was bleddy living. It's all plain sailing from here, Dusty."

"Not so bleddy sure about that, Maccy. Think you forgot something brother."

"I did, what did I bleddy forget?"

"You forget to tell Alma and the Admiral, Maccy. They're both waving at you, with the coffee bean shuffle. At least Alma is. I'm not sure what the bleddy Admiral is doing, I don't think he does either."

"Oh bollocks, I did. Ah well, sing up Dusty. 'A life on the ocean wave, a life on the ocean wave!' Are they smiling yet?"

"No, not yet brother. Did I ought to slow down?"

"No way, put your bleddy foot down. They'll be hanging over the side in a minute and it won't matter much after that. I can't think of every bleddy thing." 'Hey ho and up she rises.' "Dusty, is that Rock over there?"

"Yep, I believe it is."

"Be careful not to bump into it, we'll never hear the bleddy last of it."

"Does it matter, Maccy?"

"Not really brother. It couldn't look any worse, could it! Mind that dead cow there kid."

"Where did that come from?"

"Most likely it fell out of the abattoir or rolled down a hill. I can't see how they can stand up on a hill in the first place. Why don't they fall over?"

"I couldn't say Maccy, it's a bleddy mystery to me."

"It surely is brother. Here's the creek mouth, Dusty. Can we get up it okay?"

"Sure we can bro', we've been up the creek plenty of times. One more won't hurt. I doubt it'll be the last."

"Shit Creek!"

"Where have I heard that before?"

"Is that Alice and Lavinia sunbathing over there?"

"Could be, shall I pull in closer?"

"You could do but I don't think they'll be very happy boy. They are in the buff I do believe. Maybe a tad closer wouldn't hurt. Is that the same cow?"

"How the hell should I know. They all look the same. Perhaps they have telescopic legs Maccy, that's how they can stand on a hillside."

"Could be youngster. Morning girls, you're looking well, have you been poorly? Bleddy hell Dusty, there's no need for them to talk that way. I dunno what the world is coming to brother. I'll have a word with Michael about them. Let's get this bitch up the creek. The Birdseyes are probably on the gin by now or they might just think they are with all the rocking and rolling."

Dusty manages to steer the hulk into the narrows where the tractor can pick up the slack. The boat will need to be dragged across the land bridge and back into the lake. Between us we should be able to keep her upright, it isn't that far.

"There you go Admiral, Alma. Home sweet home."

"Maccy, you have saved us young man. We can't thank you enough."

"Just share the gin out, Alma."

She sidled over to me. "I could thank you more than enough, Maccy!"

"I know you could, Alma. There's no need darlin', I appreciate the offer."

The tub settled next to the almost completed pontoon perfectly. Bessie knows his stuff.

"That was a big crowd around the harbour to be sure, Maccy."

"T'was brother, very gratifying. Lenny, did you take any of their names?"

"Naw Maccy, I like the one I do already 'ave!"

"So do I Lenny, so do I. Good job mucker."

Chapter Nineteen

No, never, no bleddy way!

"No chance Dusty, it isn't gonna happen, never, comprende!"

"What the bleddy hell does that mean?"

"I bleddy told you once. I don't have a clue. Never mind. I idn't 'aving it. No sir!"

The kid reminds me of someone. I might call my Ma 'ma', but mostly when she isn't around. I call her Joy when she is. Every morning when I see her for the first time, it's 'Morning Joy', not to be confused in any way with 'Morning Glory!' To a stranger she is Ms Tamryn, she is my mother and she is my brother's mother! She is also prone to being a tad straitlaced but soft on the kid, soft in the head towards the kid more like. They are like each other apart from Dusty does have a slight Irish lilt to his voice, thanks to our father. Ma doesn't try to impress younger members of her sex obviously, or ours come to that.

"It's still no, Dusty." I know I'm losing. I must attempt to keep my dignity. To be fair, I've always had a problem with that. "You don't have the first idea how to run a bleddy campsite. You couldn't run a bleddy bath! Which reminds me, do you actually bathe at any point?"

"We got the space behind this place, Maccy. We do have two good fields out there. Only the rabbits use them. We got running water, well, not running, water that doesn't run very fast."

"Either one sounds like a bleddy red Indian chief. The bleddy rabbits won't be happy. Dusty, the locals will kick off big time, you know what Michael's like and the vicar. It's a bad idea. What did I tell you about mentioning rabbits?"

"Just because you didn't think of it. The fields are there doing nothing, Mac. We don't even have any bleddy cows. What you told me was, not to say, 'rabbits on a boat when they're being stroked by a woman'."

"There we are then! And, it's still no!"

"Fair enough. I'll do it now and tell you about it later, how would that be? Better early than late, better late than never. Maccy, how would a rabbit know it's on a boat?"

"Don't ask stupid questions. Yank, what do you think?" Sometimes she appears at the right time.

"Don't you all drag me into this. It's between you and your brother. I'm not taking bleddy sides. How many tents are you thinking of Dusty, what about electricity, advertising, promoting it, publicity?"

"A dozen maybe to start with, should be enough, caravans next year maybe. Easy, gas! I thought about all them things, maid."

"It seems like you have planned it already, Dusty. Anyway, I ain't getting into this. What about plumbing, showers, security? You all gotta think of all this stuff. Toilets?"

"I thought I said no." I did, resistance is futile. Now the Texan has jumped on the wagon and not a band in sight.

"Think about it, Maccy. The boy is your spit. What do you expect? Let the kid have a go."

A reminder, if needed, spit must be the most popular word and personal exercise in the States. I think about it, I don't like it. I'm outnumbered. I wish I'd thought of it myself. "I'll think about it, that's all. Now go and find something useful to do. Go and float your boat!"

"Think about it, Maccy. It sounds like a good idea. Twelve tents sure don't sound much, give the kid a chance. Jeez, he ain't even a kid. He's the same age as me dammit!"

"So, it's my fault he acts like a kid! Where did you learn all our old wives' tales anyway? You ain't even a wife yet. It don't make sense!"

"When I met you and your Ma and some other old wives, older wives."

"Ma?"

"Okay, but you know what I mean."

"Camelann Camping Company Limited."

"What?"

"Camelann Camping Company Limited, it's what we'll call it."

"Good idea, Dusty."

"Jesus, why don't you two go into partnership? 'Limited' yeah, that's you alright, good description! Reminds me of when you were at school. I always got C's, not sure you even managed that."

"Cool yank, thanks Maccy."

"Pardners!"

"It's partners!" I know I shouldn't have said it, I just wish I had remembered not to have said it!

"Not where I come from, Pardner!"

"I could see determination in her eyes, it isn't a pretty site.

On thinking about things, my brother may have finally had a good idea. It'll help fill the Maltsters with luck. The pub would gain, I'd gain, we'd all gain. I did lose the argument obviously! Maybe it's no bad thing.

"Okay, we'll do it, a one-year trial, one season."

"And you are? Sorry, it's just me and Dusty. You ain't included. You turned up your nose. We don't need another pardner, do we pardner?"

"I turned my nose up?"

"I just said that!"

"Bleddy Yanks, they get everywhere. They spit everywhere."

"You didn't say that in Kansas, Brit, I sure didn't hear you complaining then. Hey Dusty, we can do fishing stuff in the lake. Your brother tried to fish in Kansas. He never did catch anything though, I had to do it for him. He was too squeamish, too tight to bait his line, or he might have forgotten. He sure did try though. You should have heard the catfish laughing."

"He never caught anything in Padstow either!"

I ignore the taunting and make another mistake. "The Admiral and Alma can do the accounts." What am I saying? Time to open the doors. It's a tactical retreat by me. I might get some peace and quiet behind the bar. I leave them to it. Secretly, I think it's a great idea, I hope they succeed. The yank is fitting in just perfectly.

Lavinia appears and takes over from me at the bar. She smiles suggestively and winks, all the usual innuendos outpour. Ignoring her threats, I get myself a coke, take a cigar and slide out the rear door. A few minutes' walk and I am standing beside the small expanse of water. The water is level which is helpful. The rough ground around it will need flattening somewhat. It shouldn't be too difficult.

The three Muscovys are doing what they do best, take-offs and landings. Families and kids might like watching their antics. The birds are growing fast. They shouldn't be too much trouble; the lake is far enough away from the road through the village. They can have regular wing clips. More birds will be attracted which might be a good thing so long as they leave the eels alone. They'll eat well now the Birdseyes are out here; namely prawns, lemon slices and cherries.

Little Petrock itself hardly changes, the occasional new build or a renovation is about all. It's not easy for the cars to pass each other but they manage, they have to. A lot of cottages would need to be demolished to widen the road. It won't happen in this century. To be fair, there isn't much of it left. They would have to knock the pub down in any case.

On looking around both fields, there doesn't appear that too much needs to be done; a few lumps and bumps to be levelled out, a five-bar gate wants some repairs - Bessie will put that right. The lad was never a close friend at school, though he's done well since joining the crew, we get on and he's a good Chippy. We would need to find another gateway;

two entrances and exits would be useful. At present, there is only one, it is a double entrance. The gap separates two fields, one of which is mine, the other isn't. Not easy! The lake doesn't all belong to me, the opposite land doesn't either. Some negotiating will be needed. We still need some more fish that don't like being caught too often. No need to make it too easy for potential anglers. Hopefully the less they catch, the longer they will stay!

The other half owner of the lake is or was the owner of the cows we lads had ridden some years ago. He may still have the beasts, he may not. It seems he has forgotten the incident. Either that or he needs the money. We talk, discuss and argue. Even the Alsatian seems to listen with his one erect ear, the other is half missing due to an entanglement with a speed boat. The dog was swimming too fast and caught up with the boats' propeller! I half expect the mutt to butt in at any time.

"It's my lake." Bird begins.

"Our lake! We both own half of it. We can hardly have exactly half each. One side might be deeper than the other Now we can go all legal and get solicitors involved, or we can come to an agreement. Solicitors are expensive and this can go on for years, maybe forever. It'll need dredging somewhat, won't be cheap for either of us."

"How much are you willing to pay me, Mr Tamryn?"

"Nothing!"

"Nothing?"

"Yep, near enough!"

"Is that a boat, where did that come from? Is that a boat?"

"Where? Give me a pound, I'll give you one of mine. We share. You'll want water, I'll want water. We put markers on both sides and neither of us cross the line without agreement from the other. The fish might obviously. Deal?" We manage to forget about the boat question.

"Spit!" The old farmer spits and holds out a hand.

"Spat" I agree and offer my own wet hand. "We share the water rights without disagreement?"

"Agreed. That's that. I'll get the deeds drawn up, you get the bottle."

"Fair enough, Brandy?"

"Doubles!"

"Agreed!"

That's the way we do things in these parts. Both parties are happy, and we get a tad pissed. My neighbour must be short of readies as he rolled over easily. As for the cows, they're probably in a burger by now. The Muscovys are frolicking about in the middle of the lake as if they have understood what had just occurred.

"Whose ducks are they?"

"Mine, Jill's, ours."

"What do they taste like?"

"Duck, more than likely."

"Wouldn't mind trying one. I wouldn't mind trying one."

"That's two, I'll reserve you a table at the Maltsters. We're getting pissed together, might as well have a meal together sometime. Give me a shout and I'll sort it drekly." He makes it sound like it can go back on the lake if it doesn't taste too good.

"Will do, Mr Tamryn. Will do. Will do."

"You are?"

"Arthur, Arthur Bird. Arthur Bird! Who does that bleddy boat belong to?"

"What bleddy boat?" So there are two Arthur Birds present which could constitute a whole one.

"That boat, that boat!"

"That boat belongs to my accountant."

"Tell your accountant to count his lucky stars it isn't on my side!"

I ignore the last order, we do need to get on. Arthur Bird, course you are. "I'll get the ball rolling with the land registry." Bird nods, I snigger.

Agreement is reached between us, enough of the brandy has been consumed and we depart on good terms. I resisted the opportunity to borrow a jug of milk. As I walk away from the gateway I hear the old feller cackling as he follows his own path. I wonder if he's pecking at the ground. I decide not to look, he might well be. I don't think I can handle it. I still need to find some more fish. I also need a digger. I didn't have to look far.

Padraig agrees to come up with some ideas about dredging. He too wants a share in the lake. So, the lake belongs to all of us in effect. Dusty has the campsite with all the add ons. We'll provide the water sports. Not sure what they will be, I hear wedding bells once again, waterside weddings. I propose the idea to my partners. Dusty wades in so to speak.

"How deep is the bleddy lake?"

"No idea, you bathe in it, or so you say. One more slimy thing in there shouldn't hurt."

I have enough staff to look after the Maltsters. Lavinia, Jill and Jack can handle anything. Ma and Padraig will be around if required. Dusty will be busy with the sea bus. I need to spend some time in Padstow, it's about time the crew got to know the yank better; they will! We pack a couple of bags and leave. MJ never leaves her side and insists on coming too.

"Time you met the rest of the locals." I begin the guided tour. Not all at once as I want to save some. First stop is the Mermaid and Bow, and Lenny. The yank wanders off with the youngster while Lenny and I get down to fishy business.

"I need some more fish. A couple of dozen, mebbe more. Make sure their gagging."

"Go to the chippy mate, that'd be best. Gagging, you want randy fish? How will I knaw they're gagging?"

"Can't say buddy. They should be living and breathing. Don't forget they need to be freshwater fish. They need to be able to swim."

"I thought they all did unless they're dead, maybe knackered through a lot of swimming. Must take it out of them, all that exercise. How do they sleep?"

"It's a mystery, Lenny. Anyway, we need the breathing and swimming kind. They can sleep all they like out of season."

"Where's Alice?"

"She's gone shopping with the yank. Shouldn't be long, there isn't that many shops left. Shopping in a café doesn't really work."

The huge door of the Mermaid and Bow opens suddenly, the boy appears looking upset. "Dad, the yank and Alice are fighting on the quayside."

Lenny was outside before me. Lenny gets excitable about the women in his life, especially when they're in trouble. The boy is right but there's no need for us to get involved. We stand and watch as the two girls get the better of their adversaries. It is a sight to see. I already knew what Alice was like in a rough and tumble, in more ways than one. I had no idea how the yank could perform in street fighting. If she isn't a 'Black belt of something' I'm a dustman! It was all over far too soon. Two local girls slunk away, battered and bruised. My Texan wife is settling into Cornwall nicely! She crosses her chest with one arm and bows at the departing local girls. I have no idea what it is all about!

"Well done yank, will you teach me that stuff?"

"Sure I will if it's okay with your Dad, MJ. I'm qualified!"

"In what?" I ask. I didn't have a clue what she was doing. I have never seen anything like it. She was like a bad tempered ballerina!

It occurs to me Alice and Miss America are now bosom buddies in a manner of speaking. It is a predicament, with potentially my second wife who has no children becoming friends with Alice. Which means her boy might become friends with my son, who no longer has his mother. I'm gonna be right in the crap one of these days.

"Savate!"

"What the hell is 'Savate?"

"It's pronounced Sav 'at. It's toe fighting. Toes and balance, that's all you need. It's French foot fighting, a martial art where you can only use your feet, your toes. No fighter should kick above or near the groin unless they want to really hurt someone. I was taught by the grandson of a master. Can't tell ya no more than that, it was a promise to my tutor. I can't even disclose his name. I can teach but I can't tell. I am what they call a 'Tireuse. Sav 'ate means 'Old shoe"

I daren't ask any more for fear of finding out too much. She might have to kill me. I hate death, especially when it might be my own impending one. I stay quiet. I refuse to call her an 'old shoe'. I might change my mind at a later date.

"Bleddy hell, what happened there, Maccy?"

"Sorry Lenny, I can't say! It's not allowed." I cross my chest with one arm and bow.

"Maccy Tamryn, don't you dare take the piss or you'll get some of the same!"

"So, Miss America, what else are you good at. I would have asked when we met. I didn't like to while you had a mouthful of watermelon seeds."

"I break horses."

"Maybe you should be more careful in future. They can be valuable."

"I break horses in, so people can ride them, you tosser. Which reminds me."

"What of?"

"I need a horse."

"To break?"

"To break in and ride. You got your own, I want my own."

"Fair enough. You can use ours."

"Oh sure. I need one that can run, can't do that with three damn legs. They're over the hill! I need a young one I can train myself, yours can only run on the spot!"

"How much?"

"No need to worry, I have my own money. I have all I need."

"Yeah, well you don't need any, I have all you need." I lied, at least I think I did, it was a grey lie! Wow, I nearly slipped up then. I won't be doing that again! It seems like I have a monster I didn't even create. "I suppose you'll want a fishing rod too. How much do you have maid?"

"It's a fishing pole, not a rod. I need to get me a mount, I'll start looking. We need stables Maccy, need a paddock. A horse needs its own space. More than you can spend Fish Man!"

I decide not to ask any more questions. I don't think I can take any more, she's scaring me now.

"I need me a four-wheel drive and a box."

"Rolls Royce don't do four-wheel drives as far as I know."

"Darn it! Are you sure?"

"Anything else I can get you ma'am? I got a question for you, Tex."

"Go on, ask!"

"If you're from Texas, why were you in Kansas?" I curse myself for not taking an obvious hint.

"Oh that. Well, my kin had business interests in Kansas, a house too. We lived there, our ranch is there, all the cattle are there. Your stream is the boundary between us."

"Why do you take so long to say your words. It's like waiting for thunder after a flash of lightning."

She glares, I wisely - unusually for me - change tack.

"Boundary? Cattle, how many cattle?"

"You said a question, not half a dozen. Let me think, around forty, last I heard."

"Forty cows? The old git next door has more than that. He did have."

"Forty thousand, Maccy. Mostly for beef. We keep a herd of milk cows too!"

"So, are they born with milk already in them?"

"I'll ignore that. I lost my parents as I told ya. It just leaves me, and you. Lucky me. I should have told ya before Maccy, everything my parents and I had in Kansas is mine. I don't have any siblings. You might be the richest man in Cornwall soon enough; if you play your cards right. I'm selling up the ranch and all. I ain't going back there, everything I need is here. It's one reason I took so long to get here. There was so much to do, lawyers and such, land agents. Anyway, are you listening to me, Fish Man?"

I nod. It was all I could think of. At least I didn't nod off! "So, how much is it worth, this farm of yours. How big is it?"

"Not certain yet. I'm waiting for the papers to get here from the lawyer, might be a while. How big, no idea. I've never seen all of it. Forty thousand acres, I guess that's about one for each cow. Might be less. Anyway, the agent says I should get around the asking price, less the agents' fees and lawyers. Should leave us a tidy amount. Maccy, where are you going?"

"For a swim."

"Where?"

"Where do you think, in my lake." I stop and turn. "One last question. Are you rich?"

"Could be Brit, could be. Does it bother you?"

"Can I think about it? One other thing, you said I might be the richest man in Cornwall. How would that come to be?"

"Not now, Maccy."

Author's note:

*Savate (French pronunciation: [sa'vat]), also known as boxe française, savate boxing, French boxing or French foot-fighting, is a French combat sport that uses the hands and feet as weapons combining elements of English boxing with graceful kicking techniques. Only foot kicks are allowed, unlike some systems such as Muay Thai, which allow the use of the knees or shins. Savate is a French word for "old shoe or boot". Savate fighters wear specially designed boots. A male practitioner of savate is called a tireur while a female is called a tireuse. The sport was once part of the Olympic games. Circa 1924

Chapter Twenty

To be, or not to be?

"What the hell did you do that for, you tosser!" I was looking in the wrong direction and never saw Lenny's uncelebrated impression of Pete Townsend coming. Story of my life!

"What do you think? Stand up, now. You can have some more of the bleddy same."

"I don't need or want any more, Lenny. It's not my bleddy fault."

"Why didn't you bleddy say something?"

"What like, you were sold a pup, only it's a bleddy goat?"

"It's eaten everything, Maccy. There's nothing left!"

"You bought it. Why hit me, go find someone else to lump!"

"If I'd found anyone else, I would've already lumped them. I did find Michael. He locked himself in the bleddy chapel. I didn't buy it. I got it for nothing, t'was a bargain!"

"Wish I was with him, Lenny. He and I could have played snooker all day instead of getting lumped by you. You could give it back for nothing."

"T'was the goat's fault, Maccy. It ate my mother's oven gloves and she couldn't get the chicken out of the bleddy oven. I 'aven't bleddy eaten all day. You knaw what I'm like when I'm bleddy hungry!"

"I do now. Where is the bleddy animal anyway?"

"On the sofa watching the tele'. Some bleddy farming programme with that idiot from bleddy Newsround, no, not her, the other one."

"Noel Edmonds?"

"No, he was the one from Swapshop."

"Lenny Henry?"

"Who is Lenny Henry? Forget about it, tidn't that important. Come to think about it, neither was Swapshop."

"You left the goat on the sofa? You won't 'ave anywhere to sit when you get home boy. Why is it watching that?"

"I believe he likes woolly jumpers!"

"You should have put one man and his goat on or in your case, one man and his impostor. He might have liked that. Best you get back and get it down to the abattoir mate. I'll have some for the restaurant."

"You bleddy won't. I'm keeping 'im."

"Where?"

"I 'ave got me a mate who does have a bit of a farmyard effort."

"Serves the bugger right. Who might that be then?"

"You, you bugger!"

"Get stuffed. You just damaged my hearing, I can't hear a word you're saying."

"Sorry about that mucker. I was a tad riled."

"No, really? I'd take you on mate, I do have too much to do. I'll save it for now. Be warned, when you feel it, it'll be me massaging your neck, very tightly!"

"Fair enough. I don't understand Maccy, why didn't someone bleddy tell me?"

"Beats me Lenny, I'm totally puzzled. I suppose they didn't want to get your goat!" I couldn't help it, I have been waiting to say that.

"You bastard, it 'idn't bleddy funny."

"Come over to the Maltsters with me, we'll find you something to eat before you kill someone. If you're still alive you can do that after you eat Lavinia's cooking. I'll help you. Get your goat, he can walk along with the dog, the one that isn't impersonating a dog." Actually, he is borderline. The disfigured mutt had appeared from nowhere.

"Might be best to be honest, mucker."

And that's the way we are. It's why Lenny Copestick is my best mate and I am his. It is unlikely it will ever

225

change unless Lenny happens to find out the name of his nephew's father! It'll be a different kettle of fish if that happens.

We two do nothing by halves, we don't play fight! We sort of did today to be fair, but it was just a one off. We two will be fighting again in no time at all, it is our way. The bloke needs to eat. Lenny, the human goat! On thinking about it, the pair are perfectly suited. It won't be long before they are arguing over who will eat the quilt. Yes, they will probably share the bed unless Lenny has a woman in it. They still might! Maybe I should re-phrase that. I wouldn't want anyone to get the wrong idea.

"Any afters mate?"

"Why don't you go and see your goat, you could eat each other! I'll have a fiver on the goat to win."

"Billy Lenny!"

"Billy should be enough mate otherwise you'll never stop thinking about him. Is it a male, did you look underneath?"

"Underneath what?"

"Underneath the bleddy goat!"

"I didn't like to, tidn't right."

"So it might be your Nanny then."

"I'm warning you, Tamryn!"

"You could call it Billy the Kid! Or Nanny the…., whoa Lenny! I promise, no more mate." It was a close thing, I couldn't help myself.

"Hi Lenny. How's the puppy?"

"It's a goat, Miss Yank, tidn't a dog at all."

"Is it, well I'll be darned! How about that? Just goes to show Lenny, you never know what's around the corner 'til you get there and ya'll still might not know. Is it a Billy or a Nanny?"

"Tell her, Maccy."

"Nope! You tell her." I feel a nasty glare coming on, the hair on the back of my neck doesn't know what to do.

"Never mind Lenny, there's always a silver lining. Maccy, what happened to your face?"

"Lenny bumped into it."

"Accident?"

"Not really darlin'."

"Come on Lenny, I'll buy you a pint. Did Michael come out of the chapel yet mate?"

"No idea Maccy, still there when I left, haven't seen him since."

"No problem, we'll check on him tomorrow. Tonight, he can practice what he preaches, better still, preach what he practices. It will be beneficial. One good thing mate."

"What's that?"

"By the time you get home the chicken will be cold, you'll be able to get it out of the oven minus burns. You and your new friend can pull the wishbone together. If you win, you can wish you had a bleddy dog."

"Best you block your ears up maid."

"Don't you worry yourself Lenny, I can cuss too."

"Did your ball come back yet, Lenny?"

"How would you like yours to disappear?"

"Understood mucker!"

"Maccy, someone should have said something. You knaw what it's like for me. I'm not as stupid as I sound. nor as daft as I look. I'm a simple bloke who likes the simple things in life, like cuddly things, animals and suchlike and Lavinia. I get the feeling sometimes folk are laughing at me behind my bleddy back, Maccy. Tidn't on, it's not nice. I'm like Bessie without the weird bits, like you without the looks, like the yank, without them, you knaw, them things. I wanna be liked for being me but I don't have much to show for it like you buggers."

"Come here Lenny, let's hug. How's that mate, any better? It's not true Lenny, we all like you. We'd be lost without you. We appreciate you. Just one other thing Lenny, it is bleddy rude to point at a woman mate."

"She started it! Thank you, Maccy. I knaw, that's me saying all I did have to say."

"See you later Lenny, try not to take things to heart."

"The yank is right Lenny, stop worrying. Just one very last thing mind."

"What would that be old friend?"

"Billy likes you too!"

"How do you knaw that then?"

"He's eating the bottom of your jeans mate."

"They're my bleddy new ones, effing animal! I'll kick your arse you little git!"

"Kid, Lenny, it's a kid. The clue's in the name mate. Billy the Kid!"

I think I did rather well there. I've straightened Lenny out, probably only temporarily. I suppose in all honesty he helped himself. Next in line is Peter, a good man to have around. I'm about to make him an even better one. Lenny is manager of the Mermaid and Peter is about to become his equal. I'm about to put it to him. I don't know much about him. Then again, I don't know much about many of my staff. I do however have a gut. My gut tells me if I'm doing right or wrong.

"Peter, what do you think of it buddy?"

"What do I think of what, Maccy?"

"This place, the Maltsters and Little Petrock, all of it."

"Yeah, it's all good. You do have some weird staff but who am I to talk?"

"Exactly! Here's your keys, you're in charge."

I'm not certain if it's fear or shock I see in Peter's eyes.

"Where are you sneaking off too, Maccy?"

"Nowhere mate, I'm taking a backstep. We have plenty to be doing around here. You, Lenny and Alice run the pubs and I'll be getting on with the rest."

"I hate doing rotas, Maccy."

"Don't worry, the yank will do those for both places. What do you think?"

"Fair enough, now bugger off, I'm busy."

"Good answer, Peter. Let's do this! Just one other thing mate, we need to get ready for potential weddings, on the lake."

"It's a bloody pond with a big boat on it."

"Lake!"

"It's a small lake with a big boat on it!"

"See, that's better. Now can you say 'bleddy'?"

"Bloody!"

"No, try again."

"Bluddy."

"No, it's bled-dy."

"Bled-dy."

"Now say it fast."

"Bleddy!"

"Now say, 'it's a lake with a bleddy big boat on it."

"It's a lake with a bleddy big boat on it."

"One more, Peter say 'wosson'!"

"What?"

"Nothing like it, 'wosson'!"

"Wosson."

"Excellent."

"What does it mean?"

"No idea mate. Perfect, next patient please!"

"Doddle! Can I go now?"

"'Ang on while I make your certificate out. It's only temporary, you'll get your permanent certificate when you've been here fifty years. Where were you born, Peter?"

"Devon."

"Okay, you might have to wait a tad longer, I'll have to check with the authorities. Come back and see me later. Next patient please!"

"So, tell me, what's this malarkey all about mate?"

"Simple Peter, trade building, most especially in the season. Team building too."

"Go on, enlighten me."

"Why do the furriners come here every year and when they stop coming, another lot take their place. Half a million of the buggers come here every year. So, they like it. Why do they like it?"

"Because they like to annoy us?"

"No, my friend, they like what we do, they like what we are. Who can blame them?"

"Right, I'm from Devon, I sort of know what you mean. Tell me why you want me to talk like you?"

"Because we're gonna do what no one else does. We're all gonna talk like locals. That's why the bleddy emmets come here, Peter. There's no one else like us, the buggers are infatuated. So, if all the staff talk the same, like they are proper locals, we'll always be busy, won't we! Also, if we all talk the same, no one is left out."

"I'm not so sure. I don't have to say 'ooh arr' all the time, do I?"

"Naw, course not, they'll all think you're from bleddy Devon if you do that, it would be pointless. They would just stop off in Somerset! If they wanted to be in bleddy Somerset or Devon they would book a holiday there. They wouldn't have to come this far would they! So they need to come here and if they come into one of my pubs, they'll not want to leave. Look at it this way, Peter. They get a proper Cream Tea here in the Duchy, with everything in the right order, they get proper Cornish Pasties here with turnip in them, not bleddy swede. Where else would they get that? Now they'll get a proper Cornish welcome from our staff and they'll come back again, see? And another thing, we do 'ave Newquay and Lands' End. You can't get that in bleddy Devon. When you was bleddy hitchhiking, who picked you up?"

"You did, Maccy."

"There you go see, who else would be stupid enough to do that on a dark night?"

"A Cornishman?"

"Right, I rest my case. Hospitality see, you don't get that anywhere else."

"You want bleddy locking up Maccy, you're mad."

"Mebbe, but I won't be bleddy poor! Repeat after me: 'I won't be bleddy poor.'"

"I won't erm, be bled-dy poor."

"You've cracked it my friend. Now all we have to is teach the others."

"Which ones?"

"Them that don't talk like us. There's Jill and Jack for a start, not sure where they come from. Padraig, he's bleddy Irish, Lavinia, the yank. No, best forget about the yank, she needs extra tuition, I better do that my own self. She 'ave made a start mind. Dusty, my brother, he's half bleddy Irish, we can sort him out with a whack on the side of his head from a piece of four by two. After that anyone we give a job to working in the pubs. Bleddy simple."

"Bleddy simple!"

"See mate, you're nearly there already. Where is Devon by the way?"

"Dunnaw!"

"Wow, Peter mate, you have cracked it. Now spread the word. Tell them there's a prize at the end of the month."

"What's the prize, Maccy?"

"I'll think of something. I knaw, a free pasty tasting up down at Callington. That should do it. Just the one catch though mate, that'll be for the worst loser!"

"Okay, I'm off, you've convinced me."

"Where to?"

"To spread the word, Maccy."

"Just one last thing Peter, don't try and enlist Lenny. That might be painful."

"Who for?"

"You, Lenny already has his own language. He can get a bit touchy about such things. You work on the kids and the Birdseyes, I'll sort out the yank and Lavinia. Tell you what, try Methy Mick too."

"Who is Methy Mick?"

"The local Methodist minister. Oh bugger, I forgot about Alice, bleddy hell. You have a go and if it idn't working, I'll try. We might just have to sack her. One last thing, tell the others not to encourage the emmets to talk like we do."

"Is 'Methy Mick' on drugs or methylated spirits?"

"Probably, maybe he's the Methylated Minister."

"Don't you think the emmets might enjoy talking like you, us?"

231

"They might and then what, they won't bleddy come here, they can stay at home and talk to each other or themselves. We don't want that!"

"Knaw, we bleddy don't. It would be madness. It would be like building a bleddy monster, like Frankenstein!"

"That's right, Peter."

"Maccy."

"Ahh, Lavinia, what's wrong with you?"

"No idea, nothing as far as I know."

"Are you sure, you do look a bit peaky." At least I didn't say rough as a dogs' guts!

"Do I, I do? I might be feeling a bit sort of overworked and underpaid."

"I see, okay, take this note to the nearest job centre. Just joking Miss, go away and cook some Hogs Pudding."

"Thank you Maccy, I feel better already. I could make you feel better if you'd like me to?"

"I'm good thank you, Miss. Why did you come here?"

"I can't remember. Shall I send the dog in then?"

"Only if you're sure it's a dog. Does it look like a dog?"

"Not really, it looks more like a goat."

"Right, send it away with a flea in its ear, please."

"Where will I find one of them, Maccy?"

"Have a look in his ear, Lavinia."

"What for?"

"Meet me at the lake in fifteen minutes. I've got something I want you to do."

"Why do I have to wait that long?"

"It's the rules Lavinia, bring a pen and paper."

"Okay, I'll be there, ready and waiting, you weirdo."

It's time for a nice quiet smoke by the lake. Maybe a spliff!

I am suddenly approached by the three Amigos. They sit at my feet and stare longingly at me from below. It might not be 'longingly', how would I know, I can do double Dutch, I don't do triple duck. An ugly Alsatian joins them. Maybe they are here for elocution lessons? Lavinia is early, no surprise there. I know what she thinks she wants. When hell freezes over; still not a good enough reason. The yank has followed her. Thank god for that, I'm safe.

"Okay class, sit!" Even the three Muscovys do as they're told at my command. This will be easier than I thought.

"What's happening, Maccy?"

"Stop talking at the back, yank. We are here to talk proper maid."

"Repeat after me: 'we are 'ere to talk proper maid'."

I get two replies, neither of which are of any use. "Again!"

The yank sounds like James Cagney, Lavinia sounds like the Kray twins. The ducks sound like ducks!

"You yank, forget about Texas, Lavinia, forget about being a cockney. You are both Cornish today. Say 'weem bleddy Cornish, you bugger." There is little or no change. "Again, keep saying it over and over. Alice, thank you for joining us. Say 'weem bleddy Cornish'."

"I really don't think I can do that. I'm not in the mood."

"You have to do what I say, Alice."

"Better than working I suppose. Go on then, I'll have a go."

"Right, this is what you do 'ave to do."

"The customer might say 'are you local miss'?"

"You say, 'ais I'm Cornish my luvver', like I would, then you say, 'what can I get ee', my 'ansome', try that. The ducks stare, the women stare. I stare, into the abyss. "If you're not going to do this proper like I, you might as well bugger off you tossers."

"If you're not going to do this proper like I, you might as well bugger off, you tosser!"

"That's good, much better. Same again this time next week! Class dismissed."

That all went better than I expected.

"Lenny, is that you?"

"I bleddy 'ope so, who's askin'?"

"Tis me, listen mate, 'ow long with the rooms?"

"Same as before, we 'aven't changed them. They're still the same size."

"Are they finished yet?"

"One is more or less."

"So, more or less, mate?"

"Yep, that's about the size of 'n."

"So, the same size as before then!"

"Near enough I reckon."

"And it'll be ready drekly?"

"Jack says to say, about now."

"Great, when will the other be ready?"

"Bessie says end of the week."

"Which week?"

"He 'idn't sure mate, maybe this one or another, which one do you want?"

"The nearest one. Okay, keep me up to date, Lenny."

"I will, but I better check with Maccy first, 'ee don't like me telling strangers 'is business. Who shall I say called?"

"Elvis!"

"Elvis is dead, Maccy."

"I forgot. Lenny, don't tell me anything else as I know he does have a suspicious mind!"

Sometimes, just sometimes I could cheerfully strangle my mate. I doubt he would even notice.

On the positive side, Padraig and my ma are to be married. It's good to have married parents! Not before time. It's music to my ears. The Irishman had collared me as I was leaving the building. He explained in detail he had asked ma and she had accepted. Dusty and I are about to get full-time parents. There is just one snag; The Maltsters is to be the venue for the reception. Can't wait!

Chapter Twenty-One

Two for the price of two.

Only once before have I been present at a Tamryn wedding. Today I will be present at two at the same time. My jigsaw like Celtic family is about to become completed. The pictures for the album are all but there, so far with no pieces missing, apart from Dusty. My brother is almost always missing. Dusty will take his place if he values his life.

As strange as it may sound, Joy and Padraig would finally become mother and father to their twenty-odd year-old kids, as a joint enterprise. Well, to be fair, Joy already had been for some while, all the while in fact. Padraig already wasn't but is about to be, providing there are no last minute hitches, except the most important ones obviously.

I just can't help wondering if they both know what they are getting themselves into. I decide they do. In any case, it is none of my business, nor that of anyone else.

Padraig has been planning for a while I believe, so have I, but we haven't discussed it between ourselves. I think he knows what I have in mind. It will all work out on the day, I'm fairly certain.

The kid has already made off early this morning after drinking enough black coffee to fill a small bucket. He must get to Newquay and collect a large cake I had decided my acquired culinary skills could not produce. He'll probably come back with a family size pasty from St Agnes. I have far too much to organise than take on the catering. Now if I was a celebrity chef I'd be living over the other side with all the others who are buying up half of a place known locally as Rock. The title serves the population right, they are welcome to the nondescript piece of the Duchy.

Dusty insisted to me late last night, while still reasonably sober, it would be easier to take the sea bus, his coastal cruiser, rather than risk sharing the ten-mile round journey - where's a crow when you need one - with 'half a million useless emmets' that weren't sure where they were going or where they'd just come from and possibly why in both cases. They tend to drive in the middle of the road to make it easier for them to turn around when they are lost, occasionally their caravans do stay attached; there's no guarantee obviously. My brother would get there as fast as he could. Dusty left on his mission with his T-shirt on the wrong way around, inside out and a slice of something very black sticking out from one corner of his mouth. His belt was undone, and it may not be long before he loses his trousers. Dusty is a consistent trouser loser! The dangling food was possibly Marmite on toast, it might just as easily have been burnt bread.

He had company when he left. I couldn't see who or what it was. I had a worrying thought and had tried to shake it off. Where is Lavinia? Dusty is potentially in danger of being disrobed.

When it all begins today, I will be fully employed in making sure the Maltsters is prepared in every way possible to do its duty. My family and our friends know that the time we have is not to be used for farting about, especially in the buggering about sense. I will be present at every turn to remind them.

I am not and have never been a serious cider drinker and do not intend to be again. Unfortunately, I had decided to try just one pint of the stuff about midnight, another at one, one more at two and so on. It had been enough, far too much in fact after what had gone before and those pints had cost me my early morning awareness of anything of a human nature. The locals call it 'rough' in these quarters, I know why. When you're not used to it, perhaps if you are, you're just gonna feel rough as rats a short time later. No hair of the dog with this stuff, not unless you're looking for an early grave, simply because the grave would most likely be already occupied by others with the same affliction or possibly by someone taking a nap.

For me, I must play my part just like the other bar staff and family members. I know clockwork isn't ever going to be applicable; nothing that involves this family ever is. If Dusty and I messed up it could eventually be sudden death. A sort of Death by Chocolate, without the chocolate bit. A different kind of brown stuff could be hitting a fan if my brother and I fail.

I have one task to perform before getting involved with organising the big day. A fast trip to Wadebridge would bring a solution. I did it, got there and back in less than an hour with the one most important item left to complete the day. Nobody even notices I am gone, which is a worry. I hear you ask what the item might be? It is the one thing necessary at any wedding. I couldn't leave it to the last moment. In fact, it was indeed pretty much 'last moment'.

Time is passing, guests are arriving in the shapeless shape of Blencathra, the size of an oak tree and the Cap'n, Bligh or Cecil. Any name will do, he will answer to all of them. Bligh does seem to have his teeth in, I hope they are superglued. His distant relative, the celebrated Admiral Bligh of the Bounty wouldn't be seen without his teeth. I have my doubts the two are related but have never aired them, not to his face anyway. * The Admiral was born in the Duchy at 'Tinten', a farmstead close to St Tudy. From what Lil the tart told me a few years ago, our Bligh was born over the border. Oddly enough, I read somewhere recently the actual Admiral Bligh of the Bounty was also born over the border, in Plymouth! Maybe the old sod is telling the truth after all. They might be related.

I have regained my faculties. My brain is functioning almost fully, I am in overall control in a feeble sort of way. Maybe it is the arrival of Blen', thought by many to be the last surviving member of the oddest tribe on the planet, from somewhere in the centre of Borneo. Somewhere in the back of my head, Reg Presley's voice begins an old Trogg's favourite, 'Wild Thing'! 'You move me'. Blen is mostly immovable whether awake or asleep.

Dear Blencathra could be the love child of two Easter Island statues. There is a close comparison, the chiseled features, the gargantuan torso and the strange garb which she has decided is fitting for a wedding between two humans. I think about this latest thought. I am relieved that's all it had been. I have just witnessed the appearance of a vertical railway sleeper and a giant Swan Vesta safety match, complete with red tip, too damp to ignite. Gog and Magog, Cornish royalty, have entered the building. Breaking the mould is an often overworked phrase. Blencathra looks like she is still enshrouded in hers. She resembles an Egyptian Mummy only without the intricate gold carvings and decoration around the facial area. Less a 'boy king', more a Viking, Mrs. Thor, goddess of thunder.

"Cap'n, Blen', my lovers. I'm bleddy glad to see you both." It's not true, it just feels like it is for a split second. I have lied easily at their entrance.

"Maccy, you naughty boy, how's my pub, my 'ansome, I 'ope you're looking after it proper?" She sipped her sherry as my reply didn't arrive. Truthfully, I am glad these two great friends have managed to attend. I have no need to look after their old pub today; Lenny and Alice will do that for the lunchtime trade, then close up and be at the Maltsters for the important stuff later.

"Maccy, you watch your behavior today, or I'll be round there to give you what for if you idn't bleddy careful. You're not too big to go over my knee, my lad, so think on!"

The thought of myself over Blen's knee is extremely scary. I ignore her threat. I wouldn't wish it on anyone, friend or foe. I haven't even commenced to misbehave so far. I'm already being threatened for something I had not even considered so far.

Like a twisted branch hanging on for dear life in a force ten, the Cap'n creaks and cackles alone and loudly. The rest of us are too afraid to even hint at a smile.

"Now, I'll 'ave me a lovely cup of Cornish tea, Maccy my 'ansome. None of that bleddy Yorkshire stuff. He will too." Blen' points at the matchstick man who has no chance at all of disobeying. Obviously Bligh doesn't have a death wish.

"I'll get on it straightaway Blen, and do you 'ave two lumps 'n milk?" There it is again, I can't help myself. 'A Tamryn inuendo in action'. Blen' looked at me with something that may have been akin to smoldering lust in her eyes or it could have just be severe indigestion, maybe a combination of both. I do recall the adage: If you play with fire, you'll get burned and the thought of this makes me step back a little. I don't even want a scorch mark, I don't believe I have never considered myself to be flameproof.

I notice the kids are here. These two are the enigma twins. They have been using the Mermaid and Bow for as long as I can remember, at least as long as I have. They are acknowledged, fully paid up members of the crew. For the life of me I have no idea what they are called, I've never asked. None of us know much about them. I seem to know dozens of people, friends, acquaintances, most of them nameless. It does save me from trying to remember everybody. The two come in of an evening, get a drink and spend three or four hours exploring various parts of each other. They are expert. Bessie is here, he isn't nameless. He wasn't christened Bessie, his full name is Soul Beswetherick. Very often in times past this has been preceded by many of us locals with 'Arse'. Over the last few years we have become more affectionate towards him and just call him Bessie. He is an excellent carpenter, a useful man to have around. Lastly, Michael, who is to take the service. His first wedding. Worried, me? Of course I'm worried!

Michael has been a big part in my life. We have grown up, maybe it is wishful thinking - weights and measures might be unhappy and call it misrepresentation - we have stood by each other through thick and thin since we began to walk and talk and get into trouble. There could be no better friend. I would mention the Alsatian in passing here, there is little to say about the ugly, deformed mutt. He wasn't born deformed, he sort of grew into it. His hygiene standards are ridiculously high, he is ugly, he is there when I need him. He's my dog and I'm his man. It has not always been this way.

And now to Lenny. No, forget it, I'm not even going to try. You should already be aware of Lenny's idiosyncrasies. Possibly his parents hail from somewhere on Bodmin Moor.

There is another present. I can't describe her apart from her strange demeanor. Slight in stature, weird dress sense - my opinion only - what do I know? I know the black fur coat with shoulder pads isn't real fur, a cat wouldn't be seen dead in it. If it is cat, I hope it isn't a Tom, it might start spraying all over the place. She is steely eyed, yet there is a smile behind them. I feel I should converse with her but am unsure what to say. She may have been beamed down, there may be a language barrier. She wandered in an hour ago and has not spoken to anyone as far as I know. Already she has made countless trips to the ladies. I haven't been counting. I dare say Lil has a stopwatch. I could ask her to make out a full report if I was slightly interested. She must have spoken to someone at some point, either that or she brought her own crockery and a flask.

The woman is dressed as if she is to attend a wedding, which she is doing so far but without an invitation as far as I know. If she has one, I have no idea who might have issued it, neither does Lil. 'Never seen her in my life' Lil had stated. She has strange hair, it is curly and straight at the same time, she might as well stay for now. She has a box of what might be confetti in her lap, probably homemade from old bank statements. A baccy tin rests on her table. She both looks like she belongs here and at the same time is out of place. I consider one more weird waif or stray won't do any harm. The woman fits in, as the Maltsters has its fair share of the same today. One more enigma won't hurt, whatever her name might be! I glance away as a look on her face might be saying, 'don't dare mess with me'. It's that look few can muster, a look that can easily switch between stare and glare. She can't be local, she would smell of fish. Must be an outsider. I half smile as I walk towards her nervously. It might be due to my cider induced hangover. It isn't!

"Hello, do you have an invite, Miss?" The stranger has bugged me on and off. I decide it is a good time to confront her extremely gently.

"Um do I need one Mister Tamryn? If I am in the way here, I'll finish my coffee and be about my business."

"No, I didn't know if you had been invited. Maybe on the bride's side?"

"Not as far as I know."

"This is a family wedding sweetheart. The Maltsters isn't really open for business today."

"Your barmaid served me with coffee. I paid for it. I haven't paid for the extra creamers which are in my handbag. I did ask for powdered milk."

"I realise that. I'm sorry, cows around here only give the usual liquid version. We use Coffeemate."

"A cheap brand I believe. How am I to know your pub isn't open? The door was wide open, so I used the gap it left. I'll use it to leave by when I've finished my coffee. Is that acceptable to you Mister Tamryn?"

"Do you have enough sugar miss?" She looks in her handbag and shakes her head.

"There, help yourself." She did as I suggested and tipped half a dozen packets into her bag. My head is shaking now.

"How do you know my name, Miss, er...." I nearly said, 'pain in the arse'!

"For some strange reason I saw it over the door as I came in. I assume you are the landlord. I'll be equally surprised if your answer is yes?"

"Yes I am. Please don't rush, Miss. I have to go, we are pushed for time as you can imagine." She didn't smell of anything. She isn't local. She doesn't smell of the sea. I've always wondered about 'fish wives'. It sort of makes me think the fish wife should be married to a fish. There is something odd about this woman and I can't put my finger on it. She is confident of herself. She has managed to get my back up. I can't think why?

"Thank you, Mister Tamryn. Good luck to you and much more importantly of course, to your bride. She will need all she can get."

"Can I ask why you have confetti if you've not been invited?" I ignore the thinly veiled insults.

"Yes, you can."

"Then why?" She makes me want to bang my head on a wall quite hard.

"I always like to be prepared. It pays to be prepared."

"Okay, well enjoy your drink, miss. I'll let you know when they arrive."

"I'll try. When who arrives?"

I duck back. Men in white coats, I'm thinking. I'm losing my touch. I decide I had done my best to deter her involvement in the day. Somehow I'm certain my hastily arranged plan will not work. I have things to do. It is time to find out where my little brother is with a cake. I leave the weirdo at the table and don't look back. I feel she is glaring at my retreat. Thankfully there are no immediate stabbing pains. I'll check the cutlery later.

The Admiral and Alma arrive and take my mind off the strange one. I am surprised the Birdsalls didn't bring their own drinks with them. These two live on a floating gin palace on my lake. I leave the introducing to the yank. I wink at her as I walk away, she might be nervous. I will talk to my friends, who are also my accountants, later. I cook food while the Birdsalls cook my books. Bet they do a better job than I do in the kitchen.

The Bligh's receive their beverages, Blencathra steers the matchstick man to a table, where she settles him in with the flat of her hand on his chest and a 'sit there, don't move and behave yourself you bugger or else.' That is achieved without her even speaking. She almost had me doing it, from a distance. Bligh knows his place, he does now. The two give each other some rope, it's always pulled in before either of them hang themselves or each other. In all seriousness, suicides can be shared jointly, murders cannot. 'Would you mind killing me please?' 'Only if you kill me first!' Doesn't work, does it!

It seems the odd woman who was around earlier is gone. I can only think she may have made another visit to the bathroom. I'll have to check on the soap and toilet rolls later. I doubt she would have left as she had confetti. I don't think people leave a wedding before it has even started. She probably sells her unwanted Christmas presents at car boot sales. Who doesn't? The last time I went to a boot sale, I forgot to take the crap I wanted to sell.

There is still no sign of Dustys' return with the wedding cake. It is easy to tell I am getting a tad nervous and not just because of a lack of icing and marzipan, Dusty has his duties in the chapel to perform. He is to be my best man. My brother is so far absent, as is the cake. I feel a tad nervous, will soon be followed by short tempered. I am contemplating suicide for myself. I realise it's pointless. If it works, my friends will think I'm a miserable bastard and I deserve the consequences. If it doesn't work, I'll be a miserable bastard and deserve the consequences. I best stop thinking about such things and keep the status quo!

I did manage to get five minutes under the tree in the garden with a cigar packet. It is the only time I will skive all day. I'm nervous. I think about Jen' and wonder if she is here watching what will become a Tamryn shambles. I wouldn't put it past her, I'm sure she would if it were possible. Then, what do I know?

I do know the odd woman is still bugging me but not why. My thoughts have returned again to the stranger who has made herself temporarily at home. I haven't seen her talk to anyone and have seen no one approach her. I don't have time to ask who she belongs to. I don't intend approaching her again. She must be a friend of Miss America. That'll be it. Nothing to worry about. Case closed. Case closed? Fat chance, something is niggling me!

A Muscovy snatches at my discarded cigar butt and dips it into a puddle before swallowing it. I can't tell if it has a strange diet or it's just against smoking!

Author's note:

* William Bligh was born on 9 September 1754, but it is not clear where. It is likely that he was born in Plymouth, Devon, as he was baptised at St Andrew's Church, Plymouth on 4 October 1754, where Bligh's father, Francis (1721–1780), was serving as a customs officer. Bligh's ancestral home of Tinten Manor near St Tudy near Bodmin, Cornwall, is also a possibility. Bligh's mother, Jane Pearce (1713–1768), was a widow (née Balsam) who married Francis at the age of 40. Bligh was signed for the Royal Navy at age seven, at a time when it was common to sign on a "young gentleman" simply to gain, or at least record, the experience at sea required for a commission. In 1770, at age 16, he joined HMS *Hunter* as an able seaman, the term used because there was no vacancy for a midshipman. Because the Bounty was rated only as a cutter, it had no officers other than Bligh who was then only a commissioned lieutenant, a very small crew, and no Marines to provide protection from hostile natives during stops or to enforce security on board ship. To allow longer uninterrupted sleep, Bligh divided his crew into three watches instead of two, placing his protégé Fletcher Christian—rated as a Master's Mate—in charge of one of the watches. The mutiny, took place on 28 April 1789

Chapter Twenty-Two

Going Overboard

The phone rings and I snatch at it. I'm sure it's not always as loud. It is my brother. "Dusty, what the hell's happening, where's this bleddy cake boy."

"Cake, cake!"

"Where? No, no, no. No bleddy way. I'm not in the mood for this Dusty."

"I bleddy told you to drive round, you tosser."

"Stuff the bleddy emmets."

"What 'ave 'appened to 'n?"

"What's wrong with it?"

"A what has gone, where?"

"How the 'ell did that 'appen?"

"Why the bleddy 'ell didn't you notice?"

"Don't you have a spare outboard?"

"You 'ave a bleddy woman out there with you. No wonder you're 'aving bleddy problems."

"I know what her bleddy name is, chuck 'er overboard. You should have taken a rabbit, then you'd never come back, early or late. Get that bleddy engine started. Tell Lavinia she's sacked, tell yourself the bleddy same."

"I know you don't work for me, you never will now."

"If you chuck her over the side you won't need a bleddy condom for Christ's sake."

"You dopey tosser, Dusty."

"Can't you do something?"

"Not that. Can't you do something about the bleddy engine?"

"Syphon it out."

"Call out the RAC at Sea."

"You've got two hours to get back here, without her preferably. Tie the outboard to her; then throw her over. Ring me in an hour, let me know."

"Okay, be careful, you plank." He should be walking one for taking a woman – did I say 'woman', I'm using that term loosely. "You useless bugger, why don't you ever bleddy listen to me?"

The yank has been listening. I attempt to explain. "That was Dusty, he have had a bleddy breakdown. He's got the bleddy cake. Daft bugger thought I said Hake. He have left Newquay behind and has broken down at sea. I thought he was having me on. I told him to drive around there but no, he wouldn't bleddy have it, said the roads would be too busy, full of 'bleddy emmets'. He's gone and got seawater in the fuel tank. The cap did come away and he don't 'ave a spare motor nor much spare fuel. Now the bugger can't find a bit of tubing to get the crap fuel out of the tank. The bleddy tosser took the idiot with him and he's pissed off that he can't give 'er one. I hope she can row!"

"Took who with him?"

"Lavinia."

"Is that bad, Maccy?"

"I can't think of anything worse, can you?"

"Is there any good news, Brit?"

"There could be. They could end up on the bleddy * Doom Bar."

"That would be good?"

"It couldn't be worse."

There was me thinking I was talking to some poor local bugger who had got a wrong number and was afraid to tell me. I forgot, she can't be used to this sort of thing. There can't be much call for boats in Kansas or Texas or wherever.

"Presuming I know what you're talking about, what's he gonna do now, Mac? What do you mean, 'give her one'? What's Hake? So, where has he gone now?"

"Nowhere, he's still where he was, in a bleddy circle. Why do you ask? Are you on something?"

"You said he's pissed off and called him a tosser. What's he going to do now, Maccy?"

"He's gonna be buried at sea. The bugger's gonna call me back in an hour. He's out in the bleddy Irish Sea somewhere with a cake and a tart. He's got seawater in the fuel and he isn't going anywhere I don't believe. He'll be in New York bleddy harbour and trying to chat up the bird with the big torch by this time tomorrow."

"And what will you do if he doesn't get back here in time?"

"Dunno, you'll 'ave to give ma away or be Padraig's best man or woman. I'll give ma away. Best I do, 'er bein' my Ma. You can't give someone else's Ma away. Let's wait one hour anyway and see. I gotta get back to the kitchen. You call me if you hear anything before, yeah? You better get dressed, darlin'. Put your best on."

"I already bleddy did, damn you!"

She looks totally confused and bewildered. I know the feeling. It's my fault anyway. Do I really need a brother? Unfortunately I do right now.

A large ugly bloke is attempting the impossible. He is trying to block my path. Now he wants to chat. I'd rather talk to my dog, there's a good chance the Alsatian is more intelligent, a tad uglier, it's difficult to choose between them.

"When's he back?"

"If you're talking to me, I can't say. Later I believe. Who might you be, a waiter?"

"When's that, later when? A waiter?"

"No idea. Sometime after now I s'pose, drekly. Yep, thought you might like to wait outside." This could be Lennys' long lost twin. He could take up writing poetry. It would be less painful for him in the long run, I decide.

"I'll see to him drekly then."

"That'd be best, after me. Best you got back to your village now lad." This village idiot is getting me to talk like him now. I'm betting he's from St Issey. I'm not saying St Issey has a dearth of idiots. They do have at least one, they did have, now he's missing, he's here and imitating a nuisance.

Luckily the phone rings again as our conversation, if it can be called that, comes to a stuttering end and the bloke waddles back through the door like a Muscovy hooked on cider, in the direction from where he'd come if he can remember. It is my brother again.

"Maccy, no better, it's no good. I can't get the bleddy thing started. Call out the bleddy lifeboat. I've sent off all my rockets, they didn't go very far, just fell in the water a couple of yards away. I believe it would be best you call them. Gotta go now, my mobile's almost out of bleddy credit."

I did as I was told and had to wait for thirty seconds until the crashing noises died down the other side of the kitchen door. It's amazing what a few saucepan lids and sharp pointed implements will sound like when thrown about a kitchen. I am imagining someone has been pinned to the back of the door surrounded by sharp knives. The bloody caterers are here. Going by the language, Gordon Ramsey and his whole family, what's left of it, have dropped in. I snatch at the phone as I hear the front door open again.

I watch as the old woman who looks like she had caught her face in a combine harvester as it was reversing or perhaps she had got her face stuck in a food mixer while it was mixing her make-up, came in. I know who this latest visitor is. It is Lil the old tart from the Mermaid and Bow, a crew member. She is looking smart. The smart tart who always gives the impression she's been hacked in the lower face area with a meat cleaver. She doesn't look as though she is in fighting mood like the last person that had come in unannounced and so I make her welcome and I believe I was glad the deceased, One-Armed Frank wasn't with her, although I suppose he could have been. He never did like to miss a do! I get Lil a drink and sit her down with the Cap'n and Blencathra. The three looking like they were in a dentist's waiting room and rightfully so, in

Bligh's case. The dentist and his nurse may need to work overtime.

I am still trying to swear down the phone. It's the coastguard station and I give them Dusty's details, as much as I know. There is just an hour before the wedding service should be taking place at Michael's chapel.

A minute later and I assume Padstow Harbour is echoing to the sound of something known locally as the maroons. They'll be out to Dusty in less than half an hour all being well, it does depend on the tide and swell and a decent compass.

"Hiya Lil darlin', you're looking almost bleddy edible today. You made me look twice, bird!"

Lil grins and waves across to me as I wonder about the stroppy large bloke with the bit between his teeth. He said he would catch up with my brother later. I get the impression he isn't looking to buy him a beer, more likely a wheelchair. I won't be pushing it unless it's over the edge of the quay.

Just about every member of the crew is here now. If Dusty turns up sometime soon, we'll have a full pack.

My soon to be father is fretting now. "Nothing to worry about, Dusty will be getting a lift back with the cake. Everything's just about ready. The caterers can look after anything we've forgotten. Think I'll let Lavinia look after Bessie when she gets back, if anyone can straighten him out, she can! Pad' tell the organisers to make room for four at the front before you go up. Ma can be as late as she likes. It'd be best she is."

The large idiot appears again. "Look mate, he's not here, same as he wasn't before." Talk about Groundhog Day! "What's the problem?" I decided to give it one more try. I might get through eventually.

"No problem mister, apart from my girlfriend thinks she's bleddy pregnant."

"Dusty isn't a bloody midwife, you tosser. He can't help himself, let alone help a woman about to give birth. You need a doctor. You'd best be taking her to the hospital." I knew what the fat git was inferring but thought to relieve my tension with this perfect opportunity. It is working fine. "So what do you want my brother for?"

"I'm thinking 'e 'ave been tinkering with 'er, while my back was turned and them buggers down at the Bells 'ave said the same. Chris says he believed it was someone from here that did part her hair."

"So, you're here to thank him then for looking after your interests! I have warned him not to go near pregnant women, especially if they come from St Issey."

"Oh yeah, I'll be showing my gratitude drekly, 'tis only right I should. Best you stay out of it mister lessen you want some of what he's got coming." The pointing finger is missing me by miles. I'm tempted to smile.

Now I could be wrong, I again get the impression this bloke isn't about to buy Dusty a beer and give him a good old slap on the back and be looking to hand over an invitation to a christening. There is a smidgen of threat in his voice. I would do well to warn my brother somehow before he gets back into the village. If he gets back into the village before it isn't too late, which wouldn't be long now. I think of a better masterplan. "What's her name, pal?" I ask.

"Glenda."

"I thought so. Don't think it was my brother, buddy. He doesn't have great eyesight though."

"Why not? He'll need more than a pair of bleddy glasses when I've finished with him!"

"Easy mate, it was me!" I moved sideways, his fist got lost and now he's lying down.

Jack helps me carry the idiot across the road to the churchyard where we leave him to ask for forgiveness. I'll talk to Dusty later. I'm beginning to feel better now. I ought to get the bloke a doctor, on second thoughts, I maybe won't.

"He don't look too great, Maccy."

"To be honest Jack, he didn't look too great before I hurt my knuckles. We'll chuck a bucket of water over him.

Not now, later. We could drop him in an empty grave if there is one. That way he won't have to go far."

The next three-quarters of an hour are mostly spent looking at watch faces and those being worn by the various other guests sitting around the bar and hanging around in the doorway, not forgetting the regular sounds coming from under a table. I couldn't see the bloody dog. I know it's there and without an invitation. It should be upstairs on a bed with the goat, washing. Not my bed obviously.

There is just thirty minutes left now before the cars will arrive and we would have to leave for Michaels' chapel. Talking becomes a waste of time. Something big and noisy is outside. I don't have time to look. I just hope the silencers haven't all dropped off the wedding cars simultaneously.

It is time for me to change, otherwise I won't be in my place. Fifteen minutes later, I am dressed and ready. It is a complete surprise, Dusty is back. I didn't realise it but the noise from outside was signaling the return of my brother, a cake and a tart. It sounds as if it is circling the building and makes it shake a little as it almost settles on the roof. It isn't on the roof, it's in the carpark. Just as a helicopter appears to be climbing again and reels over the village, Dusty enters unannounced. My brother is announcing himself. He seems to be in a state of levitation. He is taking levitation to a whole new height. His body has entered through the Maltsters door in what most would call a prone position. It is some inches from the ground for a few seconds. My brother is followed by a yokel and in much the same way. I work it out and conclude somewhere just outside the now wide open door is a free-for-all. This did cheer me up and take my mind off everything else that should be going on. I have no idea whatever as to the location of the precious cake.

"You got yourself a ringside ticket, Padraig", I ask. It is my father who has propelled the second flyer it seems.

My father winks painfully as he leaves again with a determined growl the Alsatian couldn't possibly compete with.

Dusty's own voice is a little muffled, swollen lips will do that, I am just able to understand what he says.

"There's three or four more of the bastards outside, Mac."

My guess is Padraig is holding on to one or two of them even now. "Well what are you waiting for brother? You're always bleddy late! What were you thinking taking the nutjob with you."

"You knaw what I was thinking! She didn't want to know!"

"Next time don't think kid. Don't let any part of your body think about Lavinia. I bleddy warned you."

"Don't worry Mac, she's lined up Peter."

"Poor bastard! So anyway, who brought you back safely. What's her name brother?"

"Oh, Selina was in the neighborhood with some of her friends luckily for me. **She's a pilot in the RAF now, Search and Rescue."

So Selina came back after all. About ten years late. Better late than never. I couldn't be happier for my sibling. Dusty brought her home years ago, she stayed a while and then suddenly disappeared to take up flying obviously. It's understandable.

I step outside just in front of my now recovered partially half dead sibling. He has trampled the hands of his first attacker who had landed just inside the door and there is all hell let loose and waiting to be paid for. I am doing rather well considering I am in a firm headlock. Padraig has two of his own in progress now and there is something of a stalemate which Dusty and I decide should be broken.

I would have much preferred to spectate today. I thought it would be bad manners. I did manage to ask my brother another question as he and his two associates were almost static for a second or two. "They don't usually drop rescuees off at home, do they?"

"Made a deal with the helicopter boys, and girls of course. Good lads they are. Ouch, bleddy 'ell you bastard that's my eye. Told them they could have a free ride on the Newquay run, if they put their foot down. Selina was piloting the chopper. Get off me you tosser!"

A fourth lad is scrambling around on the floor with an inflated eye of his own and a slightly leaking nose; it isn't ketchup. Dusty is correct, there are five of them in all and after cutting off communication, I make for the nearest and we two went at it like, well we went at it until I believed them to be rendered harmless.

I turn my attention back to the task in hand. One of the pair, the ugly heavyweight I'd met a couple of times earlier has eventually woken up and is already moving back in on Dusty, while my brother attempts to regain his breath. He's already lost part of a tooth. I am free to spectate now as I get my own breath back.

My nose closes around a fist, who's owner I never see. It is time for me to show my stuff again as my earlier opponent comes back for another try and with encouragement from the other Tamryn, I am on my way. I couldn't let the side down. Then it is all over, more or less. I hear a woman's voice, it is getting louder and clearer. I believe it is Glenda, the pregnant maid.

"You bleddy idiot, I bleddy told you it wadn't him, nor the other one. Why don't you listen, you useless bleddy tosser?"

I could hear the voice of the village girl as she ripped into the local idiot with everything she had. It is this interruption that brings the fighting to a close which is good as I am getting hurt now. I much prefer pain to belong to someone else, my brother would be a good candidate right now.

This last exchange is at least interesting to watch as the girl snatches at a bunch of her feller's hair which has the effect of halting any further violence from him as she shakes his head with it.

"It wadn't him, I already bleddy told you."

"Who was it then?"

"It was you, you daft pillock. I 'aven't been with no other bugger. I bleddy told you. Now come away before my baby becomes fatherless or you become a bleddy eunuch." She tugs at his hair again and the badly bashed boyfriend does as he is told as she leads him away. I feel a tad sorry for the lad, nothing more.

Ma and the others suddenly come out from the Maltsters and the remaining three, slightly damaged locals slink away without another word unless you count 'ouch, bleddy 'ell' and 'I think he broke my bleddy nose', or 'my nuts 'ave gone up behind my bleddy ears'.

My guess is they have all been drinking early at the Bells and Chris the landlord has been winding them up. I realise it should have been the remaining four slinking away. There is still one of the would-be St Issey Commandoes unaccounted for.

The puzzle is soon solved to everyone's satisfaction, especially mine, as I get the chance to see the great 'undefeated' heavyweight champion of Cornwall, Blencathra, in action. Her victim is being used as a sofa and unmoving! I don't blame him. The last thing I would want to do in this life is move with Blencathra sitting on me. She might get the wrong idea!

"Maccy, that Glenda is a bleddy good liar."

"I know Dusty, I know."

Author's notes:

*The Doom Bar has been used in poetry to symbolise feelings of melancholy, and has lent its name to the flagship ale from the local Sharp's Brewery.

**The Royal Air Force Search and Rescue Force (SARF or SAR Force)

Chapter Twenty-Three

Let us all Unite.

With my good hand, I pick up the sacred undamaged cake which had been resting under Lavinia's ample chest area throughout the melee, for want of a better word. It's possible the 'melee' was going on inside her clothing, hence my being careful. Something is moving about in there. I suppose I should be thankful she kept the cake in a safe place. Due to the padding it was unlikely to get badly damaged. The Alsatian must have a sweet tooth as he follows me doggedly - no pun intended obviously - into the kitchen.

The door hadn't quite shut behind me as I issued an abrupt order to anyone who might be interested. "Get that tramp out of here now!" It was fairly abrupt as abruptness goes. Definitely it was a bad move on my part. Sitting on a stool by the rear door is the scruffiest - I use the term loosely - human being I have ever encountered. The mutt is handsome by comparison. This isn't my immediate problem. I grab at his collar, it is not a smart move as the item comes away from the coat. The wearer is unaware. I shove the ragged item into my pocket sharpish.

Lavinia understandably, believes I was talking to and about her. I am instantly convinced as she attacks me with a large serving platter. I don't believe it is made of silver foil, more like lead. Anyway the aluminum item collided with my head a handful of times. It might have been two handfuls!

"What the hell are you doing, you idiot?"

"You can't talk to me like that, you bloody moron."

"I wasn't talking to you, and it's bleddy."

"You won't be able to talk at all by the time I finish with you. How dare you call me a tramp!"

"I didn't call you a tramp. I called the tramp a tramp."

"Liar! What bleedin' tramp?"

I pointed out the obvious. "That tramp. It's 'bleddy', not 'bleedin'!"

"Whose tramp is it?"

"Not mine Lavinia, I'd know if it was mine."

"You could be related!"

"Thank you, you could be ejected. Maybe you should think before you lash out maid."

"Sorry Maccy, did it hurt?"

"Pretty much."

"Good, watch what you're saying next time. It was only tin."

"Tin has killed before maid!"

"Where?"

"In tin mines."

"Liar, tins don't come from mines."

"No, of course they don't, I'm sorry, Lavinia."

I am careful not to mention Copper mines. Dusty, with our soon to be recycled parents re-enters the Maltsters just in time to bring this ridiculous exchange to an end.

"Dusty, get rid of the tramp. Peter, you better help him, my brother isn't used to throwing things out unless toys from a pram count!"

"Right Lil, out, Maccy said you have to sling your hook."

This is not helpful as Lil immediately bursts into tears. She says a lot that shouldn't be repeated. How does an eighty-year-old woman know such things? To be fair, I don't think I want to know the answer. I calm her down with a gin and something. I do know people need to cry at weddings. We haven't had one yet and everyone is already bawling, swearing and yelling, not forgetting fighting!

The fight is continuing between Blencathra and the fourth and final member of the St Issey militia who is crying his eyes out, a bit like Lil, and begging to be released from the nightmare of being bested by a distant, not so distant most likely, cousin of the Incredible Hulk. I love surprises. It is a relief to see that none of her clothes have been ripped apart as she had obviously pounced on the poor sod. She is growling a tad; under the circumstances it is to be expected. I feel a small amount of sympathy for the lad. I don't like to overreact, my hypocrisy only stretches so far.

The indomitable Blencathra is continuing to play her part in the defence of the Maltsters. It's possible this might all be innocent. It might constitute some strange courtship maneuver by her. Blen' might fancy the poor kid, she may be distantly related to a Praying Mantis, she looks like she might eat him. He hasn't even performed yet, they are still at the foreplay section. Blen' retains a vice-like grip on the remaining attacker and even now is straddling him and threatening further agony by shoving a knee into his throat. Worse still, his face is being roughly licked clean by the Alsatian. I have time to wonder what the dog did last!

Face licking isn't my thing except under certain circumstances. I never have partaken of this pastime but I'm apt to try anything once, providing a certain ex-landlady of the Mermaid isn't involved.

The Cap'n is sitting calmly, passing every kind of injurious and pain inducing instruction to his beloved, slathering wife. I say slathering, I might mean panting. I refuse to comment further, though not to feel sorry for the lad would seem churlish. As they say, all's fair in love and war. If they don't they should. I doubt the five lads from up the road will be out on the beer tonight. This last one might have a semi blind date with Blencathra, or possibly even the dog, to look forward to. She is not done yet, neither is the mutt it seems. Hopefully the lad and the dog will walk off into the sunset with Blencathra.

I had called out firm orders. I couldn't help but wonder as I'm sure we all did right then, who they were directed at. I didn't want to make another mistake while I'm still suffering from my previous one. 'Stop that now, get off him you ugly bleddy animal, heel, leave him be now, you ugly fat beast!'

And there is no telling twice as both human and canine let go of the stricken lad at the same time. The lad slunk away sulking and checking his bits. A repeat of this day may never arrive. I hope not. Dear Blen' has no idea. Once again I consider taking up prayer. Padraig looks across to me, smiling as he winks with his good eye. He knew! He knew, I knew, most of us knew. I just hope she didn't know. One thing that did puzzle me, I had always believed punch ups happened after a wedding ceremony, usually at the reception, never before.

The dog wanders embarrassingly away to the bar and settles in next to the tramp, who is even now serving itself from a beer tap. At last it seems the mutt has found a home here. I will remind myself when I get time, to get a new pool table installed. There isn't a lot of space underneath the one we have. Blencathra stands back and looks rather pleased with her days work, which only took her about ten minutes. There is something resembling a smile on her face.

"Is it always like this, Maccy?" Peter asked in a quieter moment.

"Not always, no mate. Welcome to my world. It will get better yet mind."

"Reckon I'm going to stick around then. Think I might like it here."

"Good, can you get rid of the tramp, Pete."

"Course I can, if you're not including me, which one!"

"Take your bleddy pick mate." I whispered, wouldn't you?

Blencathra and Bligh continue discussing the ins and outs of the fight.

"You should have gouged his eyes my lover, I bleddy told you. You dig your thumbs in and their eyeballs pop out, couldn't be simpler my lover." Bligh continues convincing himself he had been taking part in an advisory role. He's almost convincing me.

"The boy 'ad had enough, Cap'n. No sense me over doing it."

"You should 'ave crushed his nuts dear."

"I believe I did, 'ee was squeaking some when he left. It's been a while, I feel better after that."

"That's alright then, sit down here and get your breath back, maid."

Ma is not at all happy. I suspect she would soon forgive and forget. Maybe not forget. It was her wedding day after all. My own also. It's possible Blen' could utilise two chairs during the service. I resist making the suggestion, life is far too important. There's no point in setting her off again.

I needed something to take my mind off the recent melee. As if by magic it materialises in the shape of Bert. Actually this isn't quite true, it might be the shape of the woman who is holding his hand and pretending to help him walk.

"Bert, good to see you buddy and you've brought a friend, or is it your sister?"

"She might be, she might not be. I don't remember 'er around the house when I was a tacker, so I don't believe we are related. Everything is above board and shipshape, mister."

"I beg to differ old friend, she don't look like a ship to me, a figurehead, maybe? She has a certain charm."

"'Tis my companion sorta. She 'ave 'eard I did win the lottery and she 'aven't let go my 'and since. Sorry my dear, Maccy does have a dirty mind. Maccy, this is my bleddy carer. 'Er did have to come with me or I couldn't come at all."

"In case you got bleddy lost getting here?"

"Ais, that's right."

"It's okay, Bert. I knawed what she is as she does have her watch on upside down and black fishnet stockings do usually give a person a clue."

"I 'ad 'e fooled for a minute ya bugger."

259

"You did, Bert. Have a really good day matey and you, Miss."

"Thank you, Mister Tamryn."

"Don't call him mister, woman, he'll get ideas above 'is bleddy station! I have the feeling he's had one or two already!"

"Get yourself one on me Bert and one for your friend."

No clothes were severely damaged during the scuffle. A good brush down would have to suffice. My brother has a blood dribble down his chin, it has seeped from a split lip. I just have the one slightly swollen eye, the other is still working perfectly. There is no time for Joy to explode now as the three beautifully polished cars pull up behind each other in the narrow lane that leads off from the Padstow and Wadebridge road. I had spared no expense and had made sure there was space for us all to get to the chapel in comfort. It's only up the road. There is a church right across the road, but the vicar is a tad crazy!

It's a good job it's daylight as we have to cross the humpback bridge. The sound of infants wailing might set the Texan off. They might set me off. They will definitely set Lenny off, they always do.

Dusty took just five minutes to don his glad rags and clean the drying blood off his chin in the kitchen, much to the annoyance of the caterers who started throwing pans again. It must be some sort of culinary competition. It sounds like a bad orchestra rehearsing for a concert. Five minutes later the cars pull to a halt on double yellow lines in the narrow back lane. Jack, Jill and Lavinia - who has made a half decent attempt at looking well dressed, she still has the pillows - are all waiting at the door for our arrival.

Everyone who should be here, is. Gulls yell as they dive and soar skyward again, as if in hope the Tamryn wedding feast might be conducted here in the street outside the chapel at any moment.

"Maccy, I don't want to be a bridesmaid today."

"Why not?"

"I would prefer to be a bride."

Here's something I hadn't thought of much. Why do the women always leave these things until the last minute? "Okay, you should go change into your best clobber then maid, you can't get married looking like that. Who's the lucky man anyway?"

"Don't push it, Tamryn!"

Michael is already primed it seems. The Texan has pre-empted my plan.

"I need a bridesmaid!"

"Do you need one right now?"

"I'm warning you! What kind of question is that? I need someone with me, I don't have anyone to give me away."

"I'll sort it. Give me five minutes. Dusty can give you away, or Lenny. No, Lenny is my best man. Peter can give you away, I can give ma away. Sorted! Where's Lavinia when she's needed. There's only one thing I can do. I approach the confetti carrier with some trepidation. I am pleased now to see she is still here.

"Excuse me Miss, are you busy? Have you finished your coffee?"

"She glances around the room. "Does it look like it, Mister Tamryn? I have done some basic nursing. How can I be of use?" She checked her now empty cup.

"I don't need a nurse. I'm looking for a favour, Miss."

"How long have you been looking?"

"Thirty seconds."

"That's not long, Mister Tamryn. Do you have any idea what this favour is?"

"It's quite simple, I need a bridesmaid."

"Really, need or want. Isn't it traditional for a groom to have a page boy?"

"No, no miss, I don't need a bridesmaid, my fiancé needs a bridesmaid. Well, can you do it?"

"I can do most things Mister Tamryn, as you have already suggested. I suppose I could do bridesmaid. Obviously, I wouldn't do it on a permanent basis. I don't go from wedding to wedding offering a bridesmaid service. I do have references. I need time to think about it. I don't have a dress. I don't wear dresses."

"Neither do I, you look okay to me!"

"Yeah, yeah, okay? I don't do okay. Actually I think I might be busy. You were rather rude to me earlier. Should I say insulting?"

"I'll pay miss, what do you want, please, I don't have much time. I don't have any time. I apologise."

"I need a job, regular work, here. Or do I? Go on then. I do need a job and somewhere to sleep, Mister Tamryn. I will even apologise for my provoked petulance if it will help."

"It's a deal, we'll talk about it later." I need my head testing, one more nutter. Come one, come all!

"I will need my own room too. What is her name?"

"Who?"

"The woman you're supposed to be marrying, the bride, you wally!"

"Charming! I'll let you know when I find out."

"I'm Lyndsey, my name is Lyndsey, if you're interested."

"Okay Lyndsey, you're hired. Please just stand next to my wife. We'll talk about the other thing later. I mean my bride, she's not married yet. If she was, I wouldn't need you. You can sleep in Dusty's room. You might have to throw the dog out."

"Do you know which one she is. The wedding hasn't started yet, you can pick anyone right now, except me obviously. That wouldn't do. Your dog is called Dusty?"

"Could be. Dusty is my brother."

"I think I would rather sleep with the Alsatian."

"Me too, maid!"

Michael gives me a one fingered salute as a hand appears from under his cassock. He follows it with a thumbs up. I don't reciprocate, preferring to stay on my best behavior as I stand next to my bride, who is standing next to Lyndsey. I stay motionless as does my bladder, thank god. I may have pissed myself many times, I won't do it in my wedding suit. Michael has spent a lifetime being uncouth. He's a bit rough around the edges to be a minister but he knows all the proper words for these situations; which is a godsend, so to speak. Ma and Padraig stand at the front centre. I take her hand and prompt her to move forward. We stand in line with my parents. Ma looks across and realises then what is happening. She stays silent and just smiles, as I was confident she would.

She wears an amazing dress and a dazed expression. It is a beautiful moment. There is no further threat of violence. Maybe later! To be fair, I've had enough for one day anyway.

Last trick! I whistle shrilly in the chapel and he appears. The old Indian in full Comanche regalia walks forward and stands next to my bride, where he will in fact give her away. She only has time to say one word as Michael takes control of the proceedings.

"Grandfather!"

Michael mumbles into my ear: "You jammy sod, how did you do that?"

"Never you mind loser, just watch and learn."

"Tosser!"

"It takes one, Michael. You wouldn't know class if smacked you in the face and introduced itself."

The ceremony is otherwise commenced and completed in normal fashion, as far as I can be certain, by Michael, who didn't seem at all surprised at the disheveled appearances of most of the male attendees. Michael had been prepared for the changes in the service. Why wouldn't he? My mucker is smart, he knows the drill. After all, Michael, myself and Dusty have grown up together in Lannwedhenek! Don't ask, I have no idea. Michael had used the weird word at the end of the service. I hadn't a clue what he was on about. Most likely he'd made it up.

Blencathra had not a mark on her as far as I could see. I wouldn't want to see any further. I know my mucker will be disappointed he wasn't involved in the knuckle swapping. My friend is a man of the people, he likes to mix with his parishioners, which is only right. It was fortuitous Lenny wasn't about. The police would have just had a complete round-up. We would have married behind bars and got a free honeymoon, minus the honey and the big cheese!

There are two surprises for me, one pleasant, the second I don't have a clue what to think. I haven't had a chance to ask her so far, what with the mild fracas of earlier. I make a decision to ask her at the first opportunity. Alice has attended with Lenny. Alice has hold of young Danny's hand. It brings a lump to my throat. I will have to tell the yank one day. I hadn't thought about this.

Lenny arrived and had made sure everyone who mattered was in attendance. I hope he never finds out the truth about the boy or his mother, and I come to that. The service itself had gone off without a hitch, obviously there were the important ones. Dusty and I now have our family complete and, on our return, with Michael and the other members of the Mermaids' crew back to the Maltsters, we are greeted with the spread the caterers have been noisily preparing all morning. Michael has taken his frock off. I suggested it suited him. I backed off in case he felt like rearranging some of my features. He did make some whispered comment about going away anywhere, Michael isn't great with directions, so not unexpected!

For a moment or two I stop eating as I look around at the faces of my friends, family and one or two other odds and ends I have accrued over the last few months and years. Not so long ago, most were complete strangers.

I watch as the proud faces of Padraig and Joy beam out over the seated and slightly battle-scarred congregation. For myself, I think about the newest members of the crew, two of which, instead of being here would still be living in a ropey old caravan in a field at the back of a pub somewhere down West, Lavinia; I'd better not say too much, she will take everything literally. Peter would still be standing by a roadside with his thumb sticking out. They all fit in here, I hope they will stay. Finally, my wife looks right at home. I can't say much about the very latest acquisition. She is Welsh apparently!

After the shock of losing her parents and her sudden marriage, the yank told me 'My day is made, Fish Man!' She has forgotten my name already. It appears I'm to be known as 'Fish man'. It was just one incomplete fish. I'm not allowed to forget it. I didn't murder it.

Lastly there is Dusty's rescuee, Selina. Apparently, she isn't just a crew member of the helicopter, she had flown it. That's Dusty for you, fall in shit, come up smelling of roses. Maybe he has the beginnings of his own crew. Knowing my brother, he may not have thought about it at all.

I watch Lil as she chews and smiles while crumbs of still warm pastry drop away towards the floor, her eyes all the time on the wedding cake in the centre of the two tables. Even Lil's make-up is unusually well put on. Though she still isn't much better looking than my dog – it has finally become my dog - maybe she thought smartened up she'd get some trade later.

Somewhere beneath the table the Alsatian with only half its face is still the proud owner of the cleanest dog's bollocks in the county. He'll be starting again soon enough. When we first met, he wasn't my dog. Just spending twenty-four hours together, seven days a week does not constitute ownership.

I listen intently as my new wife speaks, a single star gleams and hangs from her neck. Her poignant words make me proud as she makes a little speech of her own. I stand beside her as she thanks my parents for now being hers. As she seats herself, I ask her about the one thing that has been bothering me. "Why only one star?"

She replies. "Easy, Hombre, I'm from Texas, the Lone Star State. We might only have one, but boy do we let it shine!"

"But I was in Kansas. I've never been to Texas"

"You still haven't, Brit. There's nothing small about Texas. Hombre, our place is on the border with your gaff!"

I am none the wiser. I'm sure I will be at some point. She is learning fast, I'm a tad slower. 'Gaff?' Oh dear, what have I brought her to?

Padraig interrupts our exchanges. "To each and everyone that are our family and those that are our friends, thank you for allowing me to come home to my family."

I think about this, it's perfect. I complete the formalities with one last sentence. "Our Ma may have changed her name today, Dusty, Maccy Junior, my wife and myself are still and always will be Tamryns."

The Irishman smiles on, seemingly content, as does the Indian. I'm not sure I've ever seen him smile before, I haven't seen him spit lately either. Maybe he has given up smoking whatever it was he kept in his peace pipe.

I look around at all these people. Everyone a friend or relation, my family and crew, except for just one sitting at the far end of the seated congregation. "Get that bleddy tramp out of here!" I can't believe my ears as a chorus of voices shout in unison "which one!" He is halfway through a pasty. "Let it finish its pasty first then someone take it outside and throw it in the lake please."

"Don't you dare!"

This is a surprise. The Welsh woman gives me a filthy look for some reason. I feel in a charitable mood as I retract my order to evict the grimy human.

The day is far from over and has been full of incident, almost all down to my brother. A good family day out! It has been a Tamryn wedding. On thinking about it, it's the first one I ever attended. Nothing out of the ordinary. People might have Alsatians and tramps at their weddings everywhere.

"Maccy, I hear tell you boys had a bit of a scrap?"

"It wasn't much Lenny, bit of a knock about mate. Handbags mostly."

"Oh, so it was the bleddy women again. They always start the bleddy trouble."

"No Lenny, I meant it wasn't very rough. Not like when we do get to scrapping!"

"That's because the women weren't involved."

"That's right mate. Best keep your voice down."

"So, who had the bleddy handbags then?"

"I don't remember, Lenny. Think the mutt was looking after them. Gotta mingle mate, you too."

"Where, who with?"

"Anywhere, anyone, that's what it means."

"I know what 'it' means. I'm not as stupid as I look."

"You're right mate. Now mingle! Wait, before you do that turn the new lights on outside."

"Lights? What bleddy lights, mucker?"

"The illuminations I asked you to put around the place."

"You asked for bulbs Maccy, they haven't bleddy come up yet mate."

I don't know what to say. I believe it best I keep quiet for now. I will keep myself in the dark, to coin a phrase. To be fair, Lenny is right, I did ask for bulbs. I did ask for colourful. I did ask for it by asking for it. I may kill him later.

I notice the newcomer is nowhere to be seen. It could be she is one of these people I've heard about. They just go about attending funerals of people they didn't even know, now it's weddings. This one must go to weddings in the same way, though she did deny it.

"Maccy, my love."

"Yes, my bird?"

"Shagged out, you were going to tell me?"

"It, er means sort of very tired."

"In what way?"

"Like really knackered."

"Like you will be in the morning?"

"Yeah, probably." I'm not sure if this is a threat or a promise? I'll know by breakfast time. It's none of your business!

"Your room is ready Mrs, Mister Tamryn."

"Thank you, young lady." I had spoken too soon. One minute she is nowhere, next minute she is standing next to me. I have to admit, she is more than useful. There's no law against being discreet, not something I know much about to be fair. She reminds me of someone, I just don't know who. She makes me nervous, I don't know why. One worrying point is, she got me talking strange, almost but not quite posh. I suppose I might have done before. Maybe the case isn't closed, maybe it only just opened.

On a more serious note, it has been quite a day. Another thing, where the hell is Lannwedhenek when it's at home? "So why did you call the old feller, Grandfather, yank?"

"Why shouldn't I Brit, he is my grandfather. I thought you knew."

"So that's why I sent for him, I was beginning to wonder." I never had a clue. It never crossed my mind! "What are we going to do about him after today? We can't tell him to sling his hook."

"No we can't tell him to do that, whatever it means. He can stay as long as he likes, Maccy."

"He sure can my Comanche wife. You should know, when we met the second time at the creek, I wondered if you two were related due to the constant spitting!"

"I'm just part Comanche. He needs somewhere to sleep. Where do you suggest?"

"No problem, he can sleep in the yurt with the kid and Peter, he should be used to sleeping in a tent. It's big enough for the three of them and Dusty said it would come in useful. The old feller might tame my brother, then he can start on Lenny. No, not Lenny! How long is he staying do you think?"

"No idea, our people don't like to move. Our ancestors had to move on far too often in the old days. He might stay for good."

"Yeah, yeah." I'm not sure why I sad that!

"Be careful, he might hear you, Maccy. Don't say I didn't warn you!"

"One good thing did come out of our wedding."

"Just one brit? This better be damn good. 'nu nahaniatsa Rio' Macdonald' - Rio."

"I found out your name do you need that many, Mrs Rio Dona Marina Tamryn?"

"Now you know why I never told you."

"Rio!"

"Yes?"

"Is he going to sleep outside the door all night?"

"It's a custom of our tribe."

I shout down the stairs. "Lenny, turn the lights on now mucker!"

"I will mucker. How's that."

Suddenly it is broad daylight. With luck the plants will all go blind and won't know where to grow!

Lenny shouts back up the stairs. "Maccy, there's something missing."

"How do you mean, what's missing?"

"Outside. The pub sign is gone buddy."

"It's not April 1st yet, Lenny."

Chapter Twenty-four

The Aftermath

There's nothing like a good old hitching to bring friends and family together. The lack of a shotgun is always a good sign. Just one or two interlopers popped in and out, they didn't stay long, we made sure of that. We let the tramp stay. It wasn't fightable. I have no idea what happened to it. Asleep in the bus shelter most likely.

I take to the office. I'm alone, I need to do some quiet thinking. I take out the flimsy folder I had taken from the newspaper office in McCarthy City. It is full of old faded paper clippings. On flipping through the slim pile I eventually discard the folder through boredom. I pour myself a coffee and decide to look again. After that, the folder will be put away for someone else to discover in a hundred years or more from now. Maybe I should start my own folder. It might be best not to bother due to what would be a general lack of interest.

Sipping at my coffee, I return to the wad of papers again. I notice with surprise the name of the editor of a yellowing broadsheet, George A Benford! I see little else of interest except Ulysses S. Grant is president of the USA.

The clippings are mostly just torn reports on local goings on of the time. It seems the town continued on until at least the early nineteen hundreds, into the twentieth century. I guess after that it must just have just been Renee. She might have lived alone for quite some time. Just how old was she? Very few of the graves in the cemetery had dated signs over them. The wooden crosses must have dried and crumbled away, less than a dozen remain. I only know of a handful of the occupants of the plots because of what Renee had told Dusty and I on our visit to the cemetery almost ten years ago.

Lyndsey suddenly appears and wants to talk. I wish she would stop creeping up on me, she makes me nervous. Her request sounds more like a command unsurprisingly. Like Queen Victoria asking for an audience with her Prime Minister. This immediately makes me more nervous. We sit in the office, which looks remarkably like a box bedroom, most likely because that's what it is. The room is so small, it's more of an alcove, we should have stood outside and talked.

She immediately picked up the folder from the desk - it's just a table - and looked inside. After fingering through a handful of pages she took one aside and dropped it on the desk in front of me.

"You found it then I see. There, you should read the headline."

"Tafflyn Evans is once again mayor".

I read the headline without picking up the scrap of paper. "Yes, so?"

"Tafflynn Evans was my great grandfather, Mister Tamryn."

"So you have already seen this Lyndsey, you have been to Kansas too, you've been to McCarthy City?"

"Yes I have. I didn't like to take it away, so left it where I found it. Then you must have found it. I left it all for you inadvertently. What do you think the confetti was made of, old advertisements from the paper? I thought that would amuse you. Why do you think I came here, Mister Tamryn? You see I do know who you are, I've known since I arrived here. You didn't know who I was, who I am. We are cousins I believe. Not sure how it works but my great grandfather was partners with your great grandfather. Somewhere along the line Tafflyn Evans and Henry Tamryn became related through marriage. All this makes us cousins Mister Tamryn, it's why we're here. I didn't know for sure until I got here myself. You getting married was just coincidence. I thought you would like a surprise, the confetti was it! It was only advertisements as I said. I did take some pages of the newspaper to read. I was in The Ring O Bells along the road here one evening a few days ago and some of the locals were talking about a wedding, it became obvious it was yours. I invited myself and again heard the name Tamryn as I had expected too. I knew then I was in the right place. By the way, Chris says you owe him a pint and a pool match and various other things. Your brother borrowed his lawnmower apparently."

"Dammit, this all changes everything. He can wait. The old sod never forgets anything, except his wallet. I didn't borrow it, Dusty can take it back. Chris doesn't have a lawn anyway. It's not much use to him."

"What does it change, Mister Tamryn?"

"Renee's Will. She left everything, the whole town to Dusty and I, as she could not have known if there was anyone else from our families left. Now there is, you! The old girl told us she knew about Cork. Ma used to get letters from Aunt Patricia, but they had stopped. She was great aunt Patricia, but you know how things get changed the older you get. Could you not keep calling me mister? I'm Maccy to everyone but the mad vicar and any passing taxman. The reverend calls me all sorts of everything but I never call the tax inspector. Would anyone in their right mind?"

"I certainly would if it was essential, um ….. Maccy."

"I realise that. It's surprising what people would do if they have nothing to do."

"There is only me, I am alone, I am the last! Your great aunt Patricia in Cork passed away a while ago. You need to tell your ma, I doubt she knows yet. She should be told, Maccy. I've been doing searches for some while; I came up with you people. Aren't I the lucky bleddy one! Yes I might not have been invited to your lessons, I have however learned. There is no one left of my family now. Patricia left me her ** 'Blackhouse' near to Blarney Castle a short distance away from Cork. It's not for me but it belongs to the family in a way. Some of that house must belong to you and your family. I think you should see a solicitor on your way to seeing a psychiatrist. Maybe the other way around would be better served."

"So what is your last name again, maid?" If anyone is unsure as to the meaning of 'forthright', I suggest you speak to this woman. Ignore her at your peril, I don't intend too.

"Evans, Lyndsey Evans, same as it was before. I am not a maid in the true sense of the word, or am I? Maybe I am, I don't really know. The word maid has so many different connotations. I will retract my statement so that I might do some further research cousin. I will let you know in due course."

I looked at the clipping again and hardly knew what to think or say. The woman is telling the truth of that I am convinced, about McCarthy City anyway. I have no idea what else she is talking about. She lost me ten minutes ago. She doesn't need money as she has my aunt's house, our aunt's house. She should buy herself a new coat and take the old one to the vets or an animal sanctuary. Let it live in peace or better still give it a decent burial. My head begins to spin, I get myself a beer, it doesn't help other than to encourage the motion. I offer to get her a drink from the bar, she refuses and requests a mint tea!

"Extra strong mint?"

"Very amusing, Maccy!"

"You know where the kitchen is, maid." I wasn't deliberately being inattentive, just letting my new-found cousin know she can do and get anything she wanted.

"We need to inform Dusty before we tell ma and Padraig. I have to tell Dona Marina too. What do I say, Lyndsey?" I had to repeat her name, it helps me remember I now have another living relative. The more the merrier I say. She is strange but aren't we all when we want to be and at times when we don't!

"I agree. I know how it must seem, I was nervous of even telling you, Maccy. It is indeed a small world, do you not think? Just tell them. One other thing, Maccy Tamryn."

"What now, is there more?"

"Yes I'm afraid so, there is indeed. Please don't yell at me, it is about your um tramp."

"What about it, whatever it might be? It's not my bleddy tramp! I've never seen it in my life before. Where did it sleep? I don't know any tramps except Dusty."

"In my room with me!"

"You slept with a tramp, why would you sleep with a tramp maid?"

"You were correct, Maccy, she isn't yours. She is in fact my tramp, she is my mother, yes the 'tramp' is my mother, most probably she is your aunt. Your ma should know. I haven't worked it all out yet. I haven't seen her for ages until the wedding. You two are related. We all of us are. How strange it is Maccy, that you asked me to take part in the ceremony. In fact I was not intending to tell anyone about my mother, I am not sure she even knew I was here, I didn't know she would be. I hadn't reckoned on that happening, not at all."

"I'm as surprised as you are. You're serious about the tramp aren't you!"

"I think you should be a little more polite towards her now Maccy, you two are kin whether you like it or not, you're related. I don't know who I feel most sorry for."

"Nothing counts more than family, Lyndsey. Bring it on!" I'm related to a tramp, what a lovely surprise. She and my brother should get along very well. I must admit I had my doubts, having no beard or a mongrel on a piece of string tended to give me a clue. I don't think I have been related to a tramp before. "I'll talk to Dusty, you get yourself a brew and we'll get a family meeting started. They should all be told right away. Just out of interest, Lynsey, what did you do before you came here?"

"Teaching. I'm a teacher, I'm between jobs, I was!"

So she is a teacher. Why am I not surprised?

For the second time in a day we are all in the same room, not the box room obviously.

"Button it everyone. Ma, who do you think this is?" I pointed to Lyndsey, just in case my mother had no idea who I was talking about.

"I have no idea Maccy, how am I supposed to bleddy know?"

"Anyone?" I waited a full half minute. Nobody has a clue. "Let me introduce you to Lyndsey, Ma, Rio Dona Marina, Padraig, Dusty, this is Lyndsey, our cousin. She is the last remaining member of the Evans family. The Evans family, not the Addams family, strangely enough, it is possible!"

"Okay Maccy, we get it. Who are the Evans family that aren't the Addams family?"

"Dusty, remember the story of Great Grandfather Henry Tamryn?"

"Sort of, yeah."

"Henry died saving a man's life and his wife, Renee, eventually married his partner, Tafflyn. Renee is Lyndsey's great Grandmother. Not the Renee we met, but her mother. I'll let you all think about it for a while."

"I think it's my turn now husband. Welcome to the family cousin, Lyndsey. Now listen girl, best you get yourself out of here while you still have your darned sanity. It sure won't last long around here. Take it from me."

So my wife can do a sense of humour but not where shooting fish is concerned. After that it was pretty much a free-for-all!

"Dusty, go get the Birdseyes."

"You go and get them, they might be busy."

"Do as I say, boy. I need to talk to the other idiot."

"Which one?"

"Doesn't matter."

"Lenny, is that you mucker."

"Bleddy 'ell Maccy, if it isn't me, why are you bleddy ringing me, I could be anyone!"

"Yes or bleddy no, you tosser? What do you want anyway?"

"No idea I thought you knew! Yes or no what?"

"Is it you?"

"I can't say."

"Lenny, get everyone together and bring them here."

"Where's here?"

"Where I am."

"I don't know where you are, do I? If I knew where you are, you wouldn't have to bleddy inform me mate."

"Lenny, it's me, Maccy,"

"No sorry you must have dialled wrong, bugger off."

"You bleddy tosser!"

"Come here and bleddy say that!"

"If I come there, you won't need to come here. Lenny, get a bleddy mini bus and bring the whole crew, everyone and come here. Get a thirteen seater, that way you and they might not get here at all. Shut the Mermaid!"

"Okay, Maccy. What about the goat?"

"Just leave your wash basket out for him."

"Why?"

"It'll save you having to do your washing. Bring the bleddy goat if you have to. Put a muzzle on him, that way he won't eat everyone's clothes. He must have grown, what's he look like now?"

"Like a goat that have been half eaten. He eats his own fur."

"And what about Lavinia?"

"She doesn't have any fur Maccy. I wouldn't let her hear you say that. I'm like putty in her hands, Maccy."

"Lenny, are you tinkering with that maid? Get her to repair the broken window then."

"Knaw, what broken window?"

"I'll take that as a yes then. The one the goat gets in and out of, you can't miss it, it's incomplete."

"The one Alice threw the girl out of!"

276

"That's the one. We only have the one broken window mate. I think it's time to get it repaired. Either that or get the door blocked up."

"Lavinia is sitting on my knee, she's a bit busy, we both are."

"Does Peter know?"

"Who? I think he is nesting elsewhere now mate."

"I don't need to know. Minibus, Lenny!"

I got away with that reasonably unscathed. Now for some peace and quiet. On second thoughts, it's party time!

"Um, Maccy."

"Yes, Lyndsey?"

"I still need the job, you did promise!"

"Excellent, you're hired, do you know how to hide a goat, Lyndsey?"

"I will check my contract of employment before I speak to my solicitor. I will of course get back to you promptly."

"Will secretary be okay, maid?"

"It would be most acceptable, cousin. I will give my solicitor a miss this time. As is my right, I will receive a contract of employment?"

"I best let you draft your own contract Lyndsey, that way you can sign it yourself; cut out the middle man. Now, if you could just hide the goat when it gets here, maid." I have to win sometimes. I think it might be a while before the result is officially in!

"Hide it where?"

"Put it in the cellar. Lyndsey, the tramp, your mother, who is she?"

"Just my mother, Maccy."

"Get hold of her; not like I did, invite her to join us."

"Why?"

"She's family, isn't she? What is she called by the way?"

"Yes, I am afraid she is. Thank you Maccy, it's very thoughtful of you, she is Elizabeth!"

Lyndsey stands on the stairs smiling in silence. She still makes me feel nervous. I wink, it might actually have been a nervous twitch.

"Wosson, Maccy?"

"Lenny, I have no bleddy idea mate. Don't ask so many questions. Let's get a party started mucker."

"It won't go on really late will it, Maccy?"

"Oh yes, Lenny, I'm sure it will go on very, very late." I'm not certain it will stop. It hasn't so far!

"I'll go and find Lavinia then."

"Best you do mucker. I think we might need more bleddy glasses."

I shudder at the very mention of her name, as I take one more nervous look back at the now empty stairs. Sometimes I get the feeling I don't make decisions, I just do what I'm supposed to do. I believe we all do. We don't have a choice, we just read the script. I do know it's getting more like the bleddy Waltons here every day. Now for a good night, Que Sera. Dear old grandad used to love Doris Day!

Epilogue

How anyone can fit so much into such a short time is almost beyond me. Obviously it isn't completely, as I did it. If I suffer from a bout of long term boredom in the future, I know I would do it all again. Can one get enough of a good thing? In all honesty, no!

The crew continued to sail along with me as I took on The Maltsters Arms, a mile or two outside of Padstow, inland obviously! One-Armed Frank had fallen overboard in The Mermaid and Bow some years ago now. Jen' lost her way but has our second son to hold her hand and walk beside her on the journey to the unknown. New stowaways have come aboard and swelled the numbers: Lavinia, Peter, Jill and Jack, the Yank, not forgetting Lyndsey, all have joined the ranks of the ill-advised. Lenny's new pet has no idea what it is letting itself in for. It surely has to be better for the animal than being a main course in a Moroccan restaurant. Only time will tell!

I pulled up the anchor and went fishing in a manner of speaking. I caught just the one. My brother, Dusty, acquired a Yurt, Ma and I got married. Not to each other, it could have been heavily frowned upon by members of the legal profession.

Siblings, Alice and Lenny, took time out to entertain at the police station in Wadebridge. They were eventually let go with a caution along the lines of, 'Don't come back please'!

At the completion of the Mermaid and Bow, I stated 'this is not the end, it is just the beginning'. My sincere apologies for that. However, I must apologise once again by partly repeating myself; this is not the end, it is somewhere in-between. The future might see my anchor drop firmly onto the 'Bar of Doom'!

Every story must have an ending, so far it is unreached. The Mermaid and Bow the beginning, the Maltsters Arms at Little Petrock is not the ending. 'The Bars of Doom' might provide finality. The origination however is still to come. Maccy's Great grandfather, Henry kindly left the family a diary or two, which hopefully will constitute – bear with me here - a final ending from the very beginning.

Martyn

Acknowledgements

In no particular order, I would like to thank Teresa, once again for sticking with it, knowing how tough it was the first time. I rightly add Lionel 'Mac' McCarthy, who in a strange sort of way introduced me to Macdonald Tamryn, twenty years ago. Thank you Tim, for the artwork. I thank my family for their encouragement and for not dying of boredom throughout my constant wittering on. I will show my appreciation to so many people in Little Petherick, St Issey and Padstow for their warmness, co-operation and offered information. Jay and Marie, thank you for allowing me to enter the Maltsters Arms, Ashley and Debbie, thank you for allowing me into the Millhouse AKA The Mermaid and Bow. Thank you so much, Charlotte, Jane and Dudley for allowing me to return and linger in the home of Macdonald Tamryn. My thanks also go to Gordon of Woking, to Chris at the Ring O Bells, St Issey and to all who have encouraged me to continue sharing Maccy's story.

I also thank Wikipedia for providing me with confirmation of certain historical facts.

I will thank Maureen, for allowing Jay, Teresa and I to set eyes on the original sign for the Maltsters Arms of Little Petherick.

Lastly, I say thank you to the most important people of all, those who have read and enjoyed the 'Mermaid and Bow'.

Martyn

Dydh da!

The Mermaid and Bow by Martyn Benford

Macdonald Tamryn, a budding teenage entrepreneur, believes he should become the next landlord of Padstow's, Mermaid and Bow public house. Maccy moves hell and high water to achieve his aim. As a seventeen year old he has little experience, however he does have vision. He will put it to good use. The small clientele, 'the crew' a mish mash of eccentricity, supports the youth in every way, allowing him to slowly but surely succeed in his endeavour. Not an easy task for the now eighteen-year old in the early eighties.

****

Little Petrock by Martyn Benford

With ten years of experience behind him and now with an even larger ego, Maccy Tamryn embarks on yet another dive into the muddy waters of mien hosting by acquiring the Maltsters Arms at Little Petrock; a decent enough stone's throw from Padstow and the Mermaid and Bow. Maccy once more takes everything in his stride whilst press-ganging new recruits to the ship's company.

****

The Bar of Doom (working title) by Martyn Benford

Almost ten years pass and Maccy, his family with new wife Rio, a Texan, plus an assortment of eccentric staff newcomers, will attempt to bring the Mermaid and the Maltsters into the twenty-first century. A tough ask but Maccy knows all about eccentricity personally, a dreamer and a grafter, most importantly a Padstownian; he is well-equipped to succeed.

282

****

Martyn Benford:

Author: The Mermaid and Bow and Little Petrock

Facebook: martynbenford

email: martynbenford@gmail.com

****

Martyn Benford books are available to purchase from:

Dydh da, Unit two Hornabrook Place, Padstow Cornwall PL28 8DY

We are an Eco friendly gift shop and gallery; showcasing Cornish produced gifts, Art and Craftwork.

Facebook: Dydh da

email: dydhdapadstow@gmail.com